P9-EBZ-803

RUNNING SCARED

RUNNING SCARED

Jon Burmeister

ST. MARTIN'S PRESS   NEW YORK

ST. MARTIN'S PRESS   NEW YORK

St. Martin's Press
175 Fifth Avenue
New York, N.Y. 10010

Affiliated Publishers:
Macmillan & Company, Limited, London
—also at Bombay, Calcutta, Madras and Melbourne—

For Lesley

I must place on record that the task of writing this book was greatly lessened by the unstinting help of Rob and Rosie Maspero, who certainly know their Cape Town; also my thanks to Steve, Diana and all the others who lent expert know-how in technical fields during my stay in the shadow of 'Big Daddy'.

Jon Burmeister

'In the quiet of the railway station,
Running scared.'

Paul Simon, *The Boxer*

Prelude

On a warm tropical evening in fading summer, an African physician named Dr. Tshanga typed a letter to a colleague who lived nearly two thousand miles away in Cape Town at the tip of the continent. He carefully sealed, stamped and addressed it, then personally carried it to a letter box nearly a mile away, fastidiously side-stepping the droppings of *homo sapiens* that lay about the achingly dry streets. With the drought as bad as it was, he reflected, cholera would be catching up with this mass of unhygienic humanity very soon. Then he shrugged, weighed the letter rather tentatively, worried a moment about the vagueness of the address and finally posted it with a sigh. It fell with a little hollow papery thud inside the box.

At precisely that moment an American named Ernie Slade who lived and worked in Cape Town, stopped on the pavement a hundred yards from his home. While the traffic of a gigantic modern city roared past, he coughed paroxysmally into his handkerchief and then stared in horror at the two bright spots of blood that soiled the snowy linen.

While the letter fell and while Slade coughed, a sixty-three-year-old bachelor, Major John Shannon, now retired and living in Kalk Bay, was giving an interview to a friendly reporter from the *Cape Argus*. Recounting his tiger hunting days in India, for which he was quite famous, Major Shannon mentioned regretfully that he had never bagged his fiftieth; forty-nine remained his score. He said it with a touch of humorous regret that made the reporter smile sympathetically.

What was not known to either of them was that Major Shannon was dangerously and homicidally insane.

These two unrelated events concerning unrelated people had the effect of changing the shape of the doctor's letter. They turned it into a bomb. And all because of the identity of his patient.

He happened to be the President of the Republic of Gamba. That Gamba, which is not its real name, was an impoverished, barren, heat-struck overpopulated and underdeveloped country containing 30,000 sheep, 50,000 cattle and at least 62,000 baboons according to an embittered agricultural officer, that its people lived on a subsistence level and that it had no major industries is of no consequence whatsoever in an era of Noisy Minorities.

The fact remained that the President was an internationally famous and powerful man.

Bobo Lunda, big-hat of half-a-dozen international committees, ex-Chairman of a U.N. colonialism study group, anti-U.D.I. and anti-Dialogue, had been listened to in Whitehall and Washington, in Paris and Peking, in Moscow and Havana, if not for his pertinency then certainly for the trumpeting bellow in which he spoke when he was three parts full of Highland Feather, which was most of the time. And in all these places, in fact wherever he went, the Tiger of Gamba, or Old Iron Hand—or Old Bottle-head to his enemies—never failed to include in his windy harangues an especially withering blast for a country he referred to sometimes simply as the White South and sometimes more fully as the Imperialist Neo-Fascist White South, depending upon which side of the Iron Curtain he happened to be at the time.

Which made it strange that he should choose the Republic of South Africa, his old whipping boy, as the country in which he would undergo advanced medical investigation and treatment, and stranger still that he should settle on a hospital in Cape Town, that city which he had once referred to as 'the nipple of Africa's under-tit', and 'the crummy orifice through which the life-milk of Africa is drained away'.

Always a Strong Man and rather Churchillian in his personal attention to detail, he had uncharacteristically allowed everything to be done for him, from the initial inter-governmental pulse-feeling to the final twenty-five-page printed and bound report handed to him by a Deputy Minister of Foreign Affairs who was one of Bobo's favourites. He read it from cover to cover, then acquiesced with a meekness denuded even of a truncal snort and called for another glass of Highland Feather.

Some heads were shaken. All this was very unlike him.

But the explanation was really quite simple: Bobo was seventy years old, ill, scared, and afraid of dying. So he wanted medical attention that ranked with the best in the world; he wanted it as soon as possible; and he wanted it regardless of cost. As for his choice of Cape Town, he had spent a while at the University there many years before the war and had pleasant memories of it. Age, as it often does, was harking back to youth.

Dr. Tshanga's letter arrived at its destination one week after posting. It read:

My dear Dr. Zodiack,

I doubt whether you will remember me but I knew you at Guy's. I keenly recollect the occasion when you were penalized in front of your posts and Newport won the game in the last minute. In fact I was one of those who assisted you from the Coach and Pair several hours later. It is a long time ago but one cherishes these light-hearted memories.

I have the honour to be personal physician to His Excellency the President, Mr. Bobo Lunda, who is also my very dear friend, and I write with two objectives in mind. The first is to enquire whether you would be so kind as to undertake the investigation of his case, details of which are set out in my attached notes and which need not be dealt with in this letter except to say that I can take things no further up here amongst the rocks and heat and scorpions and goddam baboons. I lack facilities, so I entrust him to your very capable hands.

The other objective is to request you to make arrangements for the President's admission to the Joseph Schwer Memorial Hospital. I have the temerity to ask this only because I know you are a patron of this exclusive institution.

Apart from awaiting your very kind confirmation all other arrangements (including at governmental level) have been made. May I ask for your earliest reply and in conclusion tender my sincere congratulations on your meteoric rise to fame? I have followed your career in the newspapers with great interest.

Yours very sincerely,
H. Harecourt Tshanga.

The tongue-in-cheek reference to Zodiack's midfield misdemeanour which had cost Guy's an important match, nearly cost President Lunda the services of a really brilliant doctor. Zodiack was something of a publicity hound. He was intrigued by the idea of having such a famous man for a patient but he made the mistake of showing the letter to Sisters Hobart, Strange and Meadows, who laughed immoderately at the first paragraph. Dr. Zodiack explained hotly that he had given away the penalty only in retaliating for what he described as 'repeated felonious assaults' upon him by one of the Newport wing forwards. But the idea of the long, moody and darkly elegant doctor bashing away at the nose of a husky Welshman in the armpit-and-groin nether world of the scrum only made them laugh all the more. Furious, Zodiack tossed the letter aside and sulked. A day later, tempted by the prospect of fame and mollified by the winning tones of the last two lines, he grumblingly sent off a cable of acceptance after contenting himself with the remark that Harecourt Tshanga had always been a creep, anyway.

The cable formed the last link in a causal chain. The Gamban government notified the host government that final arrangements had been concluded. Harecourt Tshanga artfully persuaded Bobo Lunda to swallow some Antibus tablets and then, presenting the President with a fait-accompli, put him in charge of Bobo's own Chief of Police, the lantern-jawed Captain Cyril Crutchley, who took him away into the bush where Bobo, for three days in succession, fought a magnificent one-man battle against a slavering pack of green-eyed wolves, beating the last of them to death with a Number Seven iron before Crutchley would bring him back, shaken from the terrors of cold turkey and withdrawal but dried out for the first time in years.

In Cape Town governmental and other machinery ground into motion and a number of unconnected people were drawn into the scheme of things. A broad-shouldered craggy-faced colonel in the Criminal Investigation Department of the Police, one Albert Pahler, was abruptly taken off other duties and directed to command the security aspect of President Lunda's visit. The urgency of the work forced him to keep long hours and he became grouchy because he had to cut out the squash he liked to play three times a week. At forty-four Pahler was reigning champion of his club, an ex-Western Province cap and fitter than many men of half his age.

A young schoolmaster named Ian Douglas who appeared to be constructed of whipcord and high-tensile steel, read a buff-coloured memorandum during a history class. It informed him in military jargon that G Company, Fourth Battalion, Cape Town Highlanders, had been detailed to form the guard of honour at the airport on the occasion of the President's arrival. There would be extra drills and practice parades in the evenings. Douglas, who had more entertaining ways of spending his leisure hours, crumpled the memorandum into a ball, threw it with deadly accuracy at the head of Johnson Minor and decided ungraciously that he would have to cut down on his screwing.

Eight-year-old Francina van der Merwe took home a letter from her school principal informing Francina's parents that their daughter had been chosen to present a protea, South Africa's unlovely national flower, to the President upon his arrival. The letter requested their consent, which her father gave upon condition that there would be no hand-shaking, please.

The Secretary of the Joseph Schwer Memorial Hospital, one Warren Clunes, took the first of a course of 15-milligram tranquillizers and headed a piece of paper with the words 'What to do before B.L. arrives'. He headed another 'What to do after B.L. arrives' and finally scribbled on his memo pad, 'Racialism in the Joseph Schwer—does it exist?' like the beginning of a treatise. He had a tendency towards impassioned over-organization and since the death of his widowed mother his nights had been free except for a regular half-hour he spent locked in the toilet with a copy of *Playboy*. Clunes began to burn the midnight oils.

Ernie Slade, who was now regularly coughing blood, was employed at the Joseph Schwer as Orderly–Ambulance Driver. He was given a sheaf of stapled Xeroxed data entitled, 'Arrival of the President of Gamba—Vehicle Movement Chart'. The part that concerned him was sub-headed, '(9). Ambulance. Joseph Schwer Memorial Hospital', and began, 'Take entrance "B" on left side of International Hall and park in Bay 4 on right of "G" Company, Cape Town Highlanders at exactly 1600 hours...' Slade was on his way for the annual para-medical staff chest X-ray. He shoved the booklet into his pocket and forgot about it because he had more on his mind. Again, today, he had produced blood on his handkerchief.

The Cape Town representative of Highland Feather, a tubby little man called Aaron Fuskin, seriously weighed the possibilities of getting Bobo Lunda to endorse his product and wondered whether, if the President refused, he could somehow be conned into being photographed with a bottle of it in one hand.

Major John Shannon received a small parcel brought to his door by a messenger from one of the air charter companies. He took it through to his gun-room, tore off the wrapping and disclosed a reel of recorded tape. Alone amongst the trophies of his tiger-hunting days he played it back on his own recorder, smiling faintly as he listened to the voice. He ran it through, in all, four times, then placed it in the fireplace and burnt it, crumbling the gummy ashes with a careful foot.

The tape had put him in a cheerful mood. He hummed as he went through to the bathroom, stripped, checked his weight on the scale he kept there. Naked he was a lean and muscular man without the plucked-fowl flesh of advancing age. He showered, humming above the blast of the water, dried himself briskly, then prepared a solution of Effecton which he used to keep his hair raven black. He was busy rubbing it on when he jerked violently erect, quivering, staring at himself in the mirror above the wash basin. Blindly he fumbled his way out of the bathroom and walked with a fast but stiffly unnatural gait to the living-room where he poured himself a very large glass of whisky, drinking it quickly and then immediately pouring another, standing rigidly at his little bar while he fought some terrible internal struggle that left him limp and sweat-drenched. But after ten minutes the strange attack had passed. He returned to the bathroom, reapplied the Effecton and while he waited for it to work he read the afternoon paper.

The President of Gamba, it said, was due to arrive in Cape Town in exactly four days' time.

Chapter One

Warren Clunes was a square chubby man, a dapper dresser if one's taste ran to heavy diamond tiepins and cartwheel cufflinks, a twinkle-toed, nimble-footed little chap who seemed to skip when he walked, as though he were about to sing, 'Girls And Boys Come Out To Play'. He bobbed about like Noddy, timing all his movements with a small man's exactness, so that Ben Zodiack appeared to shamble next to him with all the grace of a Himalayan bear.

'You must calm down,' said the bear weightily, 'or the excitement will bring on a period.' When he thought of Clunes frantically buying Tampax he wanted to laugh and cry at the same time. He stopped at a door in the long corridor, unlocked it with his own key and entered.

'I can't help it,' Clunes skipped in after him, chirruping. 'This is the end product of nearly three weeks of intense activity.' He dumped a briefcase on the desk that occupied most of the room. 'On this I have really done my thing. Clune's Climax. Warren's Work. I am now short-circuiting. I have fuses blowing and bulbs popping.'

'Where are the other two?' Ben Zodiack lit a cigarette and fell disjointedly into a chair. He was tall and dark-haired and moodily sanguine, handsome in a hollow-cheeked Gregory Peckish manner.

'On their way.' Clunes soft-shoed himself to a seat. He began fishing paper out of the briefcase. 'The Clunes Way to Success. Duty schedules. Gamban national dishes. There are three, and one is goat poached in curdling milk. A short history of the Joseph Schwer for visitors and pressmen. I tell you, over these I have burned the midnight oil.'

'You've got it to burn.' The Lincolnesque figure gloomed at him across the desk.

Clunes flushed, but it was true. His mother's death a year

ago had foiled a flowering Oedipus Complex, leaving him with a budding narcissism and his nightly lavatorial courtship of *Playboy*. Otherwise he had nothing to do outside of office hours.

He lost a little of his ebullience. 'Maybe so. But there was no one else to do it. Want to see some?'

'Not really.' The doctor's mood was decidedly snappish. 'Just fill me in generally.' He yawned and stared at Clunes out of baggy eyes.

Clunes fizzled a little more. 'I can wait until Hobart and Slade get here for the—er—briefing.' His small white hands ran an impromptu scale up and down the desk. A heavy gold dress-ring gleamed. 'Meanwhile, Ben, I want to say a big thank you, an overdue thank you, a thank you that covers past and present.' His bottom lip quivered as he flung himself into florid rhetoric. 'Your rising star has towed the Joseph Schwer along in the gold of its tail. Your patronage of this institution has got it out of the red for the first time in years. And now you are sacrificing valuable time to go with Hobart and Slade in the ambulance to meet President Lunda. You have done, and are doing, a power of good to the Joseph Schwer. Don't think I don't realize it every day of my life and say, "Thanks, Big Ben Zodiack".'

'It is a marriage of convenience, Warren.' Ben didn't know whether he should clap or call for an encore. Clunes always rehearsed this sort of thing, so that it invariably sounded silly. 'I like working here. My patients like being here.' He shrugged. 'The Joseph Schwer and I scratch each other's back.'

There was a tap at the open door and Clunes twisted in his chair. 'Ah, Sister! Come in.' He rose, bobbing about, one-two-threeing with his little feet.

Everybody knew that Clunes had pets and that Horrible Hobart was one of them. Sister Crowbar. Painful Jane. Only twenty-two, brilliantly competent, a gold medallist and midwifery prizewinner, this paragon of nursing perfection should, by rights, have been bell-breasted and hairy, with a crop of warts. Instead her lace cap balanced on corn-blonde hair below which was a delicately retroussé nose, soft woman-lips untouched by lipstick, a figure that was girlishly boyish, and what are known as 'good' legs. God had been kind to her. He had even managed to make her look like a virgin. Which was a big laugh.

Painful Jane walked briskly across the carpet and stopped at the side of the desk. She put four X-ray envelopes in front of the doctor. Small pink hands, with the beginnings of a chilblain on one finger. Hobart got them all the time. Nobody was perfect.

'Good afternoon.' This greeting could have been addressed to Ben and Clunes together, or individually, or to the wall. She regarded Ben with a pair of impersonal grey eyes that had the warmth of steel. 'These are the last of the routine staff chest X-rays. Mine, Sister Meadows, Sister Strange, And Ernie Slade.'

'Thank you.' He knew that if she undid her tight white belt the skirt of her uniform frock would drop another eight inches and hang low on her calves. Hobart could never seem to get anything to fit her and was always pinned and tucked, but it didn't matter because she looked so good. Which was, of course, why Clunes had chosen her to go to the airport.

Clunes jigged into his chair, six-eight time. 'I very much appreciate, Sister, the way you have given up your spare time, I know you're on night duty.'

'It's a pleasure.' She nodded quite regally and sat down in one of the spare chairs with a smooth economy of movement. Ben, looking up, caught movement in the open doorway. A man in white stood there, one big-knuckled hand extended to knock.

'Here's Ernie.'

Clunes aahed him in and ushered him to the other spare chair with almost as much enthusiasm as he had displayed for Hobart. This was Pet Number Two, this Ernie Slade who moved with an unconscious grace, wore white slacks and a short-sleeved collarless tunic buttoned right up to the neck, but who gave the impression, always, of ragged jeans, and bare feet gripping a sea-drenched deck. He had the wind in his face, this brown man, and horizon eyes.

'All squared away, Ernie? Ambulance rearing to go?'

'Yup.'

'Got your copy of the Vehicle Movement Chart?'

Slade touched a hand to his tunic. The heavy hair on his wrist was bleached gold. 'Yup.' Noisy Slade, he was called. His weather-faded blue eyes rested on the X-ray envelopes, then rose to meet Ben's. Neither said anything and Slade looked away.

'This is a great day in the history of the Joseph Schwer.' Clunes had begun to over-breathe with excitement. 'The President's stay must begin well. Nothing must go wrong at the airport.' He considered his two pets with affection. 'The only hazard I can foresee is the Press. Say as little as you can because they will probably ask you all sorts of hairy questions. Keep your answers short.'

'That's easy for Ernie,' Ben said.

'Remember that silence is golden. The Joseph Schwer is delighted to have President Lunda as a patient. We are not concerned with colour, politics, ideologies or—or anything else. We just want to heal the sick, with God's help.' Clunes swallowed emotionally. 'I know I don't have to tell you to be courteous and polite to the President. Good luck.'

'Keep a stiff upper lip,' Ben said, 'and fire when you see the whites of their eyes.'

Jane Hobart managed to turn a snigger into a cough. Clunes fiddled in his briefcase. 'Here are your identity pictures. Please pin them on.' He produced three Polaroids and gave one to each face that belonged. They were in plastic shields and bore the name of the subject, Colonel Pahler's spidery signature, and the rubber stamp of the Police.

Slade stood up. 'I'll go bring the ambulance around to the front.'

'Good boy, I'll come with you.' Clunes jumped to his feet and chassé-ed to the door. People were saying there was something on between him and the ambulance, it was so dear to him.

In the new silence Ben pinned his identity picture to the breast pocket of his white bush jacket. 'Sister Hobart?'

'Yes, doctor?' She rose, slim and gravely lovely.

'You left your toothbrush in my bathroom. And your Sequins.'

She went a little pink in the cheeks. 'I wondered where they'd got to. How do you feel this morning, Doctor?'

'Rough. All those Scotches. And you, Sister?'

'Rough. I have an aching back and a dislocated elbow. You're a very robust lover, you old bastard.'

He began to twinkle at her. 'Want to call it a day?'

'No, damn it.' She met him as he came forward, put her arms around him and her head against his chest. 'I missed you like hell, afterwards.'

'So did I.' He kissed her with warmth that turned into fire. Both of them were breathing heavily when he pulled away. 'Don't arouse me, Sister, we have to go and fetch that old twit from the airport.'

'Damn him.' She kept her arms around Ben. 'When does Flora come back?'

'Just short of a week.'

'Think you can fit me into your busy schedule before then?'

He grinned. 'I might. You can sleep until noon tomorrow. That's enough for any red-blooded girl, even one on night duty. Then lunch somewhere. A swim in the afternoon. Dinner at my place, with the coldest bottle of Late Harvest you've ever tasted. How's that sound?'

She brought her face very close to his and whispered. 'That sounds very, very groovy, Doctor darling.' Then she kissed him suddenly and ran blushing to the doorway. She blushed very easily, this girl, every part of whose body he had kissed less than twenty-four hours before.

Ben extinguished his cigarette. 'Let's go fetch the President, huh?' He joined her at the door, grinned and hugged her briefly. Then they left the room and walked along the corridor towards the entrance, their brisk footsteps echoing in the mid-afternoon quiet. Once, for a brief moment, she reached out quickly and touched his hand.

Slade had parked the ambulance in the shade of the overhang in front of the main entrance. Clunes had wandered off and he felt cold standing next to it in his thin whites, with a fierce, newly-risen wind tugging at him, so he moved into the sunlight and lit one of the cigarillos he fancied. Quite suddenly he began to cough. He said in a ragged voice, 'Oh shit,' and dropped the cigarillo, where it was picked up by the wind and whipped away.

Slade buckled over. He put his big hands on his knees, coughing until his eyes streamed, until he felt something come into his mouth. He reached blindly for a handkerchief, fumbled it to his lips and spat into it, closing his fist over the handkerchief until the paroxysm had passed. Then he straightened, opened his hand and stared at the three big spots of scarlet blood amongst the phlegm.

He cleared his throat. He said, 'How 'bout that, now,' and put the handkerchief back in his pocket.

Always, when this happened, he wanted to run. Ginny's lap was warm. He could picture the freckled thighs, the little pouting bulge between them, her fingers in his hair, his muffled laugh when she said she wanted to sleep, the scent of her strong in his nostrils.

It's no good running. Godammit, you some sort of a kid or something? The way she opened the door, when he came home. Always, 'Ernie!' *Like I just popped out of a submarine.* Always surprises. A lost kid. An old lady who got funny turns at the bus stop. A dove with a broken wing. Finding parents, telephoning an old-age home, making a cage out of an apple-box. *Look, can't you spread some of this charity around the neighbourhood?* Nights. Next to the pool. *See the Southern Cross, up there. Okay, you looked long enough, now look down here, lookit Ernie's submarine.* Ernie! Oh God, Ernie, I'd die without you!

He moved away from the pillar. Big Ben and Sister Crowbar were coming out of the entrance, ducking into the wind, so he made himself smile at them. Going around to the passenger door, he looked lean and healthy.

'We can ride three up in the cab.' He extended his hand to Jane Hobart and she took it, holding on to her cap with the other against the wind's insistent pull.

She said, 'You've got thin, Ernie, have you laid off the doughnuts?' and disappeared into the cab. Slade looked briefly at Ben. Then he went around to the driver's door, opened it and climbed in. The big engine burst into a clean rumble. Clune's Concubine. Slade engaged gear and they moved down the driveway towards the wrought iron gates that stood open.

'What ails President Lunda?' She looked too young, he thought, for the authority of the wine-coloured epaulettes on her slim shoulders, too young for the expertise she had shown last night, too young for the professional indifference of her question. 'It would help to know in case he falls down frothing at my feet at the airport.'

He saw nothing unusual in her ignorance. When you knew how to nurse you were told that so-and-so was admitted to such-and-such a ward and there was this-and-that wrong with him and you either knew what to do or they told you what to do, and you got on with it. And Hobart was one hell of a nurse.

'He has an anaemia.' They nudged through the gates and turned on to the road. Old oaks linked hands overhead, shutting out the wind and letting the sunlight through in golden filtered bars. A squirrel scampered through fallen leaves.

'How bad?'

'I don't know. That creep Harecourt Tshanga could only take it so far. Lunda complained of excessive fatigue, attacks of dizziness and loss of weight. He had an enlarged liver and spleen. Failed to respond to iron treatment.' Ben shrugged. 'Obviously the anaemia is of more sinister importance. Perhaps it's pernicious, perhaps it's leukaemia. Who knows? We'll settle the old guy down and run some tests on him.'

'A bone marrow biopsy,' Jane Hobart said.

'There speaks the gold medallist. But first we'll get some blood, X-ray the old boy and run an M.A.O.'

'And if it *is* leukaemia?'

'Then we'll send him home to die. Warren doesn't want dead Presidents cluttering up the corridors of the Joseph Schwer. It's bad for business.'

They reached the freeway. Slade swung left, accelerated, weaved across to the fast lane. Jane fiddled on the seat and produced a crumpled Argus. It welcomed the President in dignified fashion but it hadn't forgotten the under-tit of Africa or the crummy orifice bit. Bobo Lunda would have to make amends. 'Anything interesting in here, Ernie?'

'Yup.' Slade passed a sawn-off Volkswagen. Mixed up amongst all the unisex hair and beads and braless shirts were a haystack of students. 'There's a story about an old guy called Major Shannon. He lives in Cape Town now but he used to hunt tigers in India. Shot forty-nine altogether and he's real mad because he never got his fiftieth.'

'Tough,' said Jane. 'I bleed for him.'

'I bleed for the poor damn tigers,' the doctor gloomed.

'We on time, Ernie?'

'Yup.' Slade took the long tight turn that would bring them to the airport freeway. He glanced at the dashboard clock. 'Twenty minutes to touch-down.'

The Air Force Lieutenant closed the communications door

leading from the flight deck and put his back against it, looking aft down the long rows of seats. There were only five passengers. *Five little nigger boys* ... He couldn't remember what had happened in the rhyme to reduce them to four.

They had scattered themselves about the interior of the big cabin. The Lieutenant, remembering the list he had seen before take-off in Gamba, placed them mentally as they sat: quite close to him was the President's personal valet, a certain Private Fula seconded from the Gamba Rifles. Next came Lunda's male secretary, small and sparrow-like, blinking nervously behind glinting spectacles, and about six rows behind him slumped the President himself, heavily asleep, his baronial snores rumbling stereophonically through flared nostrils. Finally, so far aft that they seemed deliberately huddled near the toilet door, the only twosome whispered and then fell silent under his glance. These two were Deputy Ministers in the President's Cabinet and were on the plane at the personal invitation of Lunda himself. They were corrupt but efficient, they were the President's swingers, his get-things-done boys. Their mission on this trip was to raise loans, land contracts, and negotiate aid for the betterment of their country. And if they picked up a little on the side it was one of those things, people had been doing it for a thousand years.

The Lieutenant moved quietly along the aisle and paused a moment next to the slumbering President. So this was the famous Bobo Lunda. Or notorious, depending upon one's point of view. Even in sleep, he wore his famous green woollen tribal cap and clutched his horsetail fly-whisk in one loose-fingered big hand. The cap had a primitive zig-zag design worked in yellow around the edges and was a good-luck omen. The fly-whisk had gone everywhere with him since it had gained renown in 1945, bobbing like a banner at the head of the crowd that had stormed the Governor's residence to demand—and get—land reforms.

Whether one were an admirer or a detractor of this old man whose name was a household word all over the world, there was no denying, the Lieutenant thought, that he was god-awful ugly in any man's language. Below the cap was a huge trunk-like nose that had been battered in Gamba Central Prison in 1947 by warders who had homed to it like fair-goers to an Aunt Sally. He had a wide thick-lipped barracuda mouth, set like a wound in a Punch-and-Judy jaw and, when they were open, little flaring threatening yellow eyes. Even the big steel-rimmed Dickensian spectacles, which might on most people have intruded a hint of olde-worlde charm, of tea-around-the-hearth and well-children-did-you-enjoy-the-ramble, on Bobo merely produced a sort of all-the-better-to-see-you-with menace.

There was a book lying on the President's lap. Curious, the Lieutenant bent over to see the title *Thoughts of Chairman Mao*, he guessed; they regard it as required reading.

It turned out to be *The Wind in the Willows*.

Baffled, the Lieutenant went back to the flight deck. The pilot, a shirtsleeved Major, looked up and grinned. 'Is the old guy still asleep?'

'Yes.' The Lieutenant took his seat. 'I'm surprised we can't hear the snoring, it's loud enough.'

The Major laughed. 'Take over. I'll go and wake him as diplomatically as possible. Probably get a strip torn off me but we can't have him all bleary-eyed when he meets the welcoming committee.'

'On schedule so far?' The Lieutenant lit a cigarette.

'Yes.' The Major moved away. 'We'll be landing in about twenty minutes.'

The man in the airport bar had thinning black hair pulled straight across his brown scalp. He had a narrow thin-fleshed face with a strong patrician nose and slightly hooded eyes. Wide shoulders pushed against the dark blue of a light, expensive casual shirt. A bush of slightly greying chest hair showed at the open V neck. Pastel slacks clung at the thigh, showing the ridges of quadriceps muscle. Perched on a bar stool, Major John Shannon had hooked the heels of his cream-coloured shoes on the rung. He was talking to a textile executive who was waiting for his flight to be announced. They had met by reason of being the bar's only two customers for a moment and the fact that the man had, diffidently at first, identified him from the open *Argus* that lay on the counter between them.

'I used a Mannlicher ·375,' Shannon said. 'It's a nice, clean, hard-hitting weapon. But there were others: a Holland and Holland Express; the ever-popular Winchester ·270; an old Snider once, believe it or not—remember that bit from Kipling?

23

"A Snider squibbed in the jungle, somebody laughed and fled...''?' He shrugged indifferently.

'Go on, go on.' His name was Davidson.

Major Shannon's hooded eyes fixed on him. He leaned slightly forward. ' "And the men of the First Shikaris picked up their Subaltern dead, with a big blue mark in his forehead, and the back blown out of his head".' A muscle at the corner of one eye jumped. A tiny convulsive shudder ran through the athletic body. 'Rather effective, what?'

Davidson groped for his scotch. He could not look away. The hooded eyes held him. 'You say it so well. I was never much cop on Kipling, or any form of poetry for that matter.'

'But you're interested in guns, eh?'

'Not really.' Davidson's little red lips sucked at the drink. 'I was more interested in your experiences; you know, the thrill of the hunt. Goodness, I don't even know how a gun works!'

'It's very simple.' Shannon's lips peeled back from his tobacco-stained teeth. 'A rifle is a woman, my friend. One places a cartridge in the breech between her thighs, so to speak, and then with the bolt one pushes it home and squeezes the trigger. The short straight firing pin, hard and commanding, strikes the soft nub of the percussion cap, which gives way. Heat is engendered. It is a fierce, rending heat. There is pinkness and redness. There is an explosion. The lips of the cartridge part in the ferocity of the orgasm and and the bullet is ejaculated.'

'I've never heard it put ... quite that way.' Davidson gulped at his drink, fascinated like a mouse, his glance locked with Major Shannon's midnight cat-eyes.

'Death is always so dramatic when it is fired from a rifle,' said Major Shannon. He stared broodingly at the other man. 'Yet I could kill you with my hands very easily. That's your flight being announced, isn't it?'

Davidson jumped. 'Eh? Oh, thank you.' He slid off the stool. 'It's been so frightfully nice meeting you.'

Shannon grunted. He turned away and signalled the barman for another whisky. Ah, God, those tiger days. The tonic of sheer youth. That damned hellish fright that was so great it was almost ecstatic. And the looseness of letting go, afterwards, with the taste of whisky clean on the tongue and the pleasure of watching a beautiful woman whom you knew would go to bed with you when you snapped your fingers.

24

Wonderful, zesty days. He closed his eyes. Come, tiger, burning bright. I smell your stink, I see your big pug-marks. Come through the bamboo. Come, come with your diamond eyes, let me hear the rumble of you, big tiger, in the jungles of the night, let me live the pure hate and pure life and pure death, let me hear the rattle of the cane, the earth smashing, see the fluffy-kitten fur on your chest, the Mannlicher sights coming up...

He opened his eyes. The next bar-stool was empty. Davidson had gone. There was the roar of the plane, the thud and shriek of its tyres striking the tarmac. He said to the barman at the far end of the bar, 'Is that the President's plane?'

The barman cut through a lemon. Then he checked his watch. 'Must be, sir.'

Major John Shannon rose. He dropped coins on the bar. 'Ah, well.' He lit a thin cheroot and started to walk out. Near the door he stopped. 'You always scout around, you know. You have a look at him; if you can, you find out how he works, how he smells, what his habits are, the places he favours. It comes in very useful at the crunch.'

'Sir?' The barman, startled, was looking at him.

'It doesn't matter.' Major Shannon chuckled. 'I shouldn't give away my trade secrets, after all, should I?' Then he was gone, leaving behind only the acrid, gunpowdery smoke of his cheroot.

The hairy legs of the Pipe Major quivered in a throe of anticipation. His kilt trembled to the blatting of the drones. His right arm, held rigidly aloft, plunged down. The pipes howled into 'Cock of the North'.

Ben screwed up his face. He stood with Jane and Slade leaning against the grille of the ambulance. Slade had parked it in its appointed slot, Bay 4, on the edge of the hardstand to the left of the low dingy red bulk of the Terminal and its newer accessory, the graceless International Hall. The band was very close.

'The Scot in me,' he said, 'thrills. The Jew is in mortal agony.'

Slade was one of those rare things, an unmusical, tone-deaf sailor, and to him the pipes sounded like an alley of cats being emasculated without anaesthetic. So he remained dourly silent.

'It's thrilling,' Jane cried, clutching her lace cap. Her eyes were on the whipcord-and-steel Captain commanding the High-landers. He stood out alone, looking lean and brown and bullet-proof in his rugged combat suit. His jaw muscles bunched.

'Companee ... per ... reeee ... sent ... homs!'

There was the innocuous slither of the light FNs coming up. 'Give me the old three-oh-three any time,' Ben growled. 'You could really bash 'em around. Sounded like soldiers.'

A wheeled gangway had been pushed up to the side of the trim Air Force Transport with its drab fuselage and distinctive orange empennage. A door opened, mysteriously impelled by a blue-clad arm from within. A small knot of dignitaries clustered on the hardstand. Men and women clutched their hats impartially. A sombre Homburg escaped and went bowling away. Francina van der Merwe, tightly holding her King Protea, made a tiny blotch of colour amongst the sober-suited group in a brown blazer with green-and-yellow stripes. A rabble of newsmen and photographers prowled nearby, kept at a safe distance for the time being by a small blue-fleshed policeman of nineteen, shivering in his summer kit.

'I think we'd better go,' Jane said.

Ernie took a firm grip on the wheelchair. 'Yup.'

'All right. Forward march.' Ben jerked at his jacket. 'Hup, toop, threep, fope, hup, toop, three, fope.'

By chance they were in step. Three neat figures in white, they marched along the hardstand in line abreast, passing across the front of the Highlanders. Captain Ian Douglas swivelled his gunmetal eyes, fascinatedly watching the hypnotic brown-stockinged legs of Sister Crowbar as she quick-marched by. A cold grey eye caught his and flickered away.

'Her pants must drop off before she reaches the plane,' announced Lieutenant MacDonald nearby. 'With all our massed manhood it's inevitable.'

'Gawd, look at 'er go,' said a voice from the ranks. 'She could lead me into battle.'

'She could lead me into bed.'

'A little bugger like you? She'd inject you to keep you quiet.'

'I would inject *her*, but it wouldn't keep her quiet. More, more, she would cry, more injections, please...'

'Shaddup,' hissed Captain Douglas through his teeth.

The Joseph Schwer's three-man phalangeal march-past was too much for the newsmen. They broke past their captor and ran, and he let them go, wishing he had become a fireman. Their wave broke upon the wheelchair and they milled around, firing cameras and questions.

'Ever nursed an African before, Sister?' A flashgun popped electronically.

'Is it a heart transplant, Doc?' This was addressed to Slade. Ben went a dull red.

'That's him, you dope! That's Zodiack. Is it a heart transplant, Doc?'

'Would your parents approve of your washing a Bantu, Sister?' This from a stern man with a hairline moustache.

'Say, are you a bodyguard?' The question was addressed to Slade once again.

'Nope.'

'But you're Security, aren't you?'

'Listen, Buster, I just drive the ambulance.'

'Hey, this guy's a Yank! He's a Yank, fellers! Sir, are you on loan from C.I.A.?'

The marchers marched stoically. Ben got a word in edgeways. 'President Lunda is here for the investigation of a condition. There is little or no likelihood of surgery. I am afraid I cannot be more specific.'

'Yes, but is it serious?'

'He would hardly have come all this way if it wasn't.' They neared the dignitaries. An old lady with a folded parasol said, 'Shhhh!' The newsmen, squeezed between the two groups, quietened and spread out.

'He's coming,' said the old lady so authoritatively that a camera focused on the gaping black doorway in the side of the fuselage began to whir.

He did not walk into view. He simply appeared, seeming to fill the doorway. He was taller than they had expected, and broader, and uglier, and more menacing. The Dickensian glasses were gone. Small eyes looked arrogantly along either side of the barrel of his nose as though he were bringing them into focus before opening fire. There was a moment of hush while everyone was still, while Bobo cunningly contemplated them, a black man-eater sensing their soft white exclusiveness. Then the great barracuda mouth broke into a grin that had the width and the warmth of an estuary filled with dangerous yellowed snags, the fly-whisk whirled overhead, a horsehair penant streaming in the wind's pull, and they were clapping and cheering their unafraid enemy, this grinning Tiger of Gamba who prowled from his jet-propelled lair and rumbled a growl of greeting as he stopped before the whip-thin microphone that trembled in the wind.

One or two hands were shaken. The battery of flashguns rippled like dawn at Alamein. Then the Tiger raised his paws and instant silence came.

'That mountain over there.' He flung an arm arbitrarily not bothering to look. *'Thank you for naming it after me!'*

They had never heard that trumpeting roar before. They quailed before it like a sea of grass before a wind. Then they saw the way he was laughing at them, they saw the crackle of his eyes, they realized it was the *Tygerberg* to which he was referring, the Tiger Mountain, and they roared along with him.

This time he simply flicked a finger. Again, instant silence. 'Not many people know that I have lived in Cape Town.' He looked about, deliberately pausing almost challenging someone to wriggle. No one did. 'It was in 1923 that I spent a year at the University. And during that time I'—he lowered his voice so that it was soft and rich and full—'I fell in love.'

There was a mother-oohing from the women, who waited entranced.

'I couldn't stay. I wanted to, but I had to go on. So I went to her, I went down from the University on the hill, down to her to say goodbye.' An almost tremulous note crept into the deep husky voice. The great head wagged in regret. 'She had flung her arms about the mountain, counting it dearer than me. But I kissed her lips in Adderley Street. Goodbye, my dear. *Goodbye, Cape Town!'*

There was a breathless, startled silence. Then they understood, and they howled louder than the wind while Bobo Lunda, the old rogue, hung his head and pretended to weep.

Silence came. 'This is an unofficial visit,' growled the Tiger, serious now. 'I have no axes to grind. Having been misquoted once on the subject of your lovely city, I wouldn't want to give anyone another chance.' He menaced the pressmen with a threatening stare, then turned back to the small crowd. 'Thank you for the welcome. Now I must get on with the reason for which I came—to be filled full of pills and things, so that I can go back to Gamba filled with enough vigour'— he started to laugh, stabbing a great horny finger at them— 'so that I can get stuck into you again!'

They would have run him for Parliament on a National Party ticket at that moment and only wondered why afterwards. Amidst thunderous applause little Francina van der Merwe came forward with her protea. Bobo towered over her like a black ogre. When he bent he seemed to come tumbling down towards her. When he smiled he seemed about to gobble her up. Suddenly and without warning, she began to cry.

Bobo cast a distressed, oh-shame look at the crowd. He tut-tutted, crouching over her like a mother hen, patting her flaxen head and whispering in her ear as he relieved her of the protea and passed it on to a surprised official. Instantly, the child stopped weeping. Turning, she scuttled back to her parents. There were cries of adulation from the mothers in the group who did not know that Bobo had told her to stop it at once or he would shut her in the aeroplane and fly her to Ugly-Ugly Land.

He came away grinning, wise-cracking, calling to the band, 'Let's have "Cock of the North" again, shall we, it's rather fitting,' until he reached the wheelchair and subsided suddenly into it, turning and weakly shaking hands with Ben, Jane and Slade from a seated position, to a chorus of 'Poor thing,' from the crowd.

Officials pressed about them, concerned, but Bobo waved them away. 'Let's have a look at those boys, they've come all this way to welcome me.' And so they rolled once more in front of the Highlanders, and Captain Douglas managed to make his salute cover both Bobo and Jane. He marched with them along the ranks, with Ben and Slade looking woodenly before them, Jane blushing pinkly and Bobo crying out, 'Thank you boys, fine boys, thank you chaps,' winning even the heart of that dour Scot, Rifleman van Blerk, who was heard to comment later after his third beer in the airport bar that the President had seemed like a nice old kaffir.

They reached the ambulance. One or two last pictures were taken and then Bobo said goodbye to his welcomers. Big black Daimlers and Jaguars began to pull away. The grinning Highlanders marched smartly past towards their dismissal point outside the terminal, and Captain Douglas, trying to catch Jane Hobart's eye, wondered whether he should chance a wave. But she was bending solicitously over the President, tucking a rug over his legs.

' "The Captains and the Kings depart," ' Bobo said. He had gone suddenly grey with fatigue. 'Do you like Kipling, Dr. Zodiack?'

'In small doses.' Ben felt a sudden rush of sympathy for the old man. 'Let's get you to bed.'

'An enticing thought. The after-glow of a bath, the warmth of the blankets, a cup of steaming cocoa and my Enid Blyton. Security. I feel like a little chap.' But he clutched the arms of the wheelchair rather tremblingly, and there was no vestige of child left in him.

He signalled to his group. They were standing near the car that had been placed at their disposal, with a coloured chauffeur who was looking down his nose at them. Sullen from being disregarded, they walked slowly to the ambulance.

'My party. You may as well meet them now because they will be visiting me at the hospital.' He introduced Deputy Ministers Mango and Zaza, the Secretary, whose name was Blamemore Zinto and finally his valet Fula. Then he shooed them back to their car again, quite benignly, and turned to Ben. 'Shall we go?'

Assisted by Slade he got stiffly into the rear of the ambulance and sat awkwardly on a bunk. Ben and Jane followed and Slade closed the doors. After a while the engine rumbled into life. The big vehicle bumped gently as it headed for the exit.

They sat opposite him, a little self-consciously because they were so close together under Bobo's thoughtful scrutiny. The small yellowed eyes rested on the girl after a while.

'So young Sister Hobart, so clever and so beautiful. A gold medallist, and then the Bleeker prize for midwifery.' He simply nodded at her surprise. 'Oh, yes, I know a good deal about you. My security chaps are every bit as good as yours. You are very fortunate, my dear, to have these three assets. Use them well. Don't make mistakes you will cry for in your old age.'

Jane Hobart looked at him rigidly as though her neck had turned to marble, while the blood rose in a visible tide into the pale skin of her face. But behind the grey eyes two steel curtains slammed down as she closed him out. Horrible Hobart, immune, exclusive, and self-contained.

Bobo's thoughts seemed to preoccupy him for a moment.

Then he smiled at Ben. 'The good Doctor Zodiack. Still fairly young, too. Brilliant, forceful and ambitious. A great worker. A candle burner. Right so far, Doctor?'

Ben flushed. 'You don't get up there by sitting on your hands.'

'No, no, very true.' The great head nodded. 'One attains the stars only through Herculean effort, and unfortunately usually at the expense of people close to one. How does your wife feel, Doctor, married to a largely absent dynamo?'

Bobo had probed through the only chink in the Hippocratic armour. Ben felt the shock of vulnerability, the guilt, and the following flood of anger. 'I should imagine she feels a good deal better, Sir,' he said in a carefully restrained voice, 'than those Gambans who, having served their purpose and helped a President into power, now languish forgotten in dirty nameless jails.'

Bobo considered him without apparent anger, but two tiny fires showed in the yellow eyes, burning bright in the jungles of his brain. A manicured jungle. Neat, weeded, tabulated.

Suddenly he laughed. 'We'll make a politician of you yet. I think I am going to like you, Doctor Zodiack.' The deep bass chuckles had hardly faded away when the heavy jaw sank slowly on to the chest, the small eyes flickered and closed, and Bobo began to doze, his huge horny fingers hooked into the edge of the bunk.

He reminded Ben, inevitably, of a vulture, an elderly ungainly and arrogant vulture high up upon a mountain perch, dreaming broodingly of the place below where the fat lambs lay.

Chapter Two

From where Slade stood he could see a section of mountain between the tossing cypresses in the garden. It was a piece of the Twelve Apostles, those mountains that came away in a chain from Big Daddy's south-western flank. It was very close, a palate-smear of autumn browns and greens with angry dark clouds boiling high up across its rocky face. Rain was falling in time with the gusty wind.

Always there were mountains, Slade thought. No matter where you were at, all you had to do was lift your head and there was one or more of them looking at you. He had climbed a lot of them and he liked them. The mountains were mostly friends of his but still, it was a hell of a funny place to put a town, dumping it around a string of mountains just like that, squeezing it in between them and the sea on both sides of a continent, so that around Sea Point and Clifton and Camps Bay the road went tippy-toe along the very edge of the land as though it were scared it might slide down into the Atlantic, and around Muizenberg and St. James and Kalk Bay and Fish Hoek the road *and* the railway line, the both of them went tippy-toe along the very edge of the land as though they were scared they might slide down into the Indian. It was all very higgledy-piggledy, but maybe it was because Cape Town sprawled like this in haphazard confusion that you felt you were dealing with a woman, a real woman, so that the city centre wasn't a city centre at all but a beating heart, the roads weren't roads but veins, her arm on the Atlantic side was cold and regal, on the Indian it was warm and loving, tucking you into the curve of her waist that was False Bay. You could fall in love with her like any other woman, and like any other woman she could be contrary as hell.

Slade dropped his smoke and crushed it. He ran a hand through his short-cut blond hair. The cooling ambulance, put to bed for the night, still gave out a small emanation of heat and its contracting metal ticked quietly.

Stop playing for time. The reproof came quietly, and he accepted it knowing that it was deserved. Kicking around in the ambulance park like a kid dodging that bed-time call. Oh hell, he thought, to be six years old, worked for, thought for, fed and housed. Secure. Life was today and tomorrow, life was what-am-I-gonna-get-for-Christmas and a dog with sad eyes that chased a butterfly around and around in a beam of sunlight, life was a loose tooth, getting locked in the bathroom, honey spreading across a waffle.

Life is the taste of blood in my mouth. That one slid in through his guard, unexpectedly, bringing with it a short moment of desolation. He shook it off angrily and began to walk quickly from the doorless ambulance park, crunching across the wet wind-blown gravel on the hardstand, feeling a sprinkle of rain on his neck, rounding the building and seeing lights springing on because it was early-dark from the rain, going in the main entrance where the electronic eye opened the glass door for him, pausing before the grill at Reception where a chunky-looking man in a sportscoat checked his Polaroid and nodded him on, listening to the light tap of his feet in the corridor, stopping finally at the door of the office Ben used, stopping and letting out all the held-back breath in one long rushing sigh. And saying it. Saying it at last: *I got scared, back there. First and last time.* He tapped, opened the door and went in.

Ben had the newspaper opened out on the desk. He looked up at once and smiled. 'See the new clerk in Reception?'

'That clerk,' Slade said, 'is a cop.' He sat facing the doctor.

'You're so right. It's like putting a bulldog in woollies and telling everyone it's a French poodle. Apparently Colonel Pahler, in charge of security, thinks it's a good idea. He's got men on it right around the clock. They filter visitors and check these damn pictures. The whole staff is wearing them, from Matron Burns to the women who clean the floors.'

'Does he expect a commando raid to break the President out of the Bastille?'

Ben shrugged. 'The cops say no. They say they've got a visiting foreign Head of State on their hands and they've got to look after him. Imagine the furore if he got creamed.'

A silence fell between them as sharp and sudden and defined as the pulling of a switch, the slamming of a steel shutter, the fall of an executioner's axe. Ben lit a cigarette and Slade sat motionless for a passing minute as though carved out of mahogany. Then he smiled a little.

'Always, you used to offer me a cigarette.'

'Sorry, I——' Ben's hand, returning to his pocket, stopped. He met Slade's eyes. 'So?'

'So tell me what the X-ray says, Ben.'

Ben said quickly, 'You sound as though you've already made certain deductions. I forgot to offer you a smoke and suddenly it's got a meaning, it's full of ominous portent.'

'Did you *really* forget?'

'Yes. Look, Ernie——' Ben stopped again. He put his hands carefully on the desk. 'Okay, I deliberately didn't offer you one. Where do we go from there?'

Slade said with heavy deliberation, 'Tell me what the X-ray says.'

'Not so fast.' Ben became aware that he was mentally weaving like a boxer, dodging the words as though they were blows, and that it stuck out all over him. 'Ernie, I'd like to do a Mantoux on you.'

Slade stared at him without any animosity, in fact with a deep fondness. He let the silence run awhile. 'Ben, listen. Listen good. I'm a big boy. I'm a grown man nearly forty-one years old. I've been around, I've seen the elephant and heard the owl hoot. I know you're holding back because you don't want to scare me. The point is, *I'm not scared*. You get it, Ben? It's no good shovelling me a load of bullshit about T.B. and offering to run a Mantoux test. I'm pretty sure I know exactly what's in those X-ray plates you've got hidden under the newspaper, but I want to hear it from you, and the only reason I want to hear it from you is because I'm married to a kid who depends on me to bring in the bread. I've got to do some figuring, find out where I stand financially. Ginny is the reason I want confirmation. And Ginny is a pretty damn good reason. So Ben, tell me what it says.'

Ben stared at him halfway between anger and astonishment. 'You've made up your bloody mind already!'

'I'm a male nurse, Ben. I know the signs.'

'All right, then. You're so damn clever. Tell me what ails you.'

34

Slade said calmly, 'Carcinoma. Left lung.'

'What about tuberculosis?'

Slade shook his head. 'Uh-uh.'

'How come you're so positive? Have you had a Mantoux that I don't know about?'

'The Mantoux wouldn't help. I had a B.C.G. about three years ago, last place I worked.' He looked over the top of Ben's head. 'I just know.'

'Well, the radiologist doesn't agree with you.' Ben pushed the newspaper off the desk revealing the plates and the white flimsy of the report clipped to them. 'Listen to this, you stubborn old mule: "there is a large irregular paucity occurring in the left upper lobe of the lung related to the left main bronchus, with extensive pulmonary infiltration. The appearances are those of carcinoma of the lung; however, tuberculosis of the lung cannot be excluded."'

He raised his eyes. 'That's bad, Ernie, I know. But you've got a chance at the moment and you can't exclude it until it's been checked. You can't say you "just know". Tuberculosis mimics other conditions. It's not called the "actress of medicine" for nothing. What makes you so damn sure it's carcinoma?'

'All the signs are there.'

Ben became brisk. 'What signs? Come on, let's have them. You've leapt to a hell of a categorical one-man diagnosis and you must have worked off some basis that was more than just a hunch.' He eyed the lean figure. 'I can see you've lost weight. How much?'

'Fourteen pounds.'

'In what length of time?'

''Bout two, maybe three months.'

'Appetite?'

'Lousy.'

'Coughing blood?'

'Yup. Like just before we went to the airport.'

Ben stared at him wonderingly. 'And you never said a word. Ever had a haemoptysos?'

'Not yet.'

'You can expect one under stressful conditions. Up to half a cup of blood. Anything else?'

'Night fevers. Night sweats.'

Ben paused. 'What does Ginny know of this?'

For the first time Slade showed emotion. A ragged look crossed his face. 'Nothing. And I don't want her to.'

'Sure.' He was getting frayed at the seams at last, Ben thought. He got up and came around the desk, perching on its edge and looking at Slade. 'Ernie, even if it is T.B. it's still bad, I know. It's going to mean your spending anything up to a year in an institution. But dammit, that's a damn sight better than a disease with a one-hundred-per-cent mortality rate within twelve months, isn't it?' He watched Slade for a moment while Slade watched the wall. 'I agree that that the Mantoux tests won't be helpful. So let me take a specimen of sputum and send it away for histology and analysis. It only takes three to five days.'

He was inclined, although he did not know it, to keep people at arm's length for fear of involvement, for fear of emotion. It had helped, it had got him to where he was. But now he realized that Slade was more than an animated figure that said good morning how are you and Ginny's fine thanks. Slade wasn't just a heart and a veriuos stream, he was a real person just like Benjamin Zodiack, who fancied, liked, loved, angered, orgasmed and feared. For a rare moment Ben was able to transpose his personality and be uncomplicated Ernie Slade, with a small education and a terrible problem. It lasted only a fraction of a second and he was glad, for in that fleeting time he became very afraid. When it was gone he looked at the bristly blond head and thought: you are stronger than me.

'Okay.' Slade got up. His eyes were very clear and there were laugh-seams in the brown skin around them. For a moment, Ben thought, I nearly knew you, but I don't know you and maybe quite soon I will only remember you.

Slade looked at his watch. 'Mind if we do the test tomorrow? I figured on shooting home for an hour before I go on duty.'

'That's fine.' Ben rose. He was relieved that Slade was going, he didn't want to look at him and feel he might be looking in a certain way that Slade would understand. 'Come to me before you go off duty tomorrow, I'll be here early, I'm doing a thorocotomy.'

'Fine.' Slade flicked a hand and went to the door. There he hovered a moment. 'Thanks, Ben. Thanks for everything.'

'Hell, I haven't done anything.' It came out with surprising bitterness, in a little flood that told him medicine was for

36

nothing, all those years were for nothing. Then he checked it. 'See you in the morning.'

He watched the door close. Then he went to the window and looked out at the gathering darkness. A figure trotted through the rain to a Volkswagen in the staff rank. Slade, going home to his Ginny. What was he going to say to her? How did you behave under Slade's circumstances?

After that it seemed that there was nothing more pressing to do than sit down again and smoke a cigarette and listen to the rain trickling through the drainpipe outside the window.

People who live in the large plush homes of Bishopscourt do so because they have large plush incomes or large plush overdrafts or because they happen to be the Bishop. This is a standard rule but every rule has an exception and on a darkening Monday evening with the gusting wind and the rain in dark duet, the exception was a naked girl named Virginia Slade who liked to kid her friends that she had been called Virgin for short but not for long, so everyone had settled for Ginny. And she was an exception because the large plush home wasn't hers, it belonged to large, plush and well-upholstered Mrs. Mary Eliott-Johnson who was at present touring the Far East.

Ginny was by nature a rescuer. She would rescue, release, free from captivity, take under her care or generally succour anything that wasn't patently owned, uninjured or in the best of spirits. Once she had tried to save a healthy one-hundred-and-sixty-pound gym mistress from four feet of surf and been slugged in the ribs for her pains by her victim, who had taken this to be the playful opening gambit of a Lesbian. But she remained undeterred, and following her regular modus operandi, one sunny morning she had rescued a distressed Mrs. Eliott-Johnson from the evils of bus travel. It turned out that Mrs. Eliott-Johnson had forgotten to put petrol in the Humber and her husband—the beast—had taken the Jaguar and Mrs. Eliott-Johnson was very grateful indeed to be rescued because she had never caught a bus before and wasn't sure where to sit and was afraid the conductor might be rude to her.

Hence the house. Rent free. For seven months.

It was not a condition of her occupation that Ginny should run around in the nude. This had been caused by the telephone, which had got her out of the shower. Steamy and untowelled, she sat in an unconsciously abandoned posture, legs carelessly apart, body slumped, staring at the receiver which she had just replaced. After a while she started to laugh. She laughed heartily for a moment. Then she began to cry, ending off with a watery and reproving, 'That will do, you bitch.'

It was the bedroom telephone she had answered, not the one in the library or the hallway or the study or the games room. So she got up restlessly, prowled across to the dresser and studied her reflection in the mirror. She had one of those wholesome What-Katy-Did-At-School faces, pink-cheeked and freckled hockey-fieldish and tennis-courty, winter air and come on girls another goal for good old St. Cyps. A face framed by strawberry blonde hair, a good enough figure, chubby hips that would develop as she grew older and an overall bloom to her skin that matched the cheeks and the hair. She was, she often said, a pink girl.

She had never even seen St. Cyps. She had never played hockey or tennis. Bred in Montreal, she had been forced to drop out of school at the age of fifteen. Untrained, she found employment in a small branch of a large bookshop chain and ended up, after the passage of six years and the consumption of about three thousand novels, as manageress. At this stage she met Ernest Hobday Slade, who solemnly purchased a magazine from her, returned half an hour later and smiled, and asked her to come out with him.

When he smiled she fell in love with him.

The American and the Canadian embarked upon a peculiar marriage. Neither had any relatives or ties and Ginny wanted to see the world and what Ginny wanted she sure as hell got. So they drifted, and when the money ran out they worked. Sometimes they both worked. Sometimes they took turns. If they had accumulated a bit then neither worked, and they became the beautiful people of the beaches, swimming, browning, surfing, fishing, loving in quiet coves. The Bahamas. Trinidad. Sydney. Singapore. Hong Kong. Two years, three years, four years. Nice. Those Costas in Spain. The Canaries. Malagasy. Lourenco Marques. Five years, six years.

Cape Town. Seven years. Seven years of glorious bumming. She was a twenty-eight-year-old seasoned globe-trotter, without the set or the jet.

And now it was all going to change.

She got up, restless and excited, prowling like a ginger cat to the walk-in wardrobe across the room. She was hungry. Idly, thinking more in terms of what there was to eat, she put on a pair of Mrs. Eliott-Johnson's expensive high heels. They were a little out of fashion but very elegant. Then she took down a cloche hat and pressed it to her head. She was turning back to the mirror when she heard the distinctive sound of the Volkswagen's door closing. It was always like that. Thump. Rattle. Try again. *Ker-thlomp.* That was Ernie getting mad.

'Ernie!' The sound of the wrought iron gate squeaking open. Up the path across the hedge-to-hedge lawn, stop at the pool, gravely take a leaf or two off with the scoop, as though he were bringing in a sea anchor.

'Ernie!' Back to the dresser, drag a smear of lipstick across the pink lips. The scoop rattled. *Okay, the sea anchor's in.*

'Ernie!' *Slow down, you move too fast.* Along the hall, reaching the front door at the same time he did, seeing his shadow on the frosted glass panel. Okay, ready.

Wearing only the cloche hat and the high heeled shoes she said loudly, 'Come in but make it a quickie, this time. I'm expecting my stupid husband home at any minute.'

The door opened. Ginny said, 'Oh, my God, I've been had!'

It was Slade who'd been had, and it was not the first time. Sometimes he got quite nervous about these homecomings. But this time it was different. He started to laugh. The laugh-seams closed up in the brown skin. But then his eyes let him down and he knew it was happening so he caught her by the shoulders and said, 'Doll!' and buried his face in the smooth skin of her neck.

'Hey, hey, hey! You silly old sailor.' She took his arms and pushed him away. 'Ernie!' He saw the shock, the absolute horror, the disbelief. *'Ernie, you're crying?'*

'Crying?' He mocked her, brushing away the tears. 'Say, listen, I been sneezing all the way from the hospital, don't I get to come in this goddam door?'

She was all sympathy and apology, wonderfully absurd in nothing but the hat and the shoes, hauling him in, babbling 'Oh, Ernie!' *Like I just popped out of a submarine.* 'Darling, are you all right? Ernie, come in, sweetheart, I was just kidding——'

He was back in control, now, yet feeling oddly shaky. 'Never had hay-fever before. Sneeze, sneeze, sneeze.'

'Come on, come on!' She was pulling on one rope-like arm as though it were a hawser. The two cherry nipples danced before his eyes. He wanted to reach out and touch them yet there was no fire in him. He felt damped. 'Look, can you pour me a drink?'

She subsided and went thoughtful. 'But you're going on duty, Ernie.'

He put an arm around her. 'All I want is one vodka. I think I might be getting flu.' He steered her inside, into the big opulent living-room.

'Ernie!' The green eyes were big. She looked silly and little-girl in the hat and shoes, like a child who had been trying on her Mother's. She also looked big-girl and very desirable, like she'd been waiting to kid her husband. 'You didn't get wet?'

'Hell, the rain's not much.' He moved his head. 'Look, the vodka, do you think you could——'

'Ernie, I'm mad!' She was away from him, skidding in the stilettos to the liquor cabinet. 'We'll both have one.' The green eyes sparkled. 'You gave me such a hell of a fright when you came in! You've never had hay-fever before, darling.'

'With tonic,' he said tiredly, and sat down on the sofa before the empty fireplace.

He wished there was a fire, which was silly, it was raining but it wasn't cold. He put a forearm across his forehead, holding it there like a tired child until a hand appeared before his eyes holding a goblet with the tonic rising wine-like in little tired traceries of bubbles. Tired like him, and he had to work all night. She said something softly and was gone. He heard the tiny heels of the stilettos crossing the lounge floor, sighed, lit a cigarette. Then she was back, the hat gone, barefoot now, wearing a granny-print frock and smelling of cologne.

He drank half the vodka. It glowed inside him. 'I got the sea anchors out of the pool. There were two of them.' He said it gravely.

'Oak?'

'Oak.'

'Hearts of oak are our ships, jolly tars are our men ... Ernie, you ever miss the sea?'

The vodka. Bless the vodka. 'Yup. I miss the Ritzy food. I miss the way the Captain would take us on sightseeing tours every time we hit port. I miss the Mate darning my socks——'

She smothered his voice with her laugh and a warm palm across his mouth. 'Silly old sailor. You never, ever, want to go back?'

'One day,' he said slackly, 'when I've made my fortune, on our private yacht, I——'

'What is the state of our finances, Ernie?'

They never normally talked about money. It was a commodity, that was all, it was cabbage, it was bread. He turned his eyes on her suspiciously but she was plucking idly at a loose thread in the hem of her dress. He had a sudden horror that Ben might have telephoned her.

'What the hell makes you ask that?' His voice was harsh even to his own ears. He saw the quick look of alarm on the scrubbed features.

'Ernie!' A quick hand, warm-fingered, on his leg. He writhed away.

'You know damn well I always handled the finance. I've had a rough day. I had to meet this President guy. I had to give up time when I could have been sleeping. You haven't even asked me about it. Now you got the goddam cheek——'

'Ernie, you *are* sick!' She regarded him in astonishment. Even-tempered Ernie, suddenly yelling. Unexpected tears flooded her eyes. It was enough to shock him back to normality.

'Kid, I'm sorry. I didn't mean to talk like that.' But he wasn't really sorry. He watched her stubbornly. 'Why did you ask?'

Her mouth settled. She became plain. 'Why don't you try answering my question?'

He gave up suddenly. He was overwhelmingly tired. 'We got thirteen hundred in the Building Society savings account. My salary. The VW. Some bits and pieces. Complicated, huh?'

She ignored the clumsy attempt at a jibe. 'Monthly bills?'

'The butcher. The baker. The candlestick maker.'

'Nothing special?'

'Nothing special. No unexpected contingencies.'

'That's a big word for an old salt.'

He saw the small, withdrawn smile. He realized that there was

41

a magic about her tonight that he had never known. 'Honey?' His tone was gently explorative. 'Something is cooking. Now what is it? I got to go back on duty, I——'

She threw it at him with a quavering grin. 'You reckon what we've got is enough to split three ways?'

He goggled at her. 'Three ways?' Then he was on his feet, staring down at her. 'No! *No, Ginny!*'

'Yes, dammit!' She was standing too, the tears rolling down her face. She was coming towards him, blinded to the horror on his face, reaching for him, wanting to smother herself in him while he quaked.

'For Christ's sake, Ernie Slade, won't you give a pregnant woman a chance to be happy?'

He stared at her open-mouthed. Then he felt the cough building inside him, quickly fumbled for a cigarette, lit it, mumbled, 'Oh hell, this flu!' and wheeled away with the memory of her proud eyes watching him and thinking hell, that silly old sailor was *crying*, rushing to the toilet and letting the cough bubble out, on and on until there was a small alarming popping little low-gut explosion somewhere deep in his body and he saw the bright blood run out, mouthful after mouthful, while his trained mind said, half a cup, I got to remember it was half a cup, and he heard Ben's voice echoing in his ears, under stressful conditions you can expect a haemoptysos, Ernie, and he cursed Ben until the blood was gone, he could shakily stand up, flush the toilet, wipe his lips, walk out with his white face to join his woman.

'I'm sorry.' He had to clear his throat. Maybe she would pick up the stink of the blood.

'Ernie!' *Like I popped out of a submarine.* 'Ernie, is it all right?'

'All right?' He stared at the wall. 'You're sure about this?'

She grinned in pure triumph. 'Absolute one hundred per cent, Skipper. Doc Harrison 'phoned me just before you got in.'

'How far are you?' He held her close to him, still staring at the wall.

'Two months,' she said happily. 'Oh, Sailor, I got two months of child inside me, I got two months of living thing, Daddy!'

Slade stroked her, trying to build up some joy. 'It's gonna be a girl.'

'You think so?' She pulled away, looking at him with those

new rich eyes. 'Oh, Ernie!' *Like I just popped out of a submarine.* 'Oh hold me close, darling, I never felt so good!'

'Yeah.' Slade pulled loose. 'This is a special occasion. What do you say we have another drink, huh?'

He was marching towards the bottle even before her warm voice reached across, enwrapped him, and told him to go ahead.

Chapter Three

Above Albert's Pahler's burly body was the kind of face that makes babies cry. He had small, mean, suspicious eyes and an expression that ranged between grief and savage despair. But when he grinned it changed completely.

'Satisfied with everything, sir?' He lounged back in the chair at Bobo's bedside while the tubby raincoated figure of his assistant, Captain Maurer, hovered in the doorway.

'I am quite pleased.' Bobo looked at him over the top of his steel-rimmed spectacles. He was propped up in bed and *The Wind in the Willows* lay on his knees. Cedric Mango and the rest of his party, ill at ease in a white hospital, had come and gone and he was feeling rather alone, and vulnerable. 'You seem to have thought of everything, Colonel. I like the idea of the identity pictures.'

'Thank you,' said Pahler, who was rather proud of them himself. He cast an eye about the luxurious, pastel-coloured room. 'I hope you will be on your feet again soon.'

Bobo grunted. 'I'm allowed up but have to take things quietly. Dr. Zodiack took blood from me this evening and tomorrow I have something called a Maximum Acid Output test, and a bone-marrow biopsy. I must confess I'm not exactly looking forward to either of them.'

'You'll survive,' said Pahler with the casual cheerfulness of the disgustingly healthy. He turned his head slightly. 'Captain Maurer, there's no need to stand out there. Come inside and say good evening to the President.'

Maurer had a leanly reptilian head on top of his hippy womanish body, and little black-button eyes that were inclined to slide away. He often made Pahler think of Ka, in the *Jungle Book*.

Edging reluctantly into the ward, colour climbed slowly into his normally pasty cheeks. His eyes rested on the top button of Bobo's pyjama jacket. 'Good evening,' he said. And then, emerging after a distinct pause during which he fought a furious battle with his own inhibitions and hide-bound traditions, he ground out, 'Sir,' and cast a murderous glance in Pahler's direction.

Jane Hobart put her blonde lace-capped head around the door. 'Here's your tea, Mr. President.' She moved aside to let Slade come in with the tray. 'In about fifteen minutes I'll give you your next vitamin B12 injection and after that it's beddy-bies. Doctor's orders.'

Bobo grunted and she withdrew. Slade put the tray down on the bedside locker and there was a silence until he had followed Hobart out. Then Pahler eased himself out of his chair. 'I'll be going, sir. Glad to find everything in order.'

'Won't you have some tea?' Bobo waved at the tray.

'No, thanks.' Pahler glanced at his watch. 'It's already eight-thirty and I've had a long day.'

'Thank you for coming,' Bobo said formally. 'I was a little worried until I saw how well organized you are here. I have many enemies in Gamba and there has been talk recently of an attempt on my life. Captain Crutchley, my Chief of Police, said he was writing to you.'

'I've heard from Crutchley.' Pahler moved to the tray and poured a cup of tea, handing it to Bobo. 'There's nothing to worry about, Mr. President, I've got this place sewn up.'

Bobo sipped and nodded. 'That's a good man you've got in Slade. It gives me a sense of security to have him around.'

'Slade?' Pahler stared at him.

Bobo smiled. 'I suppose I wasn't really meant to know. But you can't fool an old bloodhound like me, Colonel. I heard some newspaper reporters at the airport talking about him.'

Pahler coloured. He said, 'Slade isn't——' and then abruptly stopped. He thought for a moment, watching Bobo with his steel-hard eyes. Then he quickly said goodnight and wheeled briskly out of the ward with Maurer half-trotting in his wake.

They found Slade halfway along the corridor. Pahler stopped and considered the calm brown face and clear blue eyes. There was not a lot of brain there, he thought, but a great deal of life.

'The President'—Pahler flicked his head in the direction of the ward—'thinks you're one of my boys.'

He had had some experiences with policemen, long ago in the alleys of his boyhood. It showed in his reserve, in the way his expression closed up. 'So?'

Pahler sensed the resentment. But he went on. 'That old man is lonely and nervous. He's taken a liking to you. I'm not asking you to pretend you're something that you're not. But there's no need to disillusion the old guy.'

Slade shrugged indifferently. His mind was busy in another quarter altogether. He said, 'Okay,' and moved away, silent and preoccupied.

Pahler watched him go. Then he shrugged and walked on with Maurer, reaching the entrance, ducking out into the windy rain and crossing to his official Fairlane. There he rested an arm on its hood and turned back to study the lights of the hospital.

'Everything seems all right.' Maurer wanted to go. Pahler could see it in the way he kept blinking against the rain in his face and moving his squat body restlessly.

'It's his first night.' Pahler wondered whether he should invite Maurer for a beer. Ever since his wife's death a year before he had boarded uneasily with his daughter Ellen who at eighteen had married a Sectist preacher and dressed like a grey owl. He was finding himself more and more reluctant these days to go home.

'Night,' echoed Maurer pointlessly. He had an irritating nervous habit of repeating the last word of one's sentence, and loose-fitting dentures produced a hiss on sibilants, making him all the more Ka-like. 'Do you believe all this nonsense about an attempt on Lunda's life?'

'I'm not sure.' Pahler moved his big shoulders uneasily inside the raincoat. He had had a sneaking sensation from time to time during the day that something was going to go wrong somewhere but one did not reveal hunches or premonitions to a man like Maurer. 'Crutchley's report mentioned this organization called the Brotherhood of the Spears. That's old hat, of course, we've all read about them in the newspapers from time to time. They're a bunch of tattered Gamban malcontents who live in the mountains and make themselves heard every now and again by blowing a rail junction somewhere. Crutchley flushes

46

them from place to place but he's had remarkably little success in rounding them up. If anybody is going to have a dip at the President then it's that bunch of clots.'

'Clots.' Maurer relished the sibilant. 'Do you think they have the power, the money, the organization, to——'

'That's the whole point,' Pahler interrupted, 'I don't. But I'm a policeman and I have to try and think of everything before it happens. Frankly, I think old Lunda is safer here than in Gamba and my main fear is that he might be overcome by the craves. He was a bottle-and-a-half man before Crutchley dried him out.'

'Out,' Maurer echoed. 'And in that event?'

'He might discharge himself quietly and go out and get boozed up, and then we'll have to find him.' All this talk of liquor had made Pahler thirsty. He finally overcame his dislike of Maurer. 'Feel like a quiet beer, somewhere?'

The Captain hesitated. 'I'd better not. Thanks all the same. I'm late as it is.' He had a wife with leg-of-mutton arms.

'Okay.' Pahler flicked a hand and watched Maurer waddle away to his own car. Then he got into the Fairlane. But he did not drive away immediately. He was reliving the scene that had come back to him several times since it had occurred that morning: the airport. A man, elderly, very fit, wearing a dark blue shirt and pale casual slacks, standing on the very fringe of the crowd, watching Bobo Lunda come down the gangway from the plane. A haughty-looking, down-with-the-wogs, God help Britain type of man, probably retired Army. Very still, intently still, studying Bobo Lunda's distant figure. Too intent. Too still. Pahler, his policeman's radar homing, had moved in next to the man, jostling him slightly. A head had turned. He saw a beaky arrogant nose, full, sensuous lips. Anger, a vicious unnatural anger.

And a red flash of madness.

Pahler put the car into gear and pulled out of the rank. He changed lanes without signalling and a car hurtled by, its hooter flailing him with indignation.

Pahler ignored it. Somewhere, he told himself, I have seen that face before.

Jane Hobart and Slade came out of Ward Three, which was

47

used for orthopaedic cases, and walked along the corridor towards her office.

'Time for a cigarette, Ernie?' She was still flushed from the effort of turning old Mrs. Kennedy, who had the shape and inertia of a beer keg.

'I got a lot to do.' They reached the office. Brummer, Hobart's fat and somnolent nurse-aid, was taking a doughnut out of the small fibre handcase that Slade usually brought to work when he was on night duty.

'Thanks, Ernie.' Brummer closed the case and handed it to Slade. 'Your wife bakes like crazy.'

'Except he doesn't eat them himself any more.' Jane studied him over the cigarette she was lighting. 'Your appetite's shot, Ernie.'

Slade took the case. 'I'm on a diet.' He smiled without humour.

Jane drew on her cigarette. 'People like that lean and hungry look. The President has taken a shine to you. And he thinks you're a cop. He told me so when I gave him his injection. What do you think of that, Brummer? Our Ernie is a sleuth.'

'F.B.I.' Brummer grinned and wiped her lips.

Slade turned to go. 'If you want me I'll be in the spare office, the one Ben uses sometimes.'

'What's this—writing your memoirs?'

'No,' said Slade solemnly, 'I'm auditing my books.'

Matron Molly Burns, known to the staff as Pussy, looked up from her desk.

'What do you want?'

Warren Clunes frugged unhappily in the doorway. 'I was going to commit the heinous crime of wishing you goodnight. But seeing you choose to adopt that tone, forget it.' He turned away.

'Come in!' Pussy barked. She had the right voice, but her body was an exception to the rule that says all Matrons have to look like battlewagons. She was slim and pretty, thirty-seven and unmarried.

Clunes entered the small office. He was so tired that all he could come up with was a slow waltz. He Blue-Danubed his way to the only spare chair.

'Goodnight,' he said fractiously.

'Don't try and get funny with me,' said the Matron threateningly. 'I've eaten big men for breakfast and you're a little chap.' She leaned forward. 'What the hell do you mean by making all sorts of staff arrangements without consulting me first?'

'Such as?'

'Such as getting Slade to stay on.'

'I thought it might help,' Clunes said wearily. 'The President is not only a man, he is a black man. I felt he might be more at ease at first with one of his own sex around. Slade goes on holiday on Wednesday for a month, so it's only two nights.'

Pussy Burns bit into a pencil. 'What you mean is that if the President has to be wiped, he would prefer a man to do it.'

He looked at her guardedly. 'More or less.'

'Hah! There are no "more or lesses" when you're being wiped. It's a very positive sort of affair.' She dropped the pencil. 'The President lived in London for three years, you know. His ideas are probably the exact opposite of yours. He would probably be as embarrassed as hell with Slade ham-handling his way around the Presidential backside.'

'Don't be coarse.'

'You seem downcast tonight.' She gave him a level look. 'Out with it. What's the matter?'

'It is not in my nature to confide,' Clunes said wearily. 'Or for that matter to whine, either. But seeing you asked, there's a new jingle going around about me. The first line goes, "You won't get Clunesie in the dunesies". Great, huh? I'm not blind, you know. I know the way I'm laughed at. All those jokes behind my back. I'm in love with the ambulance. Clunes Is Queer.'

The Matron picked up her pencil and tapped it on the desk. 'How long have we worked together, Warren?'

He shrugged. 'More than three years.'

'That's right. And in all that time I have never known you even to display interest in a woman. You can't blame those kids. At their age their minds are permanently on their fannies. They expect to see you stagger in every morning, hung over and worn out from screwing yourself to death. To them that's *normal*.'

49

Clunes was silent for a moment. Then he said, 'You tell me. *Is* it normal?'

'No,' she said softly.

'My mother died a year ago, as you know. She'd been a widow since I was five. We did everything together. Opera, theatre, bridge. I just never seemed to get around to ... girls.' He was being very calm. 'Now Mother's gone and I'm forty-eight, with so much to regret. I regret never really having had a youth. I regret being ignored by women the moment I walk into a room. I regret never having slept with one. Surely there are things you regret?'

'Yes.' She had had her fair share of living, and among the many things of which she was entitled to be proud were one or two that sorrowed her. She wept, sometimes, for the wasted years.

'I have normal desires, you know.' She noticed how his hands were trembling. 'Quite strong ones, really. I am not a homosexual. I have wanted so often, especially this past year since I've been free, to take women out. To dine with them. To screw them. To make them pregnant and then laugh at them.'

There was another silence. Then she said, 'What you need, my friend, is a drink.' She got up, unlocked a cupboard on her left, and brought out a bottle of whisky, putting it on the desk next to her water jug. 'No more looking back, Warren.' When she smiled, it changed what was basically a serious face. The smile was full and good. 'Sometimes, before I go home, I have one. For the nerves. Shall we?'

Clunes studied her. He was drained of passion. She was being very kind, after all, considering that they had never got on really well. Suddenly he relaxed.

'Strictly for the nerves,' he said, and reached for his glass as she poured.

The Joseph Schwer was a three-storeyed building. The ground floor was given over to Reception, Administration, Catering (in kitchens tucked away at the back), and seven private wards. The first floor was confined exclusively to wards both private and semi-private; and the second, the top storey, was simply known as Up There. It housed a laundry and a three-bed isolation ward, both of which had been unsuccessful. It had proved quicker, cheaper, and more convenient to have the laundry done by an outside contractor who called daily. And the isolation ward had turned out a hazardous white .elephant. So Up There was seldom visited, although there had been talk from time to time of removing the laundry and renovating the whole floor, thereby increasing the hospital's capacity. For lack of funds, and because Clunes was against it, nothing so far had been done, and the small 'locked ward' as it was called, still nearly fully equiped, was given a lick and a promise once a month by an unsupervised maid but otherwise remained more silently isolated than when it had contained measly patients.

The night staff were few in number. At night sick people sleep. If they can't sleep then they are given pills. Only emergency operations are performed. About the only thing of note that ever happens is that now and then someone dies.

So the night staff, for the Joseph Schwer's quota of fifty beds, were only six in number. Sister Hobart was running the ground floor assisted by the sloppy-figured Brummer. Sisters Meadows and Strange shared the first floor with two aids, Jensen and Novak, both of them immigrants.

Thing were quiet. At ten-thirty Janet Strange and Margaret Meadows shared a cigarette.

'You will never believe it,' said Sister Strange, 'but I had to go downstairs an hour ago and I saw Pussy and Clunesie-wunsie drinking together in her office.'

'Impossible!' Meadows made big eyes.

'For a fact. Dinkum.' Strange wagged a finger. 'And they were laughing, too.'

'Oh, well.' Margaret Meadows shrugged. 'He was probably telling her how he does it with the ambulance.'

'Exhaust-pipe?'

'Some say the ignition slot.'

Both of them laughed heartily. They were in their early twenties, with the green bar of the midwifery qualification on their epaulettes. Chunky girls, brunette, pale-skinned from night duty, firm-legged and solidly-hipped, with neat waists. They occupied flatlets in a building behind the Joseph Schwer and when they were not on night duty Meadows lived a vague burrow life, arriving at work from varying points of the compass except the poorer suburbs.

'Incidentally,' she said, 'I have bad news. I think I am.'

'Oh, not again!'

'I'm afraid so.'

'You don't look all that troubled.'

'I am and I'm not.' Sister Meadows appeared, if anything thoughtful. 'I got drunk, you see. Bombed. Stoned. Me and these three naval types. So I went into the bedroom with the one who took me there—it was at some flat or other—and then he asked me if his friend could.'

'Oh, no!'

'Oh, yes. The trouble is I was *away* that night. I was really turned on. So I had——'

'All of——'

'All three of them. And I don't know which one.'

Janet Strange digested this. 'That's what they call "love roulette".'

'And I got the bloody bullet.'

'If you could remember which one——'

'That's the trouble, I was drunk. Bits and pieces come back to me every now and then. And it wouldn't help, would it.'

'Were they officers?'

'Very much so. One was a Lieutenant-Commander.'

'Good grief. Married?'

'Not by the way they spoke to each other. You can usually tell. Or they tell you. Not many chaps hide it any more.'

'True.' Strange's face straightened. 'I want to make one thing clear, Maggie. I helped you last time. With this one you're out on your own.'

Margaret Meadows smiled unexpectedly. 'I'm in no hurry. Not yet.' She winked. 'I might even decide to blame Jimmy.'

Jimmy was the more or less steady boy friend. He was the faithful spaniel, the one who kept coming back for more despite being stood up, cheated on and regularly humiliated, he was the kind girls like Meadows usually marry. In the end. If it's not too late.

Tough cookies, these. Sly birds. But when you were brought broken off the expressway, broken and stunned and shocked, and you opened your eyes and saw them bending over you, quick and quiet and competent, you were quite happy to use the name somebody once gave them.

Angels of Mercy.

*　　*　　*

52

Slade stared at the two tablets in his shaking palm without really seeing them. Goddam night. It had the quality of death. His fever was building. He put them in his mouth and threw them back with a gulp of water. Then he went back to the desk on which lay his endless useless scribblings, the blotchy ballpoint minutiae of defeat. Foolscap. What a good name. Make a hat out of it and go sit in the corner, dunce. Class clown. Born loser.

Oh Sailor, I got two months of child inside me, I got two months of living thing, Daddy!

It was overwhelming. In seven months' time he would most definitely be dead. He wouldn't see his daughter. They would have to carry the can, the two of them. Ginny and the baby.

An empty can, his fever-sharp mind pointed out. The proof of it lay in those scattered sheets on the desk, in the jumbled figures and awkward handwriting, in the calculations made over and over again to try and prove the impossible, to try and find a mistake in what was really very simple arithmetic, to try and show that maybe you could add the savings account to the estimated value of the old Volkswagen, throw in his fishing gear, camera, a pair of Zeiss binoculars and one or two other items, tack on fifteen months of refundable pension contributions and make it total more than just short of a thousand pounds.

He went to the window and listened to the rain. Dammit, he was starting to sweat. The A.P. Cods were working. Call it a thousand, he thought, for ease of calculation, and figure out that she needed a hundred a month to live on, working in pounds, or two hundred in South African rands. The blissful days of a rent-free existence in the velvet lap of Bishopscourt would be long gone by then. She would have to get a room somewhere; a small flat if possible. He wouldn't have his widow and his daughter grubbing for a living like a bunch of dirt farmers. In ten months Estate Late Ernest Hobday Slade would be consumed. What then? Go spit on his grave? He wouldn't blame them. Ginny wouldn't want to work with the baby to look after. Except that it looked as though she had no choice. Years and years of working to pay for the creche, for nursery school, for proper school, coming home nights, dead beat, the kid running loose on the streets in some crummy suburb.

'No!'

The sound of his own voice was so loud that it shocked him. And his knuckles were red and raw where they had slammed the wall.

Absently he took out his handkerchief and wrapped it around his hand. *Bumped myself in the furniture.* Why in hell hadn't he ever taken out insurance? Why? Why? Why? His febrile mind explained dryly: because there was no need, dope. Just the two of you, two lazy, no-good, irresponsible drop-outs, two intercontinental fun-bums. Who needs insurance? Remember saying it once? Well, you did. That's what you said, you said who needs insurance.

He stalked the small empty office. So what do I do? The frustration hurt him, it caused pain in him like a blow. So he asked his mind, desperately, once more. *What do I do?*

And his mind laughed: ho-ho, went his fever-pointed mind, go rob a bank.

He stopped his prowling and stared at the blank wall opposite. His thoughts free-wheeled on. They struck the wall, bounced back like rubber and he caught them as they tried to pass him by. For a fact, he thought, I would. Except that they catch bank robbers and put them in jail.

When the telephone buzzed, he leapt. It was as though it buzzed within his mind, intimately. He went to it scared, as though it would say, I know what you've been thinking and I'm going to tell. Done sing-song, the way little girls used to, at school: *I'm going to tell. I'm going to tell.*

But it was only Hobart, saying that she was in the middle of something and would he please go to the President's ward, the old man was ringing.

Bobo Lunda was old, ill, strange, alone and homesick. All this had been bearable while there were his party to visit him, Matron Burns and that fussy little man Clunes to welcome him, Pahler to enquire after his safety and Hobart and Slade to administer to his well-being. But that had been three hours ago and by now he was just another jangly-nerved insomnolent, another nervous old man jumping at shadows while his anarchical thoughts pogo-sticked around in his mind.

So he rang, and three minutes later Slade walked in.

54

Bobo stared at him. He felt a rush of returning security so strong that affection bubbled in him. He wanted to fling his arms about the neck of this tanned, strong, calm man.

He said, out of huge relief to the man who had banished the shadows, 'My God, Mr. Slade, I would pay a prince's ransom for a glass of whisky!'

So there it was. One chance remark, and an idea entered the brain of desperate, broke Ernie Slade at that moment in his life when he was exactly conditioned to receive it. It shook him visibly. His brain, thinking with the speed of an explosion, gave him a breathless break-down of facts and figures. And Bobo, fiddling on his glasses, noticed nothing.

When he looked up, the effect had gone. Slade smiled and moved towards the bed, and if the smile was unnatural and the movement stiff, Bobo was too relieved and newly cheered to be in any way observant.

'Sorry,' Slade said. 'Scotch isn't on your list. Anything else I can get you?'

'A cigarette and a weak tranquillizer are the extent of my demands,' Bobo smiled. 'Frankly, your appearance was all I really needed. I was getting the rats.'

Slade regarded him with new interest. 'Happens that way, first night in a hospital, especially in a private ward. You get jumpy.' He produced his John Cottons. 'Have one of these. I'll tell Sister Hobart about the tranquillizer.'

'Thank you.' Bobo accepted the cigarette, waited while Slade lit it for him. 'I think I'll read for a while. Please remind Sister Hobart that I'm not on dawn patrol. I told Matron that I don't want to be woken before seven.'

'I'll do that.' Slade flicked a hand and walked to the door.

'Mr. Slade.' He stopped and turned. Bobo was looking at him seriously over the top of his spectacles. 'I would like you to know that I find your presence very reassuring. You're doing very well.'

'Thanks.' Slade flushed. 'Everything's fine.' First time, he thought, I was ever glad to be figured as a cop.

He found Hobart in her office completing a form. She looked up and smiled, neat, beautiful and efficient. 'Hi, Ernie.' Everyone said that she was nicer when she was on night duty because she got tired, and it took some of the steel out of her.

'The Pres. wants about ten grammes of Vallium.' Slade stayed in the doorway. 'Okay?'

'Fine.' Jane got up and went to the drug cupboard. She produced her key and then paused. 'Ernie?' She had gone pink.

'Huh?' He wanted to go. There were a great many things to consider and his mind was already shunting off on another track.

'You don't approve of me, do you?' She stood quite still, holding the key.

Slade sighed. 'It's nearly midnight. I got things to do. Let's leave it, Sister, shall we?'

Hobart's pinkness had turned into a red flush. 'You're so distant with me. Yet you're all buddy-buddy with Strange and Meadows and you know what Meadows is!'

Yes, thought Slade, I know what Meadows is but she's also human. He was suddenly impatient. 'Look. What you girls get up to is your own business. But if you want me to say something then I'll say that I like Ben Zodiack a lot, but that he's got plenty of faults and one of them is that he's too dumb to realize what a hell of a nice wife he's got!'

Hobart's steel curtains slammed down. She was the only girl Slade had ever known who took a personal pride in her perpetual affairs. It was the kind of involved life that would have run most women ragged but Painful Jane's clever brain enjoyed the stealth, the subterfuge and the sneaking around that was necessary.

'I don't know what you're talking about, Ernie,' she said.

'That's why I said let's leave it.' He lost patience altogether and left the room, heading back fast for the office and the scattered papers on the desk.

For the first time since leaving Bobo's ward he gave himself fully to the idea that had come to him, trying to force it into a brain that threw up its hands in horror. It kept slipping deliberately into neutral and thrumming until he rammed it back into gear. Think, he told it, and began a slow and controlled pacing of the office.

His brain divided itself into two opposing factions. It would never work, said the one side. But the other, the desperate side said, so what, there's always a chance, isn't there He is ill, said the one half, you can't haul him out of there. Oh yes, came the reply, you can, he's not all *that* sick. You haven't got the time, said the weak half, definitely on the defensive now, one more night of duty and you are going off on a month's holiday. Well, said the aggressors, it doesn't call for such a vast amount of organization, you can do it in the time that's left.

He tried a new line of approach which his rebellious mind finally accepted, although with caution and reserve. It was that there was no harm in theorizing on the principle that he was totally uncommitted, and that if eventually he decided against it then no one would ever know and he could kid himself that he'd never really meant it, anyhow.

On this basis he sat down at the desk and began to make notes. He took a sheet of paper and scrawled some headings doubtfully. He considered them, frowned, then deleted two. After a moment of thought he added three more. Gradually his mind lost its confusion and began to work with oiled precision. Midnight came and went. At one o'clock he had the foundations of what appeared to be a foolproof scheme, although quite a lot depended on luck and the manner in which people like Pahler would reason.

Luck? He sat back and stared at five pages of his awkward handwriting. When you did a thing on the spur of the moment it often worked better than months of detailed planning. And there were precedents to follow: Quebec. Palestine. Guatemala. Australia—that Quantas thing.

He lit one of an endless number of cigarillos and got up, left the office and walked the corridor to the President's ward, entering without a knock and brutally flicking on the main light.

Bobo was asleep. His big hands were clasped across his chest and *The Wind in the Willows* lay open on the counterpane. Slade moved to the bed and stood looking down at the slumbering figure. The huge feline head looked even more cruel in repose. This old guy has done things in his lifetime, he thought, for which a lot of people would have been hanged. There was no sympathy due to Bobo Lunda. Unless he remembered that, he might as well forget the whole idea right away.

He put the light off and left the ward, went back to the office, sat down, got up again, paced slowly across the room and finally turned with his back against the wall. He stared across at the desk and the terribly incriminating words that lay there.

'I'm crazy,' he said aloud.

57

He returned to the desk, put out a big brown hand and grabbed the papers, bringing them close to his face as he prepared to crumple them deliberately into a ball and throw them away. But the hand stopped. The papers lay in it, supine, so near to his eyes that he could make out some of the words. Then, very slowly, he put them back on the desk, quietly pulled out the chair and sat down.

'There is no other way,' he said wearily. He picked up the pen and began to write busily. It was one-thirty and he had a great deal to do.

At precisely that moment Ben Zodiack, in the bedroom of his home in faraway Clifton, opened one eye, stared at the ceiling, and experienced one of those stomach-fluttering dark-hour thoughts. It had occurred to him that if Ernie Slade was indeed suffering from tuberculosis then he should immediately have been suspended from duty. He should never have been allowed to circulate amongst the patients, even with only the suspicion of it there at this stage, and most of all he should never have been allowed to administer to Ben Zodiack's own personal million-dollar patient, the President of Gamba.

He sat up, switched on the light, lit a cigarette and drew smoke into his dry mouth. He accused himself bitterly of slackness and neglect and allowed his conscious mind one tiny peep at what his subconscious had known all along, which was that this was the sort of thing that happened when you got yourself involved in an affair, and infatuated to boot.

He would, he told himself, attend to his omission first thing in the morning, when Slade arrived for his sputum test. It was going to be unpleasant but it had to be done.

Then he extinguished his cigarette, switched off the light and lay back, knowing that sleep would not come easily.

Chapter Four

It was one of those beautiful days where the mountains leaned down on them, clean-faced and crisply outlined. No cloud today. No rain, no wind. It was already hot.

They were eating out on the patio. 'Only three hours sleep,' said Ginny Slade from the brunch table, 'and the man wants to go, go, go. I will never understand you, you silly old sailor.' She passed him a plate. 'Have some more sausage.'

'Eh?' Slade had woken only half-an-hour ago. He looked at her out of pouched eyes. 'No thanks.'

He couldn't have eaten if someone had paid him a lot of money to try. The scene with Ben Zodiack was too fresh in his mind.

Like Ben, the question of suspension from duty had simply not occurred to him. He had located the doctor straight after coming off duty, and the news had come like a blow in the face, with Ben's hand already on the telephone to inform Matron Burns.

'Ben, stop.' He had blurted the words out hoarsely.

'It's no good, Ernie,' Ben said sorrowfully. 'Arguing just won't work. It's got to be done and you know it.'

Slade licked his lips. 'Then why didn't you do it yesterday, when you saw the X-rays?'

Ben said nothing. He stared at Slade across the desk.

'You slipped, Ben.' Slade fought to meet the doctor's eyes. 'You made a boo-boo. I've already been in contact with the President. The harm's done. You're going to have the whole place in an uproar and there's no need.'

Ben was looking at him with puzzled and worried eyes. 'So?'

'So forget it,' Slade said desperately. 'You know what Clunes is like. He'll suspend me without pay. I might lose certain benefits. Look, I've got only one night of duty left, then I go on vacation for a month. One night, that's all. It makes no damn difference and in any case, Ben, you know I'm no danger to the patients.' He paused. 'Admit it, Ben, you know it's not T.B. It's the other thing.'

He was giving the doctor an easy way out. At last, Ben's hand came away from the telephone. 'I'll admit nothing,' he said abruptly. 'But we'll forget the whole thing. Now get out.'

Slade had left the office with the knowledge that he had used Ben's mistake, and his pity, to his own ends.

He became aware that Ginny was talking to him. 'Sorry. I didn't hear you.'

She stared at him, fresh-faced, freckled and un-made up, smelling of soap and clean girl, pink and white in a pale negligee. Ernie sure was behaving oddly. 'I was saying that your appetite is lousy. You just *never* eat anything any more, Ernie.'

'Coffee,' he said hoarsely, 'I'll have some coffee.'

She poured, and handed him a cup. 'Why don't you go back to bed? Town can wait.' She put her elbows on the table, clasped her hands and leant her chin on them, studying him with a good deal of discernment. 'You're looking kind of beat, husband.'

He sipped. The coffee was too hot. 'I'll sleep when I come back.' He got up.

'What's so all-fired important?'

'Chores. Just chores.'

'Real mysterious, huh?' She was kidding, but the green eyes had developed a speculative look.

Slade went up to her. He took her face gently between his hands. 'You behave yourself and maybe Sailor will buy you something special.'

'Old marrieds.' He saw the instant pleasure in her face. 'Hurry back, lover.'

He chuckled. Sometimes he could forget for a moment. Then the knowledge would come back like a blow in the face. 'Be seeing you,' he said quickly, turned, and walked away. He only half heard the slight sound behind him and reached the three steps that led down to the path before he realized that he had dropped something. Then he swung about and went still.

Both of them studied the little booklet whose bright vinyl

60

cover winked back the sunlight. Then slowly she raised her glance and they looked at each other carefully across the length of the patio.

'Ernie?' It was a small voice. 'Why do you need your passport?'

His heart slogged on. When he spoke he felt as though his cheeks were stiff. 'It has to be endorsed. At the Consular Office. Otherwise it goes stale.'

'In that case you'd need mine, too. We got them together. They're the same age.'

'It's in my pocket.' He forced his wooden legs to move, and came back. Bending, one hand outstretched, his jacket gaped open and something else fell with the tiniest papery tick of sound to join the passport.

It was his Savings Account passbook.

Another tableau that seemed to stretch into infinity. Then anger flooded him, anger and shame, and he snatched them up and straightened to find her close to him, looking into his face with a sweet yearning.

'Sailor, you sure are all fingers and thumbs this morning.' She gave him a wobbly smile.

He grabbed her impulsively and held her tightly against him, staring over her shoulder at the rising mountains. 'I won't be long. Two, three hours.' Then he let her go and walked quickly away, trotting down the path and turning only when he reached the wrought-iron gate. There he waved. It was a ritual. But she only raised a hand in response, standing motionless on the patio until he drove away.

Ben Zodiack was rested, well-breakfasted, relaxed and contemplative, holding the gunmetal Capri down to a grumbling thirty while he listened to the stereo tape. The car swung its long shark's-snout bonnet around the corner of Queen's and into Beach Road, threading its way around the long brown legs of Sea Point's beautiful people, tooling along the road that had the lilting, lazy, lowtide Atlantic on the left, the rugged canyons of Sea Point's rearing blocks of flats on the right.

You could, he thought, smell the money. There were the Young Rich and the Old Rich, and in the morning all of them gravitated to the sea. The Old Rich got creakily out of bed alone, the Young Rich got out in twos and multiples thereof. The Old Rich fumbled in their teeth, the Young Rich fumbled out their Dutch caps, the Old ate gruel for breakfast, the Young drank Prairie Oysters for hangovers. The Old and the Young got into Jaguars and Aston Martins and were conveyed to the sea where the Old mumbled in the sun and the Young crucified themselves in the sun so that by the end of the summer all of the heavily rich were heavily tanned. They had sprung a trick on nature, these people, they had found an elixir somewhere so that there were no In-Betweens. They had exterminated middle age; the Young retained their smooth erotic limbs and their effervescent organs until one day, suddenly, the flame went out and they were Old.

The elixir was called money.

He passed the Sea Point Pool where the beautiful people were buying their tickets to spend a day in the sun, leaving it and its Pavilion a mile behind. There was a girl in yellow walking slowly along the pavement, a very slim girl with very nearly perfect legs, and honey-coloured hair. Crimplene hugged her small bottom and smooth hips, it moulded itself to the thrust of her small breasts. She was a very regal-looking girl. He stopped the car a few yards ahead, got out and stood waiting for her.

She came on unafraid, so he said, 'Forgive my intruding so rudely but it's a lovely day and both of us are obviously on our own; I wonder whether you would care to have lunch with me somewhere shady and expensive?'

The girl stopped. She looked out to sea where a picture-card lobster boat chugged sturdily past. Then she turned her head and surveyed him with a regal smile.

'You're ten minutes late, you bastard,' said Jane Hobart.

He took her to the car and they drove away. 'I brought your bikini,' he said. 'You left that in my bathroom too, along with your toothbrush and the Sequins.'

She rested a hand on his thigh. 'I borrowed one from Maggie Meadows.'

'A toothbrush?'

She chuckled. 'I'm starving. Three hours sleep and no breakfast. Where are we going to eat? I feel like fresh oysters and a runny Chinese omelette full of prawns.'

'Somewhere high up. I feel like smoked salmon with four

hefty winds on the pepper mill and a great ferocious beast of a T-bone steak.'

She hugged his arm, snuggling against it. 'Groovy. Burn it, lover.'

So lover burnt it all the way into the City and they went to the Sable Room which is sixteen storeys up, and they ate fresh oysters and a runny omelette full of prawns, smoked salmon with four hefty winds on the pepper mill and a great ferocious beast of a T-bone steak. They looked out at the vast Atlantic and the ships going by, and when she was finished twenty-two-year-old Jane Hobart lit a cigarette with a gold lighter and put her hand on his and said, 'I wonder how the poor are making out?'

The poor weren't making out very well. Slade ate a meat pie and drank a cup of bitter coffee in a dingy Greek café in Wynberg. He gave up the pie on the third mouthful of gristle, left half the coffee, paid his twenty-two cents and walked out into the hot two o'clock sun.

The Volkswagen was parked in the lot behind the cinema. He unlocked it and got in, leaving the door open. Then he took a list out of his jacket pocket and checked it against the items on the back seat; one dog chain, twelve feet long; two padlocks of different sizes; two Thermos flasks; a Coleman paraffin pressure lamp, filled, with a mantle tied on and ready to burn; some canned food—he would get the perishable stuff later; a cheap plastic salt cellar, an enamel plate and mug; a knife, fork and spoon; a collapsible nylon and aluminium camping stretcher, light and strong. It had cost quite an appreciable amount of money.

Slade nodded, reasonably satisfied. There were one or two items remaining but he could get them later. Time was running out on him and he had still to cart all this gear some miles out on the Hout Bay Road. What he needed more than anything else at the moment was another vehicle.

He locked the car again, pocketed the keys and walked in the early afternoon heat to a telephone kiosk where he ran through the yellow pages of the directory. It gave him four used-car lots. He picked the nearest, Herbstein's Proud Autos, ('Get a Clean Car From Ethical Ed') and walked three more blocks to reach it, where he settled on a shabby brown Austin

Light Delivery van that had, 'Klein's Contractors, We Pant to Paint' lettered along its sides.

Ethical Ed was thin and morose. 'You can have it for six hundred. At that price I give it to you, I make a present of it to you. People say I'm crazy. All the time I'm told that I'm mentally deficient, I shouldn't be in this game. I should be Santa Claus or something, but I got a wife and six kids to feed and a Barmitzvah coming up next week and I need the money, I got too much money tied up in these vehicles, so is it wrong to be honest and tell it like it is, I'm asking you?'

'Five hundred,' said Slade. 'And I've got to have it right away.' In his pocket lay a cheque for thirteen hundred rands. He had drawn it out of his savings account in Rosebank that morning, leaving a nil balance.

'Five hundred, the man says. So if I'm mad, if I'm held up to the world as nuts, if I give everything away and lose money every day, why must I hold out for six hundred? You can have it for five-fifty, this clean, well-shod vehicle.' He kicked a worn tyre bitterly. 'And I can let you have it in an hour. In an hour I can let you have a fleet of trucks. I probably will, in this present mood of mine. Strictly cash, huh?'

Slade passed across the Building Society's cheque and Ed studied it. 'Fifty-seven thou on the clock and that is a genuine mileage. Because I'm such a fool I can tell you that we do turn them back. I just hadn't got around to this one. And is it dishonest? Everybody *expects* me to do it, so if I don't then they read fifty-seven thou and automatically add on another twenty and then who's wrong? And tell me, how do I know you're E. H. Slade, like this says? Understand, I'm not insinuating anything. But I've got to give you a cheque for quite a lot of change. I got to be careful. Maybe you picked this up in the street or something. You got any means of identification?'

Slade fumbled for his passport and reluctantly handed it over. 'American, hey? Sometimes I wonder where the Capetonians get to, all I see is Greeks, Ities, and Poms and Squareheads, and now I got you.'

In a mood of increasing despair he led the way across the cinders to his pre-fab office and filled out a transfer form. 'Just sign here, friend. How are things at the hospital?'

The world stopped with a jar. A voice asked, 'Hospital?' and he realized it was his own.

'Sure. You work there, don't you, at the Joseph Schwer? My Uncle Louis died there in January. Poor old guy. His bladder just couldn't take the hammering Uncle Louis gave it all his life, but he had a terrific funeral, musta been three hundred mourners. I used to see you there when I went to visit him.'

The same voice said almost soundlessly, 'I don't work there. I've never worked there.'

'You trying to be funny or something?' Ed regarded him with outrage. 'I never forget a face. It's my job never to forget a face. If I forgot a face I wouldn't still be here giving motor cars away instead of selling them, would I?'

Slade turned away. 'I'll be back in an hour.' He crunched across the open lot to the street, aware of Herbstein standing in the doorway of the pre-fab, watching him all the way.

The Southern Suburbs run in almost a straight line across the Peninsula to Muizenberg. The Capri shadowed them on the expressway, fleeing from the cold ocean to the warm one.

At Muizenberg they parked and then wandered amongst the rotting multi-coloured beach cabins that stood on spindly pilings in arch Victorian gaiety until they found one that was unlocked, and changed in it.

'Mind where you walk,' said Ben. 'Amongst all the evidence of mass copulation are bits and pieces of broken bottle.'

With a slim brown foot Jane toed a discarded condom. 'I didn't know they still used these things. Here, unzip me.'

'They are making a come-back.' Ben tugged down the zip. As she lifted the dress over her head he put his arms around her waist from behind and pulled her against him. 'You're awful warm, Sister Hobart.'

She turned around within his grasp. 'I'm more than warm. But let reason prevail. The habitués of this place must do it standing up and I think we're both a bit above that.'

'Oh, definitely,' Ben said, bringing her closer. Then he kissed her, and reason prevailed, and he let her go. But her eyes had gone heavy so he pulled her back again without a word from either of them. This time reason took a minute or two to prevail while they strained against each other, while he roughly pushed her lace bra off her breasts and felt the small nipples grow hard against his chest and they ground their bodies together in a

65

kind of fury. It took a very special last-ditch discipline to pull away and regard each other with hearts racing and breath coming hard.

'God, Ben, darling,' she said, and pushed him out of the cabin. She followed a minute or two later and they ran down to the sea and flung themselves into it, holding hands like children and letting the small waves wash over them until they had cooled off enough to go back to the sand and lie on their towels, smoking cigarettes and talking as though nothing had ever happened.

'That's a crazy name you've got.' Jane tickled him with a gull's feather. 'How did you come by it?'

'My father was a Jew.' Ben screwed up his face as the feather traced its way across his upper lip. 'My mother was a Scot. She was his second wife. The first wife was also Jewish, so I had a half-brother who was a full Jew.'

'You say you *had* a half-brother?'

'He's dead. Killed in the Six-Day War. In my case the chicken followed the hen so I didn't feel the call as much as David. 'He pondered for a moment. 'I suppose you could say that being only half-Jewish undoubtedly saved my life.'

'That's a real Zodiack Irishism.' She twirled the feather and giggled. 'I am going to say girl's names while I draw this feather across your face. Where does it tickle most?'

'There.' He sneezed paroxysmally. 'Under my nose.'

'Jane!' She said it triumphantly. 'I was saying Jane!'

'Bully for you.' He sat up and flicked away his cigarette, looking along the length of almost deserted beach. 'Muizenberg on a week-day in the off season is a depressing place and the breeze grows cool. Shall we go to my pad and frolic?'

'It's only three-thirty.' Jane turned on her back and looked up at the pale sky of Africa. She stretched like a lazy cat, a very svelte pussy-cat in a black wet-look bikini. 'The sun is warm, the sea is at hand. You must learn to appreciate the good things. How would you like to be some poor working-class dope sweating behind the wheel of a stuffy car, full of nervous tension and covered in multiple tics?'

Ben studied the smooth relaxed face for a moment. Then he grinned and said, 'You're a hedonist, Sister Hobart. It's just dawned on me.'

'What's that?' Jane sat up.

66

'A pleasure lover.'

'Oh balls,' she said, and threw sand at him.

Sweat ran down Slade's cheek. It burned his neck where he had cut himself shaving and went on to join the hundreds of other drops that had nearly saturated his shirt. He wriggled irritably as he swung the Austin van into the quiet street that ran beyond the Joseph Schwer and pulled up almost directly in front of the old laundry ramp.

The hospital had been built in a hollow, a once unhealthy trap for the run-off of winter rainfall from all the other ground about, so that although the driveway from the main street entrance was reasonably level, the road on this side ran on a line with the second floor, that part of the building known as Up There. When Up There had still functioned in its dual capacity of Isolation Ward and Laundry it had seemed a practical expedient to run a ramp out on concrete pillars to meet the side street, thereby giving easy unloading access to delivery and supply trucks. At that stage they hadn't had a Warren Clunes to point out all the many disadvantages of the idea and the fact that if the building itself had cracked at this end because of the treacherous shifting nature of the once-boggy ground, then the ramp didn't stand a chance. So without a sagacious wisehead around the Trustees had gone ahead and built it.

The ramp's cracking and partial subsidence, condemning it for any further use, had coincided with and influenced the decision to abandon the second floor. But for Slade it would still serve admirably.

He got out of the van and locked it, then stood for a moment looking about. This was a quiet residential street. Houses on the other side were screened by high hedges and stone walls. A coloured maid pushing a baby in a perambulator was the only other being about.

He turned his attention to the hospital side. Although the ramp had subsided to a depth of a foot across half its fifteen-foot width, what hadn't broken looked substantial enough. Certainly, he thought, it would support the weight of two men and one wheelchair. The dust-shrouded windows of Up There looked back at him like so many blind eyes. The first floor was a good twenty feet below him. All its windows here were frosted because at this end were the lavatories and bathrooms. From the ground floor came the hollow rattling of garbage cans and the lighter clatter of crockery. Those were the kitchens, far below him where he stood on the pavement of the high embankment.

Satisfied, he turned away and began to walk, ignoring the Austin, crossing the road and leaving the hospital rapidly behind.

He kept to the quiet and drowsy residential streets of Constantia, seeing the neighbourhood only through a filigree of patrician hedges and hearing it above the drowsy murmur of well-bred flies. A girl on the edge of a pool, slowly tumbling into the incredibly cobalt water; arch voices from a hidden tennis court; a gossip of women having tea under a striped garden umbrella.

He was nearly finished with his chores. In the hour between buying and collecting the van he had found a small travel agent's and bought an air ticket to Lusaka in Zambia: South African Airways from Cape Town to Johannesburg, C.A.A. from there. It had taken some fast walking and a distressing coughing bout to get back to the car lot within his self-imposed hour limit but he had managed it. Herbstein, busy on the telephone, had silently handed him the keys and a cheque for what was due to him.

He had started rushing from this point, driving to the travel agent to pay for the ticket, then via Constantia Neck to a turn-off on the Hout Bay Road. The van had turned out to have rattley tappets and a differential whine but it had got the trip done just inside another hour.

When he was a mile from the Joseph Schwer his fatigue hit him suddenly, together with a growing realization that he was running very late. Ginny would be worried and inquisitive. It was four o'clock already. He deliberated on the kerb-side for a moment, then crossed the road and summoned a taxi.

It took ten minutes to arrive and another twenty to get him back to Wynberg through the rush-hour traffic. At four-thirty-five he bought letter paper and envelopes from a stationer. His face was flushed and yet he was shivery, as though the day had turned cold. Recognizing the symptoms, he found a pharmacy and got a draught from the dispenser, drank it quickly and reached the Volkswagen ten minutes later.

It was nearly five o'clock. At this stage Slade drove home,

68

wondering how he was going to explain his lateness to Ginny.

That area of Cape Town known as Clifton lies beyond Sea Point. It is strung along the littoral, crammed between mountains and sea. It is the home of the four famous Bikini Beaches, of more beautiful people skinned in copper and bronze whose bathing suits never get wet, of houses that go up towards the mountain and blocks of flats that go down towards the sea, so that the inhabitants of Clifton either scale or descend steep flights of steps or drive on to the roofs of their apartment blocks and go down in lifts to their homes, where they can sit at ease and watch the cold Atlantic roll in at about a buck to the wave, calculated in direct ratio to their rent.

Clifton is the home of the modern troglodyte. It is kinky and kooky and costly and hard on the legs and wind, but it is also easy on the eye.

Clifton is beautiful.

Benjamin Zodiack occupied a tiny cottage near Fourth Beach. There was a cove which was a droop in the hem of the indigo Atlantic. It had a border of white sand done in poster paints, and worked into it in vermilion and aureole and ruby and emerald were the gem colours of the little houses and their handkerchief-size gardens. Your neighbour was the casual toss of a ball away, your access to the world was to climb a bean-stalk flight of steps.

It was a hushed, stillness-of-evening, cold-beer-on-the-verandah, enchanted type of place, and the girl in the yellow dress looked as though she belonged.

'I don't think I could ever shout in a place like this,' said Jane Hobart, 'or grow angry or feel depressed. It is too beautiful.' There were times when Painful Jane showed traces of having a soul.

Ben emerged from the shadowed interior and handed her a tall glass of beer. Then he sat next to her in a deckchair and poked idly at the small portable barbecue that winked red coals in the near darkness.

'Cheers.' He raised his own glass. 'You know, I think I am falling in love with you.'

She turned her head quickly. 'Don't be crazy, Ben.'

'What's crazy about it?'

'Everything. You're a married man. You have a ten-year-old son.'

'Does that place an automatic embargo on a commodity called love?'

'I don't want to disturb anything, Ben. I don't want to be a home-wrecker.'

He had gone stiff, hunched over the barbecue. 'What are you in it for, then—kicks?'

She turned quietly to face him. 'That was a pretty mean thing to say.'

He dropped the iron. 'It was. I withdraw it. I'm sorry. Do you love me, Jane?'

She was looking out across the cove again. 'You know exactly how I feel.'

'I don't. At least, I'm not sure. I know what I would like to think. So why not put it into words?'

She was hauntingly lovely in the faint ruby reflected glow of the coals. It was impossible to correlate Jane Hobart of the night-time with Sister Hobart of the day-time.

'Witness refuses to answer.' He tried unsuccessfully to say it lightly. 'That's right, is it, you won't answer?'

'That's right,' she said. She turned and he saw that those grey steel shutters had come down. But it was only a brief rejection. When Jane smiled it was something to see. 'Let's not waste time, darling,' she said, 'let's not dig too deep. Let's just live for the present.' She got up and stood behind him, looking down at the winking coals, with her hands gently touching his shoulders. 'The evening is too beautiful to waste.'

It was unlike Jane Hobart to waste anything.

'It's only because I love you,' Ginny Slade said through her tears. 'If I didn't love you so goddam much I wouldn't worry. Don't you want to be loved? Don't you want me to worry? Couldn't you even have 'phoned me? Hell, here I sat with the hours going by, wondering what had happened! You might have had an accident, you might have collapsed in the street. You're looking sick enough to have collapsed in the street. And then when I'm ready to collapse myself you march in looking as haggard as a three-day jag and you tell me you got held up at the Consulate. Hasn't the Consulate got a 'phone?'

Slade had his arm around her. 'I've told you, I didn't think about it. I'm sorry, but——'

'You're shivering, Ernie!' The green eyes went soft with concern. 'Oh Ernie! Darling,'—a slim hand touched his forehead—'why didn't you say you were ill? You're running a fever!'

'It's nothing,' Slade said hoarsely. He pulled away from her a little. 'Like that hay fever I had yesterday. Sneeze, sneeze, you get all flushed from——'

'Oh Ernie! Have I been horrible, darling? Oh Sailor, it's only because I love you!' She came against him, put her arms around him and her head against his chest and began to cry.

Slade stared across the plushly-furnished room, stroking her hair absently. A great feeling of desolation took hold of him. He stirred and looked at his watch. 'I better go. I go on in thirty minutes. You been sick much today?'

She brushed at the tears. 'Three, four times. I won't ever get used to it. I get madly up-tight when it happens. I suppose that's why I was so upset at your being late. Pregnant women are crazy creatures.'

'Not this one.' He got up and kissed her. 'Look after yourself.'

'And you.' She stood too, holding him. 'Take it easy, Ernie. You haven't been looking very well lately. Remember, there'll be two of us to take care of one of these days.'

He paled visibly. He opened his mouth to say something, hesitated, then began to move away. He was at the door when Ginny's voice reached him again. 'Ernie, is there anything wrong?'

'No.'

'If you're ill, don't go on duty. I'll phone Matron. You should go to bed.'

'I've got to go,' he said stubbornly.

'Please, Ernie.'

'*I've got to go!*' he shouted.

They stared at each other across the long stretch of room. Then he opened the door and was gone behind the bang of its closing.

Ginny ran through to the bedroom. At the window she pulled aside the lace curtain and watched his slim figure go down the path. Jesus, Ernie, she said within her mind, whatever it is that's eating you I hope to God you'll tell me, or get over it, I never thought I would have husband problems.

After a while she lay on the bed and tried to sleep.

Jane Hobart lay naked on the bed. Nude, she was so boyishly figured she appeared almost frail. But the slim legs clenched like steel, the smooth arms clung with a wiry tenacity, her strong heart frantically drummed, she sucked air into her lungs through her open mouth with hoarse audible breaths, her eyes were so heavy they seemed almost shut. She was drenched with sweat, she was writhing, she was shoving, she was ramming with her body upon the fulcrum of her buttocks, she was using it like a club, bruising it and hurting it in the agony of the pleasure that was turning into ecstasy. She began to cry, 'Oh, yes, oh yes, oh yes, darling, oh darling don't stop, oh my precious, my sweet, I love you, oh Ben my beloved man, my strong Ben, oh God, yes, *yes* darling,' almost singing this paean of exultation until she stiffened, her body upthrust and quivering, her lips fluttering, an actual scream exploding from her, 'Ben, ahhh, oh, God, *darling* yes!'

She stayed like that, quivering, for another ten seconds. Then she collapsed, this girl who was now neither the day-time Sister Hobart or the girl in the yellow dress of enchanted evening but a sweet-wet, trembling, exploded lover.

Minutes passed. He lit two cigarettes and they lay quietly smoking in the darkness that was lit by a moon peeping through the window. Then he said, 'You said you loved me.'

'Did I?'

'You did. More than once.'

Temporarily spent, she could chuckle. 'So did you.'

'I know. I meant it. I'll say it again now. I love you, darling Sister Hobart. I've never been more sure of anything in my life. Now you say it.'

She put a hand on his chest. 'There's no need. You know exactly how I feel.' Then she swung her legs off the bed. 'How about some coffee, lover?'

Painful Jane had reverted to type.

Chapter Five

Margaret Meadows had been moved downstairs to run the ground floor in Hobart's absence because the Joseph Schwer was less than half full and she was not needed on the first floor. Tired and distinctly irritable, she worked automatically, repacking the dressing of the thorocotomy case Ben Zodiack had done that morning. Her deft fingers moved nimbly but her mind delved in the past.

Sister Meadows was remembering the time when she had been a virgin.

Oh, she thought, to be seventeen and intact again. I've always had more fanny than sense. And now she was preggy again. Damn it, if she'd realized that five minutes on the back seat of a car outside the nurses' home six years ago were going to change her whole life she would never have gone through with it. She had been a very willing party at the time but when you were that age you had no sense. She had it now, but it was too late and it was no use crying over spilt milk.

She straightened. Her back was sore. 'You stay here, I'm going for a smoke.'

'Yus, Suster,' said Novak the nurse-aid.

Margaret left the ward and walked briskly along the corridor towards the Sisters' office. She stopped at the door, fiddled in her pockets, found her cigarettes and lit one with her gas lighter. Some of the tension began to go out of her. Quietly she put her hand on the knob, opened the door and walked in.

'Ernie!' She said it loudly because she was surprised.

Slade whirled. He put his back against the door of the drug cupboard. He had only that moment locked it, and hidden in one hand was the key he had taken from the desk drawer.

'Hi,' he said huskily.

Deep down in her subconscious, a very small voice warned Sister Meadows that something was wrong. But it was drowned

73

by her own problems. 'Hi, Ernie. I'd forgotten you were on duty tonight.' She sauntered to the desk and perched on one corner.

'It's the last time.' Slade stood rigidly against the cupboard, feeling its handle pressing into his back. His legs had begun to tremble and he wondered whether she would notice.

'You're not looking too well,' Margaret observed.

'The vacation will fix me.' The key felt slippery in his sweating palm.

'You lucky devil.' She studied him a moment. He looked really ill. 'Better see a doctor as well, Ernie.'

He nodded. 'I will.'

'How's the President?' It was, after all, her duty to check on him.

'Fine. Sleeping.'

'He's a funny old chap.' She had looked in on Bobo earlier. 'I mean, he's not like an African at all, is he, with that Oxford accent, and the way he calls you "my dear". And I don't mind, I really don't mind at all being addressed that way by a black man.' She let her imagination go. 'Maybe he'll start a craze on the Joseph Schwer amongst African Presidents. We'd have them all here, Jomo and Julius and Humphrey and Hastings and even Crying Kenneth, all in a row.'

Slade said nothing. Margaret's eye lit on Slade's small hand case near her on the desk. 'Ahah!' she said. It was symptomatic of her condition that she momentarily forgot her troubles. She was suddenly achingly hungry, salivating. 'Ginny's doughnuts, my God!' With the ease of long familiarity she reached out, but the case was snatched from under her clutching fingers. She found Slade in front of her, the case clutched to his chest in both hands, his eyes containing a mixture of ferocity and fear. He seemed to be trying to say something.

'Well, forgive me!' Margaret Meadows went a deep red.

'It's empty,' he said hoarsely.

'You don't have to be so damn rude.' She got up huffily, walked around the desk and seated herself, picking up a form and beginning to complete it.

Turning to go, Slade's sweating fingers lost their hold on the case. He grabbed at it, missed, grabbed again and caught it at the level of his knees, sinking with it to the floor as the lid flew open and bright ampoules of Vitamin B12 and intravenous

Vallium tumbled into his lap. With his back turned to the girl he shoved them wildly back into the case, conscious of sweat running suddenly down his cheeks. Getting to his feet again, he felt something else drop from his shaking hand.

The drug cupboard key fell with a little silver tinkle.

'Ernie, what the *hell* are you doing?' Meadows stood up, irritated. She began to come around the desk.

Slade swooped. 'It's okay.' Colour rushed into his face from bending. 'Dropped my car key.' He tried to grin into the serious face of the girl but his lips and his neck muscles would not obey him. He felt as though his head were wobbling on his shoulders.

Meadows studied him. 'What's going on, Ernie?'

'Nothing, Maggie. Honest, it's nothing.' A teardrop of sweat plunged out of his hair and ran down his forehead. It rested in an eyebrow, hesitating before dropping. His expression was ghastly.

'Say, you really are ill.' She put a hand on his shoulder. 'Ernie, you've got to promise me you'll see a doctor tomorrow.'

'I will.' He looked straight into the concerned eyes.

'I'll 'phone Ginny if you don't.'

'I promise.' It was only a kindly threat, he knew. She would never know whether he had or he hadn't.

'All right, then.' Margaret smiled. 'Bring me a doughnut when you get the chance.'

'Sure.' Slowly, vastly relaxing, Slade headed for the door. Her voice caught him as he put a foot into the corridor.

'Oh, and Ernie?'

He turned very slowly. 'Yes?'

'You can give me the drug cupboard key. It will save having to sneak it back later.'

He stared at her. The pit dropped out of his stomach and fell away into a void. She was waiting for an explanation. 'I've got a bit of a fever, Maggie. I took some A.P. Cod.' Thank God, he had his own bottle in a pocket. He produced it, holding it out for her to see on a shaking palm.

She was smiling. 'I guessed as much when I realized you weren't well. Don't act so furtive next time.'

'I won't.' He put the tablets back in his pocket and gave her the key. 'Sorry, Maggie. I never wanted to get you in trouble.'

'Crap. When you start pinching Speed, that's another story.'

'Sure. Sure.' He was so grateful he nearly kissed her. But his chest hurt. Another cough might be coming on. 'Thanks, Maggie.'

'Oh, forget it.' She winked and turned away. Slade went out into the corridor. Quite slowly he began to walk back to the office Ben used sometimes, where he had left the doughnuts from his hand case greasily turned out on the green desk blotter.

Warren Clunes put his hand over Pussy Burns' on the white tablecloth. The band was playing 'All Over the World' softly in the background. Cutlery clinked. A candle in a wine bottle spilt long fingers of red wax. The wreckage of the *langoustines portugaise* had not yet been removed but the big Knysna oysters were already a memory. In the pervading pink of the van Donck, high up in the Trust Building, he felt happily and contentedly pink, himself. All over. What a wonderful atmosphere, he thought, in which to get clobbered.

'Here, have some more.' With his free hand he topped up her glass with the exquisite riesling that had accompanied the langoustines like an eager choir.

'I'll be getting smashed,' said the Matron most un-Matronishly.

'Two's company.' When he spoke he felt as though his tongue were a furry springboard for his cube-shaped words. 'Enjoying yourself?'

'Very much indeed. It's been a wonderful evening.'

'Not so much of the "has been".' Clunes squeezed her hand. Perhaps in the dark pink night she could be persuaded into a confidence. 'Tell me, who started that "Clunesie in the Dunesies" thing?'

Molly Barnes studied him through half-closed eyes, the better to focus. 'Jane Hobart.'

'No!' His pet, his gold medallist. 'I can't believe it.'

She winked. 'There are lots of things you wouldn't believe about Painful Jane.' She peered at her small gold watch and pinned down the time. 'The morning is nigh, dear. Hadn't we better went?'

'I suppose so.' They got up and steered each other across the glass dance-floor and out to the lift. He felt seven feet tall and full of agro, so on the way down he kissed her, and she said,

'No, Warren, I'm not your mother, try it like this.' Getting from the van Donck to the ground takes a goodly length of time, and he proved an apt pupil, so that between re-entry and splashdown they managed to work up a cheerful breathlessness.

'A great evening,' he said as they reached his Volvo. 'Whassa time?'

'Twelve thirty.'

'Is that all? Good grief, the night's a pup!'

'It's not Sunday tomorrow, Warren, don't you think we should——'

'Nuts,' said Warren Clunes, the strong. 'Let's go to my pad.'

When Slade checked his watch it showed precisely twelve-thirty. He intended to put his plan into operation at exactly four o'clock, so there was nothing more to do in the intervening three-and-a-half hours except double-check every part of it and then try to relax.

He was surprised at how calm he had become. The shakiness that had overcome him during the incident with Margaret Meadows had gone, and the brain that had seemed so woolly was now a precision instrument of crystal and stainless steel, functioning quickly and faultlessly.

Luck, or the element of calculated risk on which he was obliged to rely to a certain extent, had dealt him two rather sharp body blows: Herbstein's recognition of him and Margaret finding him at the drug cupboard. But he was prepared, now, deliberately to shrug them off as minor disasters. If things worked the way he hoped they would, then if Herbstein ever did put two and two together it would be too late as far as the authorities were concerned—Slade would already have left the country. And Maggie Meadows would hardly be likely to relate his presence at the drug cupboard to the disappearance of Bobo Lunda. She seldom thought very deeply and in any case, according to the grapevine, she had enough problems of her own without concerning herself in those of someone else.

He got up and walked slowly to the window, looking out upon the darkened hardstand lit only on its edges by the bounce-back of lights like his. That was the way, he told himself, keep it slow and calm.

Four o'clock had been a deliberate choice. It was the really

77

dead hour on night duty and Margaret would not leave her office except to check on the thorocotomy case, or if she were rung for. Making his plans the night before, he had relied on these factors. If Margaret were busy in Ward Four with Mrs. Turner, the thorocotomy, then the whirr of the small suction machine that was busy pumping the muck out of the patient would drown all extraneous noises. If she were in her office then it was too far off for her to hear him anyway. The only risk he ran was in meeting her or Novak in the corridor, in the five yards that lay between Bobo's ward and the lift. But he had calculated that he would be exposed for only ten— perhaps fifteen—seconds, and this was where the calculated risk, or luck if one wanted to call it that, came in, but in a full twelve hours of duty it wasn't asking too much to have the corridor alone to himself for that tiny fraction of time.

There were two more risks he had to run, one minor and one major. The first, minor one, was that Margaret or Novak might enter Bobo's ward during the five minutes he needed to spend there. Here again, it was unlikely. Margaret had Slade's own reassurance—which he intended to give again shortly before four o'clock—that the President was well and sleeping contentedly. In addition, she had firm instructions not to wake him until just before the day-staff arrived, so that a check between four o'clock and five minutes later could be discounted. There was then the second factor, or risk, to consider. From just after four o'clock Bobo's ward would be empty, and it was important in the scheme of things that no one discover his absence until the time when he was supposed to be woken. If Slade's reasoning were correct there would then be no immediate alarm. On Tuesday morning—his first at the Joseph Schwer—the old man had gone out into the garden in pyjamas and dressing gown and wandered about. There would be an inevitable hiatus while the night and day staffs changed and it was therefore quite likely that no real concern would develop for about an hour. With luck it might be even more. But if Margaret or Novak should happen to check Ward Seven during the remaining hours of darkness an immediate alarm could be expected once it had been established that the President was not in the lavatory.

Again, Slade had his doubts. There were the reasons he had already considered and also the fact that from five-thirty Margaret and Novak would be moving in on the other three ground floor patients with the full knowledge that to disturb Bobo Lunda would be more than their jobs were worth.

Basically, Slade was pleased. In theory everything sounded eminently workable but in practice he knew very well how the slightest chance could disrupt the most well-laid plans. It was a case of wait and see.

He went back to the desk, took a sheet of paper and scrawled a check-list from memory. That was the idea—to see how quickly each item came to mind including times and mileages, because the plan was wrapped around a very meagre time schedule. Everything would have to be done on the dot, and when he moved he would have to move fast.

The schedule, when it was completed, was perfect. He set alight the paper, let it burn to ash, crumbled the ashes thoroughly and then let them sift out of the window.

After that there was nothing more to do than sit, and study the hands of his watch on their slow crawl towards four.

Four o'clock in the morning. A time of blue velvet darkness, light breathing that sounds like the edge of death, the sprawled looseness of life held poised to a heartbeat and the slow off-duty functions of the body. Down there inside you, automatic pilot is on. The crew are sleeping. A little dream chases itself across the face of the computer like a tickle in the nose. The needles in the dial wobble and fall again. A clenched hand unclenches. Life ticks on. Sleep is so close to death that some never wake.

Ben Zodiack stirred, touched naked warmth that wasn't his. His sleepy nerve-ends reluctantly fed the message to his brain, complete with the approximate time and other relevant data. So he awoke. He reached out and pulled her close and felt the hot buttock-warmth of her against his belly.

'I must take you home,' he said.

'Eh? Whassat?' She revolved like an eel and pressed up against him. 'Darling? Huh?'

'Come on, come on.' He reached across her and found the bedside light. It produced a yellow, sickly glow. It showed an airmail envelope propped against the lamp with big scrawly writing resounding across its face in black ballpoint. A letter from Flora, his wife.

Jane made mewling, disturbed, little-girl noises. 'Nah,' she

79

said, 'don't wanna go.' Her eyes remained tight shut.

Ben swung his legs off the bed. He grabbed a slim arm and hauled her upright. 'Get dressed, darling,' he said urgently.

She awoke at last. More or less. 'Oh Christ, this is bloody.'

His head was hurting. He started to fumble his way into his clothing. 'Isn't it just.' Every time he looked anywhere, he saw the letter. Round and generous, like Flora.

Damn four o'clock in the morning.

Four o'clock in the morning. Warren Clunes stumbled into the utility slickness of his bathroom. He found Alka-Seltzer and drank it. He scrabbled aspirins and swallowed them. He did a weaving rhumba back to his bed and fell upon it, muffling a giggle into the pillow. Great evening, said his bludgeoned brain. Just to sit there and *talk* about it, without doing anything. Because Pussy said there would be no button-fumbling or bra-pawing, no elastic-snapping or pelvis-prodding, a girl can get injured that way, and the last thing it does is excite her, and that's what you had a mind to do, isn't it? And he'd said yes, to be honest with you that is exactly what I had a mind to do, and she'd said ah-hah I knew it, now down, Fido, just you listen to me and I'll give you Chapter One of the Facts of Life but while you're on your feet you can pour me another drink.

Hooray for four o'clock in the morning.

Four o'clock in the morning. Six bells in the Graveyard Watch. If you were stand-by man on the bridge you had the feeling that you were high up amongst the stars while all the aids clever man had invented did the work for you. The Kelvin-Hughes radar was your eyes, the Telemotor was your hands, the Marconi and the Decca were your ears, the distant rumbling Diesels were your sails and all you had to do to hoist them was push a button. Being a sailor had become being a dial-watcher. If something went wrong you went Oops and called an expert. But they still hadn't invented a soul or a brain, so you could stand up there level with the stars, and have your time of reflection.

God, he thought, that's the first time since I left that I ever wanted to go back to sea.

The office was lit by cold yellow electric light. He picked up the hand case and stood for a moment, looking at the door. You are about to commit a crime, he told himself, which is punishable in some countries by death. There is an even chance, no more, that you will pull it off. If you want to forget the whole thing then now is the time. Once you go through that door there is no coming back.

He nodded in agreement with the soundness of this final caution. But there was no longer any doubt in his mind. What did it matter if he were caught? It was worth the even chance that he would not be.

Slade extinguished his partly smoked cigarillo. He jerked at his tunic, took up the hand case. *Here goes for the fifty per cent.* Then he walked quickly to the door of his decision, opened it, went out into the corridor and walked away without once looking back.

He used the stairs to get Up There. He intended to use the lift once, and once only. He wasn't going to run the risk of people wondering why it was so popular in the early hours of the morning.

They discharged him into a corridor. Directly across from him was the door to the 'locked ward', its key rather paradoxically in the lock. To the left down the corridor was the abandoned laundry, then the door leading out on to the ramp.

It was dark and cold. He took a tiny torch from his pocket, unlocked the door facing him and entered the three-bed ward. There he placed the torch and the hand case on one bed and gathered up three blankets from the neat stack standing on a tier of shelves in the middle of the room. Tucking them awkwardly under his arm he walked down the corridor past the silent old laundry, flicked back the Yale on this last door and walked out on to the ramp that jutted pale in the darkness between him and the road.

Vaguely, he could make out the oblong square of deeper darkness that was the Austin. Feeling his way across the ramp, he reached it and unlocked the rear door, tossing the blankets in and then leaning after them and constructing a rough bed. Then he locked the door once more, pocketed the keys and went back to the isolation ward.

First he checked the hand case by torchlight. He had stolen several disposable hypodermics, a box of 5cc intravenous Vallium ampoules and a box of Vitamin B12 ampoules. He removed four of the Vallium ampoules and distributed them about his pockets, then added a hypodermic. Then he shut the case and shoved it under some blankets.

The wheelchair was where he expected it to be, at the side of a bed near the door. One-handed, he took it out with him, locked the isolation ward door and pushed the wheelchair into the lift, thumbing the ground floor button.

The lift was old and slow. It took sixteen seconds from the closing of the inside gate to the automatic opening of the same gate at his destination.

Slade left the wheelchair in the car, opened the outside swing door and briefly checked the corridor. It had the deathly stillness of a sleeping hospital. Far away, near its end, he could see a glimmer of light from Margaret Meadows's office, which meant that she had the door nearly shut.

He got the wheelchair out and pushed it quickly over the pre-measured five-yard distance to Ward Seven, unceremoniously but quietly shouldering the door fully open and leaving the chair at the foot of the bed.

Bobo was quite clearly asleep, his rhythmic breathing breaking into intermittent, strangled snores.

Using the torch again, Slade found the President's wristwatch propped on his bedside locker. It showed him in a green submarine glow that the time was three minutes past four. He had started one or two minutes early, so the watch was accurate.

He reached out and took the watch, rapidly clicked out the winder and moved the hands on until they showed exactly a quarter to seven. Then he put the watch back, swept the torch across the windows to confirm that the heavy drapes were still in place, and moved to the door where he made one final lightning check of the corridor. It was empty, with only the whirr of the suction machine in Mrs. Turner's ward to break the silence.

Slade came back. He hesitated for one tiny moment at the President's bedside, aware that this was the final categorical step. Then he reached out and gently shook Bobo awake.

The President had been sleeping a feathery, old man's sleep peopled with dark dreams. He woke to find Slade in the act of switching on the bedside lamp.

'Good morning, sir.' Slade smiled at him. 'Sleep well, I hope?'

Bobo blinked. He felt very sleepy still. His eye went automatically to the watch at his bedside. Fourteen minutes to seven. 'Good heavens!' He stared at Slade. 'Is it that time already? It's still very dark.'

'That's because I haven't opened your drapes yet.' Slade nodded at the window. 'I'll do it in a sec. But first I have to give you an injection. It's connected with another test you're going to have today.'

Bobo struggled upright. His eyes were heavy. 'I don't remember any further tests!' He glared at Slade suspiciously.

Slade shrugged. 'I can call Sister Meadows if you like, but she's busy with a very sick old lady.'

Bobo considered. Then another thought struck him. 'But damn it, man, you don't even know how to give one!'

'I was put through a special course,' Slade said gravely.

Bobo grunted. 'Where do you want it?'

'In the arm.' Slade began to fill the hypodermic. 'It's intravenous.'

Bobo started to roll up his sleeve. Then his eyes caught the wheelchair near the door. 'What the devil is that for?' His fingers stopped with the sleeve half rolled.

Slade's heart sank. It had been out of the question to leave the chair in the corridor, where it would have invited attention. His hope had been that Bobo would not see it, but knowing the President's eagle eye for detail he had prepared an explanation. All that remained to be seen was whether Bobo would accept it.

'We're moving you to another ward,' he said. 'No French windows. Less access from outside.'

'But I like it here!' Bobo said indignantly.

'It's not my decision, or Matron's.' Slade paused deliberately. Then he said: 'It's Colonel Pahler's. The other ward will be maximum security. The decision was made after the Colonel had a long-distance telephone conversation with your Captain Crutchley.'

Bobo stared at him in alarm. 'What does this mean? Is trouble expected?' His heart had begun to thud. 'Get Pahler here this instant!'

'He'll be here in five minutes, Mr. President,' Slade lied. 'I can hardly get him quicker. Let's go on with the injection in the meantime, huh?'

'You're sure you don't know anything?' Thank God, Bobo was rolling up his sleeve again.

'That's fine. Now make a fist. No, I don't know any details.' Slade inserted the needle into the anticubital vein and started to feed in the Vallium.

It took very quickly. On ten ccs Bobo sagged, and Slade lowered him gently. There was a confused, last-second awareness in the President as he realized that he was sinking into unconsciousness. But it was too late. There was no resistance left in him, and before the yellowed tiger eyes shut they showed a brief and furious frustration.

Slade gave him 30 ccs in all, enough to keep him soundly asleep for a very long time. Then he pocketed the empty ampoules and hypodermic, took a small suitcase from the clothes cupboard across the room and began to fill it with clothing and personal articles from a prearranged mental check-list. It took him just over thirty seconds to fling everything into the case and close it. After that he brought the wheelchair to the bedside and had an awkward minute getting the unconscious man into it. He was breathing heavily by the time Bobo had been installed with his own suitcase resting on his lap.

Slade checked the corridor once more. Calculated risk Number One. There was the sound of Meadows's voice from Mrs. Turner's ward along the corridor, audible faintly above the whirr of the suction machine.

Hell. What he had hoped wouldn't happen had occurred. But there was no delaying. Deliberately, he grasped the back of the wheelchair and pushed it out into the corridor, walking five rapid strides to the lift, flinging open the door and pushing it with its burden into the car.

He was on the brink of following it when Novak came out of ward Four. She stood momentarily still, her back turned so that all Slade could see was her plump white-uniformed back and the silly paper cap balanced on her flaxen hair.

Staring at her, hardly breathing, he let the lift door close quietly. Through the glass panel inset he could see Bobo slumped in the wheelchair.

Novak turned around. It was as though she sensed his eyes on her back. But all she saw was Slade producing his cigarillos and apparently calmly lighting one. The ten yards that separated them concealed the violent and uncontrollable shaking of his hand.

'Ah, Meester Slide.' She always pronounced it this way. 'I had forgotten you were on, down here.' Unwittingly she was mimicking Margaret Meadows's words. 'The night goes slowly, yus?'

'Sure does.' Slade flicked away the dead match and blew smoke. 'Can I get you anything?'

'Thank you, no. I go to Suster's office for her jersey.' Novak wagged her head at the door of Number Four. 'We are being kept very busy.'

'Okay. See you.' Slade watched the nurse-aid walk away, her big bottom jiggling under the uniform. The busier the better, he thought. He waited until she had disappeared in the far reaches of the corridor, then quickly opened the lift door, got into the car and pressed button 2. The lift hummed and began to move upwards.

Janet Strange was six steps from the lift door on the second floor when the car passed by up the shaft. She caught just a flash of illumination through the panel and then it was gone. She reached the door, pressed the call button, then watched, puzzled, as the indicator stopped at the second floor. Up There. Who, she wondered, wanted to go traipsing around on the abandoned floor? Unless, of course, one of those humorists with which the Joseph Schwer seemed to abound had pressed button 2 for fun, just to hold up the works. It was surprising how often this happened.

She shrugged and trotted down the stairs. Margaret Meadows was in Ward Four, as she had expected, pulling on her dark blue jersey.

'Getting cold,' observed Meadows. 'Things quiet up your way?'

Sister Strange nodded. 'Very. Even the lift is bored. It's wandering around between the first floor and Up There.' She gestured at the thorocotomy case. Old Mrs. Turner's face was whiter than her hair. 'Keeping you busy, eh?'

'Not too busy not to have another cup of coffee.' Margaret waved a finger at Novak. 'Keep an eye on her.'

'Yus, Suster,' said the nurse-aid stoically.

They walked to Margaret's office. Janet switched on the kettle and they sat down facing each other. 'How are things?' She studied the other girl's flushed face.

'Nowhere nearer a solution.' Margaret's eyes filled suddenly with angry, frustrated tears. All the crude cheer of the night before was gone. 'I'm paying the penalty for being such a bitch.'

'Oh, nonsense.' Janet lit a cigarette for both of them and gave the other girl one. 'Look, why delay? If I were you I would do something about it.'

Margaret stared into nothing. 'I've been wondering whether the average girl has usually had two abortions by the age of twenty-three.'

'I didn't necessarily suggest that. What you do is your business. I've told you my attitude. But it's no good crying over spilt milk and you can't go back and remake your life.'

'That's true. But I can have a damn good crack at improving it.'

'*You* reform? Don't make me laugh.' Having said the words, Janet could have bitten off her tongue. Quickly, she added, 'What are you going to do—tell Jimmy?'

'It doesn't seem fair, somehow. I know damn well it isn't his kid.'

Strange came back to the desk with the coffee. 'Drink that. It will cheer you up.'

Margaret lifted her head and showed brown eyes starry with tears. 'I could never hurt Jimmy. He's so dumb he thinks he's only the second one. I gave him the routine about the singing teacher, and how he said it would improve my voice.' Her lips curled. 'He thinks I've had a raw deal out of life.'

'Maggie, listen to me.' Janet leant across the desk. 'Stop feeling sorry for yourself. You always get like this when you're—that way. You don't want to have it down and you don't want to hurt Jimmy. What are you going to do—marry three naval officers?'

Margaret stared at her friend. 'I like the way you put that.' She giggled suddenly and Janet joined her. They laughed heartily for a moment.

'That's better.' Strange stood up. 'Forget it for the present. Now, I haven't seen this President of yours yet. Can I take a peek?'

Margaret rose. 'He's Jane's cookie, not mine. But I'll come with you.'

They walked briskly along the corridor. At Bobo's ward Margaret put her hand on the door and then stopped in mid-stride. 'That's my telephone ringing in the office. I'm blowed if I'm going to answer it. Come and take a peek at how a President snores.'

'He's not snoring that I can hear.' The distant telephone shrilled persistently. Janet moved uneasily. 'These damn things always go at the wrong time.' She pushed the door half-open so that they could see part of the darkened room and began to enter. Then eight years of discipline and training asserted themselves. In mid-stride she changed her mind. 'Margaret, you'd better answer the damn thing. Bobo's not going to run away.'

They trotted along the corridor and back into the office. Margaret snatched up the receiver. 'Sister Meadows speaking.'

There was a pause. Then she said. 'Yes, Mr. Turner. She's sleeping. She seems comfortable.' It was a standard answer. There was a long pause. Then in a different voice Margaret said quite softly, 'All right, Mr. Turner, I'll do that,' and replaced the receiver gently.

'Some nut, to ring at this hour?'

'No.' Margaret stared at Janet Strange. 'That was the husband of Mrs. Turner the thorocotomy in Four. He couldn't sleep because he was worried about her. He gave me a message to give her in the morning. You know what it is?' She spoke quite slowly. 'He is seventy-six. His wife is seventy. He said, "Tell Baby I miss her. Tell her she is my heart-beat. Tell her I love her with my body and my soul. Tell her that in the morning, when she wakes."' Meadows slammed the desk. 'Now isn't that the corniest goddam crap you ever heard?' She stared at Janet with glittering eyes. 'Isn't that the most bloody stupid nonsense?'

Janet stood looking at her for a long moment in brittle silence. Then Margaret Meadows sat wearily down, put her head on the desk, and wept.

It had proved surprisingly easy to complete the manoeuvre. Once he had reached Up There, Slade had stopped only long enough to collect his handcase from the abandoned ward, then wheeled Bobo precariously across the cracked and subsided ramp without daring to use even the small light of his pocket torch. The main difficulty had been in getting the President's limp and heavy body on to the rough blanket bed inside the van, an effort that had left him sweating even in the cold of pre-dawn; and with his heart thundering.

After that all he had to do was lock the van and go by the same route back to his borrowed office, except that this time he used the stairs.

He felt the heavy dull depression of anti-climax. The desk was dusty, the carpet was shoe-scarred and the green blotter had the fat-marks on it from the doughnuts he had earlier thrown into the garbage disposal system.

So I've kidnapped a President, he thought. Hi-ho Silver, and head for the hills, write a note, collect the money, and accept their grateful thanks for letting him come back safely.

He got up and walked to the window. Except it wasn't going to be like that. Once his identity was established every man's hand would be against him. When you did a thing like this you were no longer Ernie Slade, you were It, you were a scared man running across a mountain. So the hammer would come down, and there would be this noise, and a feeling like a big sledgehammer hitting him in the back, and they would pick him up and say well, that's that, look where I got him. And then Ginny would not only have a dead husband, and no money, but a Stigma with it all, and Stigmas were very hard to live with.

Cut it out, cut it out!

The pristine crystal and honed stainless steel that was his brain would not rest. It was four-twenty-seven, two hours and eighteen minutes before official wake-up time. Two hours and eighteen minutes during which Meadows or Novak, on a chance whim, a moment of officiousness, might wreck the whole scheme with one quick peep into an empty ward. This was Calculated Major Risk Two, and all he could do was rely on his own assessment of the two women's attitude, and hang about in the neighbourhood just to make assurance doubly sure.

He went along the corridor to Ward Seven, catching a glimpse of Margaret writing in her office, and then stationed himself near the ward's door, ready to move and look busy if someone came along.

He would never know that the chance telephone call of a worried old man had saved the operation from total failure at its inception.

Chapter Six

When Alice Gregg's husband George had lost an argument with a beer truck on the Koeberg Interchange some thirteen months before, he had left her a fair amount of insurance, two small twin sons, a three-year-old Simca, an unmortgaged house on the Quarterdeck in Kalk Bay, and a neighbour who liked to watch her through a mounted telescope when she undressed at night before going to bed.

It had taken her a long time to make the discovery. Hers had become a quiet, even lonely life, after the buzz of the do-gooders had died down not too long after the funeral. A few true friends still invited her to dinner or bridge regularly and George's closest friend, a bachelor called Peter Neames, had started turning up after work and giving her a hand with the kids. This was a warming development, but she was taking a long-term view of it. Basically, she spent a lot of her time on her own, especially at night, and usually retired around ten-thirty, never bothering to draw the curtains because of the inevitable darkness of her neighbour's house.

It was the moon reflecting off the telescope lens that had first given her an inkling of what was going on. Sensibly, she had pulled the curtains without appearing alarmed, then walked to the children's darkened room and observed from their window, seeing the lean man straighten up from the telescope, apparently ponder a moment, then shrug and cover it with its protective canvas jacket.

Alice Gregg was a highly spirited girl. Her first emotional reaction was one of fury. She reported the matter to Peter, who wanted her immediately to sell, but she said she was damned if she would give the old bastard the satisfaction of forcing her into vacating.

Unaware of the explosively dangerous situation in which she was placing herself, Alice began a sort of Spy versus Spy campaign. She kept up her Peeping Tom's interest by partially stripping from time to time with the curtains undrawn, and drawing some cynical amusement out of never going the whole way. She, in turn, began a watch upon the man who had in any case always intrigued her.

In this manner she had discovered the existence of what she had named The Creatures.

They came every day, sometimes early but mostly in the evening; and they left at any time during the next morning, as bundled as they had arrived, so that she was still not completely sure whether they were male or female, although her intuition told her they were women.

God, she'd said to Peter, he's sixty if he's a day and not content with his telescope he's running a one-man knock-shop as well. And why always *two* of them?

Lying in bed lazily at six-thirty on a bright Wednesday morning, she thought about all this and decided reluctantly that for the boys' sake it would be best if she sold. No one knew what a weird old man was capable of if he ran out of girls, or decided suddenly to become ambivalent. She shuddered, but having made the decision she immediately felt better. Reaching out she switched on her portable to Cape Town's local commercial station, Good Hope.

They were giving one of their brief hourly news bulletins. 'Two criminals are reported to have escaped during the night from Pohlsmoor Prison,' came the smooth tones of the announcer. 'One is a Malay, Achmed Hassan, known as Bunny, and the other is a European, Flip Reyneke. A warder was seriously injured in the escape and is at present in Woodstock Hospital where his condition is believed to be critical. A police spokesman has stated that an intensive hunt is under way for men and an early arrest is anticipated, but in the meantime the public are warned that both men are potentially dangerous. Hassan is slim, brown-eyed, with a...'

Alice switched off and wondered whether she should keep the children home that day. They were only four years old and normally walked half a mile to a nearby private nursery school. Either that, she thought, or she would walk with them. Meanwhile there was breakfast to prepare.

She was pulling off her nightie when she heard the muffled bang from next door. God, she thought, maybe he's shot one of them. Naked, she leaned a hand on the window sill and moved one curtain slightly aside.

It had been the sound of the front door slamming that she had heard. There they went, The Creatures, swaddled in coats and pants as usual, trotting out to the Rover and getting quickly into the rear seat. Their host followed at a more leisurely pace, got behind the wheel and drove off to the clean rumble of the Rover's healthy engine.

I will, thought Alice Gregg, pulling on her dressing gown, telephone an Estate Agent as soon as offices open.

Major Shannon returned home only a few minutes after Alice Gregg had seen him leave. He parked the Rover neatly in the street, walked quickly down his short pathway, opened the un-locked front door and went straight to the telephone on the bar-top in the living-room where he dialled a number without refer-ence to the directory.

His call was answered after a short delay. 'Report,' Major Shannon said crisply. 'All right, I'll hang on.' He waited im-patiently, drumming his fingers on the bar-top. Then: 'Ready? Right, here goes. I had a look at the place yesterday. It's a very nice, very convenient lay-out. At exactly ten-thirty our friend came out into the garden and was installed in a deck chair under a sun umbrella where he was served tea and scones. Observation was made from a side-street which is off the beaten track and overlooks the garden. It would appear that this morning tea business will be a regular thing as long as the weather holds good, so I'm going to try today. You know what I mean. I should have good news for you by one o'clock, if you don't hear yourself, earlier.'

There was a pause. Then Shannon laughed. 'Luck? I don't need luck.' Still grinning, he replaced the receiver and walked idly into the gun-room. It was precisely quarter-to-seven but he did not want to delay too long. The day looked fine and the President might emerge into the garden earlier than yesterday.

Deeply preoccupied, a professional at work, he began to study the rack of rifles, examining each one in turn before making his choice.

Chapter Seven

Novak came out of Ward Seven at six forty-five. Slade appeared like a djinn from Ward Six. He looked haggard.

'Did you take him his tea?' He yawned and rubbed his puffy face but he had wide-awake eyes.

'Yus, but he's not there.' Novak never seemed to look tired, and she'd had a hell of a night between old Mrs. Turner and Maggie Meadows.

'Probably in the heads. Want me to tell him?'

'Yus, bleeze, Meester Slide,' said Novak.

She went away. Wind buffeted around the walls. Another goddam south-easter, he thought. Time lolled around, crossing its legs and yawning. Then Meadows appeared, looking ferociously efficient in full uniform cap and cape, with some of the sleep cold-watered out of her face and her mouth freshened by a drag of lipstick.

'Isn't that old man out of the bog-shops yet?' She wanted to go. In the topsy-turvy world of night duty she was going to have a breakfast which was really supper.

'He's not in there. I checked.'

Margaret looked exasperated. 'Well then where the hell is he? Killeen will be here any minute and she's always scratchy when she arrives.'

Somehow he produced a casual manner. 'I guess he's out in the garden. He wandered out there yesterday morning too.'

'Get him in, Ernie.' Margaret already had her handbag tucked under her arm.

'I also want to get home.' He didn't have to force his genuine desire to go. 'Does it matter? The day staff can handle him.'

'I suppose so.' Margaret lit a cigarette and pushed open the door of Ward Seven. Slade followed her in. She eyed the tea-tray. The electroplate teapot was sending up a little distressed whisp of steam. 'Funny that he doesn't want his tea.'

'I guess he doesn't know the time.' Slade looked at his watch. 'Can I go?'

Margaret hesitated, then shrugged. 'Sure. You don't feel like calling him a few times?'

'I don't mind.' Slade leaned against the door. His legs were wooden. 'But won't it look kind of silly, me going around the garden yelling, "Mr. President!" all over the place?'

Margaret laughed. Sister Killeen breezed in, thirtyish, black haired and blue eyed. 'Top o' morning to ye all,' she cried.

'And it's bum to you. You've got a wandering patient.' Margaret gestured with her cigarette at the empty bed. 'The President is out in the shrubbery, practising his dove-call. Better send your Arrie to find him.'

'Bejasus, he can come when he likes, I've got enough to do.' Killeen was something of a comic-book Irishwoman. She got drunk every Friday night and then she and her little husband would belabour each other, nude, around the house. It was by way of being an entertainment, she said, there being no Telly and no kids.

'So long,' said Slade from the door.

'Bye, bye, Steve McQueen,' said Killeen. Already her back was turned.

Meadows's mind was turning to fried eggs and bacon, grilled sausage, toast and marmalade. She yawned cavernously, showing small white teeth and a pink tongue. 'See you, Ernie,' she said, 'God, I've got sleep for Africa.'

'So have I,' he said, and took himself away.

But there was to be no sleep for him. He went to the staff rank, collected his Volkswagen and drove to a call-box about half-a-mile away in Constantia. From there he rang his home number.

'Yes?' Ginnie sounded breathless.

'You okay, kid?'

'Ernie! Yes, I'm fine. Sick once, is all.'

'I'll be along in a while,' he said. 'I've been held up. See you later, all right?'

There was a short silence. He could hear her breathing. Then: 'Ernie, you must be beat. Can't it wait, whatever it is?'

'I slept nearly all night,' he lied. 'Now the car is playing up. Had a hell of a lot of trouble starting it. I'm taking it in for a check.'

'Oh, poor darling.' The relief was audible as the words tumbled out. 'Get them to run you home. Your breakfast will be in the warming drawer if I'm not here.'

'Going to be busy?'

'Very. Supermarket. Cleaners. Library. I was hoping for the car but I'll bus.'

'That's fine,' he said, and rang off.

He drove a quarter-mile to a public lavatory in Main Road where he changed from his whites into the old sportscoat and flannels he had bought in Wynberg. From there he back-tracked and parked the Volkswagen in a narrow-mouthed cul-de-sac. From behind a high hedge came the drumming of rubber-soled feet, the resonant bonk of a tennis racket used well and truly, a distant cry of 'Oh, shot!' He passed a gate, caught a flash of straw-blonde hair, white panties riding high on round buttocks, long honeyed legs.

It was just after eight o'clock. Slade homed on the hindquarters of the Joseph Schwer through a down-street and in another few minutes had reached the laundry ramp and the silent parked Austin in which Bobo still lay. Only one car had come by, an old Rover driven at a doddery pace by an elderly man wearing a beret. It was now parked a hundred yards away on the other side of the road.

The dust-abused windows of Up There stared back at him. The frosted eyes of the first floor recorded nothing. Down below the embankment on ground level came the rattle of crockery from the kitchens. There was no visible movement of any human being. What time was it? Eight fifteen. Surely, they must have started looking for the old man by now?

Narrowing his eyes, he concentrated on the far-off garden. Wind swirled across nearly four acres of trees and lawns and shrubs. I suppose, he thought, there could be one or two people in there, searching. It was hard to tell.

Time to move. It was dangerous hanging around like this. He moved towards the Austin, glancing back briefly at the laundry ramp and remembering the effort of wheeling the inert Bobo across it in total darkness and then heaving his heavy body into the rear of the van. Around the blanket bed he had constructed lay a litter of old equipment left there by the previous owner, which Herbstein hadn't bothered to remove. Old tins of paint, a short encrusted ladder, a ragged denim work jacket, a coil of terrible tawdry rope. These had shown up in one brief guarded flash of the torch. While getting Bobo in, a tin had been knocked on its side, rolled back towards him while he had watched, helpless to do anything about it, and fallen on to the street with a shattering clang. Thank God, it hadn't disturbed anybody.

Satisfied with his view of the hospital, Slade looked back along the street. The old Rover was still there on the other side and its driver now had a newspaper propped before him. Damn it, the old coot was probably waiting for someone to come out of one of the houses.

Slade shrugged. Another calculated risk. The man hadn't even looked his way. He opened the door of the Austin, lit a cigarillo, started the engine, glanced back to see how he was placed in relation to the lip of the laundry ramp. Dropping a wheel in the gutter at this stage wouldn't be so clever. Then his heart seemed to stop for a long frozen moment of time as his eyes picked out the two narrow, parallel black lines that ran clearly across the cement face of the ramp and wound their way out of his sight behind the van.

Slade left the engine running in neutral and got out. Sure enough, the black lines ran right up to the tail of the Austin. The tyres of the wheelchair, old and perished and bruised by Bobo's weight, had left the clear stamp of their passage from the far exit door to the van.

There was absolutely nothing he could do about it except hope that its meaning would not ·become apparent. Thoughtfully, he went back to the cab, flicked the Austin into gear and pulled away, passing the Rover whose elderly occupant did not look up from the paper he was reading.

After some manoeuvring in minor streets Slade got into Klaasen Drive and headed for Constantia Neck, weaving and winding his way through the down-tumbling forest on either side of the road, dropping at first and then climbing, the Austin singing in third gear, the bends coming and going like trailed ribbon, the oaks getting sparse-leaved and golden now in autumn, the pines loomy and dark with deep secret shadows in amongst them. He swerved for a squirrel, reverse-aitched into second gear, and arrived at the Neck. The Old House and restaurant were on his left, the hub-like traffic circle on his right with roads spoking off it. Darkest Africa.

He took the Hout Bay road and kept on going, breaching the

valley between mountains on either side, bursting out into clear sunlight and a vista of grey-greens and browns, wind-whirled Cape Wattles, poplars and scrub on one side, sere rising barrenness on the other. Mountains, always mountains.

The old Austin's differential whine was noisy. It roller-coasted down for a while, the road gradually slackening the steepness of its descent. After a minute or two Slade cut the engine and pulled over to the verge, listening to the ticking metal noises of the van while he studied the sagging broken gate across the road.

It was the entrance to a long-abandoned property, a typical South African farm gate, a long, inherently weak structure made of metal tubing that had somehow been expected to hang its heavy length indefinitely off two lone hinges. It had lost heart and sagged. It had cracked along its bottom length. It had rusted a dark red. Grass rose around it like hair above a dirty collar.

Slade got out. He raised the cheap wire loop off the hook, lifted and heaved. The gate creaked in the knees, then let go and came open. He went back to the Austin, started it, checked for traffic but there was nothing much about at this time. Then he swung across the road and drove through. Immediately the van was almost lost in the tossing, insidious Cape wattle that covers much of the Cape Peninsula like the hair on the proverbial dog's back.

For the time being he left the gate ayawn and grassy-toothed. No one, he was sure, was going to bother about it. As he watched, a Mercedes flashed past and confirmed his thoughts. The driver saw neither Slade, the van, nor the open gate. He's late, Slade thought, and racing to get somewhere on time. Capetonians lived on the most beautiful Peninsula in the world and they never paused long enough to see it.

He went back to the van and bumped his way over three hundred yards of track so grassy that only the tunnel through the reluctant, pressing wattles showed that it had once been a road of sorts. Grass and small bushes scraped the underbelly of the Austin. He drove tensely, hands sweating again on the wheel, body screwed up wire-taut. Through the side-mirror he could see the crushed grass rise slowly erect like a tired audience getting slowly to its feet. It was smeared with sump-oil. The Austin was not built for this, it was no brush hopper, but the end came at last in a brief yielding of wattles, a tiny clearing, and a cul-de-sac in which stood the white bones of a ruined cottage.

Slade swung the blunt nose of the van into the wattles on his left. He tugged on the stubborn wheel, flipped into reverse and brought the back of the Austin as close to the old building as he could. Then he switched off and let himself go limp, his hands in his lap and the sweat coursing down his chest under his jacket.

No time, he thought, for soliloquy. He got out on trembly legs, opened the double doors at the back, gave a brief grunt of relief at the sight of Bobo still swathed in blankets that rose and fell to the even rhythm of his breathing. He left the old man like that for a moment and stumbled over chunks of crude weathered brick into the cottage.

There was no door. The floor was earth and grass and a pallid bush struggling up against one wall. Debris littered it. Slade clanked his way over broken crockery, old tins, and a holed enamel chamber-pot brown with rust-sores, to the far wall where the lightweight aluminium camp bed stood. On its blue nylon covering were piled all the other things he had brought here yesterday in the dash that had made him late. The dog's chain and the padlocks, the Coleman and canned food, all were untouched where he had placed them. Now he added from the van two cans of pilchards, a loaf of bread, a quarter-pound of butter, a pint of milk and one of the Thermoses filled with minestrone that he had got from an Italian restaurant.

He lit a cigarillo and rolled the smoke around his dry, bitter-tasting mouth. Then he spent five minutes re-arranging the equipment so that the bed was unencumbered, packing most of the stores underneath it. Afterwards he made two trips to the van, bringing in the handcase and the suitcase, the blankets he stripped off Bobo and finally *The Wind in the Willows*.

It was nine-thirty-five by the time he had finished. They will be worried by now, he thought. By now they know the old guy has gone. By now they will have gone yelling for help to Pahler. But they wouldn't have realized—or, he corrected himself, they shouldn't have—that Bobo had been kidnapped. Not yet. Not if his reasoning had been correct. Which gave him a certain amount of time.

He flipped away the cigarillo, went back to the Austin and brought Bobo into the cottage. There was no other way but to carry him. Slade stumbled, panting, over the debris, tripped at the end and almost flung his heavy burden on to the camp bed. A stay snapped with a dry carrot-like crack and the bed sagged. He staggered away, went to the doorless door and hung on to the jam, sucking for air, waiting for his heart to stop hammering, the blood-roar in his ears to cease. His chest hurt.

After five minutes he felt strong enough to go back to the bed. He checked Bobo's pulse, then pulled down the waist of his candy-striped pyjamas and studied the dressing over the iliac crest where the needle had gone in for the bone marrow biopsy. It looked clean and fresh. The surrounding area felt warm to the touch but not hot. Slade stood up holding the dog chain. He looped one end over a roof beam, locking it in place with the larger of the two padlocks. The other end he twisted around Bobo's right ankle, securing it with the smaller one.

Once the blankets were drawn over the sleeping figure there was nothing much more to do but put the typewritten note he had ready in his jacket pocket, prepared as far in advance as Monday night, next to the bed. It read:

'Nothing to worry about. There's food under the bed. You are perfectly safe. Will be back some time this afternoon.'

He stopped in the doorway, briefly checking. The chain was drawn more tightly around the old man's ankle than he would have liked but he'd had to do this in case Bobo smeared the area with butter and tried to work the chain off that way.

Slade was turning away when his eye lit on the abandoned chamber pot. It was within Bobo's reach. Handy weapon, he thought. People had been killed by these things before now. So he went back, retrieved it and flung it outside. As an afterthought he tossed his half-empty packet of John Cottons on the bed. Then he left the cottage and went to the van.

He had a peculiar feeling of suspension. It was as though what he had just completed should have brought about some sense of finality and accomplishment, but did not. He felt almost lightheaded, as though all of it were a dream, as though the clashing grey-green wattles were part of the nightmare, a background-music accompaniment, they and the *woooo* of the wind. He knew he would never forget the dust in his nostrils, the sweet semen smell of crushed grass, the hot-engine stink of the old Austin. He had bobbed like a bounding airy bubble amongst all this, studying it through the heat-haze of his fevered body.

99

And yet he could reason like a machine. I will make the pick-up back there, he thought, about a mile back. It was a chance, doing it so close to where he had Bobo, but there again he had his own theories on how two governments, one worried sick and the other accusatory, would react.

The way he was standing he was looking back, up towards the Neck. He could not see the closer ground because of the wattles, but the mountains rose grandly above the valley. Ahead and slightly to his left they were stippled with pine growth ... the back of Big Daddy. On his right, more sheer, more barren, the lower slopes of Constantiaberg and Vlakkenberg.

If they want to watch, he thought, that's where they'll be, on one or all of the flanks of those mountains, with high-powered glasses. And when they see me make the pick-up they will want to close in, they *could* in fact close in, except that he did not think they would be allowed to. Not until Bobo came back in one piece. This was his hole card, but there was never any harm in being doubly sure. An idea, a sort of insurance, had come to him.

He turned away, looking down the valley now towards Hout Bay. They could come up that way, too, but he doubted it. They would have very little time, the way he was going to work it, to get men into position. Looking in that direction, the ground flattened out into smallholdings; oaks, poplars, bursts of flowers. Heavy country, thick with vegetation, with Orange Kloof on the right, that huge gorge that cuts into the back of Table Mountain. It was narrow country because after all this was the real guts of the Peninsula, this was where it began to taper, but it was difficult country, good for the hunted man who knew what he was doing, bad for the hunters who would not—not at first for sure, anyway—even know who their quarry was.

He was reasonably satisfied. He straightened and looked up briefly at the crisp blue sky, the wind ruffling his short blond hair. *I'm not asking You for help for myself, because what I'm doing is wrong in Your book. But look after Ginny, please, whichever way it works out.*

After that there seemed nothing more to do than get back into the van, and drive away.

Chapter Eight

For Albert Pahler, morning and a hideously wet cold had arrived simultaneously. He sneezed violently, spraying the small office with germs.

'Soddy,' he said, looking most un-soddy. He honked into his handkerchief and cleared his inflamed nose a little. Then he looked blearily around the small office into which, by defeating logistics, he had crammed thirteen people.

On his side of the desk were Captain Maurer, Detective-Sergeant de Villiers who had been on duty at Reception during the night, and a grave and troubled Cedric Mango. Opposite him and overflowing in all directions were Warren Clunes, Matron Burns, a small pink gnomelike man called Kahn who was chairman of the Board of Trustees, Ben Zodiack, who had turned up to see his thorocotomy case and been invited to sit in, Jane Hobart, and the night staff: Meadows, Strange, Novak and Jensen.

Pahler had all these names before him. He recognized most of their faces from the time he had compared and then signed their Polaroid identity discs. But one appeared to be missing.

'Slade,' he said. 'Where is Mr. E. H. Slade?' He took out his Parker and absently made a cross next to the name.

'He hadn't got home when we telephoned.' Clunes had his little feet *en point* below the desk. 'Car trouble. His wife was told to tell him to get back here as soon as he showed up.'

Pahler regarded him disgruntledly. He could understand the two night Sisters and their nurse-aids having circles under their eyes, they'd been hooked out of bed after two or three hours' sleep, dressed anyhow and brought back here. But dammit, this twitchy little man Clunes had circles under his eyes, the Matron had circles under her eyes, Doctor Zodiack had circles under his eyes, Sister Hobart had circles under her eyes. Was the whole damn Joseph Schwer on a permanent whoop-up?

'We'll leave him for the time being.' He consulted his list once more. 'Sister Hobart. You had a lot to do with the President on Monday afternoon and evening. Did he seem reasonably normal to you?'

Jane considered. She was wearing thong sandals, bleached jeans and a tuck-in shirt. 'He was a bit nervous, I suppose. First night in hospital does that to people. You saw him. You should be able to judge.'

Pahler flushed. 'I meant during the entire night.' He made a note. 'Nothing out of the ordinary, then?'

'No.'

'And you were off duty last night?'

'Yes.'

Again the list. But this time it was Molly Burns who got the benefit of Pahler's gun-muzzle stare. 'Only four—or five if you include Slade—nursing staff on duty last night, Matron. Is that customary?'

'There are not many patients at the moment,' said Pussy. 'And Sister Hobart and her aid were off. There would normally be six because Mr. Slade's presence was unusual.'

'How so?' Pahler made another note.

'Mr. Clunes,' she smiled, 'felt that the President would be happier having a man around for the first two nights while he settled in.'

Warren blushed. Pahler ignored him. Instead he singled out Meadows. 'You were in charge of the ground floor last night, Sister. When did you know for the first time that the President was missing?'

'This morning, just before I went off.' A jaw-cracking, uncontrollable yawn overcame her.

'Just before seven?'

'Yes.'

'And you didn't attribute anything unusual to this?'

'Why should I? He stipulated when he was admitted that he was not to be woken at the usual time. When Mrs. Novak took him his tea she saw that he was gone. All of us thought he was in the bog—er, toilet. Then Ernie checked and found he wasn't there so we presumed he was having a stroll in the garden. That's what he did yesterday morning.'

'So his absence wasn't noted until that time. Didn't you check on him during the night?'

Margaret coloured. 'Listen, I'd had my feet run off me. Ernie was looking after the President, so he could not have been in better hands.'

Pahler dug desperately for his handkerchief and atishooed violently into it. Then he mopped his nose and said gravel-voiced, 'I'm not saying you did anything wrong. You have no idea, then, of when he took it into his head to ... to ...'

'Vamoose? No.' They were matching each other, yawn for sneeze.

There was a tap at the door and Slade squeezed in. 'Mr. Ernie Slade,' said Matron Burns.

Pahler nodded at him. God, another one with circles under his eyes. 'Sorry to drag you back, but you probably know that the President has taken it into his head to disappear. We're trying to find some sort of reason for it all.'

'I thought he was in the garden,' said Slade.

'Everybody thought he was in the garden, everybody thought he was in the toilet,' droned Pahler. 'But he wasn't, was he. When did you last see him?'

Slade pretended to think. 'Musta been just four o'clock. I told Maggie he was sleeping soundly.'

'So he could have left anywhere between say four and six-thirty.' Pahler glared at his note pad. Wherever the old fool has got to, he thought dismally, and whether we get him back drunk or sober, there is going to be one hell of a stink about this.

'Guess so.' Slade shrugged. He lit one of his John Cottons and added his contribution to the layers of smoke-smog.

A heavy-breathing silence came for a moment while Pahler digested this. Then: 'Mrs. Novak, when you took in the President's tea did you notice any signs of *recent* occupation such as cigarette smoke hanging in the air, or a warm bed, or ... uh ...'

'No, Curdle Pallour,' said Novak. There was a titter from the nurses.

Pahler's eyes watered. He glared at her, then snatched for his handkerchief and thundered into it. 'You, Sister Meadows— did *nothing* out of the ordinary happen last night that you can recollect?'

'No,' said Margaret, and handed him a yawny Roland for his sneezy Oliver. Slade breathed out, in slow relief. As he had anticipated, it had not entered her head to relate the drug cupboard incident to Bobo's disappearance.

Pahler was busy with Janet Strange and Jensen. 'You two. You saw or heard nothing unusual?'

Janet and her nurse-aid shook their heads.

The door opened with a clunk against somebody's chair and a coloured woman in a blue overall came in. She went directly to Matron Burns, handed her a piece of paper and went out again.

Pussy read for a moment. Then she said, 'That was one of my housekeepers, Colonel Pahler. We take an inventory of all patients' belongings when they are admitted. The President's ward has now been re-inventoried and certain items are missing.'

The Colonel sat up straighter. 'Such as?'

Pussy read from her list. 'One pair of beige slacks, two sports shirts, three pair of socks, ditto underpants, one pair brown moccasins, one leather belt, one small suitcase and a book entitled *The Wind in the Willows*.'

There was a murmur of laughter. Somebody said, 'It would appear that our President has discharged himself.'

Even Pahler smiled. 'So it would seem.' He tore the top page off the pad, folded it and put it in a pocket. 'Thank you, ladies and gentlemen, for giving me your time. Please regard the fact of the President's disappearance, and everything said in this room, as completely confidential.'

It was a dismissal, so the interviewees got up and filed out. Pahler made a little ceremony out of seeing Mango off, promising full reports as often as possible. Then he returned to the office and rejoined the other two policemen.

Pahler beat at the grey air. 'For God's sake, somebody open a window.' He rose and prowled around the desk, then settled his big rump on the edge so that he could look at Maurer. 'This is the last thing I expected.'

'Expected,' Maurer hissed. His little black button eyes settled on the knot in Pahler's tie. He reminded Pahler more than ever of Ka. 'The President has walked out, ja? I maintained all along that he should be treated in a Bantu hospital. He would have been more at home there. *Soort soek soort*.'

Yes, thought Pahler, and a Kaffir Is Always A Kaffir, you forgot that one. Aloud he said, 'There are three possible explanations for Lunda's disappearance. You've mentioned the first one, that he was unhappy here, or nervous about his treatment, and simply walked out. It happens in hospitals all the time, especially with alcoholics, and Lunda has only been off the bottle for a short time. Which is our second possibility, one you may remember I even anticipated after we saw him on Monday night, that his thirst got the better of him. And then there is the third contingency, the one I don't like to think about: that he was forcibly removed.'

'Removed,' echoed Maurer. 'I don't think so. No sign of a struggle. I am prepared to bet a month's pay that he walked out of his own accord.'

'I think so too,' Pahler said.

'But sir!' Detective-Sergeant de Villiers was flushed with concern. He had, after all, been the only policeman present during the night and he was well aware of the inferences that could be drawn from this. 'I was sitting just behind the desk in Reception, looking straight into the foyer. I would have seen the President if I'd been half blind.'

'You go to the lavatory like anyone else, don't you?' Pahler said grumpily. 'Apart from which there is at least one back door and one side door, or he could have got out of half-a-dozen windows. When we decided to station somebody at the Joseph Schwer it was as a general security check, and to filter visitors. Nobody ever intended it to be foolproof. So relax, boy.'

There was a silence while Pahler produced his Dunhill and plugged it with Three Nuns. He went through the pipe smoker's orgiastic ritual of light-puff-matchbox-puff-light and when it was glowing nicely he said, 'Captain Maurer, with your ability to think along certain lines, you no doubt have your own personal opinion of what happened, surely?'

'Surely,' Maurer hissed, enjoying the sibilant. He got out of his chair, entirely missing Pahler's heavy irony, and tugged his jacket down over his fat hips. He waddled to the open window, breathed some south-easter, then turned his reptilian gaze on his senior officer. 'I can tell you exactly what Lunda did. He left here in the early hours of the morning, waited until a bottle store opened, bought himself a bottle of that Highland whatever-it-is he drinks, and then found a convenient place to get drunk. We will find him paralytic in a gutter, or on Rondebosch Common or—or somewhere.'

'Somewhere,' mimicked Pahler savagely, breathing noisily.

He opened his mouth to say more, thought better, and puffed on his pipe.

Maurer at last detected a faint hostility in the air. He plunged his hands into his pockets and turned squarely to face his chief. 'You don't share this opinion, I take it. Or you have another?'

'I do indeed.' Pahler stared along the barrel of his pipe at the far wall.

'Then what is your opinion?'

Pahler rubbed the bowl of his pipe against his nose. 'It's not really an opinion. If you asked me for an official view I would agree with you. But as a policeman's hunch and nothing else, I think Lunda might have been abducted. There's no way of proving it, of course, until something else happens.'

'Happens.' Maurer stared at him. 'Such as?'

Pahler drew on his pipe and then smiled without any humour. 'Such as the delivery of a ransom note. It's the next logical step, isn't it?'

Chapter Nine

'You look absolutely ghastly,' said Jimmy Craig. He lit two cigarettes and gave Margaret Meadows one. They were sitting in his Volkswagen outside the Joseph Schwer.

'Hah-hah,' said Margaret bitterly. She regarded him broodingly out of puffy eyes. 'I would dearly love to see you after one hell of a night, three hours sleep, and then having to answer some stupid policeman's questions.'

A police truck trundled by, its long aerial whipping, its blue cab-light flicking. 'What the hell's going on? Are you in some kind of trouble?'

'For me, half the police force?' She drew drearily on her cigarette. 'I'm not worth all that bother and expense. No, the flipping President of Gamba has taken a walk. He's disappeared. But keep it to yourself.'

'God, is that all! You hooked me out of office, all mysterious, to give me a news bulletin.' He didn't know whether to be angry or relieved. 'For a moment I thought——'

'You're a clever boy. You thought?'

'I thought—well, I ...' He was blond and pale-skinned, and coloured easily. He turned troubled blue eyes on her. 'It doesn't matter what I thought. What's up?'

'Jesus,' she said, 'your choice of phraseology is so apt. You were up, that's what.'

'You don't mean?'

'I do. I haven't.'

'Oh hell.' Blanched is an overworked word, but he blanched. His stomach fluttered. 'How long?'

'About six weeks.'

'Have you seen a quack?'

She blew smoke all over him. Her breath was stale. 'James, old chap, dear boy, to qualify in my profession I have done the equivalent of four years' medicine and a year's gynaecology. I know when I *am*.'

There was a long, bitter silence. She stared through the windscreen. And eventually: 'Silence reigns. So what do we do?'

He gave her a surprisingly shrewd look, although his maturity had been delayed by his studies and a brilliant flair for the blindside break that had earned him a Provincial cap. 'Are you sure it's me?' He didn't really mean it, but people say that kind of thing at that kind of nasty time.

She went scarlet. She said, 'God, let me out of here,' and began to struggle with the door handle.

He grabbed her arm and pulled her back. 'Maggie, Maggie, I didn't——'

'Didn't? Didn't?' She got the door open and swung her legs out. 'Drop dead!'

'Maggie, they'll see us! They'll see us from the windows!' He became angry and dragged her in and slammed the door. She looked away and began to cry. She was really rather strikingly pretty, and at twenty-three some years of wassail and short sleeps on strange beds, don't damage the features. Debauchery at that age is only a roughed-out Dorian Grey.

So Jimmy Craig's anger turned abruptly into an overwhelming pity. And although he was too young to know it, love. He pulled her against him and kissed her several times. 'I'm twenty-five and independent and it's high time I settled down. There will be some arrangements to make. Can you hang on for a month?'

She went very quiet and very still. 'Jimmy, are you sure?'

His imagination and his emotions got out of hand. 'Of course I'm sure, sweetheart!'

'Oh, darling!' said Margaret Meadows.

And so they fell to planning, and kissing and cuddling, with a few coy fiddles thrown in, until he had to go or be fired by his company, and she had to go or fall asleep in the middle of an exclamation of deepest love. He drove off in a mood of temporary euphoria, full of thoughts of wedding bells and confetti and indigestible cake. She walked around the hospital to the flatlets where the Sisters lived and halfway along found herself comparing her progress with the undulating slither of a sly snake. So she began to cry again.

Such is life.

*   *   *

Ginny Slade lifted her head from over the toilet bowl and regarded her husband out of streaming eyes. 'Being pregnant is fabulous.'

He was startled. She so obviously meant it. 'Here.' He gave her the towel. 'Wipe your mouth.'

She wiped. 'Oh Ernie, that's the fourth time today.'

'It happens,' he said dully. He had slept for two hours, then taken some benzedrine to remain awake. It was beginning to work. In half an hour he wouldn't feel as though he had two cast-iron potlids poised over his eyes.

The toilet flushed noisily. 'This is going to be one helluva naughty kid.'

'I'll bet.' His mind kept darting to Bobo, slumbering in the ruined cottage on the Hout Bay road. 'What's the time?'

'Five after three. Like some coffee?'

'Great. With cold milk, kid.' Perhaps Bobo was awake by now. 'I got to go back to the hospital.'

'Oh, Ernie!' Her face was flushed from retching but it was still pink, scrubbed, Sixth Form. 'Ernie, they can't *do* this to you! Why, for heavens's sake?'

'The cop wants to talk to us again. He wants to go over the whole thing in case he missed a point.' Lying was coming so easily. 'That is, unless they find the President. If they find him they'll 'phone me not to come.' Like hell they'll find him, he thought with a certain amount of mild pride at the accuracy of his anticipation, not the way they're thinking at the moment.

'Will you be long?' She handed him his cup.

He made some quick mental calculations: time and distance. The benzedrine was helping. 'About an hour, I guess.'

'You think that silly old man has gone and got drunk somewhere?'

'Looks like it.' He lit a John Cotton. Was it his imagination or was her waist beginning to thicken?

'I think it's very thoughtless of him.' Why had he got into the habit of gulping everything these days? Fine for a nervous wreck but not a calm, slow man like Ernie.

'Yeah.' He put the empty cup on the table. 'I'm off, honey.'

She got up and went to the door with him. 'In, out, in, out. Like a drive-in bank, or a filling station. You got a drive-in home, Ernie.' She laughed, but a nervous tremble got in the way and made it wobble. 'Figure you'll be staying home a piece, tonight?'

'Guess so.' He was looking down the path already. ''Bye.'

Her throat closed up on her without warning so that she could only mouth the reply. But he did not look back. And he hadn't kissed her.

Ginny went through to the bedroom and pulled back the lace curtain. The car door thumped. Wait for it, she told herself, here comes the *ker-thlomp*. But instead the motor exploded into life, gunned, the piece of beetle-back she could see over the hedge slid out of view. Rattle and all, he'd gone.

She went through to the kitchen. Old gulp-and-go Slade. And no kiss. She opened the top of the stable-type back door and looked out into the courtyard. The neighbour's dog was a blood-shot Basset of woeful mien. In a world strangely devoid of deer, he panhandled.

'Hi, Murgatroyd.' She let him in. 'You bumming again this morning?'

Yes he said, he was, if one would call it that, and he remembered that she had some rather delectable doughnuts.

Ginny found the tin and gave him one. After he'd slobbered it down she picked him up, all adroop, and took him through to the living-room where she stretched out on the sofa. The Basset put its short crooked legs on her chest, joggling a breast, and regarded her with desperate gloom.

'Murg,' she said, 'old buddy, you're a wise old guy, you've been around. You know plenty.' Her voice started to crack and she was blinking back the tears, but she pushed on doggedly. 'I'm all alone, Murg, with no one to turn to. Be a sport, old chap, and tell me. Do you figure that silly old sailor of mine has gone and got himself a girl-friend?'

There was a twenty-year-old constable stationed at the main gate of the Joseph Schwer, hanging on to his cap and bracing himself against the remorseless buffeting of the south-easter. Major Shannon, having moved the Rover some distance away, came briskly past and then stopped in apparent surprise.

'Eh? Goodness me! Is there some sort of trouble at the hospital?'

The constable blinked nervously. His English normally hung

together without verbs and when it came to understanding this type of clipped accent he was all at sea.

'Visitor?' he asked, because he didn't know whether to use 'Is you' or 'Are you', and although he would have settled for the former, English had some funny rules.

Lout, thought Shannon. Aloud he said, 'No, no, Constable. I'm merely taking a walk. But I was a patient here a little while ago, so naturally I'm interested. Not often one sees a—hah, hah —one of you chaps in these parts.'

The boy had some down above his upper lip, a coffee-stain embryo moustache. He licked it uncertainly. In a slightly different way this man reminded him of Pahler. Very authoritative. He felt compelled to give some answer but the cautious English words that came to mind felt sludgy and uncommunicative. After a moment's hesitation it poured out: 'That kaffir that's staying here is loose.' He looked hopefully at the Major.

Shannon mulled this over. He had understood the gist of it. *Los*, the boy meant. Similar to the German. 'Really?' He fixed the youth with his hypnotic cat eyes. 'Where's he gone? Eh? Come on, young man, spit it out!'

'Don't know.' The Constable slogged along. 'He buggered off. Walked out. Big search going on.'

'Just like that? No rhyme or reason?'

The Constable began to develop a nagging, uneasy feeling that he was talking too much. But he was committed now. 'They think he wented to buy a bottle.'

'Fancy that,' said Major Shannon. So the tiger had left his lair. And for a booze-up, no less. Oh hell.

'Absolute disgrace,' he said. 'They should never have had the chap staying here.' He was about to turn away when a Fairlane nosed between the gates and paused on the pavement while its uniformed driver checked his right and left. Shannon turned and found himself staring into the face of the passenger at a distance of less than six feet. A big face belonging to a big man, high cheekbones and a blunt nose and angry little steel-hard eyes. Policeman's eyes. The face of the man who had deliberately bumped him at the airport when he stood amongst the crowd.

Shannon wheeled away. At the same moment recognition sprang into the face of the man in the car.

By now Shannon's back was turned. He headed across the street at a diagonal, dodging a labouring bus. There was a cry of 'Hang on there!' behind him but he paid no attention, using the bus as a temporary shield, trotting with it for a few seconds until he could duck into the side street where the Rover was parked. In the side street he glanced behind him once more. There was a blur of incurious faces from the second deck of the bus but nothing else. He ran at a steady trot for a hundred yards, reached the car and got in.

Puffing, he started the engine and took the Rover around in a neat U-turn, driving by a roundabout route until he reached the expressway. Once there, bundled up amongst the rest of the charging metallic herd, he let himself go loose.

'Damn fool,' he said. 'What a damn fool I am.'

'Feeling better?' asked Pussy Burns with a cynical grin.

'I thought I was going to die this morning.' Warren Clunes rose and tap-danced around to the other side of the desk. 'I was genuinely convinced that I had an hour or so, no more, but the detoxicants have done their work nicely, thank you. Clunes's Come-back.' He lit a cigarette. 'What was all that excitement at the gate?'

Pussy waved a hand. 'Nothing much. Our head Cop, whom dear Novak calls Curdle Pallour, was going somewhere or other in his official limousine when he noticed a suspicious character hanging around outside. This chap took off and Pahler decided to follow, only he omitted to brief his driver, so as the Curdle gets out, the driver lets go his clutch with a thump and Pahler three-points. The last I heard, he was sneezing and crying at the same time.'

Clunes laughed so heartily that Molly Burns could almost hear the jingling of the bell on his Noddy-cap. Then he said, suddenly sombre, 'I hope they find Lunda. This is very bad for the Joseph Schwer. If only I had——'

'Warren,' said Pussy, 'you didn't personally open a window and push him out, with a slap on the back and a "Good luck, old chap". Cut out the nonsense and concentrate on your hang-over. Bear it with pride.'

'It's not so bad that I can't tolerate a repeat performance. Tonight I think Duckling Bigarade at the Mount Nelson Grill Room would be very nice.'

'Tonight we will do nothing of the sort. Tonight you will buy some best end of neck at that Braam's in Rondebosch and I will perpetrate a tomato *bredee* in your pressure cooker.'

'Wonderful,' Clunes cried happily. 'I have a beautiful Cabernet which I will put into the fridge, and a magnificent Drambuie for afterwards.' He winked. 'Over coffee we can get matey.'

'Save it,' said Pussy, 'for the great day. I'm training you up.'

'And when it arrives, my God, we'll shatter windows. The first vaginal sonic boom.'

'You're becoming a dirty old man,' she said.

Flora Zodiack had written from Durban:

'Dear Ben,

Thank you for your letter. I'm glad you are managing without my deft domestic touch (hah-hah). Mother is much better but I might have to prolong my visit by a few days as she still experiences difficulty in getting about and has not yet got the hang of the crutches. Oscar is well, but missing you, believe it or not. I have had rather a lot of time on my hands, as you might expect, and have done a good deal of thinking about *us*. Don't you think that as one approaches middle age one's marriage is inclined to settle into a groove, and I don't mean a rut, I mean an ice-coated bobrun in which the sled can so easily overturn, or bang blindly from side to side, or even fly out at one of the corners?

'This is probably a poor comparison. What I am trying to say is that blind existence, or taking for granted, does not necessarily mean prosaic progress into old age in the rut of one of those ghastly Darby and Joan relationships—I could never bear this clean-the-car-on-Sunday-afternoons, let's-plan-now-for-our-retirement, one-poke-a-week-on-Friday-night type of life as you know it can be quite a headlong careering which ends up with everybody bruised out in the snow, shocked, hurt, and most of all very surprised. Two people nearing forty, and a kid of twelve with only half his parents.

'I think that you of all people, Ben, need the solidity of a home, a woman—I don't want to use the word wife because it's old-fashioned—to come home to, a decent kid—even though you may not think so—to kick around with when he gets a little older.

'I've said all this because I think that the way we're heading, we're going to fly out of that bobrun one of these days
unless we slow down and think. Just as an aperitif, I think
that the fact that you are home so little indicates that I have
failed you somewhere, that I lack something. I in turn feel
that my non-bridge-playing, non-gadding, non-gossiping
total fidelity is both wasted and ignored.

'Sorry to be so serious. I love you very much, my darling.

Flora'

Ben folded the letter, put it back in the tricolour-trimmed
envelope and tossed it on to the back seat of the Capri. Then he
lit a cigarette, got out, and walked through the dappled shade of
tall trees, the sound of cooing doves and distant wind, past
scattered cars until he reached the looming blockhouse bulk of
the Lower Cable Station.

Inside, there were stairs and a ticket window, and morgue-like
acoustics that turned the efficient cries of a group of German
tourists into vaulted boomings.

Alone on a hard bench sat a slim girl. She wore sensible
brogues with turned-over white socks, an Ancient-Campbell
tartan skirt, a beige blouse. A brown leather bag was slung over
one shoulder and a tam o'shanter with a scarlet pom-pom
balanced on her blonde curls.

Ben approached her. Keeping his voice down, he said: 'I have
a fear of heights, and since you appear to be a sensible person
without such ridiculous phobias, I wonder whether you would
be kind enough to accompany me to the top?'

The blonde girl considered. 'If you have this problem, why
go?'

'I am compelled to,' said Ben. 'I want to stand on the top of
Table Mountain and tell a certain girl just how very much I love
her, while the mist swirls and the wild wind keens.'

'You are an over-romantic, immature twit,' said Horrible
Hobart, rising, 'and you are just in time. The car is due any
minute and I bought the tickets.'

'I don't expect you to do the paying.' Ben dug out his wallet
and proffered a five-rand note, the equivalent of fifty shillings
and consequently far in excess of the price of the tickets.

'Thanks,' said Jane, and popped it into her sling bag. For a
fractional second Ben was reminded of a bus-conductor's satchel.

Then he dismissed such a silly comparison from his mind.

The approaching car's rumble filled the station. An announcement was made. They went up into the grotto-like docking bay with the dark little German men and their Brünhilde's, and were briefed by a jaded operator who seemed wearied by his aerial Flying Dutchman existence. He told them to avoid jumping out, or climbing on the roof, and that as the car left it would be photographed and that the photograph would be Number One.

'Turn your head away from the camera,' whispered sensible Jane Hobart.

The car was draughty and glassless and thoroughly wet from conveying water on its previous trip. Ben found a damp seat and put Jane on his lap, holding her tightly around her almost fragilely slim waist and laughing with the Germans who were just as frightened as he was. For seven minutes they soared away and up, and Jane admired the unbelievable beauty of the Peninsula as it unfolded below them, and Ben listened to her chatter while he deliberately unfocused his eyes and fought down the insistent desire to jump on to the sill, and spread his arms and sail away to distant mountains.

But after a century or so they entered a pock on Big Daddy's face and got out. It was freezingly cold. Their teeth chattered, their skin goosepimpled. They hugged themselves and each other as they left the Upper Station and ran, sometimes hopping from rock to rock like chamois, to the quaint stone restaurant where they thawed slowly over a pot of steaming tea and toasted currant buns.

Ben took Jane's hand. The restaurant was momentarily empty, so he kissed the chilblain on her forefinger. 'If I went out now into the mist and the wild wind's keening, I would die. So let me say it now. I love you. I know you don't believe me, but I do.'

She sighed. 'That's half the trouble. I do believe you. You're crazy, Ben.'

'It's happened before.'

She said nothing, turning her head and gazing out of the diamond-pane window at the cold-proof Germans photographing everything in sight while Ben sulked. She lit a cigarette and let time go by until he put money on the table and said huffily, 'I suppose we might as well go. There's a car due.'

Then Jane lifted the armoured shutters in her eyes, pointed

her little pink tongue at him, squeezed his hand, smoothed his hair and adjusted his tie. 'You're an absolute disgrace,' she said motheringly, but with a twinkle. 'There. That's better. What's the time?'

'Half-past-three.'

'Is it too early for a drink?'

'It will be fiveish by the time we get to Clifton. We can have one or two.' When she tickled him under the table he gave a grunt of laughter. 'Or three or four. I'm neglecting my practice.'

'So you need a holiday. Come, darling.' She put her red lips to his ear. 'Or three or four. And then some love? Please? Pretty please?'

'You're incorrigible.'

They got up, laughing again, holding hands like teenage lovers. Like lovers they went down in the cable car under the admiring gaze of the Germans, and like lovers they kissed in the warm dappled shade next to the Capri.

Ben started the engine and they moved off. Jane glanced into the back and saw the envelope. 'A letter from Flora?'

'Yes.' He changed gear.

'Anything much in it?'

'No,' he said, 'nothing much at all.'

The ruined cottage seemed wreathed in stillness. Somehow Slade felt that it should have a cheerful curl of smoke coming from the half-toppled chimney or a mongrel running out to bark. Even the hollow bang of the Austin's door was out of place and unreal.

Slade studied the shadowed doorless doorway that stood like an exclamation mark in the face of the small building and knew suddenly that Bobo was dead. Fright, he was sure, or his illness, or a combination of both had proved too much for the old man. He began to walk forward with dragging steps.

Then he heard the rattle of the dog chain from inside.

He ran the last few yards and burst through the doorway, hanging on to the jam, puffing and grinning, sweating, trembling with relief.

'You took a hell of a long time coming,' said the President of Gamba.

Slade came in. 'I'm sorry. I had a lot to do.'

There was an angry curve to the barracuda mouth and the tiger eyes glowed at him yellowly. 'I was, to say the least, alarmed. What if you had been killed in an accident?'

'I know.' Slade sat down on a chunk of rubble. 'It was a chance I had to take.' His eyes had grown accustomed to the indoor gloom and he saw that Bobo was seated on the edge of the camp bed, his left foot resting across his right thigh. The foot was smeared with butter.

'That won't work.'

'I know.' Bobo lifted his glance. 'It's not the only thing I tried.'

Following his eyes, Slade saw how the thick rafter had been crudely hacked about the area where the chain encircled it. 'How did you do that?'

'With the tin opener. But it's too blunt and my arms got tired.' Bobo blinked and rubbed a hand across his face.

'I didn't figure you'd try so hard. I'm sorry.' Slade shifted his weight. Even his backside was weary. 'Like some tea?'

'All right,' Bobo grumbled. Some of the ferocity went out of his eyes.

Slade went back to the van for another thermos he'd had filled in town. He brought it inside and poured for both of them.

There was a reflective pause while they sipped. After a while Bobo topped up, added some sugar, stirred noisily and then said, 'I should be very angry with you, you know.'

'Guess so.' Slade proffered his John Cottons and Bobo took one. They lit up. 'I certainly wouldn't deny that.'

'You abused my trust. I thought you were a security man.'

'Would you take it so far—that I abused your trust?'

'I certainly would.'

'Then I guess I did. And I feel bad about it. I haven't got much education and I'm not very good with words but if you say I abused your trust then I did.'

Bobo eyed him. 'You don't sound so bad with words to me, but be that as it may, you're a damn fine organizer. You must have planned this weeks in advance.'

Slade shook his head. 'I only got the idea on Monday night.'

'Never!'

'It's true, it's true. Like some more tea?'

'No thanks. In that case you're partly a good organizer and partly insanely lucky.'

'Yes, sir.' Slade nodded. 'I go along with that.'

Bobo drew on the cigarillo thoughtfully. 'I take it this will follow the normal pattern. I mean, some sort of ransom. But tell me one thing: is it financial or political?'

'Entirely financial.'

'You don't look like a crook. Why did you do it—debt?'

'Nope.' Noisy Slade clammed up.

'I wouldn't insult you by suggesting that you were purely greedy.'

Slade was tempted to leave this, but felt it might be regarded as an admission. 'I needed—I need—the money. Not for me but for someone else.'

'Whom?'

'Nope.' Slade wagged his head. 'That's it. I won't say any more. When it's all over I'll write you a letter from Zambia, or wherever I am, telling you why. If it works, that is.'

'You damn fool,' Bobo said bitterly, 'why didn't you come to me in hospital and *ask* me for the money?'

'You mean—borrow it from you?'

'Yes.'

He considered. 'No. I don't figure you for that kind of man. You'd be a dope. No security, and not even knowing me. Uh-uh. Sorry. I don't agree.'

Bobo shrugged. 'I suppose you're right. I would never have lent you the money. That was an idiot thing to say.'

They smoked for a minute and drank their tea. Then Bobo said, 'How much are you asking?'

'Fifty thousand rands.'

'That's the equivalent of twenty-five thousand pounds. You don't place a very high value on me, do you?'

'It's enough,' Slade said. 'You figure that invested at say nine per cent. It's just about enough to live on, if they're careful.'

'Ahah! So it's an income you're concerned with, more than a lump sum.'

Slade remained silent. Bobo changed the subject. 'When do I get out of here?'

'Tomorrow at six in the evening. If they play ball. And they should.'

Bobo considered. 'Obviously my presence has been missed. You realize I suppose that by now there's a manhunt on the go?'

Slade smiled. 'For me? You mean for me?'

'Are you trying to tell me that you haven't identified yourself as yet to the police?'

'Heck, no! Why should I?'

Bobo frowned at him. 'But you must have sent a ransom note!'

'Sure I have. I posted it to a newspaper on my way here. But it will only arrive in this afternoon's post. When I left the hospital they were looking for *you*, not for a kidnapper.'

'You mean they didn't think, they didn't realize that I had been——'

'Kidnapped? No.'

'Then what did they think?'

'They thought you'd gone out to tie one on.'

'That is an Americanism which escapes me.'

'They thought you'd gone out to get jugged. A booze-up.' A faintly sly smile tugged at Slade's lips. 'It figures, don't it?'

'Damn fools.' Bobo said it grimly. 'Just because I——' then he laughed suddenly. 'All right. I suppose it figures, as you put it.' He thought some more. 'But when the ransom note arrives. Then the chase will be on, won't it? You can't possibly hope to succeed in this mad enterprise.'

'I figure there's a fifty-fifty chance,' Slade said. 'For a start, I suppose you think they will be hunting me?'

'Who else? I've never kidnapped anyone. But they've got to hand the ransom over to you, haven't they.'

Slade chuckled. 'I've never kidnapped anyone either. But there's always a first time and lots of precedent to follow, like these political highjackings we read about in the papers.' He shook his head. 'No, sir, the ransom will be dumped at a place named in the note. And I didn't sign the note in my name.'

Bobo was intrigued. 'Then in whose name did you sign it?'

Slade gave him a small look of triumph. 'The Brotherhood of the Spears.'

There was a moment while Bobo stared at him bewilderedly. Thoughts tumbled around in his mind. Then he said, very slowly, 'Mr. Slade, I think I have been underestimating you.'

'Yeah, I thought so too,' Slade said modestly.

'This will make it a very high-level matter.' Bobo began to work things out. 'The South African government will be frantic to get me back and at the same time not become involved in a Gamban domestic issue. My cabinet will demand that my

safe return is made the primary consideration. In other words'
—he gave Slade a look of open admiration—'every step will be
taken to ensure that the ransom is handed over and I am
released.'

'Now you've got it,' Slade said.

Bobo narrowed his eyes. 'I hope you understand that afterwards will prove another story. The South African government
will feel humiliated. Then the hunt will be on with the ven-
geance.'

Slade shrugged. 'Sure. But look. The ransom is due for
delivery at eleven o'clock tomorrow morning. After I've collected it I will post a letter, express mail, to the same newspaper
to which I sent the ransom note, telling where you are. It will
only be delivered by about four, more likely five o'clock. It will
take the cops half an hour to get you out of here. I haven't
explained this in the note. All I've said is that I guarantee your
release by six o'clock at the latest. Anyway, at that stage you tell
them it's me who did it, but it won't do the cops any good
because my flight leaves Cape Town at one o'clock tomorrow.
By the time you give them the news I will be out of the
country.'

Bobo nodded thoughtfully. 'You're cutting things awfully
fine.'

Slade stood up. 'For something planned overnight it's got to
have weaknesses.'

Bobo put up a hand in a halting gesture. 'Don't rush off. Let's
just presume that they refuse to play ball, as you would put it.
In other words they mount a major search, however blind it
may be, and don't pay the ransom. What then?'

Slade was shaking his head before Bobo finished speaking.
'You're the head of a government yourself. Do you see it
happening that way?'

'Just say it did,' Bobo insisted. 'You wouldn't consider, in
extremes of desperation'—he gave Slade quite an apologetic look
—'harming me in any way?'

'Do I look it?' Slade met his glance squarely.

'No. I don't think you look it at all. I'm sorry, but you will
appreciate I had to make sure.'

'Of course.'

'Look, I'm rather tired of sitting around in pyjamas. Mind
unlocking me, so that I can change?'

'Sure.' Slade went out to the van. He came back with the key to the smaller padlock, and a large brown-paper packet. 'Brought you some more grub.' Dumping it next to the bed, he bent and dragged out Bobo's suitcase. 'There's quite a lot of kit in here. Hold up your foot.'

Bobo was unfettered. He changed into clothes and then once more passively raised his foot while Slade wound the chain around his ankle and clicked the padlock shut again.

'Thanks.' Slade pocketed the key. 'Know how to work the Coleman?'

'I have camped before.' Bobo shuddered inwardly at his memory of the last occasion, when Cyril Crutchley had dried him out.

'Well.' Slade fidgeted. 'Guess I'd better be going.'

'I suppose so.' There was a strange awkwardness between them. 'Will I see you again before——'

'I go? Yeah. I'll pop in early tomorrow morning to see how you are, and bring you some more minestrone if I can.'

'That would be nice. Please buy it at the same place.'

'I will. I——' Slade's expression turned to one of sudden alarm. There was this rising, rushing, fluttering feeling in his chest. He turned quickly. 'Got to go. Got to——'

His stumbling feet took him over the debris to the door, but it was too late. At the doorway he began to cough. The spasm took over and buckled him. He coughed clinging to the door-jamb, staring at Bobo with the blank-eyed face of a wounded beast, coughing and coughing endlessly on while Bobo stared in mounting concern and then struggled to the end of his chain to try and reach him.

'Dammit, I can't!' Bobo cried.

Slade felt the sudden pop in his chest, the little detonation that sent the blood spurting into his mouth to pour out over his chin and spatter on the chips of broken plaster at his feet.

Bobo pulled at the chain. He went on his knees, stretching out his leg behind, then down on his belly, arms pushed out. 'I can't reach you, Mr. Slade!'

Slade spat out the last of the blood. 'It's okay. It's over.' He slid down the door jamb, all the way down with his back against it, knees hunched under his chin, staring straight ahead of him.

Into the silence Bobo said, 'You are a very sick man, Mr. Slade.'

He wiped a hand slowly across his mouth. 'No sicker'n you.' His blue eyes burned out of a washed grey face.

'Can you manage?'

'Uh-huh.' He struggled to his feet, trying to control his breathing. 'I'll be going now.'

Bobo retreated to his camp bed. 'You're not going to collapse or anything like that, I hope.'

Slade gave him a bitter grin. 'Worried about my welfare or yours?'

'If you were to die,' Bobo said coldly, 'so would I. And I have a few things to do, yet. I'm not quite ready.'

'Yeah.' Slade hovered in the doorway. 'Look, I should give you a shot of vitamin B12 now but I'm whacked and way behind schedule. Do you feel okay? Do you think you'll be all right until tomorrow morning?'

'I haven't got much option, have I?'

'I'll give you the damn injection,' Slade shouted, 'if you really need it!'

'Go to hell!'

They stared at each other furiously. Then Slade turned away and walked out into the cooling sunlight. He got into the Austin and was about to start the engine when the voice came rumblingly and grudgingly from the cottage. 'What time can I expect you tomorrow?'

'About eight.' Slade leant his fevered head on the hard rim of the wheel.

There was a pause. Then, 'Goodbye.' In dignified tones.

'See you,' Slade said.

He started up, turned the van and bumped away between the wattles to the gate.

He was a small, nearly bald man with quivery jowls. He took in the smoke-filled office, the four grim-faced detectives, the weary Pahler behind the desk. 'What the hell is the meaning of this, being dragged in here like a common criminal?' he cried.

'You weren't dragged in, for a start,' Pahler said. 'And on top of that you've been hanging around for nearly an hour. Now

I want to know what it's all about.'

'I wanted to see him.'

'Who?'

'The President. But when I saw all the cops I thought Jesus, maybe I'd better see what's going on first so I stood on the pavement until that big goon comes up——'

'Your name?'

'Fuskin. Aaron J. Fuskin. Listen, I'm a respectable——'

'Why did you want to see the President?'

'Because I'm the local rep. for Highland Feather.'

Pahler dug for his handkerchief. He screwed up his face. 'What's thad god to do with id?' He honked loudly.

'I wanted him to endorse our product.' Fuskin's face lit up. 'Something like, "Suppliers to His Excellency the President of Gamba" on the label. Hell of a feather in my cap, eh? Hah-hah, accidental pun, huh? You know—feather, Highland Feather, get it?'

'Oh Christ. Get out.' Pahler looked as though he were going to weep.

'I'll have your name and number, sergeant. I'm a respectable citizen, you can't talk to me——'

'I'm Colonel Pahler, Mr. Fuskin. And I still want you to get out.'

'Top Gestapo, hey?' Fuskin's jowls wobbled. 'And I happen to know I'm not committing a crime. Now I demand to see the President, unless he doesn't want to——'

Pahler jumped to his feet. 'The President isn't here! He's moved! Now go away!'

Fuskin backed to the door under the force of the bull-like roar. 'I'll go. I'll go. Otherwise I know you'll pull me in under one of those funny laws of your, eh? But I've got this to say before I leave. I'm a respectable citizen. I pay my taxes. I've got a boy at the university. I've got a helluva big mortgage on my house. But I've got this to say.'

'Say it, please,' Pahler begged.

Fuskin took a deep breath. His cheeks ballooned. 'Down with the fuzz!' he cried. Then he turned and waddled out.

There was a short, reflective silence. Then Pahler grinned. 'A middle-aged hippie.'

'Hippie,' hissed Maurer. 'A jew-boy Communist, too.' His furious black button eyes still watched the doorway.

'I doubt it.' Pahler studied him with interest. He disliked Maurer even more now, if that were possible. 'Look, it's eight o'clock and I'm tired. Let's finish, shall we? Nothing on the airport, nothing on the docks, a blank on railway stations, taxis, car-hire, buses...'

'We can't be absolutely sure on Bantu buses.' Maurer, Pahler was sure, never blinked. 'So many passengers, and these people all look alike.'

Pahler sighed. 'As near as we can judge, a blank. I'm sure he wouldn't catch a bus, anyway. A blank on bottle stores, parks, drains, overgrown areas other than the mountains, rugby fields, public toilets, culverts, bars, domestic premises within a reasonable radius, hell, is there anything more?'

The detectives stirred, muttered, lapsed into tired silence.

'Marvellous.' A sneeze sneaked up on Pahler and he succeeded in making even Maurer jump. 'Oh hell. I wadda go hobe bud I can't.' All four men in the room now actually hated the sight of his pulpy handkerchief and the sound of his goose-like honking.

Pahler lifted his baggy eyes, yellowed like a hound dog, to survey the door. 'Can I help you, Sister?'

Janet Strange regarded him with cool appraisal. She had never seen a man with a more messy cold. If he went on like this the Joseph Schwer would be running an epidemic. 'There is no one at Reception for the moment so I took a message from a man called Carson who wants to see you urgently. He's from one of the papers.'

Pahler frowned. 'What does he want?'

'I don't know I'm sure. I'm not a receptionist.'

He caught the rebuke. 'I'm sorry, Sister.' What the hell was this, now, had there been a leak to the press?'

Janet relented. 'He said he's the assistant editor. And he wants to show you something very important.'

A large coin clanged in Pahler's brain. He saw coloured lights briefly and did several things at once. A detective was sent scampering down the corridor while Strange was treated to a waterily dazzling smile. As she went away she reflected that Pahler was better looking than she had at first thought.

Carson was brought to the office. He and Pahler virtually collided at the door and fumbled a brief handshake. Carson was lean and good-looking and and in the grip of tremendous excitement. He was holding a thin brown-paper parcel which was partly torn open.

'I had the helluva job finding you, everybody was so mysterious.' His eyes swept the smoggy room. 'He's gone, I take it? Lunda's gone?'

'Yes.' Pahler said the word into an aeon of time.

'I thought this was genuine.' Carson put the narrow wrapping on the desk. He fiddled at it with shaking hands, finally extracting its contents.

Bobo Lunda's fly-whisk.

It seemed to grow larger and larger in Pahler's sight until it filled his vision. He heard his voice say quite calmly. 'And a note?'

'Yes.' A neatly printed sheet of writing paper was thrust before him. He read it automatically. And then he sighed a long sigh.

'Here.' He passed it on to Maurer, waited while the Captain read it. Their eyes met. 'Now we know.'

'Know.' Maurer read it again and gave it back. 'Fifty thousand rand. By eleven tomorrow. So little time.'

Pahler suddenly wanted to snap the fly-whisk. 'These goddam little tin-pot states with their dirty little fratricidal wars!' He whirled on Maurer as though he were going to hit him. 'Get Mango and Zaza here! Don't tell them what it's about and keep them outside in the car until I send for you. I'm going to tell them what has happened but I must get clearance first. Take Clark and Kapp. Now get moving.'

Maurer left at a waddling trot with two of the three detectives. The other man fidgeted in his chair while Pahler stared at the fly-whisk.

'Can I publish?' Carson asked the question apologetically.

'No. At least, not yet. I'll let you know.'

'This is big, isn't it. It has all sorts of implications.'

'You're kidding?' Pahler blinked at him. 'I'll have to get on to somebody in the government and they will have to contact Gamba. I don't know what the—policy will be.' He picked up the empty package and examined it. 'Posted this morning, in Rondesbosch. The letter too. Why did it take so long to reach me?'

Carson shrugged. 'We get a hell of a lot of post. Eventually someone opened it. Then it came to me, of course, on the run.'

'"Brotherhood of the Spears".' Sounds like a comic strip.' Pahler dropped the package on the desk.

'A deadly one. There've been people killed up there, in this squabble.'

'I know, I know, I read your paper. And others.' Pahler smiled wearily. 'You'll excuse me? I've got a lot to do. It doesn't look as though I'm going to get much sleep.' He shook hands again with Carson. 'Thank you for your help.'

When the newspaperman had left Pahler went to the telephone. He was about to dial when he looked at the remaining detective. 'How old are you, Smith?'

'Twenty-five, sir.' Smith stood up.

'Ever been mixed up in a kidnapping?'

'No, sir.'

'Well.' Pahler began to dial. 'I'm forty-four and nor have I.'

At ten o'clock that evening Major Shannon's telephone rang. He was standing at the bar pouring himself a whisky, so he snatched it up immediately. He said, 'Yes?' and then listened. His colour heightened and eventually he burst in heatedly: 'Look here, I don't take that kind of talk from anyone! I sat there for hours hoping he would come out. The garden is pretty sheltered from the wind, after all. Round about eleven I started seeing policemen, and much activity. I got worried so I thought I'd stroll down and take a look. How was I to know that I'd see this fellow Pahler or whatever his name is?'

There was another long pause and then Shannon spoke again in a far more mollified tone. 'Oh. Well, that's a relief.' Another pause. Then: 'Damned ridiculous thing to happen. There's nothing I can do, obviously, until Lunda's brought back. *If* he's brought back, that is. Some of these kidnappings can be damned sticky. You may not—hah-hah—need me after all. But I hope you do.'

He replaced the telephone and lifted his whisky, then looked up impatiently as a girl appeared in the doorway. She was a slovenly unlovely creature, naked except for one of his white shirts that draped on her like a nightgown. She reached the middle of the carpet and stood with her bare feet apart, hands buried somewhere under the shirt, dark hair hanging in lifeless clusters on her shoulders.

'Where's Betsy?' He said it sharply.

She swayed slightly. 'Still in bed.' The pupils of her eyes were hugely dilated.

'Well get back there yourself, damn it,' he snarled. 'I haven't finished with you yet.'

The girl hesitated. 'Can I have a drink?'

'Have the whole bloody bottle.' He tossed a bottle of sherry at her. It struck her on the thigh and fell to the carpet. Slowly the girl bent and retrieved it. She regarded him dully, then shuffled out of the room in the direction of the bedroom.

Shannon had another drink while he listened to the radio. The news came on after a while, telling him that the Pohlsmoor escapees had not yet been recaptured. He switched off the set uninterestedly, finished his drink, poured another and took it with him to the bedroom.

There was an ornate, carved double bed against the far wall. He went to it, grabbed the covers in one hand and flicked them back, smiling at the two naked, shivering, dull-faced girls who lay there waiting for him.

'All right girls, it's sticking time,' he said. Then he laughed and began to take off his clothes. In a minute he was in bed with them, three examples of the vulnerability of *homo sapiens*, the genus man. Two were very nearly sub-human. And the third was irretrievably mad.

In the quiet of the night Ginny Slade put her slim arms around her husband. 'Ernie! Ernie, turn over. You've been dreaming!'

'Huh?' He twisted and automatically reached out and held her. He made choking sleep-noises. Then he said in a clear and thin and unreal voice, 'Oh Christ, I'm so tired!'

'You're burning. God Ernie, you're burning up you're so hot!' She pressed her cool face against his. 'Can I get you something, Ernie?'

He grunted again, turned once more and put his back to her. She reached out one-handed and found her wrist-watch. Ten o'clock, the luminous dial said. And he'd gone to bed at six-thirty and passed out.

Ginny scrabbled for the bedside light and switched it on. She got out of bed, went to the lavatory and threw up. In the bathroom she rinsed her mouth and washed her hands, then went to the medicine cabinet and checked it for aspirin. But there was nothing. She returned to the bedroom, shook him.

'Ernie! Ernie! You got anything for your fever?'

He came bolt upright in bed so quickly that they nearly banged heads. 'Pants pocket.' There was a sheen of sleep over his eyes. He gazed vaguely past her.

She crossed the room to his carelessly flung trousers, fiddled in the pockets and found the bottle of A.P. Cods. Something came out with the bottle, a folded, small, slippery piece of paper. A prescription, perhaps. She smoothed it out quickly, but it was only a scribbled cash slip from a hardware store: '1 12ft. dog chain. Two Master padlocks'.

Ginny crumpled the paper and tossed it aside. She took two tablets from the bottle and poured a glass of water.

'Here, Ernie. Take these pills, darling.'

He gulped noisily and fell back, at once breathing heavily. Ginny got back on her side and pulled up the covers. She touched his fever-hot body gently. He would start sweating in a while and she would probably have to change him.

The foetus in her womb made her yearn for sleep but her mind was spring-loaded. Dog chain. And two padlocks. What for? They had no pets. Even the dove in the applebox cage had recovered and flown away.

She put out the light. In the mantle of the velvet darkness she remembered an old poem she had learned in her book-store days, so many years ago:

> Light in the darkness, Sailor, day is at hand!
> See o'er the foaming billows fair Heaven's land;
> Drear was the voyage, sailor, now almost o'er,
> Safe within the lifeboat, sailor, pull for the shore.
> Pull for the shore, sailor, pull for the shore.
> Heed not the rolling waves, but bend to the oar.

She moved back and held him again. The tears came easily now, so she cried in the darkness, the lifeboat and the oar.

Chapter Ten

Slade awoke with a jerk at six o'clock, clear-headed and clear-eyed, although his chest hurt. Ginny was a mound of blankets and a tousle of strawberry blonde hair, so he got stealthily out of bed and quickly dressed, shaved, drank a few mouthfuls of milk straight from the carton in the refrigerator. Then he put the letter he had written her on the kitchen table, propped up against the sugar bowl so she couldn't miss it, let himself quietly out of the house, went down the path to the Volkswagen and coasted the car for twenty yards before letting the motor kick into life.

The Austin stood alone and rather conspicuous behind the Rosebank cinema, but it was shielded from the main road by the bulk of the building. He swopped vehicles, leaving the Volkswagen in the Austin's place in accordance with a post-script promise he had made to Ginny in his letter. Then he drove the van a mile to a filling station where he topped up the tank and bought two two-gallon jerrycans of Regular. He had taken only ten minutes to dress and shave and another fifteen to reach this point, so that the hands of his wristwatch pointed to just short of six thirty.

He made a quick final check of the glove compartment: the big Zeiss binoculars might play an important part; and without the air ticket his carefully laid plans could go very wrong. Satisfied, he kicked the six-year-old engine into life and headed through the curvy looms of forest in Constantia, making good time across the Neck and letting the van sing its differential song on the long down-run to the overgrown gate, the pressing wattles, the sound of flies buzzing and the little ruined cottage with its silent smokeless air of abandonment.

He had been conscious of gathering tension ever since changing vehicles; it was as though this brought about a mechanical Jekyll and Hyde separation into two conflicting personalities. In the Volkswagen it was all a silly dream. In the Austin it was frightening reality, and he had this butterfly sensation of ir-revocable commitment, a gulping feeling of rushing downhill without brakes and launching into a final cliff-jump with the scream forcibly buttoned down.

It was too late to go back. The ransom note had been de-livered; forces of various intent were gathering, discussing, preparing, disposing. And all because of him.

It made Ernest Slade feel very small, very alone, and very frightened.

This time he heard the rattle of the dog-chain directly after the thump of the van door. Oddly, it was a reassuring sound, not only because it meant that Bobo was alive but because it heralded company, as well. So he hastened to the doorway with a pulse-beat committed to the low hundreds by reason of his tension.

Bobo looked fairly neat for a large ungainly man who has been obliged to sleep in his clothes, so there was only a small air of rumpledness, slightly aggravated by a glint of white beard stubble.

'I look like hell,' he complained grumpily, without any formal greeting. 'And I was scared stiff in the night. All those creepy noises. Do you think that's an admission, Mr. Slade, for a seventy-year-old President to say that he was frightened?'

'Only a big man can admit to being little.' Slade joined him on the edge of the camp bed.

Bobo eyed him. 'Homespun philosophy. You're shrewder than you realize. Feeling a little better today? I had visions of your dying in the night.'

Slade smiled. 'I'm as better as twelve hours sleep can make me.'

'You look less haggard.' Bobo leaned a shoulder against the bag-plastered wall at the head of the bed. 'But I am, conversely, jaded. Does this call for some vitamin B12?'

'It does.' Slade got up, found the handcase and spent two minutes giving him the intramuscular injection. When Bobo had rolled down his sleeve he asked, 'How's the site of the bone marrow biopsy?'

Bobo ran a hand cautiously over the area just in front of his left trouser pocket. 'Slightly tender. Is that normal?'

'You'll be back this evening. If it's not they will knock it with antibiotics.' Slade resumed his seat.

'The master of the begged question.'

'Huh?'

'It doesn't matter. Is everything ready for your coup?'

'Yup.' Slade gave him a John Cotton and they lit up.

'I have had a lot of time to think.' Bobo blew smoke at the doorway. 'Your scheme is theoretically clever, of course, but examined carefully it hangs together by its toenails in places. So much depends upon the reaction of the so-called Powers that Be. Do you agree?'

'It was the only way.'

'Quite.' Bobo nodded. 'But I am the man in the middle. If your note giving my location should go astray; if somebody gets silly or stubborn; if an official makes one of those brave-sounding statements like, "We don't negotiate with kidnappers"; if any of these things chance to happen then I become another Lacrosse, don't I?'

Slade coloured. 'Look, I told you I wouldn't harm you.'

'Not directly, no. But I could quietly starve to death all the same, couldn't I?'

'I doubt it. If you like I could send a cable from Zambia, repeating your location.'

'Thank you so much. While I sit here for another—say forty-eight hours with my condition untreated.'

Slade studied him carefully. 'You've got some kind of an idea.'

'I have, indeed, and it is motivated entirely by instincts of self-preservation.' Bobo considered him crossly. 'You're a damn nuisance, getting a harmless old man involved in such a situation. Is there a telephone kiosk within reasonable range?'

'There's one in Hout Bay. But I'm not agreeing, sir, to anything at this stage. What's on your mind?'

Bobo shrugged. 'I thought I could telephone the editor of the newspaper to which the ransom note was delivered and ask him to persuade the authorities not to indulge in heroics at my expense. In other words, to pay up, and smile.' The barracuda mouth opened in a slash of heartless grin. 'I'm sure the host government would insist on standing the round.'

Slade tried to think rapidly. That chromium-and-steel computer of twenty-four hours ago seemed to have slowed down. After a while he said, 'Sounds okay. There won't be many people about now. You give your word you won't shout, or try anything funny?'

'What would happen if I did?' Bobo looked at him carefully.

'I'd strong-arm you back to the van. And I'm sorry to say that the sight of a black man being cuffed by a white man doesn't raise many people's blood pressure in this country. As long as it's quick, that is. If it goes on too long it bothers their consciences.'

Bobo was intrigued. 'And if it was a black man beating a white man?'

Slade wagged his head. 'They don't.'

'Invidious.' Bobo sighed. 'All right, Mr. Slade, I will behave.' He held up his massive foot. 'Shall we go?'

Slade had the same bottled-up feeling on the way to Hout Bay, this sensation of fear and constriction. He was assailed by doubt and regretted his decision to lock Bobo in the rear, because that left him with no one to talk to. His mouth was dry and he had a conviction of disaster. The brain that had seemed fuddled now cleared the jam and made up for lost time, hurling apprehension after apprehension at him: he had allowed far too little time for this complex scheme; setting the pick-up point so near to Bobo was a mistake, it should have been miles away; even a mechanical break-down could cause him to miss his pick-up, miss his flight; if the police had had time not only to watch from the mountains above but to cut the Peninsula in half, how was he going to get back through Cape Town to the airport?

He answered, of course, with some measure of success: the whole idea of squeezing time was to allow no one much opportunity for deep thought. It was to hasten decision, to make them reason the way he wanted; the closeness to Bobo of the ransom pick-up point meant nothing as long as the President's whereabouts were unknown—it would surely lead the police, if anything, to think that Bobo was nowhere near; and even if the Peninsula had been cordoned off here near its waist, even if all the roads were blocked, weren't the police still looking for black kidnappers? Would a white man in a well-used and honest-looking working vehicle merit more than a passing glance?

This question-and-answer routine lasted him into Hout Bay, a disappointing village when seen from the main road, containing a mixture of old and new, Cape Malay architecture clashing with glass-fronted modern shops. The picture-book beauty of the little harbour and the Bay itself is not visible from there.

Slade drove as close as possible to the Post Office, which had its two call-boxes at either end of a verandah facing the street. It was not yet seven-thirty, the Post Office itself was closed, and there were very few pedestrians about. He went to the back and unlocked the double door. Bobo got out stiffly.

He stretched, Slade was sure, only on purpose, and to make himself annoying. Then they crunched on to the verandah. Slade headed automatically for the lefthand call-box, got to it, opened the door, looked around and found Bobo at the other end of the verandah. He had the sign 'NON-WHITE/*NIE BLANKES* above his head.

'You're a victim of the machine.' Bobo scratched his pockets for change. 'Do they duplicate everything like this? It must cost a fortune.'

Slade joined him. 'They've got fortunes to spend.' He looked about tensely, crazily aware that if anything would excite attention it would be the sight of a white man joining a black man in a non-white call box. He pushed Bobo inside and let the door swing shut, fiddling for the directory.

'Careful,' Bobo said. 'That's a black book, the colour might rub off.'

'Knock it off, Mr. President.' Slade checked his watch again. 'The editor should be at home.' He found the paper's entry and the editor's home number, got a dialling tone, gave Bobo the receiver and dialled. The dial was replaced by the ringing tone and he waited tensely, hearing for himself the sharp *clack* as the instrument at the other end was picked up.

Bobo slid change into a slot while Slade, having forgotten, still frantically scrabbled. 'I like the way I have to pay for my own call. Hello. Mr. Editor?'

There was a grumbling and reluctant acknowledgement.

'This is not a crank call. I must ask you please not to replace the telephone. My name is Bobo Lunda and I am the President of Gamba. I can imagine you have some idea of why I am telephoning you.'

Slade could sense the stiffening of the man at the other end, the sudden sharp crackle of enquiry in the voice. The editor, a weather-beaten old pirate with years of newspaper work behind him, took no more than two seconds to adjust, while his heart completely missed one beat. Then he said guardedly, 'How can I be sure this is genuine?' while he rolled his eyes and made signs at his wife. She followed the line of his pointing finger and switched on the tape recorder.

'You can't be sure it's genuine, can you?' Bobo said nastily. 'Now do you want to listen or do I phone the opposition?'

'Talk, Mr. President,' said the editor. Gently sweating, he made more signs. His wife ran up with one inch of crayon and an unpaid account on which he scribbled, 'FONE COPS.'

'Do you know all about me? Was the ransom note received?' Bobo glared at Slade.

'It was received by Mr. Carson the assistant editor, but naturally I was informed.' The editor stonily watched his wife complete one circuit of the living-room and then, comprehension dawning, head for the front door and the neighbours' telephone, running strongly.

'Was the note handed to the police?'

'Er—yes.' He was not quite sure whether this was the right thing to say.

'Very well.' Bobo sounded to Slade as though he were enjoying the situation. 'Now the object of this call, Mr. Editor, is to request you to speak most earnestly to the authorities, both my government and yours, and convey to them my sincere hope that no one will indulge in false heroics at my expense. In other words, I would like the ransom note followed to the letter. Do you understand?'

'Yes, sir.' The editor regarded his tape recorder with absolute hatred: it was recording only his end of the conversation Then he had an idea; he repeated almost *verbatim* what Bobo had said.

'Correct. You have someone taking this down, I gather?'

'Er, my tape recorder.' The editor made this admission almost shyly. This was the Tiger of Gamba he was talking to, all right, this astute old bastard. 'You have my assurance I will get on to the police immediately, Mr. President. Now may I ask you one of two questions?'

'Be quick about it. I am in some personal discomfort.'

The editor wiped his brow. 'Are you being compelled to make this call, Mr. President?'

'Let's say I'm doing it for the sake of my health.'

'And if the ransom note is *not* followed, are you liable to be ill-treated?'

Bobo stared dispassionately at Slade. 'I have no illusions on that score.'

Slade wrung his hands. 'Don't overdo it.'

'You could possibly confirm that you are being held by a group known as——'

'What was that?' said Bobo to Slade.

'I said could you confirm that——'

'Don't overdo it,' repeated Slade.

'I thought I heard another voice——' The editor stopped suddenly, confused. 'I withdraw the question.'

'It is being indicated to me that I must ring off,' said Bobo. 'I do hope you will act at once.'

'I will indeed.' Through the window the editor could see his wife headed back, followed by what happened to be a throng.

'Thank you.' The editor heard the receiver replaced. He said fatuously, 'Hello?' and then replaced his own.

His wife returned accompanied by two sets of neighbours.

'Did you get through?'

'Eventually. Jack's phone had been cut off——'

'I'd forgotten to pay the damn bill, hah-hah——'

'So I shot across to Maureen——'

'They wouldn't *believe* her!' Maureen was eggy-lipped from an interrupted breakfast.

The editor picked up his telephone. 'Who did you 'phone?'

'Rosebank police station.'

'Oh God.' He began to dial.

'Come.' Maureen picked up her sorrowful Basset hound. 'Come, Murgatroyd.'

The petrol had a harsh smell that gave him a sense of indigestion. It throbbed pinkly out of the jerrycan in jetting pulsebeats, like mechanical blood. It spattered on the dry grass, the shrubs, the bushes. It bled from the can as he slowly walked, until it was empty. He threw it aside, went away for a few yards, got the other one and went on, until he had saturated more than a hundred yards of grass and scrub.

When he was finished he was again tired and it was really only the beginning of a very busy day. He desperately wanted to smoke, but although there was a wind of sorts coming up, petrol fumes hung heavily in the air. Instead, he surveyed his handiwork and tried to construct an animated map in his mind.

Back there, about a mile away, was the cottage and Bobo. Two hundred yards from him was the pick-up point, a small stunted oak in a five-yard clearing of its own, reached by another vague and grass-choked track leading from the main road. And here, in the petrol-soaked mixture of dry and green shrubbery on either side of him, was his insurance, the idea that had come to him yesterday and which he had seized instantly, giving himself no time to reconsider.

He looked at his watch. Eight-fifty. He had stipulated that the money was to be placed at the oak at precisely 11 a.m. and no later. He had a long wait ahead of him. There was no need to re-check anything. He was entirely ready, even down to the van obscured by branches from both ground observation and the possible searching eye of helicopters.

He had to stay near the petrol. One hundred and thirty—no, one hundred and twenty-nine—minutes to wait. No smoking. And preferably no movement.

He tramped back wearily in a westerly direction to where the petrol trail started. There he found a nook and sat down uncomfortably, the big Zeiss glasses digging into one hip.

Inevitably he thought about Ginny, and what this would be doing to her. He felt a crying sadness.

Chapter Eleven

In the hectic come-and-go atmosphere of Pahler's commandeered office at the Joseph Schwer there occurred a small moment of quietude.

'I had four hours sleep last night.' He and Maurer were alone. 'They lent me a bed in an empty ward. I suppose I could have gone home but there didn't seem much point in it. I was so damn busy.'

'Busy.' Maurer instantly flushed. 'I worked very hard, too. But I had to go home in the end. The children are still young.'

Typically, he had read a slight into Pahler's innocent remark. 'Captain Maurer, I——' Pahler gave up. It was just no use trying. One couldn't change Maurer, nor was Maurer the sort of man to whom he was prepared to impart that kind of buddies-together confidence which might have helped, like the fact that he disliked going home anyway, especially since his daughter Ellen now objected to his pipe and had forbidden liquor of any sort in the house. Instead he droned on, partly because he was tense and overwrought, partly because his mind seemed to work better when he did it.

'I kept thinking something was going to pop, but it didn't. In the end I went to bed. They offered me a pair of hospital pyjamas, but you should have seen them. More like baggies. So I slept in my underpants. Sister Strange brought me coffee a few times. Funny how these hospitals work. She's downstairs now with Jensen and Meadows and Novak're on the first floor. Hobart's off until Saturday, then she starts day duty and these four go off for a few days, while Killeen...' He stopped, confused. He had bought a box of Kleenex and the discarded ones lay scattered about the desk in various shapes like magnified snow crystals. 'It was a long night. Once your mind gets working...' He sighed and left it there.

'Working,' Maurer hissed. 'The man at the gate?'

'Him, and other things.' Pahler found his pipe and studied it longsightedly. 'To see him at the airport, and feel there was something odd about him, and then find him here hanging about outside and asking my bloke all sorts of questions, is too much of a coincidence. He said he had been a patient here. Well, Smith went through the records with Matron Burns for a full two years. She has an excellent memory and there is no one who comes even close to matching the description I gave them. Apart from which, I *know* I have seen his face before. In something printed. Some book perhaps.'

'Perhaps.' Maurer lit a cigarette and then added unexpectedly, 'A nut-case, maybe. The kidnappers are Bantu.'

'Could be,' Pahler spoke around his pipe. 'If the kidnappers are indeed black men—and I must accept that they are—then he probably is a nut-case, but a worrying one. Which brings me to another point. How the hell was Lunda spirited out of the Joseph Schwer without a soul seeing him or anyone else who didn't fit? No sign of a struggle. No suspicious people.'

He popped a match and held it in his big fingers, ignoring it while he glared indignantly at Maurer. 'Suddenly he's gone, like the bloody Scarlet Pimpernel. It all points to someone on the staff lending a hand, but I don't see who. Meadows has got her mind on her fanny all the time, so I hear, Hobart is a shrewd little gold-digger, Novak and Jensen are simple immigrant types with full family lives, Slade and his wife are a pair of loafers who drift around the world, working when they have to. They're drop-outs.'

'Drop-outs. You haven't mentioned Sister Strange?' Maurer stared fascinatedly as the match-flame neared Pahler's horny finger-tips.

'Janet Strange is a lady.' Pahler fixed his subordinate with a grim, challenging eye. 'She's above that sort of thing.' At the last possible fraction of a second he brought the match down upon the tobacco. 'Frankly, if there were any point in it I would consider it my duty to investigate *all* of them. But the decision whether or not to pay the ransom is being made at the moment and I'm pretty sure I know what it will be. So we pay, we get Lunda back and he gives us the identity of his kidnappers.' He shrugged. 'There's no earthly point in doing a lot of unnecessary donkey-work at this stage.'

'Stage.' Maurer worked ecstatically on the sibilant. '*Provided* we get Lunda back, you mean.'

'No, no, we'll get him back all right.' Pahler shook his head. 'This sort of thing follows a precedent, these days, all over the world. A sort of Highjacker's Code of Ethics. Abide by the terms of ransom and you get your man back. Refuse'—he sawed a hand across his leathery throat—'and they give him the works. Which brings me to the last of my three brainteasers: with this sort of political kidnapping the ransom seldom sounds in money. It usually takes the form of a demand for the release of political prisoners, the stay of an execution, that sort of thing. There's the Palestine-guerilla case as a precedent, the Quebec affair as another. Now what I want to know is: in our instance, *why* only money, and if it's got to be money, *why* so little? Fifty thousand rands in Highjacker's language is peanuts. Look at the Quantas bloke—three hundred thousand Australian dollars if I'm not mistaken.'

'Mistaken.' Maurer produced his inevitable echo absently this time. 'What did the Brigadier say about a trap?'

'Uh-uh. Not a chance. They're playing this one so bloody carefully that you feel you're being obliged to run in football boots along a pathway paved with eggshells without breaking any.'

He got up and went over to the wall where a large-scale map of the Peninsula had been hung. 'This is Constantia Neck, *here*. We're allowed thirty men, as well concealed as possible on the western slopes of the mountain *here*, overlooking the Hout Bay Road. This will be known as Observation Point One. Now *here*'—he slid a finger down in a south-westerly direction—'is Victoria Road, just at the turnoff to Hout Bay harbour. It then, as you can see, swings east to cut into Hout Bay Road. We're allowed one truckload of men there, well back from the main road. This is Observation Point Two. Theoretically, once the money-drop is made, OPs One and Two can isolate Hout Bay Road, cutting off the kidnappers at either end. Then we've got them unless they take to the bush in which case we'd still get them anyway.'

He wagged his head sadly. 'But I can't see it happening. Not a move will be made until we've got Lunda back. That's several hours after the drop-off, and by then the kidnappers will be miles away. No, all we can hope for is that one of the OPs, more likely Two, will spot a suspicious vehicle. Even then our instructions are to shadow in such a delicate way that we'll most likely lose it.' He sucked angrily at his pipe until the tobacco glowed. 'All this is known as Stage One, and it's a complete bloody waste of time. We can't hope to get cracking until we get Lunda back. Then we move into Stage Two. With no holds barred, I hope.'

Maurer said nothing, staring at the map with his little black-button eyes. Then the telephone rang and both of them jumped.

'This is it.' Pahler reached out a long hand for the receiver. He said only, 'Pahler,' and then listened, grunted at intervals. The voice went on in buzzing monologue until Pahler said, 'Okay, sir, I understand,' and put the receiver back on its cradle. Then he looked at Maurer with rather bitter eyes. 'That was the Commissioner. Like a guess?'

'Guess.' Maurer had gone paler with tension. Hesitantly, he suggested, 'Pay?'

'Yes, dammit, we pay. Fifty thousand rands in notes of small denomination will be delivered here within the next twenty minutes. You are to take the packet personally to the drop-off point in a civilian vehicle. You can have my Fairlane, it's un-marked. For my purposes I'll use a truck. It's more suited, probably.' He picked up the phone again, dialled impatiently, spoke briefly, replaced it. 'It's nine-fifteen now. That means the money will be here by nine-forty-five at the latest. To reach the drop-off point from the Joseph Schwer takes almost exactly twenty minutes at standard speeds and the delivery time is precisely eleven, so I would like you to leave here at say ten-forty so that you can slow down if you find you're going to overshoot on time. Rather that than be late. We dare not be late, these boys will probably be very brittle.'

'Brittle,' repeated Maurer. He seemed to ponder, staring with hot little eyes across the smoke-filled room.

Pahler eyed him with interest. 'You know the route?'

'Route.' Maurer looked pastily uncertain of himself, Ka menaced by an unknown quantity of a Sher Khan. 'Yes, I know the route. Will I have to do this alone?'

The reason for his hesitancy now became apparent. 'I'm afraid so.' Pahler regarded him with pleasure. 'I shouldn't think it will be all that dangerous.'

'Dangerous,' echoed Maurer, staring at the desk. Then his

normally passive face erupted into unusual animation. He swept a used tissue on to the carpet and glared at Pahler as though challenging him to make something of this defiant strike at authority. 'It's stupid! Bloody stupid!'

'You mean the decision to pay?' He took a tissue and blew into it absently. I *do* honk, he thought, considering the onomatopoesis of the word, my heart goes where the wild goose goes, my God I must pull myself together.

'Of course!' Maurer jumped up. 'It's ridiculous! For one dirty black shit of a kaffir I have to risk my life!'

Pahler regarded him with repressed homicidal intent. 'You could become the proud wearer,' he said mildly, 'of the Gamban Order of Merit.'

Maurer slapped his fat hips, provoked beyond measure. 'Colonel Pahler,' he said loudly. 'I think it is time that you and I...' Natural canniness and his overriding ambition overtook him and he stopped, quivering.

Pahler raised pouchy eyes and smiled. 'You were saying?'

Maurer remained sulkily silent. They stared each other out for a while. Then Pahler said reasonably, 'It is not quite complete surrender, Captain Maurer. We *may* spot the pick-up, we *may* be able to shadow it successfully. All this is conjecture. But you must remember that this whole thing is very delicate, you know. Gamban versus Gamban, here in South Africa on a racial rugby field. As you know, the decision has been made to give the story to the press tonight, so that as from tomorrow morning the whole world will be in on things. So the object of the Powers That Be at this stage is purely to get Lunda back and say look, fellers, he's all right. What do you think outside comment would be if we dug in our toes and allowed Lunda to be murdered? As it is, there are going to be some pretty sour cracks about our security.'

Maurer had cooled down a little. 'He should never have come here in the first place.'

'He came,' said Pahler patiently, 'because, although he disagrees fundamentally with government policy, with *apartheid* and all the rest, he respects this country's technical advancement. He likes its people. Don't forget, he lived here for a year long before——' He stopped himself on the brink of saying too much. 'Forget it. It doesn't matter.' It was too tiresome, too much like trying to explain something to a piece of wood.

'Has that transcript of the editor's talk with the President come through yet?'

'It's being typed,' Maurer said sullenly.

'Hurry it up.'

There was a laboured silence while Pahler briefly scanned a flimsy. Then he got gruntingly to his feet and began stuffing his pockets with Kleenex. 'Those two thugs who broke out of Pohlsmoor on Tuesday night raped a woman yesterday afternoon. Carved her up good and proper, too. Robbed her of cash, food and some liquor.' He tapped the flimsy. 'There's a list here. Includes, believe it or not, a bottle of Highland Feather, which brings to mind our friend Mr. Aaron J. Fuskin.'

'Fuskin. Not *my* friend.'

'No,' Pahler sighed, 'and I don't suppose he could ever be. Anyway, they're looking for these birds in Tokai, if they haven't already moved on. I may have to pull men off that job for this one, which I wouldn't like to do. Not yet, anyhow. We'll just have to wait and see.'

A sergeant appeared in the doorway, flicking a salute. 'Truck, Sir.'

'Thanks.' Pahler found his Dunhill, turned to go. 'Join me at O.P. One as soon as you've made the drop. That money should be here at any moment.'

'All right.' Maurer nodded. He deliberately turned his plump back.

For a moment Pahler studied the woman-like hips. He shook his head, turned, and walked with the sergeant along the corridor to the entrance, where he waited while the Chev. truck, idling in the staff rank, revved its engine and came to meet him in a long hard curve, tyres squealing.

Pahler put his hand on the door. Then he paused. So much had happened here since Wednesday morning, less than twenty-four hours ago. It seemed more like a week. He shrugged. There was a wind of sorts coming up, fitfully stirring the blown leaves on the hardstand. If it developed it might also have a hand in things.

He clambered into the truck and it headed along the driveway, nosed between the gates and turned in the direction of Constantia Neck.

Ginny-doll,

I've done a crazy thing, which will go towards explaining my worrisome behaviour, over the past couple of days. I know you've been concerned, kid, but I couldn't say a thing at the time. Now you're going to get the explanation you're entitled to.

First off, I got these funny buzzings in my chest and started coughing real bad. The next thing there was this blood, coming up. So I put a very simple two and two together and the answer was The Big C., the You-Know-What that's got a 100% mortality rate within 12 months. It didn't help much having the X-ray because I knew what I'd got but there was a routine staff one coming up and I had it anyway. Ben saw it and read me the report, which was exactly what I'd expected. Apart from which while he was talking hope he was looking at me in that kind of funny way I seen so often in nursing, when people know a guy is now just an animated doll who'll be with them for a while before he's gone forever, and they feel guilty because they're healthy and so they dodge your eye. I done it myself, times in the past.

When this happens you get a big scare. I'll admit it. Then the scare passes and suddenly it's okay, you know what's going to happen. Somebody up there likes you and you realize it's not so bad, you're going home really, aren't you? So all that's left to do is figure the percentage for the ones you're leaving behind, and in my case it was worse than bad. A crummy thousand pounds, more or less, and I didn't want to see my wife grubbing to keep a home going and trying to look after a little baby girl at nights when she's all beat up. I wanted my wife to stay a proud woman, with decent surroundings, and see my lady baby grow up the way a Slade should, the way I never got the chance to do.

So I did this crazy thing, I highjacked *El Presidente* from the Schwer, right under everybody's noses, and they haven't even guessed it's me, yet, although they will when Bobo is released.

I'm writing this Wednesday night. Tomorrow is the day for the ransom pick-up. This money is enough to see you and the kid through until she is big enough to help you, if you're careful. From the pick-up I'm flying straight out and will contact you when I'm in the clear.

I know you so well, Kid. I know you're not going to approve of what I done. But it's all I could think of in a hell of a hurry and the chances are that it's going to work. I don't know how long I've got afterwards: maybe five, six months, and I'd like to spend that time with you. I may even see my daughter if I'm real lucky. But if you don't want to come, if you figure it's a bad thing I done, then Ernie understands and I'll get the money to you somehow.

There's just a chance I might contact you before I blow, so stay home tomorrow. And please burn this letter because it isn't going to self-destruct like in those spy movies. The cops are bound to ask you questions and you can play it anyhow you like, but make it damn clear you didn't know a thing about it until it was done.

You know me well enough so that I don't really have to tell you I wouldn't ever hurt The President not under any circumstances. Rather than do that I'd let him go and give the whole thing up.

I love you, Virginia Mary Slade. Please forgive your old Sailor.

Ernie

P.S. I left the VW in the car-park behind the Cinerama in Rosebank.

Only one tear, one silly fat blob of a tear would she allow to fall with a plop and run a smeary channel down his letter. Then she rushed to the toilet and threw up for the third time that day. She had been trembling before, but the aftermath of the violent spasm helped to ease her strained body. She rinsed her mouth, still holding the letter firmly clenched in one hand. Then she took it with her into the bedroom and stood before the mirror, watching herself with a grave and intense interest.

No more *ker-thlomping* from the car door. No more hooking those sea anchors out of the pool. No more nights there, slippery-nude in the warm crystal water. *Lookit Ernie's submarine. Oh, Ernie!*

She looked away, down at the letter. Then she was infused with a sudden inexplicably warm glow. It ran right through her, and her eyes when she looked back at the mirror had a glittering brilliance.

'Forgive?' she said in a strong voice. 'Forgive? Oh, Ernie, I'm just so goddam proud!'

It was one of those dung-rolling beetles, too damn dumb and obstinate to go around the tuft of grass, but persistently trying to get its dung-ball through the middle, pushing and falling back, pushing and falling back, once toppling over and waving its black legs helplessly. But when he righted it, it stayed icily motionless for a minute as though fuming at this unwarranted interference.

'Good luck, buddy,' said Slade, 'it's guys like you who get places.'

He got up creakily and stretched, trying to tear some of the tension out of his iron-hard muscles. It was in his shoulders, mostly, shoulders and neck. Occupational fibrositis, he thought humourlessly. He moved away from the tiny area of flattened grass where he had been sitting. He did it cautiously, stepping slowly backwards, moving within a thin screen of wattles, his eyes fixed on the fringes of the tossing tree-tops until the lower slopes of the mountain beyond came into view, dull olive green and sear brown flecked with soldier-straight pine trees.

He took the binoculars out of their case, holding the lenses facing down until he had checked the sun. But it was away to his right and there would be no twinkle of reflected light to give him away. Only then did he bring them up and nestle against the eyepieces, watching the slope jump large and jerkily into view.

There was no need to focus. This was his seventh search. He began immediately, starting on the left and bringing the glasses slowly in halting panorama across the mountain, stopping to investigate each patch of scrub, each clump of swaying trees.

Nothing? He dropped the glasses, blinked, rubbed a forearm across his eyes. Then he brought them up again, picked out the same scarred boulder on which he had stopped, and went on again.

Strangely enough it was the truck he saw first. His glasses had jumped in elevation as he drew a breath and suddenly the truck was darkly visible, parked deep in the trees much further back towards the cut-off forestry road. It blended with the shadows and only chance had shown it to him but it became clearer as he watched, so that after moments he could make out the blue police flasher-light on the top of the cab roof and the thin metal shine of the buggy-whip aerial.

He took another breath, held the glasses away a moment. So I read you right, he thought, you bastards, you're there after all, and my insurance is going to pay off. Once more he pressed against the eyepieces and brought the binoculars slowly down in a line from the truck.

Shapes, this time, human forms vague and shadowy, again hardening with the intensity of his study. Someone moved carelessly, someone crossed a bar of sunlight, and he saw brightly the pale blue uniform, a blur of hard young face, the glitter of light off the stubby and unmistakable shape of a sten-gun.

He let the glasses drop on their strap, unaware of the jerk against his neck. There was a cramping in his stomach, a clenched-fist grab at his vitals. So there, just what I thought. If this thing goes wrong you're not Ernie Slade, you're a moving target, a running figure, with this popping behind you and the hammer-blow in the back, blood on the grass, boots scrunching, a young voice saying, hey, look where I got him.

He released all his breath and dropped his hands to his sides. The beetle was charging the grass tuft again. He sat down next to it. His wristwatch showed him the fat figures of time. Ten-fifty-five. That was three hundred seconds. To hell with it, all that petrol vapour was blowing away in the wind, he could smoke. He lit a cigarillo and drew deep and long, smothering the inevitable choking cough. Then he watched the beetle with unseeing eyes.

One hundred and ninety seconds. That was three minutes ten. Nine-eight-seven-six-five-four-three-two-one. Three minutes, now. See, it's not so long.

The beetle went over on its back. Go on, yell for help, you're too dumb for your own good. Two minutes forty. Get the beetle upright, grab him and his shit-ball in a moment of uncontrolled violence and dump him on the other side of the tuft. Now get the hell out of here.

One minute. Exactly one minute becoming exactly fifty-nine seconds, and the hum of a car going fast downhill under unnecessary acceleration. The squeak of tyres locked by big disc brakes. A Ford, judging by that rumble-thrum engine beat. Then the surge-and-die, surge-and-die, humpity-bumpity of its progress along the track. Pause. That imaginary hand had his duodenum firmly in its grasp, twisting. There was the shot-gun blast of a door closing. Rev her, Mister, you're a lousy driver but your timing is good. It was exactly eleven o'clock.

A short silence. His delivery man was by now off the track and swinging back on to the main road, probably. Yes, there was the sound of power going uphill and an automatic gear-change.

It was all movement now. Get up fast, skitter backwards, check that truck and the fuzz on the hill in one quick blurring sweep of the glasses that showed him lenses a-twinkle up there, watching for the pick-up. Drop the glasses on their strap. Matches. Two, three, make it a big flary flame.

The petrol burst into a sheet of fire black-tipped with dark carbon smoke, woomfing into life, hurling itself along the line of soaked grass and shrubs, consuming itself, consuming the fuel, eating hungrily into the green things he had scattered in its path so that as they were forced into conflagration they threw up a dense grey smoke of protest that climbed forty, fifty, sixty feet. He watched as a man below, fear-struck at the unexpected hugeness of it all, at its width and greatness, at the way the wind moved in delightedly to help, at the deafening explosive crackle of it.

Then he was away, a scared man running, fighting his way downhill with the wattles snatching at him, the scrub pulling and tripping, a foot catching in a grass tuft so that he fell sprawling, hands out to save himself, feeling the vicious burn of the gravel on his palms, remembering that same sensation thirty-five years before, remembering that same sight of blood welling through dust except that this time there was no one to whom he could run in shock for the cold water and the bite of tincture of iodine.

Up again. There was the small oak ahead of him and the packet lying on the yellow shady earth beneath it.

Slade stopped, wiping the blood from his torn hands on to his pants. He felt rubbery legged and was sweating like a blown horse, but there was no time to rest. He lunged forward, grabbed the packet, ripped away some of the paper, so that he could see the neatly packed stacks of notes. There were the green of the tens and the Monopoly-blue of the fives. Genuine. They hadn't tried a last minute switch.

'Genuine,' he heard himself say from afar. There was no thrill. He flicked a glance at his watch. Time! Hell, it was six minutes past eleven already. And the fire was getting out of hand, if he didn't move soon he would be in trouble. He could spare it only a twisted, flick-back glance but the smoke towers were a hundred feet high already and the wind had switched and strengthened, it was working its way down towards him.

He ran again. There was pain in his hands and pain in his chest, the one surface and the other as deep as though his ribs had been kicked in. The binoculars bumped awkwardly and the money package clutched under one arm was much heavier than he had thought it would be. His feet scudded on the treacherously uneven ground and he could hear his own rattley breathing. I'm going to cough, he thought, I'd better slow down. But by then he had reached the branch-camouflaged van that had seemed to hover forever in the near distance. He extended a hand, touching it to make sure it wasn't a fantasy vehicle in which nightmares were conveyed. But it was real all right, hard and hot-skinned under the wilting greenery.

He went to the driver's door, got in, threw the package on the seat next to him, kicked the engine into life and reversed in a series of over-revved jerks so that the van shook itself like a dog and the camouflage fell off. Slade turned it, pointed the bonnet along the track, flipped the gear lever into neutral, then forced himself to sit back while the engine idled with the ticking of worn tappets.

He had, he knew, to slow down. He was soaked with sweat and his heart was galloping. If he went on like this he would collapse long before he ever reached the airport. Relax, he told himself. It was an impossible instruction, but he got halfway. He placed his blood-streaked hands in his lap and took his scuffed and dirty shoe off the accelerator.

Now that you got that done, he reasoned, you've got time—about thirty seconds—for some deep thinking: for a start, the way back was closed. Too much smoke had built up and they might have slung a barrier across the road. Uh-uh. Which left only Victoria Road. That meant a time-consuming detour, a wide back-swing miles away from the airport. Estimated delay, at least twenty minutes. His watch now registered twelve minutes past eleven and he had to allow for the further hold-up of stopping to post the letter giving Bobo's whereabouts. He had undertaken to get it off by express, which meant going into a post office, waiting if there was a queue, then paying his ten cents and getting a chit from the counter-clerk. Estimated time taken up in doing this: say ten minutes with luck.

Not so bad, he thought. Even then, there would be plenty of time to get to the airport.

For the first time he allowed himself a small amount of satisfaction. Things had gone unbelievably well. The police, clearly, had been instructed to hold back. But now with the unexpected appearance of a highly effective smoke screen, there was a possibility that they might be sent in. So far, he thought, I've outsmarted them all along the line. I've read their thinking accurately. Let's keep it that way. Which meant that this was no time to sit here and congratulate himself. He could in no way ease up until his plane had crossed the border.

He coughed suddenly. It gave him a second of fright, but then he realized that it had been more of a choke than anything, and that the small cab was full of blue smoke.

The fire! He peered through the passenger-side window. God, this Frankenstein creation of his had grown beyond his wildest dreams. It was marching down upon him at the speed of a man walking, roaring ahead of the cheating wind. While he watched, a line of wattles burst instantly into flaring flame as though they had been doused in petrol. Nearer, more trees began to smoke and sizzle. A piece of charred grass floated through the window and struck the seat without sound. Soot swam about like smeary dust-motes.

The fire was less than a hundred yards away and already he could feel the heat. He put the Austin back into gear and growled along the grass-choked track, reached the half-concealed entrance to the main road, paused, checked his right and left.

The road was deserted. Uphill to the north-east it ended suddenly in a curtain of grey smoke. In the other direction it ran on emptily with only the first eddies of smoke swirling overhead.

Slade swung the wheel, fed petrol to the engine and burst out on to the road, pushing the old engine through the gears until they howled. Nought to fifty in nearly sixty seconds. Great. He was almost level with the turn-off to the ruined cottage where

Bobo still lay chained. Probably the old fellow was sipping coffee, reading *The Wind in the Willows* and wondering where all the smoke was coming from.

His feet and hands seemed to take command before his brain could consciously react. They declutched, worked the old engine back down through its gears, slowed it on its compression, steered it to the side of the road and left it running in neutral, level with the old farm gate.

His brain arrived while he stared at the gate. It started to make calculations for him. The fire was moving at walking pace. Say a mile every twenty minutes, perhaps a little slower where the vegetation thinned and it had to jump gaps. It was about nineteen hundred yards from the cottage right now. In approximately half an hour it would arrive. If the cottage didn't burn, then the heat would kill Bobo. If the heat didn't kill Bobo then the smoke would asphyxiate him. And the cottage would probably burn anyway.

Slade felt weary beyond fatigue. One could never figure the odds. That fat fifty per cent was down to a ragged and thread-bare twenty-five, because what had been intended as nothing more than a narrow smokescreen, a shrewd counter-move against the observation he had correctly guessed would take place from the mountain slopes, had turned into a wildcat bush-fire running out of control in the wrong direction.

He felt a completely unreasoning anger. Damn that old coon. Damn him. Lunda had done things in his time that could have had him hanged. Lunda had bloodstained hands and no regret in his heart. Lunda was old and sick, maybe due to die anyway if it turned out that he had leukaemia. Lunda had no pity, no sympathy, no help due to him. It was one of those things. Let Lunda die.

Slade said the words again, running them over his tongue. People died every day. They got run over, stabbed, their hearts failed, things fell on their heads. Young people. Good people. Why in God's name get Lunda out of the path of that fire? Leave him there and watch the odds-gauge shoot up again to the fifty per cent where it belonged, the fifty per cent that could become a hundred within a very short time if things came right and stayed right.

In a detached way he watched his fingers turn the ignition key. He even sat a moment after the engine had died. Who have you been kidding? he asked himself wearily. You promised Ginny. And even if you hadn't, you're the tough Ernie Slade who stopped Maggie Meadows one day from killing a bee, remember, and then in the process of getting it out of a window it stung you in gratitude.

It was good to have that little bad moment behind him. Immediately he felt a return of confidence, a rush of renewed hope. Again, he began to calculate time. It would take about ten minutes, no more, to get Bobo out of the cottage, bundle him into the van and take him along. And if Bobo was dropped a few miles from the airport on that long vista of cheerless expressway bordered by wide expanses of arid ground dotted with scrub, with only the twin stacks of the Power Station in the distance and the sign that said that this was where you turned off to Guguletu African Township, how long was it going to take him before he got picked up, let alone listened to? It was sad but true that a black man trying to hitch a ride stood as little chance of a lift from people of his own colour as he did from whites.

Even now he still had a chance to make his flight. But time was very definitely of the essence. He got quickly from the Austin, trotted across the road and opened the old gate. Then he went back to the van, started the engine in a hurry, did a tight turn in a slither of squealing rubber and a heart-snatching moment when he thought the Austin was going over. But the van came back on to all four wheels with a bone-jarring crash and he was through the gate, bouncing along the track where the grass middle strip still bore the oil-stains of his previous passages along it.

Eleven twenty. Then what seemed like an hour to negotiate three hundred yards of track. But it was only two minutes by his watch. Eleven twenty-two.

The cottage had preserved its air of surprised desertion. No curl of smoke from the chimney and that angry mongrel he always expected. But the rattle of the dog chain was there, thank God.

'Bobo!' He shouted from the window before he had even got the door open. 'Bobo!'

There was no answer. And the chain wasn't really rattling, it was a sliding, grating noise, regular like the swing of a pendulum: Scrape, pause, scrape, pause, scrape, pause. There was only this sound and the sound of the fire, a distant roar punctuated by the popping of exploding branches.

'Bobo!' He called the name harshly into the quivering heated air. There was a dark stain near him on the ground. His eyes held it for a moment, knowing instantly what it was. Then he began to run, tripping and half-falling over a chunk of debris, cursing, windmilling his arms to regain his balance. The doorway loomed. His hands reached out, gripped the jamb. He stood framed in the opening, staring with shocked eyes. Then he rushed in, stumbled over the litter on the floor, turned, put his back against the wall, heard distantly the drumming of his heart.

'Oh Jesus,' he said.

There was only about five feet of chain remaining. It hung straight from the rafter and tangled in its links was the smashed and battered Coleman, crazily dribbling paraffin across the four-foot swing of its arc while the chain endlessly and patiently scraped the wall above the twisted and mangled remains of the blue nylon camp bed.

There was blood, fresh scarlet blood, spattered about on the walls and on the ground as though a headless chicken had been swung about by the legs. There was the glitter of jagged glass, the smear of pulped food, and the air was thick with the throat-gripping stench of paraffin and liquor mingled.

Slade gulped at the rush of hot saliva into his mouth. His eyes followed the blood across the floor and out of the doorway.

'Bobo!' He lurched outside. 'Bobo!' His voice died away and he heard the distant fire, a sound of constant applause and intermittent musketry.

The blood went on. There was a trail of it dribbled on the hard-packed earth and smeared gorily on tufts of grass. It went across the small clearing and on into the wattles beyond, sometimes straight, sometimes wavering. It travelled south-west in a line almost parallel to the road in the direction of Hout Bay.

Slade plunged into the wattles. Leaves slashed at him, a small branch hooked his jacket sleeve and tore it as he wrenched loose. He splashed ankle deep through an area of boggy ground, scrambled over a dilapidated fence and paused to call again.

'Bobo!' He looked around despairingly. 'Bobo!'

No answer. He had covered at least three hundred yards from the ruined cottage and still the blood-dribble ran on. Nothing to do but follow.

He flushed a partridge in a glade, rearing back as it rocketed out in a cackle of indignation, watching its short-winged bumble-bee flight with blurred concentration while he experienced a frothy effervescent sensation in his lungs which he knew was the phlegmy lava of a cough. He gagged and hawked and kept it down, once more heading forward.

He entered a stand of light trees where the shade was flecked and dappled with sunlight. It was a hall of airy poplars on the edge of a narrow stream where water rushed busily away, and in its garden-party shade Bobo lay slumped, with his head and shoulders against a silver-barked bole and seven feet of dog chain winding from his ankle, the links a-glitter like the scales of a curling snake. Nearby, two blood-masked men circled each other slowly. Dressed alike in coarse clothing, their shirts hung in tatters, their trousers showed the skin of their legs through ragged rents. One held a crimson-bladed knife, the other clutched half a jaggedly broken bottle.

They were on the extreme edge of exhaustion but they were still trying to kill one another, wielding their weapons with slow-motion clumsiness, grunting, moaning, heavily and almost lazily slashing, stirring up a thick barred dust of leaf mould with their gaping rock-scarred boots.

Slade had stopped within the fringe of shadow. He stared in horrible fascination at this clumsy death-dance that moved slowly away towards the stream as though the gasping performers were paying painstaking care to their footwork. Then slowly, almost reluctantly, he moved his head.

Bobo was watching him. He made no move to rise or twist, or sit erect or even crawl. He slumped as though he were made of lead but the giant barracuda mouth fell open in a slack grin.

'Friends of mine,' he said. 'They came for tea.'

Slade came over in a rush, kneeling, shaking, forcing his sweat-wet right hand through the dragging cloth of his pocket for the padlock key.

Both keys came out on their twist of wire and he fumbled the smaller one into the lock. 'Get you out of here in no time at all, sir, just no time at all.'

'High bloody time.' It came out in a bass grumble and Slade gave him a faltering, relieved grin. Then the padlock snapped open, the chain fell loose around Bobo's ankle and Slade snatched it away as though it were dirty.

'Come on.' He grabbed an arm. But Bobo lay slackly like a dead weight. 'Please, Mr. President.' Slade panted. 'Come on, get up.'

Bobo's yellowed eyes were looking beyond him. 'Parity has been overcome, Mr. Slade.'

Slade whirled. Of the two men, the thinner one appeared to have stumbled. On his knees on the very brink of the stream's sharp bank, he knelt as though in supplication, body arched, hands clawing upward, head thrown back. The other man, it appeared, was holding a whole bottle, because the seven irregular prongs of its jagged edge had entered the tight-skinned expanse of brown throat. There was, for a moment, no blood. The kneeling man gurgled strangely, returning in this moment of death to the joyful throaty chucklings of infancy. Then the blood spurted in a pulsing stream as the bottle came away red-ended.

The kneeling man fell on his side. His legs scythed. He rolled on to his back, stretched his arms once more to the heaven he would probably be denied, and jerked spasmodically. A section of the bank gave way with little splashings of falling earth. Then more collapsed and the dying man was gone in a fountain-spray of water.

His murderer turned very slowly. His tiny pig-red eyes gleamed when he saw Slade and he advanced at a steady shamble, holding the scarlet-and-brown bottle from which tiny droplets of blood fell.

Slade jumped away from Bobo, his desperate eyes searching around him for a weapon, his skittering feet springy on the leaf carpet. The other man neared, grinning through the blood that completely covered his face. There were knife slashes on his bulging white chest.

Slade backed away. His foot kicked the discarded dog chain which clinked with the dullness of spurious metal. One-handed, he bent and snatched it up by a rough broken-linked end, coming erect as the man lunged in at him.

He saw the dull bloodied end of the bottle heading with the almost nonchalant accuracy of a missile for his throat. So he flung himself to one side and with his right hand whipped the chain around in a blind arc. Then he lost his footing and fell, still holding the chain.

His face struck the leaf mould. He tasted its dry bitterness in his mouth, felt its powdered dust sear his eyes. There was a violent jerk on his arm and the chain burned through his fingers but he tightened his grip instinctively, reaching out with the other hand and securing it around his wrist. But as suddenly, the tension slackened and he scrambled to his feet, jumping backwards, seeing through blurred and streaming eyes the big man with the other end of the chain wrapped tight around his throat, his face purpling, his free hand clawing at the coiled links while the other waved the bottle almost idly now.

Slade fought the man like a fish, heaving backwards to keep the chain tight, staggering past Bobo, slipping, stumbling, moving in a strange tug-of-war towards the stream. The tears his eyes had produced finally washed them clear of dust. A thick stump of branch six feet off the ground hovered before him. Instinctively he heaved his hands over it, heard the chain rattle on it, then flung himself forward and down, gripping the chain with both hands, feeling the sudden huge drag upon it, hearing the leaf mould beaten with a drumming regularity that seemed to go on forever.

It stopped eventually and there was a new and strange silence. He remained kneeling, unwound the chain from his wrist and saw the deep indentations in the skin as the chain was flicked away by the weight at the other end. There was the sodden thump of a body falling.

Slade got up very slowly. He turned on wooden legs and looked down on the black face of the man he had killed, at the gaping mouth from which a thick tongue protruded pinkly like the labellum of a charnelhouse orchid. He bent with dull reluctance, grabbed the heavy-booted feet, dragged the body to the stream's edge and toppled it in. It struck the water, plunged deep, surfaced almost immediately and floated away on the current, tossing and turning and bumping from bank to bank. Of the first man to die there was no sign.

There was blood on his jacket. The cuff was torn, there was a rent in his trousers, his shoes were caked with mud to which the flaky mould had stuck. With dragging feet he walked back to Bobo.

'Who ... ?' He gestured wearily at the stream.

'They broke out of Po—Pole——'

'Pohlsmoor?'

'Yes.'

Slade looked at his watch. Eleven fifty. Distantly the fire

popped and roared. Time was running out on him. 'Come on.' He grabbed Bobo's left arm unceremoniously and hauled. 'Come on! Please!' But Bobo remained inertly slumped. 'What's the matter with you? His temper flared raggedly. 'Get to your goddam feet!'

'Don't be angry, Mr. Slade.' Bobo smiled. 'I can't.'

Slade dropped the arm. 'Why?'

Bobo fumbled awkwardly behind his back. Something chinked against the bole of the poplar. Then he brought his hand out.

It was holding a bottle of Highland Feather.

Slade stared. There was an inch of liquid sloshing around in the bottom. 'You're drunk, damn you.'

'Absolutely,' Bobo agreed. 'Squiffo. I don't know why you're so angry. They forced me. They didn't like whisky.'

'God. Can't you walk?'

'No. I can always talk, although I avoid certain words where I might slur. But I lose the use of my legs.'

Rage descended upon Slade. 'You're gonna goddam walk. You're gonna walk if I have to kick you all the way back to the car. Because if you don't walk you're gonna burn.'

'Burn? Don't be rid—don't be silly.'

'Look.' Slade pointed back. 'See that smoke? That's a forest fire and it's heading your way. That's why I came after you, to save your goddam worthless hide.'

Bobo tried to focus. 'Goodness. Well, I'll try.' He flopped out his long arms. 'Grab these.'

Slade got him upright but it was no use. Bobo sagged against him with all the animation of a grain-bag.

Sweat was pouring down Slade. 'I'll get you over my shoulder in a fireman's lift. Now, you behave.'

It took him nearly five minutes to get the bigger man hoisted. Then he staggered to a slope in the stream's bank, concerned with the idea of putting this stretch of water between them and the fire. He splashed across unsteadily, lurched up the slope, lost his footing and fell with Bobo across him.

He got up slowly. The blood on his ragged jacket distracted him and he unbuttoned it with fumbling fingers, forgetting it as it fell.

'Okay. Let's try again. You all right?'

Bobo eyed him from the ground. 'I am feeling no pain, as they say. But you ...'

'Forget about me.' Slade bent. 'Give me your hands.'

It took another five minutes to get Bobo across his back again. Then with slow, unsure steps he turned to his left and headed south-east to cut the main Hout Bay road.

As he walked, Bobo, from his back, began to sing 'We Shall Overcome'. It was eleven minutes past twelve. Time was busy running out.

Chapter Twelve

Pahler let his binoculars drop on their strap and rubbed his eyes. 'I feel,' he said, 'like a member of the Audubon Society.'

The major to whom he was talking chuckled. 'Except that our viewing is confined to black-birds.'

They were standing thirty feet within the shade of a stand of old pine trees. Behind them on the Forestry cut-off were parked three cream-painted police trucks, and more than a score of tough-looking young policemen armed with sten-guns stood about.

'Hmmm.' Pahler had his own ideas on the colour of the kidnappers, but they were suspicions without foundation and for the time being he had to go along with the majority. 'I hope your chaps are careful with those things. We're not going to start a war, you know.'

'I always issue them when there's a kidnapping,' laughed the major, who fancied himself as something of a humorist. He glanced at his watch. 'We should catch sight of Johan's car at any moment now.' He absorbed Pahler's glance and added, 'Johan Maurer, I mean.'

'Oh.' To Pahler it was strange to find that Maurer had a Christian name. Sometimes he had amused himself by picturing Maurer bedding his wife, varying the themes from sexual mania to total impotency. 'Johan' added a definite touch of dignity which, Pahler felt, the reptilian-headed little endomorphic Captain did not deserve. Gloomily he prophesied that this discovery would put an end to those imagined scenes of high excitement or total apologia. How could you picture a *Johan* looking down at this limp thing and sobbing explanations?

He grunted and blew his nose, dropping the Kleenex and putting his foot on it. There was a glint of reflected light, sun off a hard-top, from far below on the ribbon of Hout Bay road. Two-gun Maurer, going in like a man to the drop-off point.

'There he is,' he said. 'You won't see much more from here. The drop-off point itself is obscured.'

The Major raised his glasses. 'When he leaves we may have some activity.'

'That's all we can hope for.' Pahler tried to light his pipe in the wind. 'From the road to the drop-off point isn't very far. Maurer should be back on the road in no time at all.' Going like hell too, he added to himself.

There were a few seconds of inactivity. The young uniformed policemen had come forward and crowded the gaps between the trees but they kept well in line with Pahler. Then the major said, 'There he goes. Maurer's away,' and there was a rustle and murmur from the watching group.

Pahler had his glasses raised. He caught another glint of light flashing off the Fairlane. In his mind he could hear the deep thunder of the engine as it rocketed up the road towards them. Then he swung his glasses away, lining them up as directly as possible with the drop-off point.

He saw the line of grey rise like a running fuse and did not immediately recognize it for what it was. Startled, he jerked the binoculars away and stared with the naked eye. Then he said, 'Good Christ, they're making smoke!'

The major was shouting and a babble of excitement rose from the line of men.

'It's boiling up in clouds!' Excitedly the major wrenched his glasses from his eyes. 'Do you see, sir? There's a good hundred yards of it right across the drop-off point. It's screening the entire area completely!'

'I see, I see.' Pahler beat his hands together. 'And they're trundling away at their leisure behind it.' He groaned as the smoke rose even higher. 'The wind's helping. It's moving the fire south-west. God, this is the time to get in there!'

He made up his mind suddenly, wheeling on the Major and barking orders. 'String ten of your men across the top of the road up here. Then get on to O.P. Two and tell them to be prepared to move in and close off the other end. Both road-blocks must stop and search everything that comes and I mean everything, I don't just mean Africans. I don't care if it's the Mayor, I don't care if it's the Prime Minister, drag them out and search their cars!'

Already turning, he shouted over his shoulder, 'Get the rest

of these men ready to go into that smoke!' Then he ran at full
tilt for the nearest truck where an operator waited at the radio.

The major was trotting back along the cut-off road with a
newly-arrived Maurer in tow when Pahler returned. He stopped
at once when he saw the rigid lines of the Colonel's big body,
the savage planes of his face.

'Sir ... ' The Major trailed away, waiting.

'No.' Pahler ignored Maurer and stared at the Major with
his small steel-hard eyes as though he hated him. 'Nothing doing.
The Brigadier got on to Government and Government told him
he was out of his mind. The orders are the same: wait and see.
But they will review the situation in half an hour.'

'Half an hour! But for Christ's sake, don't they realize ...'
The major looked down the valley at the smoke that now rose
more than a hundred feet. 'There are some bloody clever people
down there.'

'Everything,' said Pahler almost calmly, 'everything in me
that is policeman tells me that there is something going on behind that smoke that I should see. But I'm not allowed to do it.
Better get your men back from this end of the road. Then
radio O.P. Two and tell them to stay very firmly where they
are.'

'And then?'

'And then?' Pahler wheeled savagely on the man as though
he were going to strike him. 'We wait, man, we wait until the
bloody half hour is up, and then we try for permission again,
and by that time it will be too late.'

He walked away, his big shoulders hunched, and as he went
they heard him honking into another tissue.

Slade's labouring heart missed a beat, hung poised for an
eternity, then slogged on. His aching lungs were the bellows
that supplied air to the blast furnace that was his overheated
body. His wooden legs took steps of a few agonizing inches at a
time and each one was a jar that ran right up his body through
bone and muscle.

He had carried one hundred and eighty pounds on his back
over rough territory for nearly a quarter of a mile, and he had
been tired before he had started. Now he was finished. The van
was playing the same trick it had played at the pick-up point;

it was hovering in the near distance, never seeming to come any closer.

Slade tried to say, 'Go to hell,' to it but there was no vestige of moisture left in his mouth. Furious, wanting to kick it, he managed to produce an incredible parody of a run, lumbering for fifty yards along the asphalt until his perspective drastically changed and he found himself about to collide with it.

He stopped. Weaving, mumbling, he surveyed it. Now how 'bout that. Good old van. Still with Bobo slung across his shoulders he dug in his pockets, found the rear door key and fumblingly unlocked them.

Stuffy heat rolled out at him. Slowly, achingly and agonizedly, he bent the iron-bound muscles of his back, the vertebrae cracking like popped knuckles, and lowered Bobo to the floor, pushing him in haphazardly and slamming the door. Then, with the weight unbelievably gone from his shoulders, he moved with light drunken steps around to the cab.

He felt broken in half physically. All his movements had the slowness of the very aged. And in addition he was compelled to fight a growing detachment, a don't-care vagueness in which he observed things from outside himself.

It was a considerable struggle to force a mind that seemed to have washed its hands of the whole affair, to return to reality. He succeeded in the end, but this wayward computer of his was tired and confused. It accepted two important main headings: the fire, and the need to move. Both of these fell under time, of course.

Time? What was the time? The dashboard clock said seventeen minutes past five. He had to think very carefully to remember that it didn't work. No. No Sir, it couldn't be that time. He fumbled his wristwatch around. Twelve forty-three. Seventeen minutes to one. At the airport people were gathering, waiting for their flight to be called. Oh Christ. The column in the odds-gauge was flat. Time and the fifty-fifty had run out on him. And it had looked so good for a while. Now it was time to run.

He watched his hand reach out and turn the key, heard the engine kick into life, lifted a leg that seemed to weigh two tons and placed it on the clutch.

The van moved off. He changed gear very badly, grating the cogs. Think, he told himself. You've got a piece of very valuable goods in the back there. There must be another way. Don't give up yet, Ernest Hobday Slade.

He passed the Victoria Road intersection and went on. Ten seconds later the police truck from O.P. Two rumbled into position to block the empty road he had left behind.

Sweat had gathered in the hollows under the Fire Chief's red-rimmed eyes. Now it ran down his cheeks like tears, channelling through the soot.

'I've got seven trucks spread up the road. We've cut it off that side so it won't jump the tarmac, and we've cut it off on the mountain side, thank God. Council would've had my neck. Can't have our tourist attractions buggered up.' He scrubbed at his face, turning the soot into a streaky paste. 'I've got my boys waiting at the south-western end on the other side of the stream but I think it's going to fizzle there. I don't think it'll jump the stream. The timber thins. There's a kind of boggy area which slowed it down, then a glade and then a stand of poplars that we've cut and pushed back. Thank God for chain saws. And in a way you could say thank God for the wind. What if it had blown the other way, huh? Can you imagine a blaze that size getting into all that timber in Constantia? Jeez, the tourists——'

'I'd like to have a look,' Pahler said. They were standing on the tarmac a few hundred yards above the Victoria Road intersection with the grey smoke blowing past. It had made Pahler's nose water constantly. 'Let's start at the stream.'

'Sure.' They began to walk briskly. 'You're the boss, my friend.' The Fire Chief slapped his gloves against his rump, showering soot, and tugged them on. 'But you won't find anything, it's all burnt to hell inside there. Your birds flew long ago. Scampered like goats up the mountain and down the other side. Hah-hah. Jeez, imagine what——'

He reminded Pahler of a nigger minstrel wearing a brass helmet. Pahler sniffed and said savagely, 'Why don't you stick to putting out your bloody fires and I'll——'

'Just a sec, just a sec my good friend.' The Fire Chief hoisted a gloved hand. 'Here comes one of my boys.' He raised his voice to a bellow. 'Here we are, Fred!'

A fireman scrambled through the fence. He hooked his pants and said, 'Oh shit.' Then he ran up clumsily in his heavy rubber boots, panting. 'Captain's got some things to show you.'

He was more sooty than his superior.

'Bodies?' asked Pahler.

They stared at him. Then the fireman laughed. 'Yah, if you'd call a dead Marine a body then I suppose we've got one for you.' He and his chief laughed some more.

'For Christ's sake,' Pahler said, 'can we——'

'This way.' The fireman led them. 'Mind the fence, I nearly left the family jewels there, on the wire in No Man's Land.'

They scrambled through and plunged into high grass and scrub. On his right Pahler could see the heavy line of trees that marked the stream, but a hundred yards further on the vegetation thinned. He could make out the far bank, the amputated stumps of the poplars and beyond them a heavy pall of flame-shot smoke. Small figures in blue, their helmets glinting, rushed in and out like soldiers on a battlefield.

The Fire Chief puffed along next to him. 'Yes, we'll contain it all right, here. Good show. Where's Ropey?'

'Over there.' The fireman pointed to where a thin blackened man stood in an area of crushed grass, smoking a cigarette. He flicked away the cigarette as they approached.

'Don't know why I'm smoking the bloody thing, I got enough soot in my lungs for Africa, I tell you I could establish myself as a carbon-black factory.' He regarded Pahler gloomily. 'You the cop?'

Pahler gritted his teeth. 'Yes.'

'These may interest you.' He bent, grunting, and lifted a cloth kit-bag. 'Found one on this side of the stream but the bottle was in the poplars. It's genuine whisky.' He smiled and breathed fumily to verify his statement.

Pahler took the kit-bag and delved. His hand touched glass. He brought out a bottle and stared at the label. God, Highland Feather, with about an inch left in the bottom.

'Anybody touch this?' He looked at them with a feeling of mounting disaster.

'Only Simmy and Pool,' said the thin man. 'Simmy found it and gave it to Pool and Pool-oh brought it to me. Why?'

'It doesn't matter,' Pahler said wearily. Any idea of testing for fingerprints could be forgotten. He clamped the bottle awkwardly under an arm and brought out a crumpled sports jacket. It spilled out as he held it by the collar and the first thing he saw the blood caked on the left sleeve. Peering closely, he could make out some hairs on the right shoulder. He pinched one between his fingers and examined it longsightedly. Short. Curled like a pig's tail. Black. The so-called peppercorn hair of the Negro.

Pahler dropped the kit-bag. 'Thanks,' he said rapidly. 'You fellows have done a good job.' In the same moment he was turning and running for the fence, plunging through the grass and scrub carelessly, the bottle and the sports coat clutched in his hands.

'Maurer,' he shouted. 'Maurer, where the hell are you?'

The firemen watched him go. 'Good Lord,' said the Fire Chief, 'what's got into him?'

Slade walked very slowly into the chemist's, catching a foot on the doormat and nearly falling. He reached the counter and put out a hand to steady himself.

'Yes, sir?' The yellow-haired girl behind the counter regarded him curiously.

'I want a bottle of those Japanese liver tablets.' His voice sounded very dry, as though with age. The room revolved and he put out the other hand, almost clinging to the counter.

'Effervescent or the others?'

He considered. His mind fumbled along. 'The others.'

'Anything else?'

'A bottle of Vitamin B-Co.'

'Okay.' She moved a yard or two, stretched up the back-shelves and brought them to him. 'One forty-five.' She flicked a packet open.

Slade dragged his wallet out of his back pocket. His heavy fingers struggled with the press-stud, pushing at it while the silence ran on. His blunted glance moved from her along the shelves. Anything, anything liquid.

'Are you all right?' She glanced quickly towards the louvred panel at the end of the shop behind which the dispenser was filling a telephoned prescription.

Slade heard the words. They impinged on his brain slowly. He realized at last that they were intended for him.

'Yes.' The dry voice rustled out. 'I've been—climbing a mountain. You got'—his gaze wandered away again—'you got tonic wine?'

He fell into place in her mind. God, one of those. For a while she had thought he was ill.

'Yes.' She reached out and took the wallet from him. 'Let me do this for you. How many bottles do you want?'

'One. No, two.' He stared at her vaguely and she shivered. Could have been a good-looking man, too.

'Well, they're one-fifty a bottle. So that's four forty-five.' She took a five-rand note from the wallet, made change and gave it to him with the wallet.

'Thanks.' His blue eyes met hers but seemed to go beyond. Their vagueness was disturbing. 'Is there a call-box somewhere around?'

She hesitated and then decided against offering him the use of the shop's telephone. 'Down the road.'

'Thanks.' Slade took the packet. He lurched away from the counter on his wooden legs. On his way out he banged against the doorway.

The girl trotted to the end of the shop and went behind the panel. The dispenser looked up. 'Scruffy looking guy you had in there.'

'Scruffy, God! And did he have one helluva hangover! I've never seen anything like it.'

They peered through the panel. Slade was negotiating the two steps sideways, like an old man. She giggled. 'He said he'd been climbing a mountain.'

'More like he'd had a mountain on his back.' The dispenser laughed at his own wit.

'Funny thing is,' she said thoughtfully, 'that he didn't smell of booze.'

He reached out for a bottle. 'Probably a meths drinker.'

The girl went back and peered curiously through the door. An old light-delivery van was pulling away on the other side of the road. 'Klein's Contractors. We Pant To Paint.'

All painters drink, she thought, that's what Gran always said, it was the paint fumes or something.

The telephone rang and she went to answer it.

Ginny had been sitting next to the telephone for three hours, leaving it only when compelled to by her pregnancy sickness. Now when it rang she snatched it up.

'Hello?' She heard her trembly voice, little-girlish and afraid, she saw the fingers of her right hand turn white as she squeezed them against the palm.

There was the sound of breathing, and a fumbled slatter.

'Hello? Hello? Who is this?' She put her fingers into her mouth and bit on them.

More slow breathing. Then: 'Kid?'

'Ernie! Oh, Ernie! Ernie are you all right? God, I've been so——'

'Kid, listen.' Why did his voice sound so strange? 'We've got to talk quickly. Have the cops been on to you?'

'No. Ernie, have you——'

'Please, honey. Sure nobody's been on to you?'

'I haven't seen a soul all day. Ernie——'

'Listen carefully, kid. This thing has gone a bit wrong. There was a forest fire that blew the wrong way and ... you still there?'

'Oh, Ernie! You sound sick, Ernie! Course I'm here, I didn't say a word. What was——'

'Listen carefully. This thing went. . . . Look, there's still a way out. I still got the goods with me. Know what I mean?'

'Yes, yes. But you shouldn't have done it, Sailor. You did it for me and there was no goddam——'

'It's done. You mad at me?'

'No, I'm not mad at you. I could never be mad at you, you know I could never be mad at you.'

'I want you to join me. You figure you can?'

'Yes.' She was chewing at her nails blindly. 'I can join you if you tell me where.'

'Okay. I want you to join me so we can get out together. While I got these goods we can still bargain, you follow?'

'I follow,' she said helplessly. 'Ernie, you've *got* to tell me first, are you okay? You sound ... funny. Is it the—is your chest all right?'

'I'm fine. Listen, kid. It looks as though the cops don't know it's me, yet. They're still looking for a bunch of black guys. The heat is not on, just some things went wrong. You mustn't worry. You promise you won't worry?'

'I can't help worrying. Just tell me.'

'There was an old guy called Johnson who died at the Schwer about two months ago. He owned a house in Tokai, right out by itself on about three acres. His widow moved out and the place is coming up for auction next month. It's deserted. Got it?'

'Please, Ernie, you've got to tell me——'

'I want you to go there tomorrow early. Round six o'clock. Drive right in and park the car under a tree. If I'm not there then wait for me. Did you get the VW back from where I left it?'

'Yes, I took a taxi, the buses make me feel——'

'If you get on the Tokai road you'll see the auctioneer's signposts. It said so in the paper. There aren't any street names. You got all that?'

'Yes, yes.' She nodded rapidly, her hair falling loosely about her face. 'I got it, Ernie. Ernie, where you going to spend the night? Can't I come now?'

'No. Don't you worry where I'll spend the night.'

There were the sound of the peeps and she cried out quickly, 'Ernie, don't ring——' then stopped as a coin buzzed into the slot. 'Hello? Ernie, please darling. Listen to me.'

'I can't, I gotta——'

'Ernie, darling, can't you just forget the whole thing? You're going to ruin your health and——'

'It's ruined, kid. No, I reckon there's still a percentage. I been doing some thinking. Kid, I *have* to go.' There was a pause. Then: ' 'Bye, baby.'

'Ernie.' She said it slowly. 'Please. Look after yourself. I love you. Say you will.'

'I will. 'Bye.'

She said, ' 'Bye, Ernie, don't——' then stopped as the dialling tone rattled in her ear.

A long time passed. She breathed very deeply and let it out all at once in a long sigh. Then she got up and walked in her flouncy slippers, skirt and old cardigan into the bedroom, where she lit a cigarette and regarded herself carefully in the mirror.

'The instinct,' she said aloud, 'is to be worried and weepy. Hence the trembly voice. But it's been seven years, and all of it fun-times. Hot sand and clean fishing. This is the first bad-time. So you will keep a stiff upper lip, Virginia Mary Slade. You will get some clothes together. Tough things, no fancy threads. And food, like soup that cheers. You will busy yourself with these routinely housewifish duties and stay a woman and not look one goddam inch beyond the end of a can-opener. There's a good girl.'

She even smiled at herself. She began to turn away and then stopped, looking at her reflection. 'Oh. One other thing. You will remember that you have always borne his name with pride.'

She went away, down the long passage to the kitchen.

Slade had drunk one half of the first bottle of tonic wine outside the call-box while the van swayed to the gritty buffeting of the wind. Then he made the call, got back into the Austin and drove past the windmill-shaped restaurant, taking a turn-off to the parking area just above the beach.

There were no cars about. Clumps of sparse grass bent to the wind and sea-sand pattered on the windscreen. Hout Bay had churned itself into a criss-cross of wild blue waters. Far across on the other side, the toy-like fishing boats moved uneasily at their moorings.

Slade got out. The wind snatched the door away and slammed it for him. Leaning against it, he drank the rest of the wine quickly, shaking his head and huffing. Then he walked a few yards to a lonely tap, his feet crunching on the mixture of sand and gravel, rinsed the wine bottle and filled it with water.

When he opened the rear doors Bobo grunted. 'Huh?'

'You sit up.' Slade slapped at the soles of the huge shoes facing him. 'You sit up, damn you.' He reached in and grabbed some of Bobo's jacket, shaking him. 'Come on, come on!'

Bobo grunted again. He came upright infinitely slowly, slumping his shoulders against the back of the cab from where he regarded Slade with bleary eyes. 'What's the matter, Mr. Slade?'

'You're the matter.' Slade climbed in. The rear doors banged in the wind. 'Getting yourself goddam drunk and useless. Can you use your legs yet?'

Bobo tried. 'Not very well.'

'Well you're going to improve. We got some walking to do and this time I can't carry you. Here, take these.' He held out a hand on which were clustered some yellow pills.

Bobo looked at them with half-drunken suspicion. 'What are they?'

'Detoxicants. They'll sober you up. The normal dose is three. You're having eight. Chase them with this water.' He tendered the bottle.

'And if I won't?'

Slade drew back a clenched fist. 'I got no more talking to do.'

Bobo stared at him expressionlessly. Then he shook his head. 'No. Not you, Mr. Slade. It's not in you. You're not the kind to beat a po' nigger.'

Slade cocked his fist. They stared at each other, the one tense and the other calm. Then he lowered his arm. 'Look, Mr. President. It's for your good, too. Nobody wants to be *that* drunk. You must feel like hell. Come on. Be a good Joe and take the pills. Please.'

Bobo stretched out a hand. 'All right. Put that way, of course. Threats don't suit you, you know.' He fumbled the pills into his mouth and said around them, 'Cheers.'

'Cheers.' Slade found his John Cottons. 'You want one?'

'Thank you.'

They smoked for a moment. Then he said suddenly. 'I don't like it when you talk like that.'

'Like what?'

'That "po' nigger" bit. Not to me, anyway. You got no call to make out I'm harping on your colour.'

'I'm sorry,' Bobo said.

'Forget it. Just thought I'd say it.' He started to crawl backwards out of the van. 'Got to get moving. Keep trying to work those legs.' His feet slid off on to the ground. 'Got to lock you up now, sir.'

'There isn't a hell of a lot I can do about it,' Bobo said. 'I don't suppose you'd let me go?'

' 'Fraid not.' Slade shook his head. 'Now I got to get moving.'

He slammed the doors and locked them, pleased to see more life in his fingers. His legs were still wooden but he knew they were over-used. His body ached as a complete whole, from shoulders to groin. He felt like an undertrained discus thrower who had suddenly been compelled to run the Marathon, but the tonic wine had washed the gum out of his mouth, it had warmed him and fed him, it had killed the great bruise deep inside his chest. It had restored him to about seventy per cent functional.

He got back into the cab, returned to the main road and stayed in third, accelerating as he passed the plum-coloured Chapman's Peak Hotel on his left.

From Hout Bay the road heads very slightly west of due south as it winds towards Chapman's Peak, hugging the very edge of the Atlantic, leaving far below and behind the forgotten long cannon of the East Fort with its legendary secret steps, twisting on in an incredible feat of engineering towards the wedge end tip of Africa, grey asphalt channelled through ugly rock looking out on one of the most beautiful scenes in the world.

From this tortured road the sea below is a two-tone kaleidoscope of blue and green flecked with angry white when the south-easter blows. To the left the rock and mountain rise very nearly sheer. It is a narrow, brilliant, dangerous road. Even here, in this over-civilized southern tip of a gigantic continent, there are baboons. Less than two hundred miles away are the biggest elephants in the world.

One can never escape Africa in Africa.

Slade took this road. The old van was reduced to second gear as it howled around the curves. Up here on the edge of a mountain it was exposed to the full fury of the wind. It shook and slewed. Blown gravel peppered him viciously like tiny stinging points of shrapnel through the open window. The radiator began to boil.

He drove within his own personal vacuum, sealing off his mind to the elements. Okay, so the south-easter was blowing. He had more on his mind than the weather.

It was imperative that he got outside the ambit of the inevitable chase that was going to come very soon. It might start in the next hour, or by evening, or in the morning, but it was going to come. Around the next corner there might be a roadblock. He would not stop, at this stage, so it would all end in starred glass and a long roll down the side of a mountain and a big splash in the Atlantic. But it was unlikely.

More likely tomorrow, he thought. First they've got to wait until six o'clock because they think Bobo is going to be released now that the money has been paid. And when six o'clock comes they will give it another hour, maybe two. Then once they've made up their minds that they've been double-crossed there won't be such a hell of a lot they can do in the dark.

Tomorrow, he decided. Tomorrow those roadblocks will be up very early. And if I were Pahler I would concentrate my search in the southern waist of the Peninsula, because Pahler still thinks he's hunting a group of black aliens who are more likely to run for the uninhabited areas, perhaps to the vessel that Pahler thinks brought them in the first place.

It was important, then, that he get back north. He was on the fringe of where the search would probably start, and it looked as though he would have to spend the night in it, but come early morning he would have to move very quickly. At first, probably, the men who manned the roadblocks would be operating on a general stop-and-search basis, but sooner or later Pahler was going to tumble to the identity of the true culprit.

Bobo walked out of that hospital too easily, Slade thought. All right, the idea was to fool them and make them think he'd gone off on his own, but the arrival of the ransom note had changed all that. Pahler would immediately start wondering why there had been no sign of a struggle, or of force of any kind. Inevitably, he told himself, Pahler is going to back-check on the staff and he is going to come up with *me*.

How long would that take the colonel? Not more than a few hours, probably, once it was daylight, so he had until midday if he were lucky. But by that time, if he could collect Ginny as scheduled, they would be a very long way indeed from the Peninsula.

He reached the very top of the road, Chapman's Peak itself, changed up into third and took the van down on compression and some brake, swinging left and looking like a banking pilot down upon the true waist of the Peninsula and a new vista of the long wild stretch of Noordhoek beach, fresh from the camera-crews of *Ryan's Daughter*. At its end in the hazy distance jutted Kommetjie, Little Cup, with its thin white column of lighthouse.

Another bend, Noordhoek Valley, an olive-coloured carpet dotted with puppy-puddle pools and beyond to the east a glimpse of the Indian, gently still in the sheltering grasp of False Bay. The wind was blowing across a continent that was only six miles wide.

The road straightened. He dipped down to the valley floor through a dullness, a plethora of trees that shook themselves to death. The eternal wattles bowed and prayed. Small, poor farms flashed by. He was out of the mountains, now, travelling through country so flat that if the sea were to rise twenty feet the Peninsula would be cut in half, and the southern end would revert to the island it once was.

The turn-off up the Old Cape Road flashed by on his left and he brought the Austin down to forty, heading straight now for Fish Hoek, with a half-built housing estate erupting on his left.

Small houses—bird cages. A truck's tip-up gear whining as it spilt dirt on to a pile. Dirty-faced kids. A snobbish Corgi, conscious of royal patronage. A woman in a dressing gown and hair in curlers. Then a gap, and the sign.

It was an old weather-beaten board about three feet square. The letters were red and peeling: PEER'S CAVE. And below them, an arrow pointing vaguely to the left.

Slade jammed on his brakes and swung the wheel. The Austin rolled over a mixture of grass and sand, went past the sign, and on past the last house. Its tyres sank, spun, came free. It rolled on with wattles on either side closing in. The speedometer needle wobbled undecidedly at five miles per hour. The ammonia-stench of cattle dung entered the cab and hung there. The wind seemed cut off. The track twisted and now he was completely isolated, with only the distant drum of a car to remind him of the main road not far behind.

The Austin sank again. He fed petrol, changed down, straightened the wheel. The van slewed like a crab and climbed out of the soft ruts of its own making. There was not even a track any more, just a corridor of white sand between the wattles. If he went much further he would bog down completely.

An opening in the wattles loomed on his left. He made up his mind and swung into it quickly, coasting the Austin into a looming alleyway where branches scraped the roof of the cab, ramming it as far as it would go until it was hidden even from the corridor along which it had come. Then he switched off and sat for a moment.

A dove cried. The smell of dung was chokingly strong. The wind was gone, tossing overhead somewhere.

Slade got out. Nothing, he thought, but the dove, the dung, the wattles and the baking heat, quivering like a fevered dream.

He went to the back door of the van and unlocked it. Cigarillo smoke rolled out and struck him in the face. 'You okay?' He peered into the interior.

Bobo considered him. Slade's tanned face had developed a yellowish tinge but the blood-shot eyes were both anxious and determined. He sighed. 'I feel a little better. Those pills of yours seem to have helped.'

'That's good.' Slade stood aside as Bobo got out awkwardly and stood unsteadily next to the van, holding on to the top of a door for support.

'There's nothing good about it, Mr. Slade.' He looked around him. 'Now where the hell is this?'

'Not far from Fish Hoek.' Slade guided him out of the tunnel, leaving the van in its leafy bower. Bobo came stiff-legged and unwilling. 'See up there?' Slade pointed to a rocky ridge that ran at right angles to them. 'See that hole in the face? That's where we're going. It's called Peer's Cave.'

Bobo regarded him with astonishment. 'You must be out of your mind! I could never walk that far!'

Slade studied him anxiously. The President was grey-skinned and heavy-eyed. 'You've got to try. It's not so bad. We walk a while through this brush. Then we cross an area of sand. They figure this place was once the bottom of the sea. But it's easy walking. Only the last part is uphill.'

'Uphill!' Bobo sneered. 'My God, you must be a master of the art of understatement. Look at it!'

'Please,' said Slade, 'please, sir. I don't figure I can carry you again.'

'You're not going to lay a finger on·me,' Bobo snapped. 'I demand to be released. You've got to let me go at once.'

Slade wagged his head. 'I can't. That's the point. I just can't.'

Bobo tried reason. 'Why? You've got your money. Why don't you just scram? Take your bundle and beat it, as you would say. I will catch a bus, or thumb a lift or something.'

'No. I can't let you go.' Slade produced his John Cottons. 'Have one.'

'Thank you.' Bobo waited for the light and then puffed impatiently. 'Things went wrong, I know. You were supposed to fly out. Those two criminals getting hold of me put an end to that.' A thought struck him. 'I presume that you went back to the cottage? Otherwise you would never have found me.'

'Yes.'

'Why?'

'Because of the fire. I had lit it. I couldn't let you roast.'

'Oh.' Bobo considered. 'Then I suppose, in a weird sort of way, that I owe you my life. In two ways. Those chaps were going to kill me, you know. They were half drunk when they arrived. They got me loose and then they started quarrelling about what they were going to do with me. They fought all the way to the poplars where you found me.' He returned to his original theme. 'I can't understand why you won't let me go.'

173

'I might need you,' Slade said stubbornly.

'But damn it, man, how can you need me?' Bobo cried. 'There's no chase on yet, is there?'

'No.'

'Do they still think it's the Brotherhood they're hunting?'

'Apparently. But I reckon they'll figure it's me by tomorrow. Then the hunt will be on. Then I don't stand a chance unless I got you to bargain with. They won't touch me while I got you.'

'Mr. Slade, you can be very silly, you know.' Bobo looked at him despairingly. 'It's only early afternoon. You could leave now with your money and drive the rest of the day and the night. Seventeen hours, more or less, until daylight tomorrow. You could just about reach the border in that time, couldn't you? Or you could charter a plane or hop a ship. You've got more than enough money for the purpose. What about that, eh? How's that for some ideas?'

'They're very good,' said Slade.

'Ahah, then——'

'Except I can't do it.'

'Oh Christ!' Bobo lost his temper. 'Why? Why in God's name do you have to hang around until every man's hand is against you?'

Slade shook his head. 'I'd rather not say.'

'Oh, please!' Bobo cried. 'He says he'd rather not say. He expects me to climb a mountain but he'd rather not say!' He waved a hand at the encircling wattles and a lone dove in a tree top. 'Do you hear that, everybody, he'd rather not say! Now what do you think of that for a——'

'Shut up!' Slade shouted.

There was a short, charged silence. They quivered, both of them. Then Slade dropped his hands. 'Okay. I guess you're entitled to an explanation.' He sighed. 'I want my wife to join me tomorrow. Then we can go together. I wasn't going to do it that way, I was going to send for her, but now with everything going haywire I want her with me.'

Bobo stared at him for long moments. 'Oh. So you've got a wife, have you?'

'Yup.' Slade looked away.

'And you want the money for her? You said you didn't want it for yourself, remember? In a careless moment you said it.'

'Okay, so I want it for her.'

'And it was to be used as an income more than just a lump sum, wasn't it?'

'I know I said all that.'

'Yes, but what I want is the reason. Why don't *you* enter into the picture? You're her husband, after all.'

'I'd rather not say.' Noisy Slade closed up like a clam.

There was a long pause. Bobo looked about him, finally staring at the hole in the rock face that was Peer's Cave. Then he turned to Slade and said abruptly, 'I'll try the walk.'

Slade smiled. It was a beautiful smile. 'You're sure?'

'Let's not start arguing about whether I'm sure.' Bobo smiled too, but rather bleakly. 'Just let's get going. I feel lousy.'

They went back to the van where Slade collected the first wine bottle, still three-quarters full of water, the second unopened bottle, and his bundle of money. Bobo broke a wattle branch to use as a walking stick and slung his jacket over his arm.

'What would you do,' he mused, 'if I were to sit down, right here, here and now, and cross my legs and fold my arms and refuse to budge? Just sit there like that on the sand?'

'I'd drag you,' Slade said.

'You would never.'

'I'd drag you, I said. Don't look at me like that, I know what you're thinking. Once I stopped Maggie Meadows from killing a bee in the ward because I figured it was one of God's creatures and there was no need to hurt it ... But I've changed. You saw me kill a man this morning.' His face clouded. 'That's something I'm not going to forget very easily.'

'He thoroughly deserved killing.'

'Doesn't matter. Doesn't change things. So I would drag you, wouldn't I? Or don't you think I would?'

'Let's leave it.' Bobo jabbed his stick into the sand. 'Shall we go?'

'We'll take it real slow,' Slade said.

Warren Clunes capered into Pahler's borrowed office. 'The press are making a hell of a noise at Reception. We've already had one complaint. Can't you see them right away?' He dipped and bobbed anxiously on the other side of the desk.

'I'm ready.' Pahler pushed aside some papers and sniffed at

his inhaler, a present from Sister Strange. 'Would you mind sending them in?'

'Warren Is Willing.' Clunes went to the door and said over his shoulder. 'There's a TV crew and some newsreel boys as well.'

'Oh God.' Pahler blew left and right at his shoulders. Damn that falling hair. And his cold had reached the trickling stage. What if...?

They came in as he was knocking his Kleenex box to the floor, nine assorted men and a pale, ectomorphic woman. There was a confusion of introduction, the television crew moved chairs about and someone hung the Peninsula map on the wall behind him. Then Pahler cleared his throat and read off a police letterhead before him.

'I am authorized to make the following statement to you.'

He glanced at the mesmeric eye of the television camera and then looked rapidly away, an act that would convince half a million foreign viewers that he had something to hide.

'The ransom has been paid. It has also presumably been collected. A jacket discovered near the scene of the ransom delivery point had some blood stains on it and these have been found to belong to the same blood-group as that of Mr. Lunda. It is, however, a common group. There is therefore only a remote possibility that President Lunda might have been injured.' It was none of their business that the hair had been compared with samples taken from the pillow in Bobo's ward and declared identical.

He went on: 'Until six o'clock, the time at which Mr. Lunda is due to be released, no direct action against the kidnappers is contemplated. The concern of this Department and the two respective governments is, at this stage, only to ensure the safe return of an esteemed and respected Head of State. The terms of the ransom note have been and are being observed to the letter.'

He looked up. 'Any questions?'

A small angry-faced man jumped to his feet. 'What if they kill him?'

'I don't see why they should.' Pahler tried desperately not to sniff. 'There have been eighteen political kidnappings in the past two years. Of these, in ten cases the demand was met and the hostage was released. In three cases the demand was refused and the hostage was murdered. The rest were indecisive, like the case of Dr. Claude Fly, kidnapped by Tupamaros in Uruguay and released because of a heart attack.' He squared his shoulders and forgot about the cameras for the first time, glaring across the desk with his hard eyes. 'In answer to your question: if these people should be foolish enough to kill President Lunda then they will have reneged on their side of the bargain and they get what's coming to them.'

There was a murmur of approval. The lustreless woman turned out to have a loud and tinny voice. 'Are forces deployed for this purpose?'

'Yes,' Pahler said. 'Ample forces.' He smiled masculinely at the ectomorph and she simpered back.

The angry-faced man was up again. 'Colonel Pahler, would you confirm that this political kidnapping appears to have been motivated entirely by a desire to expose your vile policy of *apartheid*?'

Pahler flushed. 'It's not my policy for a start. I'm a policeman, not a politician. And I confirm no such thing. A Gamban domestic issue seems to be at stake.'

The pale woman quivered. 'I dissociate myself entirely from my colleague's remark.'

'You shut up,' shouted the angry man. They had broken off a pallid love affair some months before.

'Fuck off,' cried the ectomorph, her egg-sized breasts trembling.

'Take it easy,' said a lean American.

'You stay out of this.' The angry man pushed up to the American.

Someone soothed him and Pahler regained order. There were one or two more routine questions and a promise of a further press release shortly after six o'clock. Then they milled out, leaving the office filled with tobacco smoke and carelessly-squashed cigarette butts.

Pahler looked at his watch. Three forty-five. He felt jaded and depressed and very tired, so he tried to intrude a note of cheer by telling himself that this would probably all end with Lunda appearing unharmed just after six o'clock, at which stage he would treat himself to a very large whisky.

Then he shook his head. No. There were too many strange and inexplicable factors involved. And he was nursing a growing hunch that Bobo was not going to be released anyway.

Maurer waddled in but the colonel ignored him. He got up, turned, and perched on the edge of the desk, studying the wall-map. Now if I were a black man, he thought, a scared black man on the run in a strange country, I would run south because that end of the Peninsula is sparsely inhabited, a good place to hide, a good place to get back into the submarine that brought me.

Which was absolute and complete bloody nonsense. Submarine? God, Gamba was landlocked.

He was shaking his head in gloomy frustration when the telephone rang. Maurer took it and Pahler waited while the plump Captain grunted and listened, his little eyes fixing themselves on the knot in Pahler's tie.

When he replaced the instrument Pahler said, 'News?'

Maurer's pasty cheeks had developed colour-spots of rare excitement. 'Some firemen on watch duty have pulled two dead bodies out of the stream below the fire. Both male. One coloured, one white. Both covered in knife-cuts. And one has a length of dog chain wrapped around his neck.'

'Christ!' Pahler pocketed his Dunhill. 'The boys from Pohlsmoor.' He was already at the door when he added 'Did you say dog chain?'

'Yes.' Maurer half-trotted next to him. 'Dog chain.'

On the way to the car Pahler reflected that everything was becoming rather complicated.

Slade lifted his streaming face and blinked the sweat out of his eyes. Bush and scrub rocked giddily. His stumbling feet plunged ankle-deep in sand.

'Not much further. Few more yards.' He panted like a spent horse. 'Come on. Please.'

'It's no good.' Bobo sat down where he was, crunching back against a dead bush. Sand spilled over his lap from the steep, formless path. 'I'm finished.'

'You aren't, you're not.' Slade clung to a grey-fungused branch, holding himself upright against the slant.

'You're crazy.' Bobo stared at him blankly. Both of them were jerking the words out between their desperate sucking for breath.

'I'm not.' Slade peered at him as though he were far away.

He let go the branch and plunged towards Bobo, lurching from side to side as he dragged his feet loose. 'Come on, I'll help you.' He staggered and fell on his hands and knees across Bobo's legs, pushed himself half-erect and grabbed the other man by the jacket front. 'Up. Up.' He hauled on the jacket.

Bobo sagged and mumbled but Slade held him upright, spun him about so that the old man faced the slope, and then with an incredible burst of propulsive power half-pushed, half-lifted him the rest of the way up the hill.

They reached the top and fell apart, striking the ground like tumbled dolls; and there was no sound except the terrible tearing of Slade's breathing.

It was ten minutes before Slade got up very slowly. He swayed. He had a tilting glimpse of the valley floor seemingly very far below. Then he limped to where Bobo lay.

'Water?' He hauled the bottle from his pocket. His voice had the frail rustle of advanced age.

'Thanks.' Bobo hauled himself up on his elbows. There was a pinched look about the big-boned face and the eyes seemed sunken. He took the bottle and drank half the water, offered it to Slade who shook his head.

'Uh-uh.' Slade was fumbling the cap off the tonic wine. 'Finish it. I'll have this.' He gulped some of the wine. It dribbled down his chin and stained his dirty shirt front like anaemic blood.

'Later.' Bobo got fragilely to his feet. 'I thought I was going to die, you know.'

'Maybe you still will.' Slade felt cold. There was a lightness to everything, a lack of depth. It was as though he saw in only two dimensions. 'Let's get into the cave.'

They walked the remaining few yards into the vault of the overhang.

'The home of Fish Hoek Man.' Bobo peered about. 'How long ago did he live here?'

'Fifteen thousand years.'

Bobo turned slowly to look out at the valley. 'Only in Africa could you have a Drive-In Cinema and the residence of a Middle Stone Age primitive within three miles of each other.'

'He didn't look down on a Drive-In,' Slade said. 'That was a sea, down there. He fished in it.' He pointed south of the valley. 'That was an island.'

There was a reflective silence. Bobo sipped at his water. 'You propose to spend the night here? He was too weary to inflect censure into his tone. 'Isn't this a tourist attraction?'

Slade smiled with gummy lips. 'How many tourists do you figure could make that climb?'

Bobo grunted. He slumped on a convenient rock shelf and stared at Slade dispassionately. 'Where is your packet of money?'

'Oh God.' Slade blinked at him. 'It's at the bottom of that slope.'

'And my jacket?'

'Same place.'

'You've got food and blankets?'

'You know damn well I haven't. We can make a fire.'

'You're so considerate.'

'It's no good getting mad. No good at all.'

They glared at each other with very little spark. Then Slade put a hand to his chest. A catspaw of animation crossed his face. Something bubbled in his throat. He said in a gargling voice, 'Gonna cough,' and turned away. His body began to heave and then the sound came.

When it was finished Bobo said to Slade's back, 'Water?'

'No thanks.'

Bobo studied him. The tanned arms hung motionless. The wrists were heavy, the hands square, the fingers slender and well-shaped. Strong, practical hands. There was a scarlet smear on the heel of one palm.

'What's it called— I mean, when the blood comes?'

'Haemoptysos.' Slade stared at the back of the cave where Fish Hoek Man had died.

'Which means?'

'Spitting of blood from the lungs.' Slade turned at last and came to sit beside him. 'You're real curious, aren't you?'

'You should be in a hospital.' Bobo studied the stubborn profile. Even Slade's short blond hair seemed to have gone dull. It lacked sheen. 'Why don't you give this up? It's ridiculous. You're in no condition to go on with it.'

'Scared I'll die on you?'

Bobo said nothing. After a moment Slade stirred restlessly. 'I'm sorry I said that. It's just that I get mad at myself. I used to be so strong. Used to walk all over these mountains.' He waved a hand vaguely, back northwards. 'Don't talk about giving up, again.'

There was another silence. Then Bobo said, 'There's no need to turn your back when you cough. I've seen life. It doesn't frighten me. And it isolates a man, doing that. It makes a man alone.'

Slade studied him. 'When you cough like that, your soul comes into your eyes. I've seen it in the hospitals I've worked. Now I figure a man's soul is a very personal and private thing, not to be seen by anyone else.'

'I hadn't thought of it that way,' Bobo said.

Slade got up after a while. 'Reckon I'll get some wood and we can have a fire. You stay put.'

He left the cave and moved along the ridge, collecting dry branches as he went. He was bending, dragging a small deadfall out of the undergrowth, when a soft voice spoke easily behind him.

'Feeling the cold, brother?'

Slade dropped his wood and whirled in the same movement. There was no one in sight. He said, 'What the hell?'

'Like I'm here, Dad.' A head appeared over a clump of scrub. A tanned, handsome young face smiled at him. It was cloaked by a mass of tangled, shoulder-length blond hair.

'Jesus,' Slade said huskily, 'you gave me one hell of a fright.'

'Didn't mean to.' The head moved out from behind the scrub and was joined by a slim, lithe young body. Slade took in the ragged purple grandpa shirt, the dangling beads, the jeans, the dirty brown feet.

'A hippie,' Slade said.

The boy smiled. 'Like yes, Dad. Camping around the corner with some friends. Been chased around a little by the fuzz.'

Slade felt alarm. 'They after you here?'

'No, no.' The hippie shook his head. 'Little razzle in Jeffry's Bay. Got thrown out. Then we were blowing some pot at Kalk Bay and nearly got had.' He smiled. 'Like this is a place to cool off. My name's Old Hello.'

Slade hesitated. Then he said, 'Slade.'

Old Hello waved a firm young arm. 'Forget your fuelling, Dad. We got wood for Africa. It's not far.'

Slade shrugged and followed his guide through the shoulder-high scrub, uphill and around the curve of the ridge in a westerly direction until they came to a small clearing. A square of canvas had been tied to branches at one end. Long-haired bodies, scattered about, got to their feet and stared at him.

'A friend,' said Old Hello. He gestured at the gathering commune. 'Meet Mr. Slade. You got another name?'

'Ernie.'

'Where you from, Ernie?'

'Portland, way back.'

Old Hello grinned. 'I'm a displaced Aussie. These are Bush, Catch, Sloop, Byron and Fruit Machine.'

Slade nodded. They smiled. The first four were male. He would have thought that the fifth was, too, because sex was indistinguishable amongst the hair and baggy shirts. Except that Fruit Machine was in an advanced state of pregnancy.

'We're all kind of edgy.' Old Hello scooped up an armful of wood from a ragged pile. 'Like no pot. And no bread to buy it with.'

Slade took the wood. 'You got a source?'

Old Hello narrowed his eyes. 'Maybe. Like why, Dad?'

'I'll do a deal with you. If you've got the source I've got the bread. But I need something else. I need vitamin B12 ampoules for a guy with me who's got anaemia. And a couple of disposable hypodermics.'

Old Hello considered. 'This source of mine, this guy used to dispense for a hospital and got fired. He's got quite a collection. Maybe I can get it for you. But this will mean big bread, Dad.'

'I got it,' Slade said.

'That's great.' Old Hello perked up. 'All we want is some very good grass.'

'And for me, some speed,' Slade said.

'You? You don't look like you turn on, if you read me, Dad.' Old Hello regarded him curiously.

'I'm sick,' Slade said, 'and I got to keep going. Get me a little speed: dexedrine, methedrine, benzedrine. It doesn't matter what it is, get it.'

'Okay. When?'

'Give me half an hour. Then come around to the cave.'

Slade waved a hand, passing Fruit Machine who stared at him from behind huge blue tinted doughnut glasses, both hands resting on her bulging belly.

Chapter Thirteen

At sixteen minutes past seven a flash radio message was broadcast from all stations, interrupting regular programmes.

Major John Shannon was pouring a whisky at his bar when it came through.

'Police headquarters have announced,' said the voice of the announcer, 'that the President of Gamba, Mr. Bobo Lunda, who was kidnapped on Wednesday, was not released by his detainers as undertaken by them. As the deadline of six o'clock this evening has passed without further word from the kidnappers it must be presumed that they have no intention of abiding by the terms of the ransom note, and active and determined measures are being instituted immediately for their apprehension. In a message to the Gamban cabinet, the text of which was released a few minutes ago, the Prime Minister of South Africa, Mr.——'

The announcer was cut off in mid-sentence as Shannon clicked the switch.

'Damn it.' He got up, ignoring his drink, prowling to the open French doors and looking out upon the patio. 'Damn it all to blazes. That means he's dead.'

He was lighting a cigarette, staring out the lights of Kalk Bay's little harbour, when the first police truck rumbled into position at the foot of Clairvaux Road. Men spilled out and began to set up a roadblock.

Then Major Shannon's telephone started to ring.

Chapter Fourteen

Convenient night, that ally of the pale, the puffy-eyed and the poorly, had brusquely shouldered evening aside and descended firmly about the Joseph Schwer. It concealed the sleep creases and the fatigue in Margaret Meadows's face as she came out of the entrance wrapping her cloak about her, going 'Brrr' and making a run for Jimmy Craig's car.

She succeeded in getting in, kissing him and sitting down all in one movement. 'God, it's turned horrible. Won't the south-easter ever stop?' She grinned at him with that endurance of the young which is horrible to see when one is not young. 'How's Daddy? You were supposed to pop around at six, you may remember. There I was, trying to look all daisy-fresh after a nine-hour sleep, slapping ice-blocks under my eyes and spraying myself with various things, and you came not. Get held up at the office?'

'No.' Jimmy was sitting turned towards her. His back was against the door. 'As a matter of fact, after five I went to the club for a beer. I had every intention of coming on here but then I got in on the edge of a very interesting conversation and decided not to.'

'Oh.' For the first time Margaret noticed the odour of what her grandmother would have called 'strong drink'. 'What was the conversation about?' She was annoyed at having been stood up but not annoyed enough to become careless. Beggars can't be choosers.

'It was about you.'

'Me? You've got to be kidding.' Her eyes searched his face.

'Oh, I'm not kidding,' said young Jimmy Craig. 'These chaps were having a hell of a laugh about forming a club. They were going on about eligibility.'

Margaret Meadows felt her stomach sink away from her. She sensed with almost exact certainty what was going to come and yet she was compelled to be sure. 'What do you mean?'

'Eligibility,' he said as though he hadn't heard her, 'is quite easy. One has to have slept with a certain Margaret Meadows who works at the Joseph Schwer. Apparently quite a lot of fellows qualify. But then I'm only repeating what I heard from four half-drunken louts. I would much rather hear what you have to say about the matter.'

His icy, unnatural calm was in direct opposition to her shaky agony. Her face burned like fire. She felt that she was going to faint. 'It's untrue,' she heard herself say. 'So many chaps talk big after they've been out with a girl.' She started to say something else and then stopped. You could only deny something once.

Jimy Craig's long-delayed maturity had arrived. Five minutes in a smoke-filled car and it was there. 'That's true,' he said reasonably. 'A lot of a girl's reputation can be hearsay. Even sour grapes. Which is why I put it to you the way I did.' He produced a cold little smile. 'At the same time, though, you must appreciate that I got one hell of a shock. It set me thinking about all the times I've caught you out in little lies, little untruths, all the times your friends have covered for you. I've never been unobservant, you know, just deliberately blind. A glutton for punishment, that's me. The faithful spaniel. And I'm going to go on being one. I will marry you. But I want one little thing done first.'

There was a supercharged silence. 'And that is?' Her lips hardly moved. They felt stiff.

'I want a blood test.' He smiled again in quite a friendly fashion.

Their eyes remained locked. This was it. The crunch, it was called.

'It's all right.' She felt her hand on the door. 'You don't have to worry about that. The baby isn't yours. I don't know whose it is.' She was looking away, already.

'What a beautiful ride you nearly took me for.' He was shaking his head, he was looking at her with disbelief.

She said nothing. There was nothing to say. And she could not look at him. Already they were strangers. Did you bother to bid farewell to a stranger?

The door closed with a thump. She was in the dark wind, facing the entrance of the Joseph Schwer. He was shouting something from inside the car but the words were muffled. It didn't matter anyway. A stranger's words were not important.

She began to walk quite briskly back across the hardstand, not once looking back.

The night was having a fine old time. Away across the city in Clifton, Ben Zodiack lifted a shaky hand and began to dial a number. He stopped and studied his hand. Yes indeed, it was shaking. He had developed a nervous tremble. So he replaced the telephone receiver and went across his tiny living-room to study himself in the mirror. He considered his thirty-seven-year-old face. You, he told himself, are foolish, fat-headed and infatuated. You, a married man with a ten-year-old son, are all a-tremble about a twenty-two-year-old girl with a mind like a stainless steel mincing machine. You are wrong, irresponsible, immature, heartless and inconsiderate. There is no fool like an old fool, and you take the cake, you laughing-stock, you.

Having done all of which, that dogged lover went back to the telephone and tried again.

It rang in the same weary-sounding way. It was answered by the same weary-sounding maid who said she would see if Sister Hobart was in. And finally, after a delay lasting so long that he decided three times to put the telephone down, Sister Hobart herself came on the line and said wearily, 'Yes?'

'Jane?' Ben lit a cigarette with his shaky hand. 'Where the heck have you been? I've tried seven times to get you since four o'clock.'

There was no answer. The lines hummed away. He could picture her at the other end, with the curtains slammed down.

Desperately he said, 'Jane? Are you there? What's going on, darling? I mean, you agreed to come out tonight. You said I must 'phone you at four, just for final arrangements. So I tried and tried. I've been worried sick. Jane, I...' He trailed away.

'Something came up,' said Jane casually.

'But what? God, I've had four whiskies pacing around here wondering whether I said or did something ... I knew you were there all the time. I knew the maid was covering for you. Is it that I did or said something?'

'No.'

'Well—well then what in heaven's name ... Jane, darling,

look, you were quite cheerful, you didn't act upset, you agreed quite readily to come out tonight. Now why can't you?'

'I don't want to come. I've changed my mind,' said Horrible Hobart.

'God, I—oh, Jesus. Look. Look. Listen carefully. If I haven't done or said something, then why not? I mean, yesterday you were darlinging me up hill and down dale and now suddenly you won't even telephone me. I think I'm going mad.'

There was another long silence. It was not a thoughtful silence because in cruel fact Sister Hobart was not thinking. Her mind was some distance away. Eventually she said, 'All right. If you must know, I've got a date. I was asked this morning and I meant to 'phone you and tell you but I forgot.'

'A date? Who is it? His stomach clenched. 'Why couldn't you have——'

'Please, I've got to go. I'm being picked up in a few minutes. I'll see you in the morning. Are you coming to the Schwer?'

'Yes, I am, I——'

'Well, then, I'll see you and we can have a chat.'

Ben clutched the telephone as though he were going to break it. A sudden rage gripped him. 'Listen. Listen to me, Jane Hobart. I don't want to see you in the morning. I don't want to be patted on the head like Granny's little boy. If that is your attitude then——'

'I'm going to *have* to ring off, I'll be late.'

'Ring off?' He spat the words into the receiver. 'Good heavens, I wouldn't give you the pleasure. I'll do it myself!' Whereupon he slammed the instrument back on to its cradle.

He did about four circuits of the lounge, seething. He did another one more slowly. He poured a weak whisky, took a sip, then went through into the kitchen and emptied the glass into the sink. Back in the lounge he lit another cigarette, went to the door and listened to the wind, came back and stared at the telephone with a reluctant eagerness. Finally he sat down and, as though tardily regretting all this delay, zipped through the number of the Joseph Schwer (Sister's Quarters).

The same weary maid answered. Ben said briskly, 'Sister Hobart, please.'

'Sister Hobart,' said the maid, quite relieved to be telling the truth at last, 'has gone out.'

Ben put the telephone down slowly. He went with measured

tread back to the mirror, where he regarded himself once more, with a sort of clinical and bitter frankness.

'You,' he said aloud, 'have been cut down to size.'

When Pussy Burns opened the door of her flat in Newlands she found Warren Clunes jigging on the doorstep.

'Warren, this is a pleasure!' She dropped him a mock curtsy. 'Come into my parlour.'

He bobbed in. 'Can't stay, just popped around for a moment. Warren Won't Wait.'

She eyed him curiously. He was splendidly turned out in an expensive charcoal suit, cambric shirt and wide tie. Gold cuff links shone and buckles twinkled on his neat little feet. 'Well, at least have a drink.'

''Fraid not. There just isn't the time.' He produced a small tissue-wrapped package from a pocket. 'Here. This is from me, to you. Sounds like the words of some song.'

She took it automatically. 'Warren, what on earth is all this about?'

'Oh, nothing much.' He glanced about quickly. 'Beautiful flat, I must say.' Then he put his hands in his pockets and met her eye. 'Fact is, I'm leaving the Joseph Schwer. Got my marching papers today from old Kahn, right in the middle of all this hooraw over the President.'

'No!' She sank into a chair and stared at him.

'Oh, don't look so shocked.' He adjusted his stance with a neat little skip. 'I've seen it coming for a long time. The truth of the matter is that the Joseph Schwer simply can't afford a full-time male Secretary. A place like that is always battling to keep its head above water. Terrible but true. Times are hard. So old Kahn offered me the usual small golden handshake, you know, what about two months' salary in addition to a month's notice sort of thing, but I told him that if I was going I might as well go there and then, but I would take the two months' salary thank you very much.' He winked. 'So I'm jobless. Clunes is in the cold.'

'I don't really know what to say.' Molly Burns lit a cigarette and got up. 'I can't believe it.'

'Don't feel sorry for me, I can see it developing on your face.' Clunes wagged a finger at her. 'I've more or less landed a job in Durban. Did the whole thing by 'phone.' He looked at his watch. 'In fact, that's why I'm in such a tearing hurry. I have a flight in just over one hour's time. Interview is set for tomorrow morning.'

She tore away the tissue paper and opened the little box. 'Oh Warren! I——' she gulped and subsided.

It was an eternity ring. 'Sentimental me.' He blinked at her. 'I didn't want you to forget.'

'I won't. I won't, Warren.' She kissed him, surprised at the depths of her feeling.

'Now you're getting me all weak-kneed.' He took her arm and they went together to the door. 'Funny how things happen, isn't it? Ships that pass, and all that. There'll be no Big Day, no vaginal sonic boom.'

'That was just kidding,' she said seriously. 'When the time came, if it had, I would have been very ... honoured.'

'You always manage to say the right thing. Actually jokes aside, I would probably have been a total flop.' He squeezed her arm. 'You're the only girl I ever nearly had.'

They reached the landing. 'Warren, I——'

'Now, now. None of that or you'll have me dissolving. Weepy Warren. Goodbye.' He kissed her quickly.

'Goodbye,' she said dully.

'God bless you,' he said, then he turned and twinkle-toed down the stairs.

Molly Burns went back into the flat. She heard the main door of the building slam in the south-easter. But another sound went on.

It was the tinkling of a little bell.

To Pahler, Janet Strange appeared in the doorway like a Djinn. A fresh-faced, neat-figured, efficient Djinn in a rustling white uniform, carrying a tray on which rested two steaming cups of coffee.

'In view of your apparent determination to break the stay-awake record I thought I would keep you going with a little caffeine.' She advanced smiling into the office and put the tray on the desk.

Pahler regarded her with depthless gratitude. 'Bless you, my child.'

It was a marvellous opening which she seized gratefully. 'Not so much of the "child". I'll have you know that I'm a twenty-six-year-old spinster.'

'Not so much of the "spinster"!' he beamed. 'I would have put you well below that.'

'Flattery will get you nowhere,' she said archly. 'You don't look a day over thirty-five yourself.'

'As a matter of fact I'm forty-four.'

'Nobody's perfect,' said Janet, and both of them laughed heartily.

'Who is the second cup for?' Pahler winked. 'My assistant left a moment ago.'

'It's for me, dammit,' she growled. 'I like drinking with colonels. Cheers, Curdle Pallour.'

They roared again. 'You're good for me,' Pahler said. 'Cheers, Janet. Incidentally, the name is Al.' It occurred to him suddenly that he had never in his life been called Al before.

'Good to know you, Al.' She reached across the desk and they shook hands.

He told himself that he had never met such a charming girl. 'Things quiet?'

'Yes. Very few patients at the moment. Only bit of bother tonight was with one of the girls.'

'Girls?'

'Staff. Sister Meadows has had boy-friend trouble.' She stopped herself suddenly from saying more. Maggie Meadows's glassy-eyed freeze-out of the rest of the world was something one didn't talk about. It was best seen and forgotten, except to serve as a rather shattering object lesson. *There, but for me, go I. Settle down, Janet.* And Al Pahler, when he wasn't sneezing was a very nice guy.

She sipped her coffee. 'You were away for a long time. Still chasing kidnappers?'

He smiled wearily. 'My dear, I have just spent three hours at a conference hammering into shape the details of something called Phase Two, which is a beautifully vague term for the biggest manhunt this country has ever seen. Helicopters; roadblocks; police; soldiers, God, you name them we've got at least one.' He looked around. 'As a matter of fact I only came back to grab my papers.'

'You mean you're leaving?'

He shrugged. 'I only moved in here while it seemed necessary. It is clearly no longer necessary.'

She was disappointed and showed it. 'Well, heck, there's no need to run out so fast. Can't we offer you a bed for the night? That is, if you haven't got a ... a——' She blushed.

'Wife? No, I'm a widower. My wife died a year ago. My daughter Ellen married last year when she was eighteen and my son Ronald is a boarder at Rondebosch. Seemed better, without a mother around. So I have a rather quiet pad, enlivened only when Ron comes home for holidays. Funny, you know, I always wanted more——' It was his turn to colour.

'Kids?' She was seized by an odd shyness. 'About that bed. Why not stay? They've got your telephone number. When does this Phase Two jaunt start?'

'Dawn,' he said. 'Well, I suppose I ...'

'Oh, come on,' she urged, 'have a few hours of decent rest. I'll give you a lovely line in hospital baggies.'

Pahler grinned. 'Okay. I'll stay.'

'Bully for you.' She produced cigarettes out of a blue-jerseyed pocket. 'Have one. So we won't be seeing you again from tomorrow, will we?' Damn it, she thought, why the hell must I keep saying 'we' why can't I come right out with it and say 'I'?

'It doesn't look like it.' Pahler took a cigarette. 'That is, unless—er—you might...' He waved the cigarette around aimlessly.

'Might what?' She stiffened like a bird-dog with the scent of the covey coming thick and strong, but at the same time he would have to come out with it. Good beginnings were the best.

'Well.' Pahler squared his shoulders. 'This sounds rather silly, coming from a man of my age. But I was wondering if you would care to have dinner with me as soon as this is all over.'

'I don't think there's anything silly about it,' she said firmly. 'And the answer is yes, thank you, I would be honoured.'

'The honour is mine,' Pahler said. And with these olde worlde courtesies completed they proceeded to grin at each other like a pair of Cheshire cats. Then they sipped their coffee and chatted. The fencing was over. Cupid, having had rather a bad day, viewed with satisfaction the two shafts he had driven firmly home.

'Funny thing, you know,' Janet mused, 'all day I had a feeling there was something that happened on Tuesday night that I ought to tell you. Then when you were out for so long it suddenly dawned on me and it's really nothing at all.'

Pahler sat up. 'I might not think so. Let's have it.'

'Well.' Janet went pink. 'That's the whole point. There's not much to say. On Tuesday night—actually it was really Wednesday morning round about four, but still dark of course —I was on duty on the first floor. I was heading for the lift when the car passed me. I couldn't see if there was anyone in it, just the lights as it swished by. It stopped at the second floor, which is an abandoned Isolation Ward and laundry. We call it Up There, and the ward is usually referred to as the "locked ward". Nobody goes up there.'

She shrugged. 'I thought at first that it was somebody playing funny-buggers. You know, you've probably done it yourself, you get into an automatic lift and you want to go to floor three, but you press all the other buttons just to hold up the works? That happens here, sometimes. But then it occurred to me that there were only four of us on duty that night. Maggie Meadows was as busy as blazes and Jensen and Novak simply aren't the type to indulge in that kind of tomfoolery.'

Pahler stared at her. 'When Lunda first disappeared, and a search was mounted, was this place, Up There as you call it, searched?'

'I went off duty,' Janet said. 'But I very much doubt it. Nobody ever gives the place a second thought.'

'Mind if we have a look? Can you spare the time?'

'Sure.' She got up. 'But I'll have to get a key.'

Pahler joined her. 'I think you're wrong about there being four people on duty that night.'

'Wrong?' She frowned, then realization dawned. 'Oh, yes. I forgot about Ernie Slade.'

At twelve o'clock night yawned and changed guard with early morning. The wind still shrieked about the face of the cave and the sky wore a black mask of clouds as heavy-bellied as the hippie girl.

Slade felt a touch on his arm. He opened his eyes and struggled to orientate himself. Where was Ginny's warmth, why was the bed so hard, why did his body ache as though every inch of it had been beaten? Then he saw the Christ-like face of Old Hello peering down at him and things fell into place.

He groaned and sat up as though his back were broken. 'Did you get it?'

'Like complete success.' The boy had taken it upon himself to throw more wood on the fire and already the flames were leaping. Bobo sat up, bleary-eyed and silent.

'Here.' Old Hello gave him a packet. 'Three ampoules of the Vitamin B12. Two disposable hypos. And your speed. Got you benzedrine.'

'That's great.' Slade opened the packet and assembled the drugs. First he dosed himself. Then gave Bobo a massive injection of the B12.

'That's a stimulant you've taken,' Bobo rumbled. 'It won't help what's inside you.'

'It will for a while.' Slade dropped the empty hypodermic on the cave floor.

'I put your wheels back where you had them.' Old Hello tendered the keys. He hesitated a moment. Then: 'Like we got problems, Dad. You seem to know a bit about medicine. You gave that injection like a pro. Reckon you could help us?'

'What's the matter?'

'It's Fruit Machine. Like she's sick, man.'

Slade sighed. 'Bring her along.'

He put more wood on the fire and by the time he was finished they came drifting in. Old Hello and the one called Byron supported the girl between them.

Slade studied the girl. Even in the firelight he could see the lacklustre skin. Without her doughnut glasses she had a narrow little face and frightened eyes. She was wearing a shapeless skirt.

'How'd you feel?'

She opened her mouth. At first no sound came. Then, without her lips moving: 'I ... oh. Oh, oh.' And with it a splattering as though a leaky faucet had been turned on. Water spewed down her slim legs, making them glisten in the light of the fire. A puddle formed between her mud-speckled feet.

'Oh Christ.' Old Hello held her at arm's length. 'What the hell is happening?'

Slade looked around the circle of anxious, hairy faces. 'Her water has broken. She's going into labour.'

Sweat shone on Byron's face. 'Can you help, Ernie?'

'I can try.' Slade lit a John Cotton with shaking fingers. 'Bring some blankets so she can lie down. Has this girl been main-lining?'

'No.' Old Hello shook his head. 'We don't go for body drugs. They're depressants. We turn on with grass, speed, sometimes a bit of acid when you can get it. We stick to the head drugs.'

Slade grunted. He guided the girl to a rock seat and held her arm while the blankets were fetched. Then he made a rough bed out of them and helped her to lie down. He undid the skirt and pulled down her panties. The bulging belly with its distended navel lay exposed, drum-hard skin gleaming in the firelight.

'Okay.' He blinked at the exhaustion that was making his eyes burn. Soon, he hoped, the benzedrine would start to work. There was nothing more he could ask them for. Hot water and towels belonged with B-grade movies. 'This,' he said, 'is where the hair and the dirt doesn't mean a hell of a lot, does it? Does anyone know enough about this sort of thing to lend me a hand?'

There was a frightened silence. Then Bobo pushed Byron and Old Hello aside and knelt next to Slade. 'Barnum said there's one born every minute, or is that allusion too remote for you?'

'You got to remember my wife has read about five thousand books to date,' Slade grinned. 'Some of it has rubbed off, so the answer is I know a sucker when I see one. Know anything about delivering a baby?'

'In my youth,' Bobo rumbled, 'I was present at a number of tribal births. Apart from which I'm not in the habit of deliberately making an ass of myself, so you go ahead and do your thing, as they say these days, and I'll do mine.'

With which they began to work.

In the pallid grey light of the beginning of dawn Slade delivered a boy child to Fruit Machine. He slapped it, and it cried, and the seven men, the five hippies and the ex-sailor male nurse and the President, smiled upon each other, seeing new life in a place where life had begun.

Chapter Fifteen

It was barely daylight when the first helicopter growled out of the north. It passed half a mile west of the cave, temporarily filling the air with the chuffing of its rotors.

'If you're going to go then I figure you'd better go, now.' Old Hello turned serious eyes on Slade. They were standing in the cave mouth.

'You knew?' In the background the baby gave a weak and wavering cry.

'Byron's got a transistor at the camp. The cops don't know it's you yet.' Old Hello smiled suddenly. He extended a hand. 'Good luck, Ernie.'

The others pressed around. Slade waved them off and went to where the girl lay. 'Don't let these freak-outs take any of that goddam pot until they've got you to Fish Hoek Hospital. It's not far.'

She shook her head. 'They won't.' She extended a hand to the tiny head of the baby peeping above the blankets. 'I'm going to call him Ernest Bobo.' She looked at them. 'Like thanks, Ernie. And you, Granpa.'

Bobo growled. Slade flicked a hand. Then they left the cave and started down the hill.

They completed the return trip to the Austin in less than half the time it had taken to reach the cave the day before. The Austin was back in its leafy bower and, after Slade had unlocked, they sat together on the edge of the van floor and took the sand out of their shoes.

Bobo lifted his head as another helicopter chip-chopped unseen overhead. The roar of its passing was barely gone when there came the sound of trucks from the main road.

'Soldiers. They will blanket the Peninsula.' Bobo laced his shoe. 'You haven't got a chance, you know.'

The rims of Slade's eyes were red. He was bristly-chinned,

with a glint of grey in his beard. His skin was dull. But the benzedrine had lifted him out of his slough of exhaustion. 'I have while I've got you.' He got up. 'Let's go.'

Bobo grumblingly accepted being locked in the back once more. Then Slade went around to the front, started the old vehicle with a little early-morning choke and drove out on to Route Six under a bleak dark sky that threatened rain.

He drove at a steady thirty, watching the road carefully and checking continually in his rear-view mirror. Another helicopter, perhaps the first one he had seen, trailed overhead so low that he could make out the word 'Navy' painted on its fuselage.

He reached Fish Hoek within minutes, tensing up when he saw the column of stationary trucks lined nose-to-tail near the turn-off to the hospital. But the combat-suited, pot-helmeted soldiers standing about merely stared at him idly as he went by.

Slade lit a cigarillo. So far so good. No roadblock. If he encountered one he would have to bluff it out, because from here on there was only one road, that narrow vein that lay between the mountains on his left and the Indian on his right, all the way to Muizenberg.

He turned into Fish Hoek's main road. Immediately the wind seemed to hurl itself at the Austin so that Slade had to correct violently to prevent slewing into the curb.

He checked his watch. Eight minutes past six. Early still. Shops closed, bus-stops deserted. Only a few rise-and-shiners in cars, heavy-eyed and bored on their way to early-starting jobs. No sign of police or more soldiers.

There was a Simca ahead of him carrying two overalled coloured workmen. Slade stayed behind it, matching his speed with its modest thirty-five, winding with it past the Clovelly turn-off, slowing down with it as it entered Kalk Bay, watching his speedometer needle waver from twenty to fifteen to a crawling five and then to nothing. The Austin rattled in neutral.

Traffic piled up ahead. Slade's hands tightened on the wheel. The road was straight at this point and he could make out three or four cars ahead. There might be more for all he knew. He drew on the cigarillo, blowing smoke against the windscreen.

The cars moved, stopped, moved again. Each occasion was no more than a jerky, two-car-length progression. But with each gain and each thumb-twiddling wait Slade's tension mounted. The benzedrine had made him jittery and on edge and his over-stimulated heart slugged against his ribs.

They moved once more, and then Slade saw the roadblock.

Clairvaux Road, short, wide and steep, is a switchback link-up with the main vein for Boyes Drive and a number of lesser roads and streets in the area, including Quarterdeck. Two trucks were parked side-by-side on the tip of Clairvaux's tongue, so that they didn't block the narrow Main Road. Men. in blue spread out from there, moving quickly through the walking-pace jam, stopping, searching, urging on the cars that had been cleared. At this rate, by the time morning rush-hour built up, they were going to have a major traffic snarl-up on their hands that would see cars damming up, all the way back to Fish Hoek.

Which suited Slade, if he could get through this first one.

A sergeant came up to his window. Slade quickly wound it down. 'Morning, sir.' He had mean suspicious eyes set in a sallow-skinned face. 'Got anyone hidden under the seat?'

'No.' Slade forced his rock-hard facial muscles into a semblance of a smile.

'What's in the back?'

'Equipment.'

Moodily he read the lettering on the Austin's side. 'I suppose you're panting to go and paint. Okay, off you go.'

Slade sighed. He flicked on the wipers to clear a dozen fat drops of rain from the windscreen, let the clutch out and began to roll away. Ahead of him the jam was sorting itself out. The pace was still slow but at last he could begin to relax. Vastly relieved, he reached for a cigarillo. He was lighting it when the sergeant's grim narrow face reappeared at his window.

'Pull up.' The man trotted along with the van as Slade stared at him. 'Shit, stop this bloody vehicle!'

Slade braked. The bottom had fallen out of his stomach. 'You cleared me.'

'I know I cleared you. But the lieutenant's got other ideas. He wants to inspect the back. Let's have your keys, please.'

Slade switched off and got out quickly. He was opening his mouth to say something when a florid-faced lieutenant barged up, waving his hands and talking loudly. 'We can't take anybody's word for anything! Instructions are to search each vehicle completely. The sergeant had no right to clear you through the check-point.' They glared at each other in absolute hatred. Both had been on duty all night. Then the lieutenant was snapping his fingers impatiently. 'Come on, sir, for Christ's sake get this thing opened up, we're starting a new jam of our own!'

Slade handed over the keys. 'It's the small one.' He felt no fear or sense of anticlimax, just a tremendous weariness. 'But you needn't bother.'

'That's the whole trouble, I've *got* to bother.' The lieutenant stabbed the key into the slot and turned it viciously. 'What do you mean I needn't bother?'

'I've got him in there,' Slade said dully. 'The guy you——'

'What's that?' The lieutenant's voice reverberated hollowly. He emerged again, grinning. 'Your boy says you're late for the job. Real old clock-watcher you got in there, hey?'

'Boy?' Slade took two steps and peered into the back. The sergeant looked over his shoulder.

Bobo sat propped up against the back of the cab. He was wearing the ragged abandoned denim work jacket. The coil of frizzy rope lay across his lap. He held a stubble-bristled paint brush in one hand.

'Morning, master,' said the President of Gamba to the sergeant.

The sergeant grinned. Slade conquered a swaying sensation. Shock, tension, defeat. And now this. It was too much. He said feebly, 'Okay to go?'

'Sure.' The lieutenant avoided the sergeant's I-told-you-so glare. 'That's a nice old kaffir you got in there, Mister. The old ones are all the best. They know the proper way to treat a white man. Not like these young bastards you get these days.'

'Thanks,' Slade said vaguely. He went back to the cab, started the engine and drove away along the now empty road towards St. James.

Ethical Ed Herbstein regarded Pahler, an Army lieutenant-colonel and a scattering of majors and captains with indifference. The wind blew his hair awry and stray fat blobs of rain struck his Army-surplus raincoat.

'Don't know why I should be brought out here,' he said. 'All I wanted was to give some information over the telephone and the next thing *barooom barooom*, there they are running across the cinders for me——'

'Please, Mr. Herbstein.' Pahler's cold had returned in full force with the cold wet dawn. 'You wanted to tell us——'

'So I run this place, wasn't I saying? Don't you give a man a chance? And Jesus, poor old Uncle Louis hadn't died all that long ago, and I used to visit him, and I got a memory although lotsa people say I forget prices easy. In *their* favour, of course. Because I'm a fool, because I'm held up in ridicule to the whole wide world for my philanthropic tendencies, when this guy comes in I literally *give* him this very clean, well-shod van, more or less as a gift because he looked so worried. He pays me with a sound-as-a-bell cheque and then I says well how things at the Joseph Schwer, old friend, because naturally all my customers stay friends—who wouldn't, you get given things?—and he says, do you know what he says? He says I never worked there, never in my life, even when I tell him I remember him from the time I visited Uncle Louis. Hell, you can imagine my reaction, so when I read in the paper this morning—I get my paper at the crack of dawn—that this old African gentleman has been kidnapped, I think well it's funny this guy should want to conceal that he ever worked there when I know damn well that he——'

'*What was his name?*' Pahler shouted.

Herbstein looked astounded. 'Gee. Such drama. I was about to tell you. His name was E. H. Slade. I got them here, copies of the papers in my pocket. Sold him an Austin L.D.V. registration——'

'You can tell me on the way.' Pahler grabbed his arm. 'We're going back in a Fairlane, Mr. Herbstein. Just you and me. I'll drop you at the hospital and send you in one of our cars to Wynberg.' He called a sweeping farewell to the assembled officers and almost dragged the man to his car.

When they were pulling away from the command post Herbstein turned to Pahler and said in a tone of injured innocence. 'You try and help and this is what you get. Now tell me, what did I say that was wrong?'

The auctioneer's posters led Ginny along the length of Tokai Road to a dusty turn-off and a gravelled strip-road on either side of which tall trees thrashed about in the violence of the wind. The house was here, reached by a winding driveway that ran down its side and then swung right, to end in a paved turning circle opposite the entrance.

She looked about briefly. On her right was the big house, its front patio paper-littered with the droppings of the movers. There was a broken window near the front door, and the whole structure had that graceless air of abandonment that comes when the occupants go.

The house brooded at her. Somewhere a loose door or window banged monotonously in the wind. A leaf-choked swimming-pool, an overgrown lawn and a gravelled tennis court through which weeds peeped, completed a picture of recent decay.

Dead. All of it was as dead as the old man who had owned it. She drove off the turning circle, nudged the Volkswagen under cover of a tree and switched off.

The wind took the car immediately, shaking it. Branches scraped the roof. She reached over to the back seat and collected the small suitcase and wicker hamper, got out and walked slowly to the house. Rain-specks struck her, driven hard by the wind. Her feet kicked aside the scattered and crumpled papers on the patio.

It seemed logical to try the front door. She satisfied herself that it was locked, then moved a few yards along to the window with the broken pane. No burglar proofing, and the hole in the glass was just big enough to admit her hand. A point of glass scratched her wrist. She watched a tiny line of blood well into the cut. Then her fingers reached the catch and the window came loose.

First she leant in and placed the suitcase and hamper on the dusty mahogany floor. Then she swung one leg in and straddled the sill.

She was poised like that, half in and half out, when the four small boys came up the steps. They were three towheads and a carrot-top, in the six-to-eleven-years group, and they stood near her at the edge of the steps, neat, solemn and extremely curious.

Ginny licked her lips. She knew that she must look ridiculous with her hands gripping the sill in front of her as though she were trying to retain her balance on a very narrow saddle.

'Hi,' she said. 'I've lost my key. I've got to do some cleaning up. Isn't it a mess?'

One of them was clutching a small cheap transistor radio. He kicked at a piece of paper. 'The moving people did all this. They made a mess.'

'Aunty Mary cried,' said the redhead.

'Mommy gave her tea.' The transistor owner spoke in a rasping sing-song. 'Mommy said the sugar is good for shock.'

Aunty Mary would have been Mrs. Johnson, crying for the end of something, something that had been good. Ginny said vaguely, 'Yes. Now I've got a lot to do. Why don't you boys run along and play somewhere else?'

They stared at her. The transistor suddenly filled the air with tinny and distorted music.

'Please,' Ginny said desperately. 'Some men are coming just now. Big men. They will be very cross if they find you here.'

This moved them. They mooched off, the redhead turning to say, 'Mommy said we must get out because it was so early.'

'Well, you can play someplace else.' Ginny hoped her voice sounded firm. She saw their heads bobbing down the steps and then they were gone. The horrible music trailed away.

She got slowly over the sill, reached back and closed the window. Then she picked up the suitcase and hamper, trailed through the dusty empty vastness of what had been the split-level lounge and went along a passage until she found a bathroom. There was a mirror on the wall above the wash-hand basin, left there probably because it was so firmly fixed.

Ginny studied her reflection. Fright in the eyes and circles under them. Now cut that out, she told herself firmly. You've got a husband who has done a crazy thing but just remember that little homily you gave yourself yesterday. Housewifely routines, Mrs. Slade, and no focus beyond the end of a can-opener.

All very well, her reflection agreed, but at the same time we cannot deny that you have got butterflies in the tummy and a palpitating heart, that you only slept four hours last night, and there was that telephone that rang and rang and rang after midnight and had you dithering about, wondering whether to answer it, and then when you decided that it might be Ernie in trouble it rang off just as you reached out to pick it up. And nor can we deny that you have been very frightened by all the police and troops you saw on the way out, nice-looking boys until you realized that it was your husband they were gunning for, and that once your husband joined you they would be gunning for you, too. So why not admit that you'll do your best but that you're only human, and oh God why doesn't he come?

She placed her two burdens neatly on the floor, then neatly vomited into the washbasin. Routine. Fourth time since midnight. Nerves, old girl. Thank God somebody had forgotten to cut off the water, it would wash the smear away.

The tap was still gurgling reflectively when she heard the engine, so loud that it startled her until she realized that the driveway ran past the bathroom window.

'Ernie!'

She held rock-still for a moment. Then with a muttered exclamation she dived a hand into her raincoat pocket, found a comb, dragged it through her tousled hair. A quick check in the mirror and she was running for the front door.

Footsteps sounded on the patio outside. She fumbled with the latch, swore under her breath. Then the door came open and they were four yards apart, looking at each other.

There was a silence in which the papers scraped about. She saw the thin face, the red-rimmed over-tired eyes, the glinting stubble of beard, the way the dirty shirt and ragged trousers hung on the newly lean body. He had lost pounds. He had aged years.

'Hello, kid,' he said. And when he smiled it was the same Ernie who had bought a magazine from her so long ago in Montreal.

'Oh, Ernie!' she cried, and in the same movement flung herself into his arms, holding him as though she could never let go, kissing him, babbling silly little things and letting the tears at last come. 'Oh Sailor, I've missed you so, you crazy man, oh darling...'

He disengaged very gently. 'This is Mr. Lunda, honey.' Still with an arm around her he turned to Bobo. 'My wife, sir.'

Ginny saw a tall, ugly old man. When he smiled he looked as though he were going to bite her. 'It's not your fault, I suppose, that you married him,' said the President of Gamba.

She composed herself. She brushed away the tears. 'My husband has done a very silly and wrong thing, Mr. President. I know why he did it, but on behalf of the Slade family, all three of them, I apologise.'

'Three?' Bobo looked surprised.

Ginny gently patted her tummy. 'In here,' she said softly.

'Oh.' Bobo considered her for a long moment. Then he turned raised eyebrows. 'So, Mr. Slade. So.'

'Let's get in this house,' said Slade, 'before we have a band out to welcome us.'

They walked into the deserted lounge, their footsteps hollow. Ginny shut the door. She tugged at her raincoat, ran a hand over her hair.

'Now, Sailor,' she said firmly, 'this is your wife talking. I seldom turn on the heat, as you know. But the moment has arrived. I want you to give up this whole ridiculous idea. I want you to give back that money to—to wherever the hell it comes from. And I want us to drive out of here, nice and quietly, drop Mr. Lunda off at his hospital, and go home where you can have the bath you need.'

'No,' said Noisy Slade. He turned to Bobo. 'Why did you front me at the roadblock? You could have stepped out of that van and it would have been over. I was on the point of telling them.'

Bobo sighed. 'It will soon be over anyway. I know it. Your wife knows it. You know it yourself but you're too damn stubborn to give in. So in a foolish moment I decided that for you to be caught like that, by two racialistic idiots at a roadblock, was so ... undignified. You've had a good run. Much better, don't you think, to turn yourself in to a gentleman like Pahler, with the pride I know you never want to lose.'

Slade stared at him for a long time. Then he said, 'I heard all those words. Every one of them. I never thought I'd hear them from you. But I'm not proposing to turn myself in to anyone, Mr. President.'

'I don't want the money.' Ginny's voice broke. 'I don't want the lousy money. I swear I'll never touch a goddam penny of it.'

Slade turned to her. 'You heard what the President said about dignity. Don't lose yours now. And as for the money, you may not want to touch it but your daughter is going to need it, isn't she?' He shook his head. 'This is the last decision I will ever make. You've got to abide by it, kid.'

A time of moments rolled by. Then she said on a long sighing note, 'Oh well, Ernie. If that's the way it has to be.' And then she came up and put her arms around him.

'If you could break it up for just a short while,' Bobo said obnoxiously, 'I'm very hungry, very tired and very thirsty. In reverse order, come to think of it. You wouldn't by any chance have a little drop of something?'

Ginny broke away from Slade. 'Tea in a thermos. Or soup. Trust me never to let the side down. Which would you like?'

'That isn't quite what I had in mind. Oh God, I suppose I'll take the tea.'

'That's not all I've got.' Ginny fetched the hamper and the small suitcase. 'There're sandwiches—ham and tomato—a couple of boiled eggs ... oh, and I brought you a jersey, Sailor, and some fresh underclothes, and a razor.'

'You go and shave,' Bobo said, 'while your wife and I have breakfast.'

Slade left with the suitcase. He was away for twenty minutes but when he returned he looked neater, brisker. A light fawn jersey obscured the dirty shirt and the shave had rejuvenated him a little.

'I transferred the money to this grip.' He put the case on the floor next to him. 'It's easier to handle.'

'Tea or soup?' Ginny asked. She ignored the suitcase.

'Tea, thanks.' He took the plastic cup she handed him 'I figure we'd better get going. It's important to quit the Peninsula as early as possible.'

'Drink your tea first, at least,' Ginny said.

'It's too hot.' Slade put it on the floor.

Old gulp-and-go Slade. She started to put things back into the hamper.

'Leave that.' He said it quite sharply. 'Go check the front door, kid.'

Ginny got up silently and disappeared into the hall. Bobo said, 'If you get clear of the Peninsula, what about me?'

'I'm still thinking.' Slade bent and closed the suitcase.

Ginny came back. At once he could see that something was wrong. The expression on her face, the way she held herself, the way she walked. He jumped up, at once rigid with tension. 'What's the matter?'

'There were some kids fooling around here before you came. I chased them away.' Ginny's freckles stood out in her pale face. 'Now they're coming back down the driveway and they've got their mother with them.'

Slade stared at her. The knock came at that moment, frighteningly loud in the empty house.

Chapter Sixteen

Janet Strange, still in the same uniform she had worn all night, overtook Jane Hobart on her way from breakfast. 'You were strangely missing from the breakfast table. Off your food?'

Hobart was wearing an old grey cardigan, a skirt and worn sneakers. When she was sloppy, Janet reflected, Hobart was *very* sloppy.

'I only got in at five.' There were shadows under her eyes. 'Then I'm dragged out of bed and told that Pahler wants to harangue me again. What's it all about?'

Janet shrugged. 'I'm not sure. Somebody 'phoned ahead with the message to say he was on his way. And I don't think he wants to *harangue* you. He wants to talk to all of us who were on night duty on Monday and Tuesday.'

Hobart considered her with a faint smile. 'Defending our Head Cop, I gather. Set your cap at him?'

'If I have,' Janet said carefully, 'then it's certainly none of your business.'

'You never know,' Hobart said playfully with the confidence of the beautiful talking to the average-looking, 'I might be interested too.'

'No, dear, you wouldn't.' Janet smiled sweetly. 'Colonel Pahler isn't married.'

Hobart turned a dull red. There was no quick come-back. There never would be. A lot of people hadn't realized yet that Hobart, apart from being a very capable nurse, was not really clever. She was just an extremely able schemer.

Having got the worst of this encounter Hobart headed back to the point. 'What's it all about, anyway?'

Janet shrugged. 'I don't know. It may be connected with the fact that he found out late last night how President Lunda was removed from the Joseph Schwer. He was taken out via Up

There, in a wheelchair.' She saw no point in mentioning her own part in the discovery.

They entered the building and walked along the corridor. 'It's a lot of bloody nonsense,' Hobart said broodingly. 'Does Pahler think we kidnapped old Lunda? Hell, the alarms and excursions in this place. I suppose you've heard about Warren Clunes?'

'Yes. Apparently the Trustees felt he couldn't be afforded any more. He left very suddenly last night.'

'That's the story *he* put about.' Jane yawned. 'In actual fact he'd been stealing this place blind. The auditors had their suspicions so they ran a surprise check on the books during all the excitement of the President's disappearance. Clunes is into the ribs of the Schwer to the tune of five thousand seven hundred and eighty four rands.' It was typical of her that she should know the figure exactly.

'You've got to be kidding!' Janet stared at her, aghast.

'Ask Pussy if you want to. Except that she's probably in no state to answer. Seems she had a crush on him, believe it or not.'

'I liked him too.' Janet adjusted slowly to the news. 'Poor little man. He had no compensations in life except expensive cars and wines and all that gourmet food, and he wasn't earning a great deal more than we are.'

'He's just damned lucky the money was insured.' Hobart stopped at the office door. 'So all they did was fire him.' She allowed a pleasant little mock shudder to run down her lithe body. 'No scandals at the Joseph Schwer, old sport, at all costs. Let's go in and wait for the Head Cop.'

She turned the handle, swung the door open and immediately stopped on the threshold.

Ben Zodiack was leaning against the edge of the desk.

There was a long loud silence. Ben trembled visibly. Hobart withdrew into contemplation.

'Good morning,' Ben said at last.

'Good morning,' Jane smiled, a no-hard-feelings flash of warmth, then went back into her time-lapse.

'Did you have a nice time last night?' Ben drew on a cigarette with that shaky right hand of his.

'Oh.' Hobart seemed quite regretful at his having raised the matter. She gazed at him in a hurt way. 'It wasn't too bad.'

Ben studied his knees. He wanted to stay silent and retain some of his shattered pride but he was one of those people who cannot rest until the air is cleared. So he blundered on agonizingly. 'Did you wear the ruby ring I gave you? And did you offer him cigarettes from the gold case I gave you and light them with the gold lighter I gave you?'

'Well, really!' said Painful Jane.

'I think I'm in the road.' Janet Strange moved to go.

'You stay!' Ben shouted. 'You know damn well what's been going on. The whole bloody hospital saw it begin and blossom into the most lopsided romance of the century. Now you might as well watch the end.' He turned eyes that glittered like diamond chips on to Jane. 'What would you say if I told you that you were a bitch?'

Jane's lips parted. She showed her small, perfect white teeth, in what might have been the beginnings of a snarl, although it was unlikely. Hobart was simply not sufficiently interested to fight, and mere insults rattled easily off her beautiful armour. But at this stage Margaret Meadows ghosted in, a wan and lustreless blue-cloaked shadow who settled quietly on a chair.

'The audience has now assumed proportions,' said Painful Jane, 'where I am no longer prepared to participate in a soul-baring session.'

'Oh, Christ,' said Ben, both in desperation and at the unjustness of the remark, and retired to the desk.

At this stage Pahler came in. Still raincoated, he looked wet and weary. Ben got up but he waved a hand. 'Stay, doctor. You can probably help.' He grinned at Janet as he went past, turned at the window and surveyed them from there. 'This has got to be quick. Last night I found out that President Lunda didn't walk out of the Joseph Schwer, he was wheeled out. Somebody drugged him, took him in the lift to Up There and then pushed him out across the laundry ramp in a wheelchair that left tyre marks. In the light of that development it was obvious that I had to see all of you again, urgently. In fact, to be blunt it was obvious that somebody in the Joseph Schwer had participated fully in the President's kidnapping.'

He talked over their babble of surprise. 'So that was the situation last night. I wanted everyone here this morning. I even tried to get Ernie Slade on the telephone, because naturally I wanted him as well. I didn't get him, but that doesn't surprise me any more. I found out a few minutes ago that it is Slade who kidnapped the President.'

There was a moment of completely shocked silence. Then Janet said, 'But that's completely ridiculous!' The others added their protest in a disjointed chorus.

'Not Ernie,' Ben said. 'You're talking nonsense.'

Even Meadows was roused out of her far-away world. 'Ernie once stopped me from killing a bee in a ward. He said it was one of God's creatures. Then the bee stung him. Do you think a man like that would kidnap someone?'

'What little I saw of him,' Pahler said honestly, 'I liked myself.'

'Everybody loves Ernie,' said Hobart, and then turned pink.

'I know. But I can assure you that he did it. I can give you the make and registration number of the vehicle he bought from a man who recognized him, although Slade denied that he worked at the Joseph Schwer.' He shook his head. 'Look. I'm not trying to kid you into believing something that's not true. I am totally and completely satisfied that Slade is the man concerned. I'm here only because I can't understand *why*, and it will help me to know. You people are Slade's friends. Perhaps you can tell me.'

There was a short reflective silence. Then Ben said, 'It's a hell of a shock, adjusting to a thing like this. I still find it difficult to accept that Ernie would do such a crazy thing. But if he did—and I obviously accept your word on this—then he could have had only one reason and it sticks out like a sore thumb.'

Pahler went red. 'Are you trying to be funny?'

'Sorry.' Ben shook his head. 'I should have qualified that. To *me*, because I'm in possession of confidential information, the reason is obvious. It wouldn't be to anyone else, except perhaps to these girls, here, because they worked with him.'

'Ernie is very sick,' Meadows said unexpectedly, causing all the others to look at her.

'That right, doctor?' Pahler shifted his glance back to Zodiack.

'Yes.' Ben nodded. 'Margaret is a very observant girl, because it wasn't all that noticeable.' He kept his eyes on Pahler. 'There's a ninety-per-cent chance that Slade has carcinoma of the lung. The other ten is tuberculosis. So that makes him either dying or very ill. Ernie himself is convinced it's carcinoma and I think he's right.'

Pahler digested this with some confusion. 'Why the uncertainty?'

'Because the result of a test I sent off hasn't come back yet.'

Pahler frowned. 'Why should a dying man want to kidnap someone?'

'Let's extend the question.' Ben lit a cigarette. 'Why should a dying man want money? The answer is his wife. Slade has absolutely nothing to leave her. I'm pretty sure Slade wants the money for Ginny. Have you spoken to her?'

'I wish I had. The first thing I did, once I knew, was to send some people to pull her in. But she's gone, and I can only assume that she's joined him.'

There was a murmur from the girls. 'I know he was sick,' Meadows said, 'but I didn't realize he was *that* sick. On Tuesday night I caught him at the drug cupboard. He said he'd taken some A.P. Cods for a temperature he was running.'

'You didn't report it?' Pahler asked sharply.

Meadows flushed. 'Why should I? What's a few A.P. Cods anyway? Ernie is a wonderful guy. I wouldn't turn him in for a thing like that.'

Janet turned to her. 'Did you check what he'd taken?'

'No. I trusted him. Apart from which I was so...' She trailed away and stared at the carpet between her knees, lost to them again.

Janet touched her arm gently. 'Go and check, Margaret. Please.'

Meadows got up wordlessly and left the room, and they waited in unhappy silence for the few minutes it took her to return.

When she came back she stopped almost in the doorway and said to Pahler, 'There's some intravenous Vallium missing, and Vitamin B12. Quite a lot. Also some disposable hypodermics.'

'Was this used in Lunda's treatment?'

Hobart interposed. 'Not the Vallium. The other stuff was. The Vallium would have put the old man to sleep if he'd been given enough.'

All of them, for the first time, now really accepted what Pahler had told them. He gave them a minute or two while they murmured amongst themselves. Then he said: 'Every day many thousands of men die leaving their dependants penniless. But now we have a Slade, who kidnaps a visiting President just because he doesn't want to leave his wife broke. She could get a job, she could re-marry, but does our Ernie consider this? Oh no, he goes right ahead with a crackpot scheme to hand her fifty thousand rands on a plate before he dies.' He shrugged morosely. 'I'm not so sure I can believe it. A man who would do a thing like that is either a nut-case or a completely unique individual. Are you sure there wasn't something else, or something additional, like a political tie-up?'

He produced an unexpected reaction. The doctor and all three girls laughed. Then Meadows said quietly, 'Colonel Pahler, you said it all yourself. Ernie Slade *is* a completely unique individual. He is *exactly* the type of man who would kidnap a visiting President because he didn't want to leave his wife broke.'

'You genuinely believe that?'

'Believe it?' Meadows stood up. 'Colonel, not only do I believe it, I also hope like hell he gets away with it. If there were a few more Ernie Slades around maybe I wouldn't be where I am today.' She choked up and charged out of the room.

Pahler was left with the memory of a bobbing lace cap and swirling cloak. 'God save me from neurotic women. What was that in aid of?'

Hobart bared her little pearly teeth. 'She's preggers, Colonel.'

Janet Strange stood up. She gave Painful Jane a withering look. 'There but for the grace of never forgetting to take your pill, go you.' Then she clamped firm, possessive fingers on Pahler's right bicep. 'I'll see you off, Al.'

They walked down the corridor. He felt a little lost. 'There's a certain amount of feeling around today.'

'Hah! Are you kidding?' She had anger-spots on her cheeks. 'Sometimes I think Hobart is a Martian. Other times I think she is a sterilizing machine. Today I wish she was. I'd cross her wires, plug her in and short circuit her.'

He found himself feeling mildly sorry for Hobart. They reached the entrance, stood momentarily under the overhang. The rain had become less scattered. It fell steadily, driven by the wind.

'Don't come any further, you'll freeze.' He began to fasten the top button of his raincoat.

'There's just one thing about Slade that nobody mentioned.' She took over and finished fastening the button for him. 'He's got his money. But he's still got the President. Why doesn't Ernie let him go?'

'That's a very good point. I don't know. But I think an intelligent guess would be that something misfired in Slade's plans and he's sticking to Lunda so that he can use him as a hostage, a sort of guarantee of his safety.' He shrugged 'I'd probably do the same. And now I must go. I see that fat Deputy Minister Mango has parked his chauffeured limousine next to my car over in the staff rank, which means a detailed progress report delivered in a diplomatic way. I'm a little short on diplomacy as far as Mango is concerned. Wish me luck.'

'Good luck, then. And look after yourself, Al.'

He smiled. 'Concerned about me?'

Her honest blue eyes met his squarely. 'Yes, I am.'

'I'm glad,' he said gravely. Then he waved a hand and walked across the hardstand. The short fat African got into the Fairlane from his own car and then the Fairlane swept past her in a curve, heading for the main gates.

Janet waved. Then she went inside, glancing at her watch and wondering whether, with all the excitement going on, she would ever be able to sleep.

It was three minutes past eight.

Chapter Seventeen

The woman was blonde like three of her boys, stilt-legged and heavy-beamed, wearing carefully bleached out jeans and a Fred Perry windbreaker. Round Table, thought Ginny, with a touch of country.

'I'm terribly sorry.' The voice was Round Table too. 'The kids told me you'd got through the window, so I thought I'd better come and see for myself.' A pause and an apologetic smile while she tried to peer past Ginny into the hall. 'But of course on my way in I saw the van. The place *does* need doing up. I told Mary again and again, but after Fred's death you know she seemed numb...'

She trailed away and waited to be filled in. Her sons gathered like a clutch under the shelter of her overhanging bottom. The cheap transistor once more filled the air with Martian music.

Ginny said vaguely, 'Somebody changed their minds. We just do what we're told.' She kept one hand on the door. It was a hovering, I'm-busy sort of stance.

'Well, I'm sure it wasn't Mary. She was so firm about *not* having anything done. Are your instructions from the purchaser?' Tokai's curious blonde cat batted absently at an intruding child.

Ginny's gaze moved away. There was an auctioneer's poster stuck on the front door. Damn it, what was this woman getting at, the sale had definitely not yet been held, there it was, right under her nose. 'We—my husband and I—were told to do this job by the auctioneers,' she said. 'Where they got their instructions from I don't know—or care.'

The woman stared at her. 'But my dear, that's impossible!'

Ginny's heart skipped, lurched, went on. The radio blared what sounded like a fanfare. 'What's impossible?'

'The sale has been cancelled. Surely you knew?' Her green eyes had developed a probing quality. 'The notice was in this morning's paper. The auctioneers have nothing more to do with this place. A buyer was found by private treaty.' She whirled on the child with the transistor. 'Stop that racket!'

'The man's going to talk,' said the boy with the buzz-saw voice.

'Nobody said anything to us.' Ginny's strained voice fell into a sudden hush as the music ended. An announcer came on, tinny-sounding: *'Here is an important announcement.'*

'I can't understand the auctioneers not letting you know. It's almost ... fishy. I spoke to the man myself. He was going to tear his posters down some time today.' A hand came up, tweaked the zipper of the Fred Perry down an inch or two over heavy breasts. Brünhilde, girding herself for action. 'What's more, he didn't mention getting painters in.'

Ginny trembled. The pushy child scuttled past her legs. 'No one told us *not* to come.' She felt a sudden vicious hatred for this bored, nosy woman.

In the background the radio became audible again: *'...are anxious to interview Mr. Ernest Slade in connection with President Lunda's whereabouts. Mr. Slade is forty-one, about five feet eleven inches tall, slimly built, with blonde hair and blue eyes. He is heavily tanned. He speaks with a distinct American accent——'*

'Ahah!' The woman half-turned her head. 'You know what it means when they want to "interview" someone? It means he's the one. I knew they'd get him. I was saying to my husband last night that——' The head came back. 'You're American aren't you Mrs. Klein?'

Ginny felt a sliding, swaying weakness. She closed her eyes. 'I'm not Mrs. Klein.'

'But it's on the van, it says——'

'Oh, for God's sake!' The hatred flooded back and saved her. She opened her eyes. The blonde woman revolved once and settled. 'Won't you let us get on with our work!'

A huge flush crept into the broad fair face, leaving patches of its passing on her neck. 'I would like you to know that Mary Johnson *authorized* me to keep a check on this place. I——' The volume of the radio overcame even her. 'Tommy will you turn that bloody thing *off!*'

The boy's lips set stubbornly. He backed away. The radio rasped on: *'...Virginia Slade, his wife. Mrs. Slade is twenty-*

eight, slim and attractive, with reddish-blonde hair. She is
Canadian and also speaks with a noticeable accent. The couple
own a Volkswagen registration number C A 737 dash 8——'

'Tommy!' The woman screamed.

The radio clicked off. She turned, paling so quickly that a
wash of blotches was left behind.

'You're Virginia Slade.' She began to back away, her eyes
locked with Ginny's, her heavy-hipped body moving with a
dream-like slow motion. She reached out a hand blindly and
took one of her sons by the arm. 'Basil. Come with Mommy.'

Slade appeared at Ginny's shoulder. 'Clear out,' he said. 'Go
stick your nose into someone else's business.'

The blonde woman's mouth opened but no sound emerged.
As she reached the steps one foot slipped. She even fell slowly,
sprawling on the edge of the paved turning circle. The wind
whipped her hair awry. Then she got unsteadily to her feet
and began to run awkwardly up the driveway, her buttocks
jouncing under the jeans. Halfway up she stopped, bent forward
and shrieked, *'Children run! Those people will murder you!'*

Three of the four began to cry in unison. All of them turned
and fled and with their mother baying at them they disappeared
from sight.

Slade slammed the door. Ginny sagged against him. 'We got
to go. Now. Come on!'

'Ernie,' she said in a ragged voice, 'Ernie, please. I don't want
to go. Please, Ernie?'

He pushed her away. 'We'll use the Volkswagen. It doesn't
hit people in the face like the Austin. Get going, I'll follow up
with the President.'

'It's out of gas!' She put a shaking hand to her mouth. 'I got
here on the last gallon, Ernie!'

'Damn. Then it's got to be the van.' He turned her roughly
and pushed her out of the doorway. 'Go, kid. Hurry!'

Helplessly she stumbled out to the trees at the turning circle
and opened the Austin's passenger door. Bobo came striding
across and then Slade emerged from the house, trotting with
the suitcase in one hand. He and Bobo disappeared behind
the van and then Slade came to the driver's side alone.

'We've got very little time.' He started the engine, then turned
the van hard and fast. It pinked up the driveway and out into
the road. Loose wet gravel slithered under the tyres.

'The roadblocks will know about us.' She stared rigidly through the windscreen. 'If it was on the radio then the road-blocks must know. The first one we come to will shoot us up.'

'There're lots of roadblocks. They've all got to be briefed. It takes time.' He got their speed up to forty-five. 'And don't forget, most of the hunt is south of here. At the end of Tokai road I'll swing left and head back north. We may not even see a roadblock.'

Trees flashed by. The van ran unsteadily along the greasy road. Then the turn-off to the main highway came into sight. There were a few trees, a drab-coloured truck parked on the verge, men in uniform standing about. Two stout beams resting on battered petrol drums barricaded the northern side of the intersection.

'A roadblock!' Ginny began to sob. 'Stop! Ernie, stop! They'll shoot if you don't stop.' She reached out and hauled at the wheel. The van slewed dangerously and then righted as he grabbed.

'Get away, dammit!' He pushed her so hard that she bounced against the passenger door. The checkpoint rushed towards them. 'It's a new one! It wasn't there when I came by this morning!'

'It wasn't there when I passed either. But it's still real.' She slumped against the door. 'If you don't stop they'll open fire, Ernie. They'll kill me and my child.'

They were forty yards away. Slade's lips drew back. 'They won't shoot. I got to try and bust it.'

'They will. I know it.' She came towards him so suddenly that he threw up a protecting hand. But she flung herself across him without striking him, and when the engine went dead suddenly he knew what she had done, even before she held up the little silver ignition key, showing it to him and saying in a strangely calm voice, 'There. Now you can try and talk your way through that roadblock. But no busting anything. If you promise then I'll give you back the key.'

'Okay.' He sat rigid behind the wheel, refusing to look at her. 'Gimme the key.'

The van lost momentum. Slade braked and they pulled up a few yards from the intersection in line with a grinning corporal who was holding up one hand. He came forward and bent to look in through Slade's window.

'Morning, all. For a moment there I thought you were going to shoot through. Panting to go and paint, I suppose.' He had an FN slung over his shoulder and an enquiring, freckly face. 'Where's the body?' Behind him a lean young captain came strolling up.

Slade shook his head. 'No bodies. Like to have a look?'

'No.' The corporal eyed Ginny. 'I think you'll be cleared, madam.'

The captain reached them. He was handsome and walked with an unconscious swagger. His eyes went immediately to Ginny. 'Lousy morning for painting contractors and soldiers.' He smiled, showing very white teeth.

'You'll get wet out there.' Ginny's eyes went beyond him to a bespectacled radioman standing next to the truck with a walkie-talkie that buzzed and crackled.

'I am already wet, my dear.' The captain pulled back and slapped the window sill. 'Okay. You're—hang on.' He was looking at Slade for the first time. 'Say, don't I know you?'

Slade shook his head. He turned the ignition key and started the engine. 'Don't think so.'

'I've got a hell of a memory for faces.' The captain turned his back to the wind and lit a cigarette within the shelter of his slicker. 'Funnily enough I associate you with planes. You don't pant to fly too, do you?' He laughed delightedly at his own wit.

Slade produced a stiff grin. 'Not so far.' He had also noticed the radioman, who was trying to wipe the rain off his glasses one-handed while he held the walkie-talkie with the other. He had a pale scholarly face and he was frowning while he listened to the ethereal chatter.

'Hell, I've got it! The airport.' The Captain slapped his thigh. 'When the President arrived. You were there. But where-abouts?'

'I was never there,' Slade said. The radioman, still listening, had turned and was studying the van. 'Look, I'm late. I——'

'Don't be in such a hurry.' The captain's eyes narrowed. 'By God, you were the guy with the people from the Joseph Schwer! You and——'

'Sir! Captain!' Excitement rushed over the radioman's face. He began to lumber forward. 'Sir, that's the bloody van——'

The captain started to draw back. 'Get out, chum.'

Slade acted instinctively. His right fist shot out and struck the captain on the cheekbone. He had a blurred vision of the man falling before the van jerked forward, tyres spinning. Ginny screamed, 'Ernie, they'll shoot!' and then the Austin had crashed against the barrier with a noise of rending metal and splintering wood.

It took Slade a stomach-wrenching fraction of a second to realize that the beams were far heavier than they looked and that the old petrol drums had been ballasted with bricks. One of them teetered, then fell with a dull clang directly in the path of the van. In almost the same moment Slade swung the wheel violently to the right so that the van heeled, hung, brushed the fallen drum with its side and then crashed back on to all four wheels. The tyres spun, gripped and he was going away, heading south again on the road to Muizenberg.

At the roadblock the captain reached his feet as the corporal's FN thundered. He knocked up the barrel. 'For Christ's sake, man, what if the President's in the back of that thing?'

'I was shooting at the tyres,' snarled the corporal. 'The President's dead, anyway.'

'We don't know that for sure.' Captain Ian Douglas's cheek was beginning to ache. He wheeled on the radioman. 'Get on to the Muizenberg roadblock. Tell Jock McDonald they're headed his way. Then I want the Command Post.' He paused to think, still panting from the shock of the blow and his fall. 'There's nowhere else they can go, is there?'

'Nowhere,' said the corporal huffily, 'except work across to the Old Cape Road, or miss Muizenberg by taking Boyes Drive, or turn in at Westlake.'

'Westlake is a dead end.' Douglas rubbed his cheek. Blood came away on his fingers. 'You're right about Boyes Drive, though. But there's another roadblock at the foot of Clairvaux Road. That's where the Drive comes out. So that's sealed off.'

'If I were running scared like that guy,' said the corporal, 'I would turn in at Westlake. There's government forest across from the golf course. He can work his way up into the mountains behind Kalk Bay. He hasn't got a chance in that van anymore.'

'It's a possibility.' Douglas hesitated. 'I'll put it to the C.O. They can get a chopper over there in a couple of minutes.' He put his hands on his hips and stared in the direction the van had taken. 'That was one helluva gorgeous doll. Silly bitch, getting tangled up with a guy like that.'

The corporal regarded him with twenty-year-old wisdom. 'It's the way of this modern world. The dolls like a man of action.'

'Not that kind of action.' Douglas turned away and went over to the radioman.

Pahler stood in the full force of the wind-driven rain at the command post, huddled next to the radio truck with an Army lieutenant-colonel and a naval commander. The commander, red-faced and tense, was handling the ground-to-air communication himself. They were his helicopters, after all.

'Nothing yet.' Rain dripped off the peak of his cap. 'He's cruising back again from Kalk Bay. Not much traffic in this weather. He can't understand why he hasn't picked the van up yet, unless Slade has ducked off to his left around Steenberg, Sandvlei way. But there're roadblocks there, too.'

'The report from there is negative, anyway.' Pahler tried to remember Slade as he had seen him on the two or three brief occasions they had met. Was that mild man the same Slade who would set fire to a forest, split open Captain Douglas's cheek with one punch and try to crash a roadblock with a six-year-old light delivery van?'

'I don't like handling bits and pieces of units,' said the Army man fussily. His nose had gone blue. 'We've got Cape Town Highlanders, police, Commandos, a company each of First City, P.A.G. and Kaffrarian Rifles flown in last night, God, we've got anybody who happened to be training at the moment. It makes things so disjointed.' His lips pursed. 'We've even got matelots.' Then he had the grace to blush at what he had said.

The commander eyed him stonily. 'We haven't done too badly so far.' His expression changed suddenly. 'Hang on. Something's coming through.' Pahler could hear the irregular beat of the helicopter's engine while the Commander listened. 'He's spotted a brown van and is coming down for a closer look.'

'Where?' Pahler cried. 'For God's sake, man, where?' He pushed rudely up to the truck window, squashing against the Commander.

'Approaching the Westlake turn-off from our end.' There was

another charged silence. Then the Commander said, 'Here he comes again.'

This time Pahler could himself hear the remote distorted voice of the observer in the helicopter: '... brown van all right, just like the one we're looking for. We've come down to only forty feet above it. There's some lettering on the sides but I can't make out what. Swing her a bit over to the left, Jimmy. That's it. Yah, I can read it now ... Christ! It says "Klein's Contractors, We Pant To Paint". Is that the right one, Sir? Over.'

The Commander looked at Pahler strangely. 'That's it,' Pahler snapped. 'Tell him——'

He was interrupted by the voice of the observer again. 'He's now made a right turn into the Westlake road and is heading towards the golf course. There's heavy tree cover and it's hard to make the thing out but I can still see it on and off. Take her up a bit, Jimmy. No, higher. That's better. Seems to be slowing down. Very nearly level with the golf course entrance, now. Any instructions, sir? Over.'

'It's the right vehicle,' the commander said excitedly. 'Stay with it and keep reporting. Over.'

Pahler whirled on the lieutenant-colonel. 'I think the road-blocks from Muizenberg and Tokai should close in at once. How soon can you get them there?'

'Ten minutes.' The Army man headed for the next truck.

'Slade's heading for the mountains.' Pahler chewed his upside-down pipe with grim satisfaction. 'We'll ring him. The column on Route Six can cordon off the whole of the Noordhoek, then move up north while the remaining forces come down. He has *got* to end up somewhere in between.'

'Hang on,' cried the commander. He held up a quivering hand. 'My bloke is coming——'

'... trees all over the place.' The observer's voice had developed a worried note. 'He must have stopped in there but for the moment I can't see him ...'

'Oh Christ, he's lost him!' Pahler quivered. 'How in God's name can you lose a van right under your nose?'

'It's easy to be a know-all on the ground!' The commander snarled. He opened his mouth to say more and then shut it again as the observer burst through suddenly.

'... never knew a few trees could look like bloody Birnam

Wood but we're coming down as low as we dare and this damn wind isn't exactly making things ... lower, Jimmy, if you can ... I got him! I got him, Jimmy.' Excitement made the observer's voice shrill. 'Contact re-established, sir. We're sitting right on his head, with only the trees between us. I can't make out very much but I can see a patch of bonnet and ...' there was a burst of atmospherics. Pahler and the commander stiffened. Then: '... bloody great fire ... smoke all ...' There was an electronic squawk and the radio cut out.

There was a moment of silence while the two men on the ground stared at each other. Then the Commander said, 'God in Heaven, what's happened?' And began trying to raise the helicopter.

'Fire?' Pahler bit into his pipestem. 'This bastard is an expert at making smoke! He's running out under cover of it! Tell your man not to be fooled. Tell him to ignore the smoke and pull away, move a few hundred yards south-west and watch the mountains, Slade will be coming out that way. I ought to know. He's done it before.'

The commander pulled away from the microphone and stared at him. 'That's all very well. But how do I convey your brilliant decisions when I can't raise my boy? Do I get on a tribal drum or something?' His face twisted as though in pain. 'God, if they've shot him down! Do you know how much those things cost?' He started to call again, trying to raise the helicopter.

'Get on to the roadblocks,' Pahler suggested, 'and ask them if they can *see* your helicopter. That should put your mind at rest.'

He turned away and strode rapidly for his Fairlane, sighing when he saw the black official Daimler parked next to it on the sward. Deputy-Minister Mango's fat, concerned face peered out.

'Ah, Colonel Pahler. How goes it?'

'We'll get him,' Pahler said. 'It won't be long now. He's on foot and running.'

'And the President ...?'

Pahler shrugged. 'I still say Slade will not have harmed him. Slade isn't the killer type. I think Slade has kept Mr. Lunda with him because things went wrong on the Hout Bay Road, somehow, with the appearance of those criminals from Pohlsmoor. I think Slade is going to use Mr. Lunda as a passport to freedom.'

'Passport?' Mango frowned, puzzled.

'Like the Quebec thing, and others. You let us go, we give you back your man.' Pahler turned away. 'Please excuse me, Mr. Mango. I have a lot to do.'

'So have I.' Mango shook his head. 'Oh, what an affair.' He gave Pahler one of his Buddah smiles, a sad one this time, tapped his Malay chauffeur on the shoulder and the Daimler moved off at stately pace.

'Where to?' asked the chauffeur.

Mango lit a cigarette carefully. 'Where to? Oh, any call-box.'

The van slithered to a stop under the trees and in the same moment Slade was getting out and running for the rear door.

'Ernie!' Ginny stood with her hands to her ears as the beat of the helicopter's engine thundered directly overhead. The trees trembled and leaves pattered to the ground. 'Ernie, for God's sake, it's no good any more!'

He showed her a blank face over the roof of the van. 'Get the money out of the cab.' He had to shout to make himself even faintly heard. Already he was wet; his blond hair stuck to his skull, plastered there in clusters; his thin jersey clung to him.

'Out, Mr. President. Come on, come on!' The door was open and he was yelling into the interior.

Bobo got out. Instantly the wind took him and made him stagger. The rain struck him, darkening his rumpled jacket. He screwed up his face against the noise. 'It's too late, Mr. Slade. You've lost.' He held Slade's arm, shouting at him. Rain streamed down his face. 'The soldiers will be here at any moment. Don't you see? It's all over!'

'You said that once before.' Slade grabbed him, turned him the way he had on the approach to Peer's Cave, gave him a vicious push that sent him in the direction of Ginny. 'Wait there! Stay with her. Don't move away!'

He was moving all the time, crouching under the tumult just overhead as though the noise were going to strike him. He flung himself into the back of the van, fingers fumbling frantically amongst the discarded litter of the previous owner. He tossed the frizzy rope aside, pushed away empty paint cans, finally found the cold chisel and tyre lever he was seeking. Then he was on his back. slithering like a snake on the mud under the Austin's tail, feeling a stone grind into one shoulder blade and the clammy touch of the wet earth.

Ginny was calling but he paid no attention. The narrow chipped blade of the chisel was hard up against the mud-spattered under-side of the petrol tank. The tyre lever swept up in a hard, short blow. The tank boomed. A dent appeared. Mud spattered into his face. He set the chisel into the dent, tensed himself, swept his arm up once more. A slight cut within the dent this time. A teardrop of petrol appeared and fell lightly on his chest.

Once more. He grasped the tyre lever so that its edges cut into his hand. The tank reverberated again but now the chisel had gone right through, the force of the blow crushing his fingers up against the tank. Petrol gushed out and he rolled away from it, crawling out at the van's side, scampering on all fours like an ape, bending his head awkwardly to look for the thunder-ing danger overhead. If anything the helicopter was lower than ever. He could make out its dark hugeness through the thrashing foliage.

Now. He took out his matches, held four together in a per-fectly steady hand, turned his head to where Bobo and Ginny stood a few yards away. Bobo had his arm around the girl's shoulders and they were staring at him as though hypnotized.

'Get ready to run!' He didn't wait for Bobo's slow nod. The matches flared and in the instant of their lighting they were gone in a scooping underhand toss into the petrol soaked-mud beneath the Austin.

There was a moment when he thought that the matches had landed short. He made six scrambling paces away from the van, turning back, looking not at the Austin but overhead at their leafy cover, seeming to wait an eternity that was another second. Then, as though a hand had swiped a cloth across a slate, the leaves were gone. They vanished. For a moment he saw the dark rain-glistening belly of the helicopter no more than twenty feet above him, made out the word 'Navy' printed in clear white capitals along its port side. A pointed yellow finger reached up, touched the helicopter between its wheels. One tyre smoked, popped and drooped. Then all of it was gone in a rushing cloud of oily black petrol smoke that rushed straight up and engulfed it.

'Run!' He slithered towards them, panting, grinning his delight. 'Run!' A straight arm was flung out, pointing south-west, commanding, imperative. 'He's not going to bother about us. Run!'

They ran, impelled by the huge pushing hand of the explosion behind them. They ran, impelled by the relentless jabbing hands of Slade who was always behind, belabouring them on over a rain-slippery track, through clutching scrub, over treacherous boulders until they had somehow covered four hundred yards and were on the fringe of the mountain, looking down at the toy-fire of the Austin below, the streamer of black smoke that tore away towards the south-west, and the helicopter fluttering beyond it like a wind-driven butterfly.

Breath sawed in and out of their lungs. The rain coursed down their faces. Slade grinned. He felt elemental, all-powerful. 'That birdman's got enough to do without watching us.' He sucked for breath. There was a great ache in his chest as though a balloon were being inflated inside it. 'Come on. We got some walking to do.'

Neither of them moved. Slade buckled over. He put his hands on his knees. 'For Christ's sake, let's go.'

Ginny's hair clung to her face. 'You never used to talk like that.'

Slade's head drooped. 'I got no time for manners, kid.'

'You've changed, Ernie. You're not the same. You've gone mad for this money.' Her eyes glowed at him out of the pale face.

He straightened. 'Have I?' He saw her distantly, as though through a spyglass. The world spun, threatening to throw him off. He clung on.

'Look, kid.' It was his voice talking, although he heard it from outside himself. 'This is the last leg. We got to go on.' He felt his lips move in a smile. 'We got to come out of the rain. It's not a hell of a lot further. Do it for me, kid. Please. It can still work.'

'It can't.' She looked little-girl and forlorn. 'It never could. But I'll do it for you.'

'Why?' He had suddenly to ask this important question.

'You know why. It's because I love you, Sailor.'

He went to her and put his arms around her. 'Kid, I——'

'Ernie!'

They clung together for a moment. Then Ginny said, 'All right, Sailor. Let's walk. Ready, Mr. President?'

Bobo studied them both with almost painstaking care, as though he were looking inside them. Then he nodded, the rain dripping off his big nose. 'Which way?'

'That way.' Slade pointed.

They began to walk.

Chapter Eighteen

Major Shannon came out of the bedroom just as the telephone began to ring. He shut the door carefully and then leant against it, closing his eyes.

He was drenched with perspiration and his face was slack, as though he had passed through some tremendous physical ordeal. There was a rent in the shoulder of his expensive linen shirt and a smear on one cuff.

The telephone rang on. He opened his eyes, lifted his right hand and stared at it as though it did not belong to him. Then, very slowly, he walked through into the lounge, reached the bar-top and stared at the instrument for a full ten seconds before finally lifting the receiver.

'Yes?' he said dully. He leaned an arm on the bar-top, cradled the receiver between shoulder and neck and looked out at the gusting rain. Kalk Bay huddled as though for shelter between mountain and sea.

'Oh, it's you.' He listened for a minute with his interest gradually increasing. Animation returned to his face. 'There is, I take it, no positive assurance that our bloke is still alive?' Another pause, then: 'Yes, I agree it seems likely if this chap Slade is the idiot he appears to be.' He flicked a wrist to look at his watch. 'I'll give it a try. The area, fortunately, is very close to me. I should be under way in about ... oh, about fifteen minutes. What was that?' He went silent for a moment. His lips slackened and his glance swept towards the passage that led into the bedroom. He said reluctantly. 'I've been here all the time. It's just that when the phone rang I was ... having a little nap.'

He put down the receiver and went back down the passage. At the closed bedroom door he hesitated, shut his eyes again for a moment, appeared to steel himself to something. Then he opened his eyes and entered.

Fifteen minutes later Major Shannon reappeared. He was now

ruggedly and practically clad in tough alpine boots, corduroys, a woollen shirt and a nylon windbreaker. He went quickly to his study and contemplated the rack of guns on the wall.

'I'll settle for you.' He reached out and lifted the rifle off its its brackets. It was a gleaming Winchester .270 with a Lyman telescopic sight mounted above the breach. Shannon weighed the weapon in his hands, nodded, then stooped and took a box of cartridges from a drawer.

In the hall he stopped to don a fawn raincoat, keeping his right arm out of the sleeve while he fastened the buttons awkwardly with his free left hand. Then he grasped the rifle by its muzzle and slipped it inside the raincoat, holding it concealed there, the empty sleeve of the coat flapping as he left the house, ducking into the wind, crossing Quarterdeck Road and heading straight up for Boyes Drive.

Shannon walked with an easy ground-consuming stride, so that he reached the Drive in quick time, crossed it at an angle and then without hesitation began the steep climb up the side of the mountain, following a narrow and nearly vertical path.

From her living room window Alice Gregg watched the rain-shrouded figure assuming doll-like proportions. The empty sleeve of the coat had now been filled, and Major Shannon's right hand was holding what seemed to her to be a stick.

The idea had come to her from the moment she had seen him leave the house. It was now or never, and she fought down all the doubts that flooded her as she found her own raincoat and slipped into it, put on an old beret George had worn when he climbed, and left by the kitchen door, crossing directly to Shannon's house. The rail fence between the two properties was no obstacle. She climbed it the way she had so often stopped the children from doing, and thirty seconds later she was grasping the ring of the grinning gargoyle-head knocker on the front door.

The knocking echoed inside the house. Alice knocked again. No answer. No stir of movement. She tried the handle and it responded. The door swung silently open.

'Hello! Anyone home?' She put a tentative foot into the hall. Now that she was here all her early resolve gave way and she came close to panic-stricken flight. But the thought of the tiny climbing figure shored up her toppling courage.

'Anyone home?' She called again.

There was no one in the lounge. A finger-smeared whisky goblet and a telephone stood on the bar top. Outside the rain washed over the canvas jacket of Major Shannon's telescope.

Her lips tightened. She went firmly down the passage. That damn man and his frigging spyglass.

The toilet and bathroom doors stood wide open for inspection, followed by two sparsely-furnished and obviously spare bedrooms. There was only one door remaining, and it was shut.

Alice tapped upon it. Again, there was no response.

She was now convinced that the house was empty. With only the smallest hesitation she opened the door.

Alice Gregg stood on the threshold frozen in horror, staring at the bedroom that was painted in blood, and the two rag-doll forms that adorned the bed propped in hideous, obscene, clown-like postures.

Fright exploded within her. The room revolved. Then she whispered, 'Holy Mother of Jesus,' and ran for the telephone.

Chapter Nineteen

The Fairlane screeched to a halt behind the ambulance parked in Quarterdeck Road. Pahler jumped out followed by Captain Maurer and strode through the little knot of rain-coated, morbidly curious spectators into the house.

Alice Gregg was seated in the lounge with the florid lieutenant from the Clairvaux Street roadblock. He had just made medicinal use of Shannon's brandy bottle and as a result a little colour was coming back into her face.

'Where are they?' His bulky figure and savagely angry face somehow reassured her.

The lieutenant had jumped up. 'Being brought through.' He read off a slip of paper as ambulance attendants emerged from the bedroom and came past, manoeuvring their stretchers with difficulty in the narrow passage. 'Chrissie Adams. Betsy Berger. Seventeen and nineteen years old respectively. No fixed address. Both mentally retarded. Berger used to get picked up for drunkenness from time to time. Both well-known whores.'

'Whores,' Maurer hissed through the sibilant. 'White trash. They got what they deserved!'

'Do you think so?' Pahler only turned to face him, but there was so much menace in him that the Captain took a pace backwards.

Maurer went white. 'You know what I mean. They've got themselves to blame for——'

'Oh, forget it.' Pahler watched the door close behind the ambulance men. 'It's only one of society's problems. There're plenty of others.'

The lieutenant fiddled with the cap of Shannon's brandy bottle. He realized how ridiculous he must look and put it down sharply on the bar top. 'There's a rifle missing from the gun rack in the study.'

'Oh, sure.' Pahler turned from the door to contemplate the

rain-dimpled patio and, far out, the grey lashing sea. 'It follows. Our tiger hunter wants to complete his half century.' He turned to the woman. 'Feel well enough to answer a few questions, Mrs. Gregg?'

She smiled falteringly. 'The brandy helped. I'll try.'

'Good show. First of all, can you point out the route he took? There is more than one way up the mountain from Boyes Drive.'

'Yes.' She nodded positively. 'But I'll have to show you from outside.'

'That's fine.' Pahler helped her to her feet over her protests that she was all right. 'We want to get a helicopter down on him right away or things are going to get awfully tricky.'

They walked out on to the pavement. The rain had in no way lessened. 'There. Up there.' Alice Gregg clung to her late husband's beret. 'He came out of the house with an empty sleeve to his raincoat. That's what first took my attention. He walked very quickly and without hesitation.'

So would you, Pahler thought, if you wanted to be in at the kill. 'How long ago was this?'

She looked at her watch. 'It's nearly ten o'clock now. It must have been ... oh, about fifty minutes ago.'

Pahler winced inwardly. To be that much behind a professional killer like Shannon was an eternity. It could be eternity for Bobo Lunda.

'Thank you.' He patted her arm. 'In fact, thank God for you.' He turned to the florid lieutenant. 'Smart work in getting on to me so quickly.'

The lieutenant blushed. He had had some agonizing minutes that morning wondering just how he was going to tell his superiors that he had stared straight at President Lunda from a distance of a few feet and failed to identify him. What's more, he had called him 'boy'. Later maybe, he thought, when it was all over, provided it turned out well, of course, he might.

'Thank you,' he said, but Pahler was already heading for his car with Maurer in his wake. The doors slammed, the big engine rumbled and the Fairlane pulled off with a spin of tyre.

They drove for five minutes in a brittle silence. Pahler had reported Shannon's approximate route as soon as he got back to the car. Then he left his radio open but the helicopters, with two tasks now in hand, growled about the tormented leaden sky like frustrated bees in a fruitless search for honey.

230

'I knew,' Pahler said eventually, 'that I had seen that face before. It worried me not being able to place the bastard, especially after encountering him twice in circumstances where I couldn't help but become suspicious. It was such a typically British face if you know what I mean. I thought in terms of polo, politics, Consular officials, visiting business barons ... the last bloody thing that entered my head was a retired tiger hunter, and yet I'd seen the story in the *Argus* last week-end.' He clenched his fists. 'God, where in hell was my memory? The moment that Lieutenant whats-his-name from the roadblock got me on the blower it all came back: John Shannon, sixty-three, keep-fit fanatic, twenty-five years as assistant to some junior Rajah or other, and most important of all, one short of his half-century in tigers, poor bloody things. Hell, it follows. Shannon is loopier than the Mad Hatter and Bobo Lunda's hide is striped, in our crazy Major's mind. So now we're hunting a kidnapper and his victim who are in turn being hunted by a nut-case. And don't know it.' He turned his head to look at Maurer and said unpleasantly, 'Have you got anything to offer that is reasonably intelligent, Little Sir Echo?'

'Echo,' said Maurer.

'Jesus Christ,' said Pahler.

After that they drove in silence.

Pahler's radio began to squawk as he was getting out of his car near the command post. But he ignored it and trotted towards the truck where the group of officers around it had gone into a tense huddle.

The naval commander held up a rigid hand when he saw Pahler's bulky figure nearing. There was a moment of super-charged tension while a tinny voice rattled incomprehensively. Then the Commander raised a grinning, triumphant face as Pahler arrived.

'We've got them. Right underneath the chopper, pinned down in an open area. Slade, his wife. *And* President Lunda.'

'Christ.' Pahler pushed in. 'Don't let's lose him this time.'

'You've never had a car set alight more or less directly under your balls.' The commander looked at him coldly. 'This boy of mine won't budge. And Slade has run out of cars.'

Chapter Twenty

The helicopter found them as they were crossing a stretch of stony ground where coarse clumps of grass and shrub struggled for survival. It swooped down from the north behind them, the noise of its arrival lost in the wind until it burst upon them, almost instantly overhead. Grass writhed under the down-draft of the rotor blades. Rain-spray was flung like shining tears. Their sodden clothing crawled about on their skin.

Ginny dropped the suitcase. The three of them stood together, craning their necks at the huge dragonfly hovering above them. A face looked curiously down at them. Earphones bulged like muffs.

'So that's it, Sailor.' Ginny put her arms around Slade. She had to shout to make herself heard. 'The last leg. We can come in out of the rain, now.'

Slade shook his head. 'No. I won't just . . . give in.' Rain ran down his face and dripped off his chin. The wet collar of his shirt fluttered like a pulse.

Bobo took two limping steps towards Slade. He put a hand on Slade's shoulder. 'Ernie. There's nothing else you can do.' He stared at him out of a grey exhausted face.

'There is.' Slade picked up the case. 'I can walk. Come on.'

'Ernie, no, damn you!' Ginny held his arm with both hands, keeping him back. 'Ernie, so far we've done all the crazy things you wanted. But there're limits. It's over, Sailor. Don't you understand?' She peered at him through the rain, smiling hesitantly, shouting above the overhead tumult as though to a difficult child. 'Listen carefully, Ernie. You can't win, any more. You——'

Slade cut her off. 'That thing up there can follow us. But it can't shoot us and it can't bump us on the head with its wheels. Let's go, kid.'

Ginny stared at him helplessly. Her sodden raincoat hung on her exhaustedly drooping body. There was a hole in the knee of her left stocking and a smeary cut on the skin. She had fallen twice.

'Please, Jesus. Please help me. Get this man to understand.'

'No.' Bobo was suddenly shaking his head, suddenly smiling. 'No, Ginny. We are the ones who can't understand. When you've gone this far you don't just give up. You go on. You go on until they knock you down and tie you. But you never just *give in* if your name happens to be Ernie Slade.' He put out a commanding hand. 'Come on, my dear. We're part of this. Let's go.'

'Hell.' Ginny dropped her hands. 'Should I be proud of you, Sailor?'

Through the haggardness of his almost total exhaustion he produced one of his smiles. 'If you want. If you figure I'm worth it.'

'I figure you are.' She sniffed. 'I'm crazy, but I figure you're worth it. Lead on, darling.'

They began to walk. The helicopter hesitated as though astonished at this decision. Then it buzzed and caught up with them. The observer frowned down and made halting gestures with one hand.

'Don't look up,' Slade said. 'There's a little rift up ahead. We can get into that.'

A quarter of a mile away Major Shannon mounted a small rise. He saw the helicopter and the three stark figures walking steadily beneath it. In the same instant he fell neatly forward, touching the sodden ground springily. The rifle came up with smooth and practised precision.

'You damned interfering bastard,' he said calmly, 'poaching on my preserve. I'll have to do something about you first.'

The lens of the telescopic sight settled on the bubble of perspex canopy and then moved swiftly to the right. The tail rotor became a shining disc quartered exactly by the cross-hairs. Shannon squeezed off the shot.

Slade heard the vicious clang of the bullet's strike and jerked up his head. Already the helicopter was moving out of its steady pattern, rising straight up towards the cloud with an irregular, weaving motion. The engine howled. The machine spun, dipped, rose again.

'Run!' Slade reached out and pushed Bobo in the back. 'Run for that hollow!' He saw a white streak appear on a rock that was level with Bobo's knee. Directly after it came a distant popping sound. But he ignored it and hounded them on until they reached the shallow, steeply-banked cleft and tumbled into it.

Slade shepherded them under the overhang of a gnarled and misshapen tree. 'Some nut was taking pot-shots at you.'

'At me?' Bobo leaned against the bank. 'You're mad.'

They were talking jerkily, missing out unnecessary words. 'That helicopter. Its tail rotor was shot up.'

Bobo stared at him. 'Nobody ... would shoot at me.'

'Somebody did.' Slade glanced briefly at the heavy sky. It was empty. The wind still howled overhead. Rain filtered steadily through the sparse leaves of the tree and dripped down on them but they were inured to it.

'How far?' Ginny had a look of drowning about her. The skin of her face seemed slick.

'One mile. No more.' He forced a jerky hand through the dragging cloth of his trouser pocket, brought out the bottle of benzedrine and dosed himself. 'Come on.' He plunged away heavily. All his movements were unco-ordinated, as though his limbs were pulled by strings.

'Is there shelter?' Bobo began to limp after him. 'My hip is rather painful.'

'Cave.' Slade produced a parody of a grin. 'Back to square one, huh? This area is full of caves.' He flung a hand out ahead of him. 'That way.' He had developed two clown-spots of rouge-like flush on his cheeks. The cough that he had held so long at bay threatened, but he fought it down. 'Come on. Let's walk.'

Somehow he managed to fuss along behind them, driving them at little over a snail's pace. To Major Shannon, now half a mile behind, they had appeared to drop out of sight. He walked slowly, bent over, unhurried, searching for tracks, still cursing the rain-speck on the eye-piece of the Lyman that had spoiled his perfect shot. It was only just after noon and he had some five hours of reasonable light still remaining. And eight cartridges. They were more than enough. If it got dark it didn't matter, really. His fit body had been maintained in its present condition for just this kind of endurance. The Tiger would be there, burning bright, waiting for him.

He smiled to himself as he went along, finding smudges of footprints and instantly beginning to gain on his quarry.

Chapter Twenty-one

The sun didn't set that day. A grey twilight gathered and seemed to hover, as though reluctant to give way to night. It was that time when objects lose their definition, and nothing is easy to see.

Pahler approached a fire that burned under a shelter half on the rim of the mountain. Its light was pink, not yellow, as though it had borrowed from absent sundown.

'Douglas, isn't it?' He peered at the slickered figure across the flames.

The man got to his feet. 'That's right. You beat me three-two in the closed championship.'

'Hell, yes.' Pahler remembered his satisfaction at the time, the triumph at driving into exhaustion a man not many years less than half his age.

They shook hands. 'That's a nasty cut Slade gave you.' He eyed the captain's swollen cheek with its strip of sticking plaster angling down towards the chin.

Douglas smiled sourly. 'Only five stitches. That chap can use himself. One clout from behind the wheel of a car, seated, and yet it felt like the kick of a mule.'

'He used to box in his young days.' Pahler sucked his upside down pipe. 'God, what he didn't do. You'd be amazed at the people who've contacted me now that the news has broken. Consular officials, a fellow whose ship's in port—he used to sail with Slade, the little Italian greengrocer Slade used to buy from, a Methodist minister. All of them want to tell me something about him. He had a hell of a life; one of those tough kids who ended up in a sort of Boy's Town. Used religion like a pillar.' He sighed. 'Not a soul says anything bad about him. But he's out there in the rain, sick, and I've got to hunt him. Slade, his wife, an old man and a murdering nut. Wonderful combination, isn't it?'

Firelight flashed off the captain's eyes. 'This man Shannon has given everyone the willies. God, there are so many of us ringing this area that he could never get through.'

'Hah!' Pahler grunted. 'Then where is he? Shannon hunted the big cats for twenty-five years. That means deliberately losing yourself in the bush, not eating, not drinking, not sleeping, not moving for hours on end. Because if ever you stop stalking, the cat stalks you. Shannon's out there somewhere, near Slade, watching, waiting for daylight.' He knocked out his pipe on a boot heel. Sparks cascaded and died. 'Keep an eye rather sharpish, will you?'

'I will.' The captain walked a few yards with Pahler.

'I believe the helicopter Shannon shot up landed rather heavily in your area today.'

Douglas gave a grunt of spontaneous laughter. 'I've never seen two such frightened chaps in my life. The pilot said it was like riding around the sky holding on to a witch's broom.'

'I'll bet.' Pahler pocketed his pipe. 'I'd better be off. Got a few more places to visit.'

'You should turn in,' Douglas suggested. 'You look pretty clapped, sir. There's not much you can do tonight.'

'I'll wander around for a while.' Pahler grinned and gave the captain tit for tat. 'When you're fit you don't really feel the pace all that much.'

Douglas laughed. He tossed off a casual salute. 'It wasn't the fitness, it was that damned lob into the corner. It will be different, next time.'

'Says you.' Pahler brought out his torch, flicked it on. It showed a distinct beam, now. The night had come. He walked away, and Douglas followed the bobbing yellow cone until it was lost to sight.

In the darkness of the night Slade nudged the girl sleeping at his side on the cave floor. 'Ginny. Hey, kid. Wake up. Please, kid.'

'Huh?' She moved restlessly. Then full consciousness came and she jerked upright. 'Ernie, what's the matter?'

The tiny flickering fire winked. His eyes were pockets of shadow. 'Bobo's sick. That biopsy site is badly infected. He's running a pretty high temperature and wants water. Now listen.

I left your raincoat outside. Go get it. Pick it up real careful and bring it inside. There should be enough water trapped in it to give the President a drink.'

She shivered. Then, like a reluctant child: 'Why can't you go, Ernie?'

His voice was slow and patient. 'Kid, I never would have asked you unless it was because I can't. I'm running a fever myself. If I get wet I won't be getting up in the morning.'

'Oh. Okay.' She got up. Her legs were so stiff that she over-balanced and nearly fell. Then she ducked through the cave's small shrub-whiskered entrance and groped in the darkness for the raincoat.

From inside came the sound of his frantic coughing.

Ginny whimpered. She found the raincoat and bundled it from its ends. Water sloshed about at the bottom of the fold. She fumbled her way inside, straightening, holding her burden care-lessly, her eyes seeking him.

'Ernie? Ernie where——' Firelight shone off her sleep-puffed eyes, sparkled on the rain-drops in her hair.

Slade reeled from the shadows at the back of the cave. 'I'm all right.' He knelt next to Bobo's quiescent body. One hand lifted the grey-speckled woolly head. 'Gimme that water.'

She moved next to him. Slade took the raincoat with one hand underneath the bulge, guiding it. 'That's it. Hold steady. Come on, Mr. President. Open that coal-hole. Water's here.'

Bobo blinked, gulped. Water ran across his cheeks and over his chin. His eyes had a glazed sheen. 'Why's the fire so small?'

'Because there's a limit to the dry wood I found in here. Any other complaints, you put them in writing to the manager, I just work here.'

Bobo lay back. He even managed a dry chuckle. 'You're the second most stubborn man I've ever known, Ernie. Would you agree?'

'I don't know. I'm not so sure that I like to take second place. Who's the other guy?'

Bobo's eyes were shut but he grinned. 'Me.'

'Oh. Well then that's different. Okay, if you say so.'

'We're similar in lots of ways. I would like to say that our characters are altogether the same but unfortunately there is one very marked difference, one trait in which we are totally opposed.'

This was fever-talk, said through the ravages of ague. 'You go to sleep now,' Slade said. But he and Ginny remained crouching next to Bobo.

'I have no such intention.' The yellow eyes opened, stared at the cave roof a moment, flicked to them. 'Where do our characters differ? Do you know?'

They shook their heads. 'No.'

'Humanity.' He searched their faces. 'Ernie has it. And I do not. I remember such a long time ago, there was a priest who was one of my opponents. He was a very genuine man. I should have listened to him. I should at least have heard him out, and tried to persuade him to my views. But I didn't. Do you know what I did, Ginny?'

Ginny knelt too. The raincoat fell away and water ran over the damp floor. 'What did you do, Mr. President?'

'I burned his church down. To the ground.' Bobo's voice quavered like the old man he really was. 'I still have this picture in my mind of Father Shomo wading ankle-deep through the ashes, weeping. It was such a terribly wrong thing to do, wasn't it?'

They said nothing. He reached out a fumbling hand and took Ginny's arm. 'You must understand, my dear. To have humanity is not to be soft. If you'd seen me lighting that fire, Ernie, what would you have done?'

'If it had been *my* church,' Slade said, 'I'd have killed you. Then there wouldn't have been any ashes to walk through, and weep about.'

Bobo grunted. 'There, you see?' His words ran into slurs and he began to mumble.

Slade bent closer. 'Mr. President. Can you hear me?'

The old man swallowed noisily. 'Yes. My throat is dry again.'

Slade said, 'Mr. President. Listen carefully. Comes daylight, I'm turning this in. It's all over. You'll be back in hospital by nine o'clock.'

The eyes flicked open. Bobo came up on one elbow so suddenly that they jerked back. 'What did you say?'

'We'll see the night out here. But at daybreak we'll find the nearest cop or soldier and they can take you to hospital.'

Bobo stared at him unblinkingly. 'Because I'm ill, I gather. And what about your original object? Will you abandon that?'

'It hasn't worked,' Slade said.

'What you mean, really, is that you're giving up, don't you? You're throwing in the towel.'

Slade hesitated. Then he said, 'Yes.'

'So.' Bobo pushed himself completely upright. 'You and your wife will be jailed. They may or may not give her bail, I'm not particularly interested in that aspect at the moment. The money will be impounded by the police to be used as Exhibit "A" when they try you. And I will be put back in hospital where I will either die or be cured. That is more or less an accurate summing up of events, isn't it, commencing from tomorrow?' When neither of them answered he barked, 'Well, isn't it?'

Slade looked away. Ginny whispered, 'Yes.'

'Quite. So all our hardship, all our suffering, all our toils and travails, will be for *nothing*.' He almost spat the last word out. 'Slade, you look at me. Are you going to tell me that you're giving in? You, of all people?'

Slade at last looked at him. But still he said nothing.

'You would never be Ernie Slade again.' Bobo stared at him for a moment. Anger worked across his face. 'You slob, why don't you admit it's because of me you want to do this? I'm sick and you've got nothing to treat me with, so that horrible streak of humanity has started working at you. God, I'm glad I haven't got it! Ernie, listen to me! So far you've kidnapped a President, screwed twenty-five thousand pounds out of a tough government, set alight to a forest, got me out of the hands of two murderous escaped convicts, delivered a baby, knocked down an Army officer with one clout, and blown up a helicopter. And I'm prepared to bet that there's an hysterical woman in Tokai who will swear that you personally tried to rape her after pushing her down a flight of steps.' He took a deep breath. 'God dammit, Ernie, I didn't go through all that just to surrender tamely!'

There was an excruciating silence in which only the sound of Bobo's harsh breathing could be heard. Then Slade said, very slowly, 'If I don't ... give in. What then?'

Bobo crumpled slowly until he was lying quiescent again. 'That's better. Now you're talking. Hell, for a moment there you had me worried. As to what you do, that's your department. Just promise me there'll be no more talk of giving in.'

Slade's eyes met those of his wife's. They looked at each other with a depth of understanding they had never known before. Then he said, 'I promise.'

239

Bobo mumbled something. Then he began to snore. Slade rolled over on to his back. The fire burned like ice next to him. He stared at the ridged ceiling of the cave. 'Kid. Hold my hand.'

Her fingers took his. He said. 'That's good. Everything will be fine in the morning. Remember that.' His eyes closed. Then: 'What was that I said?'

'Everything will be fine in the morning, Sailor.' She watched him as his breathing deepened and he fell into a fitful sleep of exhaustion. At that moment she felt the first faint, hesitant stir of movement from the new life she held within her womb.

In the darkness of the night Major Shannon lay crouched in a form he had created. He was warm and very nearly dry. Rain spilled off a simple but effective overhead shelter. He was curled within a nest of boulders like the great cat he really was. He purred, thinking of the morning. He had found them when the light was just too bad for a shot and then they had disappeared into the round 'o' of the cavemouth. Now he was camped virtually above them, forty yards back from the entrance.

There would be trouble in the morning, he knew. The soldiers would find them. But even in that event the two humans and the Tiger within the cave would have to emerge. There was no alternative. There would be plenty of opportunity for that last, simple shot.

He smiled, staring unblinkingly out into the night, waiting for the day.

Chapter Twenty-two

Pahler discovered just after midnight that there were limits to the endurance even of a man who played six hours of squash a week, smoked only a pipe and used his Scotch rather than letting it use him.

He was cruising alone between roadblocks when he had the sudden sensation that he had lost control of his eyelids. Each of them weighed five pounds and were about to crash down with a clang, leaving him blind.

It was an alarming experience. A roadhouse loomed up as a splotch of vari-coloured light in the darkness and he considered the administration of several strong cups of coffee. But then he shook his head. The roadhouse fell behind. No. He would fold over the counter in a row with the drunks who were trying to sober up.

He felt, in fact, like a drunk. So, like a drunk, he homed. Without any conscious decision emerging from his muzzy mind he went arrow-true to the Joseph Schwer. He left the Fairlane parked any old how in the staff rank and stumbled through the entrance, where he leaned against the reception desk and asked for Janet Strange. A startled coloured girl on the night switchboard told him no, Sister Strange was Off, and lived in the flatlets behind the main building.

Pahler thanked her and weaved his way out. The hush of the sleeping hospital had increased his aching need for sleep and he struggled to keep his eyes open. Walking around the main hospital, he found the darkened flatlet block and pushed open the door to the foyer.

Janet Strange's name was on a card inserted into one of a small row of mail boxes. 1A. Thank God, that meant ground floor. He teetered to his left, squinted at a number on a door and pressed the buzzer.

She answered on the third ring, barefooted and wearing a

241

pink woolly nightie, with her short dark hair in curlers. Her face registered a mixture of alarm and bewilderment, which was nothing to the way Pahler felt.

'Hi,' he said. It occurred to him vaguely that he abhorred this term of greeting. He grinned crookedly. 'You wouldn't by any chance have a bed for me? Even a couch or a carpet will do.'

Her eyes darted around the hallway. 'Come in, dammit! You'll get me fired!'

Pahler found himself in a small neat lounge. He threw himself into a two seater sofa and looked at her blearily.

'You're drunk!' said Janet Strange.

'Drunk?' He laughed hollowly. 'I wish I was. I think I had three hours of sleep on Wednesday night. When I eventually got to bed last night I spent most of my time staring at the ceiling. Tonight is—what's tonight?'

'It's Saturday morning. It's nearly one o'clock,' Her face changed. She grinned. 'Curdle Pallour, you're bushed.'

He blinked. 'You got a Scotch by any chance?'

'Scotch? *Now?*'

Pahler's brow lowered. 'Listen,' he rumbled, 'When I ask——'

'All right, all right!' She flew to a sideboard and opened a cupboard, bending and peering inside. 'There's a bottle here with about one inch left in it. I don't drink. Somebody gave it to me. It's called Highland Feather.'

'Oh God! That'll do.' He could see her bottom quite clearly through the nightie. It was a nice bottom, he thought, small and round and firm. It hadn't jiggled when she'd walked, either.

'Water?'

'Just a dash.'

She brought the glass. 'Cheers.' She sat down next to him and curled her toes. She smelled of talcum powder and clean girl. 'How goes the hunt?'

'We'll get him tomorrow unless Shannon does first.' He told her about Shannon in a few blurry sentences. Then he drank the whisky in two large unmannerly gulps. 'I'm thinking of leaving the force when this job is over, you know.'

'You?' She looked quite alarmed. 'I thought you were the true dedicated cop. Why on earth?'

'One always reads about cops who want to start chicken farms. I couldn't bear it. I've got a lot due to me in pension contributions and so on. I want to buy a caravan and be a bum for a while. Then I'll invest in a house and look around for something not too bothersome, like industrial security. Maybe I'll start my own firm. Pahler's Patrols. Which suburb do you prefer?'

'Me?' She blinked and blushed. 'You mean ... ?' Her eyes narrowed. 'Al, if you weren't drunk, you are now.'

'I was never more sober in my life.' He grinned and stood up. 'Where's this bed of yours?' He saw an open doorway and went through on his own. She dashed after him.

'I've only got the one bed!'

He fell on to it, thereby deciding the issue. 'Room for two,' he mumbled.

'Like hell.'

'What're you doing?'

'I'm undressing you. You can't go to sleep like that, like a hobo.'

His answer was a snore. She stood a moment in deep contemplation. He lay there like a baby with his shoes and socks off and his pants halfway down. One big toe twitched.

'Al Pahler you big oaf,' she said in a soft voice. Then she completed the undressing to the extent of managing to remove his trousers and jacket. She got the blankets over him, looked about the room, said to no one in particular, 'I'm damned if I'm sleeping on a two-seater couch. If you can't lick 'em, join 'em.' With which she slid in next to him.

The pillow was soft and he was very warm. Janet Strange felt a deep and womanly contentment. Her eyes closed and she fell away into sleep.

It seemed like five minutes later that she woke. She stirred and muttered and rolled over. Then she touched him and sat bolt upright, staring at him in the faintest of filtered morning light while her thoughts fell into place.

Damn, it was the telephone ringing in the foyer that had woken her. At that moment Pahler jerked spasmodically. He creaked up alongside her.

'What's that?'

'The phone in the foyer.'

'Whassa time?'

She peered at her bedside alarm. 'Quarter to five.'

'God in heaven. Better answer it.'

'Why?'

'It might be for me.'

'You! You didn't tell them ... ?'

He came awake at last and looked sheepish. 'No.'

They stared at each other. Each decided at the same moment that the other looked like hell, and were not the slightest bit put off by it, which is the way of the world.

Then Pahler grinned. He said, 'Good morning, darling.'

'Ahhh,' she snarled. She scrambled out of bed, carelessly exhibiting some tanned thigh and untanned pink bottom. 'It's always the bloody woman who——' She disappeared into the lounge. He heard the front door slam and then the telephone stopped ringing.

The cement floor of the foyer was cold under Janet's feet. Rain streamed down the glass of the main door. 'Hello?'

There was the buzz of coins being inserted at the other end. A woman's voice said, 'Who is this?'

It was an Americanism, Janet knew. The rest of the world said 'Who's *that*.'

'Janet Strange speaking.'

'Thank God it's you, Sister Strange. This is Virginia Slade.'

All the blood drained out of Janet's face. She clutched the receiver. 'You mean ... *Ernie's wife?*'

'Yes. Please. I've got to talk quickly. I'm in a call box in Kalk Bay.'

'But how did you get through the——'

'——Cordon? I walked through. It was still dark. They didn't see me.'

Janet shivered. A picture came to her of a young woman walking alone through unlit darkness in wind and rain, avoiding patrols as though in enemy country. It *was* enemy country, to her.

'What can I do?' she said.

'Please listen carefully, I've got to say all this at once.' Virginia Slade's voice changed as though she were reading from something. 'Ernie says that the site of the bone marrow biopsy that was done on President Lunda has become badly infected. He has a high pyrexia and periods of delirium. He needs antibiotics urgently. Right now, really. Ernie said I must ask for you or Margaret Meadows. He wants you to get hold of Ben Zodiack and come through the cordon. Bring a stretcher if you can and have an ambulance waiting at the nearest road point.'

'I can do all that,' Janet said rapidly, 'but it would be impossible for us to get through the cordon without them realizing what was going on. And we don't know where Ernie is.'

'I was coming to that.' Virginia Slade's voice had the drone of the very tired or the very shocked. 'I have with me a note signed by President Lunda guaranteeing safe conduct to my husband and me from where Ernie is now, to the American Consulate. It requests the Consul on behalf of the Gamban Government to admit us, and let us stay there until Ernie is well enough to fly out. It also asks the South African Government to honour this undertaking.'

'I see.' Janet's hand trembled. 'That means I'll have to get hold of——'

'Yes. Get Colonel Pahler. Ernie trusts him. If you come to the Kalk Bay railway station I will be waiting outside. I will guide you from there.'

'All right, Mrs. Slade. I'll do it.'

'Thank you. Ernie has one more condition. The soldiers are not to come closer than four hundred yards from the cave. Only you and Dr. Zodiack are permitted to come in. Ernie first wants to see an official written guarantee by the South African government that all these conditions have been agreed to. You must bring it with you.'

'I'll tell Colonel Pahler.'

'Janet.' For the first time animation was infused into the voice. It became shaky and feminine. 'Janet. Please hurry. Sailor is also very ill.'

'I'll make them hurry.' Janet blinked. 'Goodbye.'

She dropped the telephone without looking and ran for the door of her flat.

It was still swinging from its cord when she and Pahler emerged five minutes later, Pahler unshaven and rumpled and Janet in uniform and a blue raincoat. They went to the front of the hospital and waited on the hardstand. Its swinging was slowing when Ben Zodiack's Capri came roaring through the gates and did a fast tight circle, tyres smoking as it pulled up. It paused only long enough for them to tumble in and then it was gone again.

They were going to bring Ernie Slade home, at last.

Rain dripped steadily off Pahler's old felt hat, which he had jammed on to his head against the snatching hands of the wind. He looked from Janet to Ben Zodiack to Ginny Slade, who stood bareheaded like a forlorn waif. The rain ran down her cheeks like tears and dripped on to the ragged, sodden raincoat. Her legs were criss-crossed with cuts and scratches. She studied him out of huge exhausted eyes.

They stood about a quarter of a mile from the black dot of a cave-mouth, with the drabness of dripping grass and scrub and rain-slicked rock between. The wind howled across this open space, buffeting them.

'You're sure that's the right cave, Mrs. Slade?' Behind Pahler stood the Navy commander, the lieutenant-colonel, Captain Ian Douglas and a sprinkling of other officers and men. A machine gun pointed its murderous snout at the cave, its crew crouched tensely behind it.

'I'm sure.' The wind struck Ginny Slade, making her stagger. It was as though she had become frail in the last twenty-four hours. 'Can we go now? Bobo and Sailor are very ill.'

Pahler hesitated. 'I'm obliged to abide by this condition of your husband's that we can't close up, but I still think it's damn silly.' He looked around at the grey, deserted landscape. 'Okay, you can go, but first let me give you this.' He fiddled inside his raincoat and brought out a sealed envelope bearing the South African Government crest.

'Here.' He pushed it into her raincoat pocket. 'If that doesn't satisfy your Ernie then nothing will. Some hot telephone calls were made in very high places to get it done.' He patted her arm and smiled. 'Good luck, Ginny.' Then he turned to Zodiack. 'Got your little black bag, Doc?'

'Yes.' Zodiack licked his lips. He glanced around nervously. 'What's this about a telephone?'

'Give your bag to Sister Strange.' Pahler stooped and straightened. 'This is a field telephone. I want you to carry it. Mrs. Slade can pay out the wire. The idea is to talk to Slade once you're inside.'

'Okay.' Ben took the clumsy instrument. Pahler gave Ginny the small fat reel of wire. 'One final check before you go.' He turned to Douglas. 'See anything?'

The Highlander Captain lowered a pair of powerful binoculars. He shook his head. 'Nothing. We have quartered the area and there is no sign of Shannon. I can't understand it. With all this activity he must have seen us.' He paused and then added hopefully, 'Unless, of course, he decided that things were a little on the crowded side.'

'Not him.' Pahler shook his head. 'Shannon is as mad as a March hare, and he wants his fiftieth tiger.' He sighed and flicked a hand. 'All right, you three, better get going. Good luck.'

They began to walk away, with Ginny slowly and awkwardly paying out the wire.

'I want everybody to keep their eyes skinned.' Pahler gazed uneasily about. 'I'm quite sure those three aren't in any danger. Or Slade, for that matter. It's Lunda who's the target.' He singled out the Commander. 'Your chopper's late, isn't it?'

'On its way.' The Commander looked hopefully at the sky. 'Should be here in a minute or two.'

'Keep in touch,' Pahler said, 'it's the quickest way we have of getting Lunda to hospital. But he can keep an eye out for Shannon before we need him.'

'Okay.' The Commander began to call up his pilot. Pahler turned away, noticing that in the rain and the wind his hands were perspiring.

On the roof of the cave, magnificently concealed in his scrub blind, Major Shannon watched and waited, smiling.

In the darkness of the cave Ginny knelt. 'Ernie! Sailor! Darling, I'm back!'

Slade stirred. His eyes opened. 'Kid. Thank God. I been worried as hell.' Their hands fumbled and met. She kissed him tremblingly.

'Everything's going to be all right, Ernie. I've brought Ben and Janet.'

Slade got up very slowly, like an old man. Ben was crouched next to Bobo, giving him an injection by the light of a torch held in Janet's hands. 'You stubborn old mule.' Ben grinned, looking up quickly. 'And you've won, too. Show him the letter.'

Ginny tore it open. 'Here.' Her breathing was quick. 'Read it, darling.'

Slade tilted the letter to catch the torchlight. He read it quickly. Then with it still clasped in one hand he took Ginny by the shoulders and looked straight into her eyes. 'We can come in out of the rain now, kid.'

She looked at him as though she had never really known him before. 'I know, Sailor.' Then she put her head against his chest. 'Ernie, I'm so glad.'

He kept his arm around her, turning with her to look down on Bobo. 'They've agreed, sir. They're going to let me go.'

The President's eyes were open. 'God help the world, with you running around loose.' Then he grinned. 'I'm glad, Ernie.'

Slade said to Ben, 'How is he?'

'He'll be fine. I've pumped him to the eyeballs with chloremphenical.' He closed his bag. 'This clumsy device is a field telephone. Colonel Pahler wants to talk to you before we move. Here you are.' He gave Slade the receiver. 'You press that buzzer, there.'

Slade held the receiver to his ear. There was a crackle and then he heard Pahler's voice, tinny and distant. 'Slade?'

'That's right.'

'Is the letter in order?'

'It's fine.'

'You're coming out, then?'

'Yup.'

'Fine. Now listen. Do you know why that helicopter got off your back yesterday?'

'The tail rotor was shot up.' Slade's speech was slow, like his movements. 'Some nut took a shot at the President, too. Didn't miss by much.'

There was a heavy-breathing pause. Then Pahler's voice came again. 'It's a long story. There's a lunatic called Shannon on the loose up here. He's an armed killer and his target is the President. Got that?'

'The guy who shoots tigers,' Slade said. 'It was in the *Argus*.'

Pahler was wishing he had Slade's memory. 'That's right. The tiger hunter wants the Tiger of Gamba. Get it?'

'Yup,' said Slade. He watched Ginny in the light of the torch.

'All right. Now listen. We couldn't get a stretcher in there. Can Lunda walk?'

'I doubt it. Hold on.' Slade turned. 'Reckon you can walk a little way, sir?'

'Nobody is going to carry me,' said Bobo heavily.

Slade put the receiver back to his ear. 'He says he can.'

'Fine. Tell him to come out first. Then you. Then Dr. Zodiack and your wife and Sister Strange. We've got a machine gun mounted out here and we haven't seen anything so far but come straight out and if it's possible come out *fast*. Got it?'

'Yup. Okay to move now?'

'Yes. Get going. We'll be waiting.' There was a pause. 'And Slade?'

'Yes?'

'Good luck, Ernie.'

'Thanks, Colonel.'

He replaced the telephone and rose slowly. 'Time to move, everyone.' Only the benzedrine was holding him together. It had made all his senses needle sharp but it could not speed up the slowness of his worn-out body.

Ben helped Bobo to his feet. He put an arm to support him but the President shrugged him off.

'I am going out there the way I came in.' He glanced at Ben along his trunk. 'On my own two large feet.'

'Come on, then, let's see you do it.' Slade smiled. 'You first. Then me. Then the rest of you. Let's go.'

'Here they come.' Pahler was sweating. 'Everybody on their toes, please.'

From the cave mouth Bobo had emerged, straightening as he cleared the overhang. Behind him Slade came out, pressing up quickly against the President. Pahler saw the blond head turn, watching.

They seemed like dolls from this distance. A black doll and a white doll in rumpled, ragged clothes. Three more dolls following up behind. Five dolls now, all told, seeming to meander idly towards him.

'God, I wish they'd hurry,' said the Commander.

'They're going as fast as they can.' Douglas had his binoculars trained. 'By their movements the old man and Slade are very tired.'

Pahler found that he was trembling. Rain had found its way down inside his raincoat and ran in icy trickles along his spine but he failed to notice it. He heard the bee-buzzing of the helicopter and turned to the Commander.

'Your boy see anything?'

The Commander shook his head. 'Nothing. Absolutely

nothing. Either Shannon isn't here or he's concealed from air observation.'

'Bring the chopper down,' Pahler said.

The Commander moved away. Pahler watched his five dolls threading their way in single file towards him. And while he watched the five became six. A sixth doll had appeared, not from the mouth of the cave but on its roof, a neat, slim, booted and ruggedly clad doll who stood poised with a statuesque deadliness.

'God!' Pahler forced his stiff lips into movement. *'Slade! Behind you! Shannon!'*

It was too late. Too far and too late. His voice had to carry across so much distance and the wind tore it away. He stood rooted, waiting for the first doll to tumble and become rag. But the second doll's head had turned as though he had sensed the danger. It flicked, only a fraction-of-a-second movement coupled with an instantaneous arrow-like forward fling of the slim body.

The second doll met the first. They seemed to hang together for an eternity before they fell, but then they were tumbling forward as though in slow motion while Pahler heard the popping of the shot and the sudden thunderous racket of the machine gun exploding into life next to him.

The sixth doll had flicked back the bolt of its rifle. The brass cartridge case made an arc through the air. The bolt was coming forward again with neat unhurried precision when the burst struck. Four bullets hit Major Shannon in a line up his body, shattering a kneecap, a hip, penetrating the stomach and piercing one lung. He let the rifle drop quite idly and then followed it in a long diving sprawl from the roof of the cave, hitting the ground outside its mouth and seeming to bounce before coming to rest.

They began to run forward. All of them ran with the sound of the helicopter roaring in their ears.

Slade lay on his back on the rough ground. Shannon's bullet had taken him just below the shoulder-blade and passed right through his body in that fractional moment when he had pushed the President out of the line of the shot. There was blood all over the front of his jersey, wine-red in the centre, pinkened from the rain on the edges.

He saw the dull leaden sky and a circle of down-peering intruding faces. He stared up at them out of shocked eyes, hearing the sound of his breathing.

'Kid?' He smiled when he felt her hand, saw her rain-streaked face close to his.

'Sailor,' she cried, 'Oh Sailor!!' She held him, her body bent over his as though to shield him from any more hurt.

'Is Bobo all right?'

'I'm all right, Ernie.' The big dark face intruded in his vision, drawn and concerned. 'Ernie you crazy damn fool, you and that humanity . . .'

'I'm sorry,' Slade said. 'I'm real sorry for all the trouble I put you to, you and all these other nice people.'

Bobo took his hand. 'Ernie, you're going to be fine, my boy.'

'I never seen a tiger cry,' Slade jeered. Other faces intruded in his vision. Pahler's. Janet's. Zodiack's. The doctor was doing something to him. Then there came a rushing of wind, a pulsing down-draft that stirred his blond hair and made it ruffle in the wind. His thoughts wandered. 'Got to get out from under that chopper,' he said. 'We can still walk.'

'No more walking.' It was Pahler talking. 'You're going home in style, Ernie, inside one of those instead of under it.'

'That's great.' Slade felt himself carefully lifted and placed on a stretcher. 'I want Ginny and Bobo with me.'

There was the sound of a door sliding. Ginny's and Bobo's faces stayed with him, bobbing and blurring. Then the helicopter's rotors whirled and he was whipped into the heavy grey skies over the mountain.

Chapter Twenty-three

By the following Wednesday the rain was only a memory. An idle westerly wind blew, gently moving the cypresses in the garden of the Joseph Schwer. The finely-etched mountains butted their heads against a faultlessly cobalt sky.

Janet Strange was standing near the entrance, enjoying the sun, when Ben Zodiack joined her. 'Can I give you a lift?'

'No thanks.' She blushed. 'I'm waiting for Al Pahler. He should be here at any moment.'

Ben smiled. With the colour in her face and dressed in a summery blue linen frock she looked quite pretty, although she really was almost plain. 'Thank God his cold's better. I've never seen anything like it.'

'Here's Al now.' Janet waved as Pahler's broad-shouldered figure appeared in the gateway and began to walk briskly along the drive. 'We're going to see a caravan he wants to buy.'

Pahler came up, rather old-fashionedly dapper in sportscoat and flannels. He shook hands with Ben. 'How's the President?'

'Fit enough to rule Gamba until he dies of old age,' Ben said. 'Janet has probably told you that his trouble was pernicious anaemia, which is easy enough to cure. All Bobo needs now is a rest. He overdid things with Ernie.'

There was a short silence. Ben fiddled undecidedly for a moment. Then he spoke entirely for Janet's benefit. 'I must go. I'm due to collect my wife and son from the airport in an hour. It will be wonderful to have them back.'

'I'm very glad for all of you,' Janet smiled.

Zodiack said awkwardly, 'Some people take a long time to grow up. But it usually happens in the end.' Then he flicked a hand in farewell and strode away to his car.

'Now what,' said Pahler, 'was all that about?'

'Jane Hobart. She runs a straight man and an affair. Always

the two together. He was the affair. The fourth one that I know of.'

'And the straight man?'

'She's got a new one. Ian Douglas. He latched on to her after seeing her at the airport when Bobo arrived.' It seemed so long ago, now. 'Whenever she wasn't ducking around corners with Ben she was dating him.'

'That,' Pahler lit his pipe, 'is their problem. I am taking you to view eighteen feet of elegance. It's got a double bed and a shower and one of those chemical things in case you wake up in the night. It's not far and I walked because they're fitting the hitch to my car. How do you like the sound of it all?'

'Marvellous. Especially the double bed and the chemical thing.' She took his arm and they began to walk towards the gates. 'I can't quite believe you've resigned. That grim cop. You frightened the hell out of me when I first met you.'

Pahler produced a mock snarl. 'I've hung up my raincoat. Incidentally, my successor is having some fun sorting out Shannon's things. We will never know the whole story, but it is clear that Shannon and Crutchley, Bobo's Chief of Police, were old buddies from their days in India. Between Cedric Mango and Crutchley they were going to start a new order in Gamba, and it's not for me to say whether it would have been any better or worse than the one Bobo runs. But they chose the wrong methods. Crutchley knew that Shannon was half potty so he worked on him in two ways: paid him a goodly sum of money and egged him on with that fiftieth tiger idea which of course appealed to Shannon's mad mind.'

'Bobo is very hurt. He trusted Crutchley more than anyone else.' They reached the gates as a taxi drew up. Both of them stopped when Ginny Slade got out.

'Hello, you two.' Her face had regained some of its old pinkness. She was older, more grave, with a lot of the ebullience gone, but there was still that look of the newly-showered hockey player. She would always have it.

'Come visiting?'

'Yes.' She had a rolled magazine in one gloved hand. 'He was all worried because I missed yesterday.'

There was a pause. Janet said, 'Are you okay now, Ginny?'

'Yeah, I'm okay.' She fiddled with a glove. 'Any time I get the glooms I remember what Ernie said after we got him out of the helicopter. Right here he said it, at the Schwer. He said, "Ginny's lap is warm and freckled and her hand is in my hair".' She studied them with great care. 'I figure that sounds kind of like poetry, like the beginning of a poem. I'm going to remember it all my life. In any case, Ernie isn't the kind of guy you forget, is he?'

'No,' Janet said, 'no, he isn't.'

They walked slowly. Pahler said, 'Is anyone going to tell her the result of the tuberculosis test that Ben did?'

'That it was T.B. after all? That Ernie went off half-cocked and died for nothing? No. It's best left alone.'

'True.' Ginny was just going around the curve of the driveway. They waved, and walked on.

Ginny waved back, then turned and walked slowly to the end of the driveway, on to the hardstand. She looked up at the blue sky. The tiny breeze ruffled the sleeves of her black dress. She thought about the poem she had once recited in her mind before she had known what the heck Ernie was doing. Sailor would be seeing fair heaven's land, now, but the voyage had never been drear. No. Not with him. God, Ernie Slade, she thought, I'm going to miss you.

She stood a moment, a small figure in the centre of the huge hardstand. Then she turned away and began to walk briskly towards the garden, where the old man in the wheelchair sat waiting for her.